The Watch in the Box

And other short stories

Jim and Kate Tuttle's Murder Mysteries

VOLUME ONE

Pat Ely

PAGE PUBLISHING, INC.
New York, NY

First originally published by Page Publishing, Inc. 2019

ISBN 978-1-64462-837-9 (Paperback)
ISBN 978-1-64462-838-6 (Digital)

Printed in the United States of America

Contents

PART ONE

The Watch in the Box

Prologue

The house was not large. It was a smallish one-level home that had probably been built in the late 1800s or early 1900s. But what it lacked in size, it made up for in style and beauty. Flowers bloomed in a wide variety of colors everywhere you looked. It was well manicured with no sign of a weed to be had. There was a porch that didn't date back to when the house was built; it was new or at least newer, made out of red cedar. It appeared to be maybe two or three years old. Even though it was an addition, it fit in perfectly with the rest of the house and didn't detract from it.

The city streets in the South Capitol Neighborhood, which is aptly named due to its proximity to the state capitol building, were narrow. Very narrow. Yet people still parked on the street, making it impossible to pass an oncoming car. One person had to give way to the other, let them pass, and then pull back out into the more or less single lane and continue on. Knowing this, I had parked in one of the capitol parking lots and strolled to the house that now stood before me. I had needed time to think about what I was going to say to the occupant, and I always have been able to think well when in motion. Plus, it was a gorgeous summer day, and I wanted to get out in the sun some. Replenish the old vitamin D.

Reaching into my jacket pocket, I felt the object that had brought me here. It had taken me a good deal of research to get me this far, and I was hoping it was not a dead end.

Having set this meeting up with the occupant of the home by phone, I didn't have any clue what to expect as I walked slowly up the cracked sidewalk. All I did know for sure was that she was no spring chicken.

Stepping up onto the porch, I took the last two or three steps and stopped within reach of the front door. The door was a stained glass affair that was the type you couldn't see clearly through but could usually see movement. Rapping softly, I waited for a response. I didn't see any movement coming my way. *Why did I knock so softly?* I thought to myself. I knew the old lady who lived here was seventy five years old, plus or minus a year or two. Maybe she couldn't or didn't hear my knock.

As I raised my hand to deliver a more substantial request for entry, I detected movement. I lowered my arm and waited.

The door slowly opened, and the owner smiled at me and said, "Good afternoon. You must be Mr. Tuttle."

The woman matched the house to a T. She was dressed in what my mother would have called a housedress—a loose fitting floral dress with a matching belt around her waist. She was very fit, it appeared to me, for a mid-seventies person, whether they be man or woman.

"Jim please, and you must be Mrs. Walker," I replied.

"Call me Betty please. Come in, come in," she said as she backed away from the door, holding onto the handle with one hand and gesturing with the other like Vanna White on *Wheel of Fortune* might do. I'll bet she watched *Wheel* in its regular daytime slot.

"Thank you."

I stepped into an entry with a small table with flowers that looked like some in the yard I had just passed by.

"You have a lovely garden. The flowers are spectacular."

"Why thank you, Jim. That is how I try to stay in shape. I work in my yard for a minimum of one hour a day. It usually stretches out to two or more. Lots to do," she said with a smile.

This woman had no signs whatsoever of the terrible maladies that can afflict a person as they grow older. It appeared she had kept arthritis, Alzheimer's, and even early senility at bay. This is beside the fact she was in the physical shape most sixty-year-old women would like to be in but can't seem to find the time to get there.

"Why don't we sit out on the back deck, if it's all right with you?"

"Sounds great," I replied.

"Would you like some iced tea? Or lemonade? Perhaps a beer?"

Not one to usually turn down a beer, especially on a nice day, I decided I wanted to keep my thoughts clear today.

"Lemonade would be great. Thanks."

She left to go retrieve the lemonade, and I looked out over the lake, at least what I could now see of it. When this house was built, I am sure they had a beautiful view of Capital Lake and Capital Forest in the distance. Now the trees on the hillside below had grown to the point it was a peekaboo view at best.

Betty returned with the lemonade on a tray bearing a picture of the capitol dome. Setting it down, then handing me a glass, she finally sat and looked at me.

"So when you called you said you thought you might have something that belonged to me?" she asked.

Not quite ready to jump right into it and just hand her the item in my pocket, I decided to stretch it out just a bit. It was a beautiful day, and I was enjoying sitting on her deck. Plus, I couldn't just hand it to her with no back story.

"Betty, I run a jewelry store for a living. It's kind of a long story, but in a sense, because of that, I became interested in looking for old jewelry and coins with a deep seeker. Sorry, a deep seeker is a type of metal detector that can pick up signals of metallic objects that may have been buried for years. The deep seeker allows me to pick up metal clear down to around three feet below the surface of the earth."

"Oh my, that sounds like it might be fun," she replied. Her eyes never left mine. She was intrigued I could tell with what I might have that belongs to her.

"It is a lot of fun," I replied. I still had a little more to tell her before I dropped the item in her hand.

"My brother in law, Barry, and I hunt together. The landscape varies a great deal. From clear cuts where forests used to me to dark

9

timber where the forest still remains. On one of our trips, he asked if I had ever tried looking for coins and the like around the 'old growth' stumps. Now I know from my research, you are well aware of what I mean by old growth."

Her face had changed. She now had a quizzical look that I knew was not from my asking or, more correctly, telling her about old growth timber.

"Indeed, I am aware of what old growth is. Or should I say was."

"The stumps that have springboard cuts in them is where I was looking for coins. I figured, well, Barry figured that jumping up and down from the springboards, the loggers might have had coins fall out of their pockets from time to time. I was up in the old Bordeaux logging works area, looking for coins, when I came upon the item I have that I think belonged at one time to you."

If I had her hooked earlier, now I was reeling her in. She sat forward in her chair, set down her glass of lemonade on the table beside her chair, and put her hands together in her lap.

"I used to live up there."

"I know. In the research I did to find you, I found out your father owned a store in the town that sprung up in the heyday of the camp. The hard part, though, was actually finding out if you were still in the area. Had to spend a good deal of time going through old records at the courthouse."

"You did some very good research. My father's name was Willets. First name Israel. He opened the store with a bank loan, certain he could make it up in Bordeaux. Put the family farm outside Oakville up for collateral. He did make it. I worked in the store until I got married at nineteen years old."

I had found out her maiden name from an old bookkeeper from Bordeaux. More information gleaned from my research.

"Which, in a roundabout way, is what brought me here today. Your husband's name was William. William Walker, correct?"

"Yes, it was. He died in a logging accident just after we were married. We were man and wife just two months when he died."

"Did you happen to give him a wedding present?" I inquired.

I noticed her hands were now gripped very tightly, one within the other. Her knuckles on the exposed hand were white and stretched out like Saran Wrap over a bowl.

"I did. My father gave me a gold pocket watch that he had just purchased for himself. It was actually gold and silver. Even though he was doing well, he didn't have the kind of money to buy a solid gold watch. Silver was much less expensive. Why do you ask?"

Reaching into my pocket, I pulled out an old pocket watch. It was inside a leather pouch, which was used to protect it from the elements you might endure as a logger. Rain and sawdust being two of the big ones.

I slipped the watch out of the old deteriorating leather and held it in my hand. Rolling it over in my hand, I read aloud the inscription on the back: "To my William. Love forever, Betty, 4-15-1924."

Betty went as white as the proverbial sheet.

I held the watch out to her. She opened her hands, releasing the pressure she had put on them, and took it from my palm. Then tears streamed down her face.

"Are you all right?" I asked, afraid it may have been too much of a strain on her to see it again after all these years.

It took her a full minute to answer. I could sense the wheels were turning hard in her brain. She finally responded.

"That is the watch I gave to William. I would know it anywhere. But it is impossible you found it in Bordeaux."

"Why is that, Betty? Didn't you live there when you gave it to him?"

"Yes, we did. But you see, it is impossible. That watch was buried with him when he died."

CHAPTER ONE

The sun shone down through the firs, casting bright beams down to the forest floor like beacons from a lighthouse might emit on a clear night.

It was my day off. Since my wife, Kate, was working, I had decided to grab my metal detector and head to where I knew an old logging camp used to be to do a little searching.

A customer of mine, a retired man around sixty-five, had gotten me hooked on the "sport" of metal detecting. He would come into my store with a full baggie of gold about four times a year. Rings, watches, neck chains, you name it. He told me his tale one day over coffee.

Seems when he retired, his wife wanted to go to Hawaii. He loved the sun, but the thought of lying out in it was, to him, like lying back and having a root canal performed. Without Novocain. So he had bought a metal detector, set his wife up on the beach to gather the rays, and headed out into the surf. He would go to Prince Kuhio Park, where many tourists would go to sun bath, swim, or simply play in the water. What most people don't think about is that they have just greased up with boatloads of suntan lotion, oftentimes leaving their jewelry on while doing so. The lotion, of course, is slick. They would go swimming or play with their kids in the water and never notice that they had lost their jewelry in the process.

In the two years I had known him, he had brought in probably fifteen *pounds* of gold jewelry. Some of which had precious gems in them. Diamonds, emeralds, sapphires, and rubies aren't affected by saltwater, so he would have me dismount the gems from their settings and then send the gold to a refiner for cash. I would guess that he had made roughly $50,000 just on the gold alone. I never did ask what he did with the gemstones, but he likely sold those as well.

At first, I was appalled someone would take advantage of someone else's misfortune. Then he told me a story about finding a wedding band that was engraved with the previous day's date. He had taken the time to call every single hotel in Waikiki, no small task, and found a couple who had been married the previous day. He returned the ring to the very happy couple. I guess even gathering as much gold as King Tut, he did still have a soft side.

Once I started using the metal detector, I was hooked. Sure, you find all kinds of pieces of metal—old bolts, nuts, nails, and the like—but occasionally you do find something worthwhile. I once found a Morgan 1893-S silver dollar that I subsequently sold for $2,000. I was hoping for something similar today.

The forest I was now searching in was one that once housed a huge logging camp, the Bordeaux Logging Works. It was founded by the Bordeaux family's Mumby Lumber and Shingle Company and the Mason County Logging Company. In the early 1900s, it had its own post office, stores, and hundreds of loggers. There was a hotel built to house the loggers, but that didn't last too long. Wanting to live in better surroundings, houses were built and even a school was erected.

I had a personal reason for choosing this particular sight. My grandfather had worked here in his twenties. The stories he had shared about how, during the glory days before his time, if someone was killed in the woods, they would simply pull the body off to the side and then, when the day was done, take the body down and report the happenings.

People who venture into the old growth forests, at least where the old growth used to stand, are amazed at the size of the stumps, some of which would measure seven to ten feet through at the bottom. Often when I take someone new into the woods they ask why there are holes chipped out of the sides of the old stumps. I would explain that the loggers would cut out a seat for their springboards. Springboards were six to eight feet long with carefully crafted tips that would be seated into the axed-out holes in the stump. A springboard, once in place well above ground level, would then hold a faller, the logger who was in charge of cutting down the tree, and a bucker, his mirror image on the opposite side of the tree. The springboards were positioned in the tree high enough up so that the long two-man crosscut saws they used would not become tangled in any brush at the bottom of the tree while they were cutting it down. With one logger on each side of the giant tree, standing on their springboards, they could fall the tree much easier than trying to do so it at ground level.

The second question I am usually asked is why the old stumps are not level across the tops. To fall a tree so that it goes in the direction that the faller wants it to go, the faller would undercut the side of the tree that they wanted it to fall on. This was done by sawing an angle upward from the bark at about a thirty-five- or forty-five-degree angle, to approximately 30 percent of the way to the middle of the tree. Then making a level cut on the same side, equal to where the previous cut had ended, they would remove the pie-shaped piece, creating a large mouthlike cut once it was removed. Then the fallers would go to the back side of the tree and, making a cut level with the level cut on the other side, would begin the process of cutting the tree down. Once the back side was weakened by cutting into the tree, perhaps 30 to 40 percent of the way to the top of the mouth, the tree would start to fall. It would fall toward where the chunk had been cut out and land exactly where the faller had intended it to fall. Occasionally, a tree would twist because of being caught up in another tree and not land right where it was intended, and that is when accidents, including deaths, occurred. When the tree fell, the stump would have a level cut running about a third of the way through it, and then the angled cut from the under cutting would create a sloping effect on the other side of the top of the stump. If a faller tried to cut all the way through a tree in a straight line, the weight of the tree would, at some point, tip toward where the cut started, and the saw would become stuck forever. That is why they had to do the undercut and the back cut on trees as well. Otherwise, there would be saws stuck in trees all over the western United States.

I was going to focus on the old stumps that had springboard cuts in them. My brother-in-law mentioned that he bet loggers climbing up or jumping down to run as a tree fell might have coins fall from their pockets. I agreed with his logic, so here I was.

Having worked around maybe a dozen old stumps with nothing to show for my efforts, I finally heard the ping in my headphones from something buried down about a foot and a half. Excitedly, I unhooked the shovel I had attached to my belt and started to dig. I went down about two feet, then switched back on my detector and stuck it in the hole. No sound emitted from the detector. As I rose back up, the detector came to life as I swung it over the pile of dirt and needles I had set aside from the hole. It pinged loudly, so I knew I had removed whatever treasure had been under the earth's surface, and it was now lying in a pile of dirt. I hoped it wouldn't be a tooth from a saw or an old broken pocketknife.

Sifting carefully through the soil, I didn't see anything that appeared to be metallic. Just dirt, rocks, and more dirt. I lifted my headphones from around my neck, put them in place, and picked up my metal detector. I ran it over the pile I had created by sifting, and there was no ping at all. I moved it over the pile of rocks, and it made the familiar *ping-ping-ping* sound.

What the heck?

I got on my hands and knees to look through the rocks, this time more closely. Rocks come in all shapes and sizes, so I took my time. One stood out as I looked at the pile. It was a bit too symmetrical in comparison to its brethren. I picked it up and brushed the dirt from it. It wasn't until then I realized it wasn't rock at all but a small leather pouch. I unzipped my fanny pack and reached inside, searching for my old toothbrush. They come in handy while removing dirt from objects. Stiff enough to get the job done, soft enough not to damage anything that might be damaged by a wire brush, for instance.

Carefully brushing off the dirt, I finally noticed what had been pinging me. Inside the leather pouch was a pocket watch. I removed it from the pouch by gripping the crown or winder, as some call it, and then separating the leather from the front and the back of the watch carefully, I slowly removed the watch from its resting place.

It was beautiful. What looked like gold was, all along, the outside edge of the watch. The body appeared almost black. I licked my finger and then scrubbed a spot of the black. It cleaned up a little, revealing a shiny silver color. It very likely was silver. It must have corroded over the years it had been underground.

Shaking out a little dirt that was inside the pouch, I placed it in my fanny pack. I removed a handkerchief I always carried along with me and wrapped the watch inside, then stowed it away in the pack.

Being excited about the find and having not found anything else thus far, I decided to head for home and clean the watch up. I meandered along steadily but really not in a hurry to leave the woods. The woods have been a big part of my life. When fall comes, you can always find me in the woods hunting—deer, elk, even mushrooms. I just love to be outdoors. Maybe it was because my job required me to be in just the opposite environment, but when I could get some fresh air, I took full advantage.

Driving back to Olympia, only about a twenty-minute drive or so from Bordeaux, my mind was clinging to the fact I may have, once again, found something of pretty decent value. I knew a good deal about watches—well, jewelry in general, really—and I knew if indeed it was a silver-and-gold pocket watch, it would garner a pretty good price if I decided to sell it.

My thoughts were also about whose watch it had been. Was it an old logger's watch? Seemed unlikely. Loggers never made that kind of money, and even if they did, how many of them would spend it on a truly expensive timepiece?

I turned into my driveway, shut down my truck, and jumped out. I put my metal detector in its spot in the garage and took off my boots. I knew Kate wouldn't be home for an hour or so. I hoped that would give me time to clean up the old watch and look in some of my antique jewelry books to get some sort of value. Unlacing my boots, setting them aside on the concrete floor, then entering and washing my hands in the mud room sink, I finally was able to remove my fanny pack and look at the watch once again.

As I was walking into the kitchen, where I knew I had some silver polish under the sink, I took out the watch and removed it from the handkerchief. Setting the watch on the counter, I reached under the sink for the polishing cloth and silver polish. I knew that, as dirty as this watch was, I was going to be springing for a new polishing cloth when I was finished cleaning it up.

I put the polish on and let it sit, per the directions. After the allotted time, I started wiping it with the polishing cloth. I knew the polish wouldn't hurt the gold, whether it was gold-plated, gold-filled, or solid gold. Even at that, I tried to keep it on what I assumed were the silver portions of the watch. As the cloth became blacker, the metal became brighter. As the back shined up, I noticed that the blackness had remained on portions of the smooth back. It was engraved! How cool!

Removing my toothbrush from my fanny pack, I put some silver polish on the bristles and rubbed it over the dark engraving, brushing it like I might my bicuspids. It was almost impossible to wait for it to dry so I could rub it off and see if I could read the inscription.

After four or five minutes, I took the cloth to it. Then wetting the toothbrush, I scrubbed it again and then redried it. The inscription was now readable.

The watch had obviously been a gift from a woman named Betty to a man named William back in 1924. Birthday? Wedding? Hard to say at this point. I stared at the inscription, thinking about all the possibilities. Then I heard the door open from the garage, and my lovely wife entered the house.

We had been married for two years in 1977, but it seemed like only two days. The honeymoon was still not over. Good for us.

"Hi, darlin'!" I called out.

"Hi there yourself. How was your day in the woods?" she said as she walked into the kitchen.

"Pretty cool actually. Look," I said as I handed her the watch.

"Oh my god. This is beautiful. Look at the date! Where did you find it?"

"Up in Bordeaux where Grandpa used to log. It is silver for sure, and I think 14 karat gold trim."

"What do you think it is worth?'

"No clue yet. I just got home with it a few minutes ago. I am more interested in the people. I wonder who they were…or maybe are."

"You think they may still be alive?" Kate asked.

"Why not? If this watch belonged to a logger, let's say in 1924, he was twenty. That would mean that, today, he would be seventy-five. No reason to think that he didn't beat the odds and live this long."

She looked at the watch again. "Maybe Betty too. Maybe she is still alive."

"Sounds like fun to maybe track them down and return the watch to its rightful owner." I was thinking about my customer returning the ring to the newlywed couple. How cool would that be? Finding a seventy-five-year-old, plus or minus, and returning something they had lost years before sounded like it would be a great way to spend some time.

CHAPTER TWO

I knew it was going to be a challenge to locate Betty and William if they were still alive. Not really having any sort of a starting point for my search, I decided to ask a friend of mine who was a modern-day logger about it.

He suggested trying *Loggers World* magazine. It is a publication for loggers and about loggers. Although in looking into it I found they had only been publishing their magazine since 1964, I felt like they might be able to lead me to someone who might know about what I was looking for, if it even existed. I was in search of a list of loggers who worked the Bordeaux site in 1924.

Spending my not-long-enough breaks and lunches at work, I dug into the magazine and sent letters to the managing editor and board of directors. I thought that maybe one of them might be able to help me find out if a list even existed. It was awhile before I finally got a response.

There was a member of the board who knew a guy who had worked for the Bordeaux Logging Works who had done payroll. He was living in Chehalis, just south of Olympia. He even had a phone number for the guy. Maybe this was my start.

The man's name ended up being Harlan Saunders, not Sanders like the Kentucky Fried Chicken founder but Saunders. And no *D* at the end of Harlan either. I called him and spoke with him on a Wednesday. My next day off I could actually meet him face-to-face was on the following Wednesday. He said he had a partial list and a good memory, so he might be of some help. I thanked him and waited as patiently as possible for Wednesday to roll around.

Mr. Saunders lived on a small farm, maybe a couple acres. At seventy-eight, he was still active. I could see by the cows in one of the fields, the large vegetable garden that was springing up pretty well, and a well-manicured yard.

Approaching the house, I was met by a dog the size of a small car. It was a mixed breed. Something with shepherd and heaven only knew what. He stood his ground as I walked up to the little four-foot fence that surrounded the house on all sides.

As I flipped the latch on the gate to enter, he emitted a low growl. The sound alone was more than a little scary, but add that to the size and structure of the beast emitting said sound and it became almost terrifying.

The front door opened, and the man I was looking for stepped out.

"Kill, come."

The dog lifted its head, looked one last time at me, and turned and walked to the porch.

When I had heard *kill*, I assumed he had changed his mind and wanted me dead for just wanting to ask him questions. As it turned out, the dog's name was Killer. A name had never been so fitting for an animal, at least when you looked at his appearance and then matched it with the moniker.

"Mr. Tuttle, I presume," Mr. Saunders said.

"Yes, and you must be Mr. Saunders."

"You can open the gate now. Killer won't hurt you."

Opening the gate slowly without ever taking my eyes of the monster dog, I stepped through and walked at a steady pace toward the house.

Upon reaching the porch, I thrust my hand out, he followed suit, and we shook hands.

"Please call me Jim."

"Only if you call me Sandy," he replied.

"Thanks you for allowing me to visit, Sandy. I promise I won't keep you long," I said, not really hoping it would be a short visit. I wanted answers to questions I was hoping he could supply.

"Not a problem. I don't get a lot of visitors." Probably not with a wild animal named Killer guarding your place, I wanted to say but refrained from doing so.

"Come in please."

He turned and opened the door. Killer gave me the once-over but remained still. Watching him like a hawk, I slowly walked past him and into the house.

The inside of the house was tidy, but I wouldn't say clean. I noticed there was dust on the tables in the small living room as I stepped into it. Kate would have had a fit if I let someone visit without vacuuming and dusting the house.

Sandy was a pretty good-size guy. I am no slouch, rising six feet one from the earth to the top of my cranium, and Sandy was every bit as big as I was and looked as if he could be stronger than me even at his age.

"Hey, it's such a nice day. How about we sit out back on the patio?" Sandy said.

"Just fine with me."

"Can I get you anything? How about a beer?"

Being my day off, I thought, *Why not?* "Sounds great, Sandy."

I followed him into the kitchen, where he removed two bottles of Rainier Beer from the fridge. Opening a drawer that was on one side of the fridge, he produced an opener and popped both tops for us.

"This way."

I followed him across the worn linoleum and out a door I assumed correctly would take us to the patio.

Killer was waiting for us. But this was a totally different Killer than had met me out front. Tail wagging, tongue hanging out that made him look like he was smiling, he strolled over to me and stood looking up at me.

"Once I let someone inside, he figures they are okay. Go ahead and pet him. I think he likes you. He is usually a bit more timid when he is first getting to know someone. Someone who has come through the house I should say. You try to walk into the yard and he doesn't know you, well, let's just say the outcome might not be favorable for you."

Reaching out my hand to let him sniff it, I was surprised when instead he licked it. Tail still wagging, I greeted him.

"Hi, Killer."

That was all it took. He came close enough for me to pet him, and I did. His coat was a bit like the texture of steel wool, and as he licked my hand, I noticed his tongue had dark purple spots on it.

"He likes you. You now have a new friend."

"Cool, I don't have too many friends with pink and purple tongues."

"Oh, that's because he's part wolf. Not sure how that happened exactly, but he came from Montana. A friend of mine in Billings found him on the side of the road one day. Looked like he had been running for days. Totally exhausted. He took him home and nursed him back to health, but his wife laid down the law and made him give him up. He knew I had lost my wife and figured I could use a companion. Great dog, but I see him eyeing the neighbor's sheep sometimes, and it almost gives me a chill. He minds well though, so I am not too worried about him taking any of them out."

Ah, the dust question was answered. No wife to make him keep it dust free.

As we took seats around a glass-topped table, in relatively comfortable lawn chairs, Killer lay down next to me and continued to wag his tail and stare at me. I reached down and petted him, stroking his fur, and then turned to Sandy.

"Thanks again for taking the time to talk to me."

"Shucks, that's all I got now, time. And probably not too much at that," he chuckled his response.

"Oh, I don't know about that. You look to be in pretty good shape," I replied.

"I suppose you're right. Well, what is this all about anyway?"

As I recounted the story of finding the watch and then telling him about cleaning it up and finding the engraving on the back, he watched with rapt attention. He appeared to be listening intently but seemed to be carried off to a bygone day.

"So to make a long story longer, I am trying to find out whose watch it was and then see if they might still be…uh, around the area still."

"You mean still alive and around this area?"

"Well, yes."

He sat motionless for a time and then, reaching out, grabbed his beer and took a long pull.

"I took some time off that summer, 1924. I had been working straight for three years without as much as a day off. We had hundreds of employees on the books, and even though I loved the woods, and Bordeaux in particular, I needed some time without the sound of saws and voices. I took a whole month off. Went to Long Beach and stayed in a little hotel near Oysterville. Quietest time I had spent in darn near a lifetime it seemed like. Maybe I can still help though. Got a good memory for an old fart. What names were on the watch?"

I pulled out the watch from my pocket and handed it to him. He took it carefully from me as if it were made of glass instead of precious metal. He read the inscription, moving his lips ever so slightly as he did so. He got that thousand yard look into his eyes again, and I sat quietly, figuring he was remembering those days so long ago.

He finally broke from the memories and spoke.

"Boy, no last names. William was a pretty popular name back in my day. Guess it still is. I bet we had twenty or twenty-five Williams or variations of the name working in camp at any given time. Maybe thirty."

"I kind of expected you to say that."

"But the good news is, I think I know who Betty is. Or was."

Suddenly, I felt my heart rate quicken.

"Really?"

"Weren't too many Bettys in a logging works. Only one I can think of was a cute little thing. She worked in her daddy's store, along with her sister Clara. Family name was Willets. She was probably around twenty when I last saw her. When I came back from my little trip, she wasn't working there anymore. Never gave it much thought.

Too many dang things to catch up on after being off a month. You know."

As Sandy was talking, I had taken a small pad from my coat pocket and began to scribble notes on it. If I could find out what happened to Betty Willets or maybe Clara Willets and if either was still alive and living around the area somewhere, maybe I could return the watch to Betty after all, if it was indeed hers to begin with.

Then realization struck. "I'll bet Betty was a pretty common name back then too, wasn't it?" I asked.

"Well, I guess it was. Met lots of them back in those days."

Rats. I was so excited thinking that Betty Willets was the *one* that I hadn't given a thought to the fact that most men didn't have wives in the camp. Some did for sure. There were houses up on the hill by then. Betty could have been at home on a farm or in a small town, living nowhere near the camp. The only good news Sandy had given me was that he only knew the one in camp.

"Gee, sorry, Jim. Here I thought I was helping, and I probably just muddied the water."

"Not at all, Sandy. At least I have something to work with now. You helped a lot, really."

When he had mentioned that there were a lot of Williams, I thought I would take a chance and ask him about my grandpa. Chances are he wouldn't remember him, but it didn't hurt to ask.

"Mind if I smoke?" Sandy asked.

"Not at all. Feel free."

Sandy pulled a crushed up pack of Marlboros from his pocket. He lit up and took a long drag. "Should stop smoking, but what the heck, no one wants to live forever, right?"

"Well, I want to make it as long as I can," I replied with a smile.

"I've lived long enough. Time comes when a man thinks enough is enough."

Sandy took another long drag and blew out the smoke with a contented look on his face.

"Hey, Sandy, you happen to remember a William with my last name, Tuttle?" I asked.

"Sure do. Everyone knew Bill. He didn't go by William up in the woods. You related?"

"Yes, sir. He is my grandpa."

"Well, I'll be damned. He was a hero up there, you know."

Hero? No, I didn't know.

"What are you talking about, Sandy? How was grandpa a hero?"

"Saved a man's life. Guy named Decent. Henry Decent. You ever hear about it?"

Now it was my turn to sit silent for a minute. I had heard the story at least two dozen times.

"Yeah, I heard it many times. Never heard the word *hero* out of my grandpa's mouth, but that would be just like him. He always tells me to let your actions speak louder than your words."

Grandpa had been working with Henry that day. They were using peavey, a long woodened handled tool with a metal point on the working end. There is a hook on a hinge that works in conjunction with the point. A worker would use the tip by sticking it into a log, and then by tipping the handle end skyward, it would engage the hook and the log. Then pushing the handle away from the worker's body, the hook would roll the log away from you. The worker could then pull the handle back and reset the tip and do it again to roll the log farther away.

There is a steam engine with large pulleys attached to spools holding the heavy cables used to drag the logs up hill to a landing for loading onto trucks. It is called a donkey. The donkey would blow its whistle when it was going to start pulling, allowing workers to get out of the way of the log as it moved along the ground. Grandpa and Henry's job that day was to work the logs around a large old growth stump that happened to be in the way of the logs as they were being drug up the hill. The log wouldn't stop, so they had to work quickly to roll it around the stump so that it didn't impede the logs' progress.

They were keeping up with the donkey until a very large log came along. They couldn't roll it. It was just too heavy. They heard the donkey blow its big steam whistle, which meant another log was on its way.

They both frantically tried to roll the big log out of the way. It wouldn't budge. A much smaller log came up the shoot and hit the big log and stopped dead for a moment. Then because it was still being pulled by the donkey, it flipped end over end in the air as the donkey continued its relentless pulling.

Grandpa saw it coming and ducked. The log flew over his head and straight at the old growth stump Henry was standing next to. Henry saw it coming and dropped his peavey, releasing the handle with his right hand, basically like throwing the handle away from his body. In doing so, his arm extended out from his body as the log barely missed taking his head off. However, the extended arm was hit directly by the log and pulled Henry off his feet. As he fell to his right, following his arm that was now fully engaged with the smaller log, he hit the ground with his extended arm resting on one of the roots of the old growth stump. The smaller log fell on top of his arm, pinching it between the root and the log and severing it from his body before continuing its upward climb to the top of the hill.

Grandpa had seen the whole thing happen. He fell to the ground, sat down, and took off one of his boots.

Removing the lace, he ran to Henry and tied the lace around the now stump of an arm. He helped Henry to his feet as others rushed to help.

It turned out Henry's arm was crushed. They rushed him to the hospital. He survived the incident and actually went on after getting some schooling to become the only one-armed game warden in Washington State history.

Having never thought much about the story, I could certainly see now where grandpa had been a true hero that day. Quick thinking had saved Henry's life.

"Bill got promoted to rigging slinger the next day," Sandy said, breaking me out of reliving the story in my head.

"Never heard that either. But I suppose, as I said, that's just Grandpa."

"He still with us, old Bill?"

"Why yes. Yes, he is. And I bet he would love getting together and talking old times with you. I should be seeing him Sunday, and I will bring it up."

"Would be great to talk about those days with someone who was really there, no offense. I never got to talk to him much back then. I lived in the hotel. I think he lived around Oakville."

"None taken. Out of curiosity, what was it like back then living in a hotel all the time? I think I would get cabin fever and want to get out some."

"Oh, it was all right. I lived in a single room since I was considered higher up than the loggers and, of course, made more in pay. I could afford it. I didn't have a wife or anything. I didn't get cabin fever as you call it, but I did need that vacation…Maybe I did get cabin fever." He chuckled.

"Listen, Sandy, I have to get a move on. It was great talking to you. I will let Grandpa know I ran into you and give him your number."

"That would be fine. Pleasure talking with you, Jim."

"The pleasure was truly all mine, Sandy."

Rising from my chair, I realized Killer had not moved. He still lay next to my chair. I bent and stroked him and told him he was a good dog and he'd better be nice to me the next time I came back.

"You relax, Sandy. I will go around the house and leave you to your afternoon. Thanks again."

"Thank you, Jim."

Strolling around the house, I noticed I was being followed by Killer. He was in happy mood though, tail wagging and all. I opened the gate, making sure to shut it behind myself, reached over one last time, and told Killer he was a good dog, turning and heading for my truck.

I had a lead. But how do I find Betty or Clara Willets?

CHAPTER THREE

Have you ever noticed how, when someone tells you something that they would never be kidding about, many times people will respond with "you're kidding?" That was the response I gave Betty when she informed me her late husband William had been buried along with the watch she now held in her hands.

"Sorry, I know you're not kidding. It was just a reaction to your statement."

"No apology necessary. I have done it myself when people have called and given me disturbing news. I did it once when someone called and said their husband had died," she replied.

She then went into silent mode again, staring at the watch that had once been owned by her father, then her husband. Buried with the latter. When she finally spoke, it was not something I had expected from her.

"We have to find out who dug up William just to get his watch."

This morning when I woke up and got out of bed, I would have been happy to know that I was going to be returning the watch to its rightful owner. Little did I know that the watch had been stolen from a grave, probably worn in the very same logging camp that William of the watch had worked and then lost by them only to be found by me.

Now here was Betty of the watch, asking me to help her find out who had dug up the watch from her dead husband's grave. Why she would want to know now that she had the watch in her hands was beyond me. I guess people just want to know who could desecrate a grave for the likes of a watch.

"I work full-time, Betty, but you know what? I will be happy to spend some time with you trying to figure this out. I think I will get my wife, Kate, involved, if that's okay with you."

"Why, of course it is. If it weren't for you, I wouldn't have the watch back and would have never known that someone dug up my poor William." As she said this, her voice had cracked with emotion. "I would be happy to meet your wife and even more pleased to have someone else helping us out."

"Well, Kate will be a help. She is a good, logical thinker. She thinks her way through things methodically, and I am happy to say she usually gets it right in the end. It's me you might have to worry about."

"Oh, I doubt that, Jim. You seem pretty sharp for a man your age. You see so many young people throwing their lives away these days that it's nice to know that not everyone is a criminal or a drug addict like the news is trying to tell you whenever they get the chance."

"I heard that. The news makes me feel worse about the world, not better. I have gotten to the point I hardly waste my time with it anymore."

"Well, it's nice young men like you that give me hope," she said as she reached out and patted my knee.

"Thanks, Betty. That is really kind of you to say."

Although she looked nothing like her, she reminded me of my grandmother whom I had lost just four years before—kind, gentle, and sweet. But just like my grandma, I felt that under all that was a toughness that, if exposed, well, let's just say I didn't want to find out how tough she was, at least not if that toughness were directed at me.

"Betty, like with any story, there is a beginning. I think we should start there."

Sitting in the sun, enjoying a glass of lemonade and good company was great. But if she really wanted to get to the bottom of all this and truly find who had taken the watch from the grave, it made sense that we start from scratch.

Betty sat quietly, appearing to be looking for the words to begin what I felt would be an interesting but sad tale. Finally, she took a deep breath and began.

"William and I, as you have probably already figured out, met in Bordeaux. I worked in my papa's store, and William was a timber faller. What most people who knew him didn't know was that William had been a very good student when he went to secondary school. I guess now they call it high school. Anyway, he was what most would now call a straight A student."

She stopped to take a sip of her drink and then continued.

"William had a dream. He wanted to make something of himself. He didn't plan to be a logger his whole life, like so many did. William wanted to either be an accountant or an attorney. Working with numbers was his passion. But he also wanted to help people. I think that is where being a lawyer came into play. He told me stories of people who had been cheated out of their property, their farms, why, even their livelihoods. William wanted to be a champion for those folks he felt were being cheated."

"I'm sorry, your lemonade is empty. Would you like another glass?" Betty asked.

"If the offer of a beer is still on the table, I think I could go for one about now. It's afternoon, isn't it?" I asked with a smile.

"Certainly is. To make you feel more comfortable, I will join you."

She rose and, taking the tray and glasses, walked to the back door and disappeared inside. She returned with the tray, complete with two bottles of beer, two mugs, and a small bowl of barbecued potato chips. A woman after my own heart. If someone told me they would give me a pallet of barbecued potato chips and a matching pallet of beer, I would tell them to gently set them down in my driveway.

"Would you like a glass?"

"No, thanks. I like drinking from the bottle."

She chuckled and said, "So do I, but proper ladies use a glass. Since we are in my backyard, however, I will do as I please."

Still standing, she took a bottle opener from the pocket of her dress, popped the caps, and then handed me one of them.

"To new friendships," she said as she raised her beer.

"Hear, hear!"

We clinked the two bottles together and each took a cool drink.

"Where was I?"

"You were telling me about William's dreams."

"Well, enough about that. I just wanted you to have a little background on him. We met in the store one day. I was working stocking things on the shelves that had just arrived by truck. I had only been working there for a short while. Papa wanted me to learn the business so that someday he could let me take over. Papa always wanted to take Mama on a nice trip somewhere exotic. Anyway, William came in, and as our eyes met, he stopped and just stared at me. Honestly made me a little nervous for a minute. There were plenty of roughnecks and thugs in a logging camp. Having never seen him before, I wasn't sure which of the two categories he fell into. To be fair, there were lots of nice men too. The nice men treated me with respect even though I was only nineteen at the time. The others were rude and obnoxious."

"I'll bet. You were likely one of just a few girls, or young women I should say, working in the camp. They probably got lonely living in the hotel and some probably forgot their manners when they saw a pretty girl."

"In some cases it was a lot more than not using their manners, but we can talk about that when the time comes. But yes, besides my sister Clara and me, unmarried women were nonexistent. Here stood a young man, covered with sawdust, staring at me. He had a wool buffalo plaid hat on, I recall. He took off the hat, ran his hands through his hair, wiped his forehead on his sleeve, and then smiled at me. I will never forget his first words to me because they made me laugh. He asked me if we had any bag balm. Do you know what bag balm is, Jim?"

"Actually I do. My grandpa owned a dairy farm from 1955 to the mid-'70s. Always had cans of it sitting around the milk house."

Bag balm was invented around 1900. It was a salve for helping keep cows udders from getting chaffed due to milking twice a day.

"So you can see where I might find it funny."

"Indeed. But I do know we have a can at home now. I use it on my hands when they get chapped and rough from working outside around the house or cutting firewood."

"Well, as I told you earlier, we owned a farm near Oakville, and of course, we used it as well for the prescribed reasons. It just hit my funny bone when this big, tall strapping man asked for something used on cows when the nearest cow was likely ten miles away."

Her eyes took on a sad look. "Then I saw his hands. William was a hard worker. Fallers were generally very strong, with big hands and shoulders from sawing down the trees with those big saws. Chainsaws weren't used a great deal before 1930. Anyway, his hands looked like the bark from a tree. Rough, scaly, they looked awful. I immediately apologized and told William why I had laughed. He never got angry, wasn't in his nature. He just smiled and nodded. I got a tin of bag balm and handed it to him. I told him it was on the house. He insisted on paying for it. Said he wouldn't think of getting something for free. That was just the way he was." Then she smiled—the kind of smile that puts the sun to shame.

"He introduced himself to me, very formal like, and reached out his big hand to me. I told him my name as we shook. His hands were so dry and cracked I felt even worse about laughing. But William had a way of making you feel that everything was okay with just a look. We became friends that day. However, it was more than that. Do you believe in love at first sight, Jim?"

"I have always been a romantic. Yes, absolutely. When I met Kate, I knew I was going to marry her. She was everything I wanted in a woman—smart, beautiful, easy laugh. Yes, I do believe in love at first sight."

"I fell in love that day. William started stopping in when his day was over, and I couldn't wait to see him walk through the door of the store. That happened in February of 1924."

"So you only knew him a few months before you were married?"

"Yes. As I said, it was love at first sight. And just like you, when I first saw him, I knew we were going to get married."

We had both finished our beer, and Betty asked if I would like another. I begged off. Looking at my watch, I realized it was nearly three. I wanted to get home before Kate and make her a nice dinner. Then Betty started talking again, and I was mesmerized.

"As I had said before, there were lots of men who weren't at all like William. One of them was William's bucker."

I knew a bucker was basically an apprentice faller. Too new to the job to have the expertise to fall trees but handy with a saw and axe. My dad always fancied himself a timber faller because he cut down trees for firewood. His expertise was not that of a faller. I can speak to this from personal experience. One day he fell a tree with me in the fall line. I ran and was just clipped by the treetop. A bucker maybe, but Dad was no faller.

"David Jones was his name. Davey, everyone called him. He was crude. He would say things to me that were astonishing, maybe just trying to get a rise out of me, but I thought not. My thought was he didn't have any social skills, particularly with women. Then one day, William came in just after Davey. He heard Davey make a comment to me that was awful. Just awful. I won't repeat it, but I remember it to this day. William walked over to Davey, spun him around, grabbed him by the suspenders, and then led him to the door and threw him out. He followed him outside and, without ever raising his voice, said something to Davey. I saw terror in Davey's eyes. It was the last time I ever had to worry about Davey saying anything to me again."

"Wow. Did you ever find out what William had said?"

"No, I didn't. But William was a big man. Davey was a might smaller. I always thought maybe he threatened him with death. Never did find out though. Davey died up in Bordeaux just a couple months after William." She lowered her head, and I saw the white knuckles reappear as she gripped her hands together once again. "Freak accident, everyone said."

"Tell me, how was William viewed by the other workers?"

"William was well-liked, not just by the other workers but by the Bordeaux brothers. The brothers who started to company. Somehow, they learned about William's aspirations. I still don't know how, and they had told him to keep working hard, saving his money, and when he was done with college, they would entertain hiring him as either an accountant or a lawyer, whichever he decided to pursue. That is, or should I say was, wonderful of them. They sound like pretty decent bosses.

"There's more to it than that too. The Bordeauxs gave William and me a wedding present that was totally unexpected. They told William that when he was ready to go back to school, they would loan him the money to pay for his college, half of which he would not have to pay back as long as he came to work for them when he completed his schooling. He would have to work for them for at least three years to repay that portion of the debt."

"Wow. That was really above and beyond. Why do you think they would do something like that?"

"They were businessmen. They both knew if William was a hard worker in the woods, they were betting he would be a hard worker no matter what profession he chose. I think they figured that since everyone liked him *and* he was a hard worker, they could get someone who could really move up in the company, having started at the bottom."

I wasn't sure how to bring this up, but curiosity got the best of me. Maybe it is a person's morbid fascination with death.

"Betty, if it's not too hard to tell the story, how did William die?"

Her hands gripped together even tighter than they had previously, which I would have deemed impossible. This was not going to be easy for her.

"It was an accident. He and Davey were falling an old growth tree that was about six feet through. A load of work, to say the least. As the tree finally started to fall, Davey ran as he should have, but for some reason, William was late getting started with his run."

"Why do they run?" I asked. I thought I knew the answer but wanted to hear it from her to make sure my assumptions were correct.

"When a big tree, well, any tree really, falls to the forest floor when it is cut down, as the big branches hit the ground, they act like a slingshot in a sense. It is hard to explain, but it is called kickback. The branches are usually bent up when the tree is standing. When they hit the ground and flex, they then push the entire tree back toward the stump. And I should say this is done at an alarming rate. Fallers and buckers know to get out of the way. Fast. As Davey told the story, he had run to what he figured would be a safe distance, heard the tree hit the ground, turned to look, and watched as William was hit dead on by the tree as it kicked back. Davey said he never could determine why William had not run like he usually did. But this time he didn't, and it was lethal."

Betty stopped and took a ragged breath. I could tell this was hard on her, reliving the death of her husband. Tears started to flow. I reached out and put my hand on her hands and told her how sorry I was for her loss. It sounded a bit trite, but I meant it down to the bottom of my soul.

"How long were you married?"

"We got married in April, and William was killed in June. First day of the month. We had two wonderful months. I think about him every day. Still. Wished we would have had a lifetime together."

My mind began to wander and wonder.

"Betty, did anyone else but Davey see this happen?"

"No. They were the only team in that area. They did that so that there was less danger to the other teams as the trees fell."

"This may seem like an odd question, but did anyone benefit from William's death?"

She stopped and stared at me like I had two heads. I hadn't thought that question through very well.

"Jim, I got nothing from William's death but heartache. We didn't have an insurance policy or any such thing. At our age, we thought we were kind of bulletproof, I guess."

"I'm sorry, Betty, I wasn't referring to you per se. I'm sorry it came out that way."

Now she raised her face to the treetops surrounding her home and stared some more. I wasn't sure if she was thinking of William, the way he died and all, or if she was giving thought to my question.

"Well, I hadn't much thought of things in that way. Do you think maybe it wasn't an accident?" she asked.

"I don't know. But when you said how hard he worked and how good he obviously was in the woods, it doesn't seem like William would make what I would call a rookie mistake."

After she pondered a few seconds more, she responded, "Davey was promoted to faller, and he got to choose his bucker, who just happened to be his roommate, Harvey Trumble. I guess you could say they both benefitted from William's death."

Interesting.

"Getting back to the watch, who could have seen you put the watch in the coffin with William?"

"Only about two hundred people. The Bordeaux brothers let everyone who wanted to take the day off for the service, which was unusual. Usually, the camp kept working when someone died. It was just another way the Bordeauxs showed the respect they had for William. I hadn't intended to put the watch in the coffin, thinking I could carry it always as sort of a remembrance of William. At the cemetery, I changed my mind, and in front of everyone there I opened the coffin so I could put it in with him. I decided he would always carry it with him and that somehow seemed more fitting at the time."

"How often did you visit the grave in those first few weeks or months?" I was having some thoughts I wouldn't share just now with Betty, but I wanted to get some answers from her if possible.

"Every day. I moved up here to Olympia and lived with my aunt. I couldn't stay around the camp. Too many memories. I would walk to the cemetery and talk to William. Sometimes for hours. I did that for, oh, I don't know, maybe two or three months. I was devastated when William died."

"Yeah, although I didn't know where you went, Sandy told me when he got back from his vacation, you were gone and he never saw you at the logging camp again."

"You talked to Harlan?" she asked.

"Yes, I did. That is where I started my search for you actually after I got his name from a fellow who worked at *Logging World* magazine."

"All be darned. I still see Sandy once in a while. He calls more often now that his wife has passed, God rest her soul. She was a nice person. I met her a few times over the years."

"I have to get going, Betty. I want to thank you for sharing your life with me, at least the early days. I have a lot to think about, and I think Kate could add some insight as well. That is, if she doesn't get mad because I don't have dinner ready on my day off."

She laughed out loud, and it was good to hear. She had shed tears today, and I was happy to leave her with a smile on her face. And an old watch in her hands.

CHAPTER FOUR

Walking back to my truck in the parking lot at the capitol, I let the beauty of the day envelope me. The sun was shining through the old fir trees and illuminating the lawns of homes that were close to a hundred years old. There was a slight breeze, so it didn't seem hot, just warm as I strolled back.

Retrieving my truck, I headed home, backtracking the way I had just traversed on foot. I realized I needed gas and something for dinner or else I would have one irate Kate. We had a deal, whoever was off when the other was working was responsible to make dinner. I had already decided to cheat and stop and get a pizza and some beer. It just so happened the gas station on my way home had a pizza joint in the same parking lot.

Swinging into the station, I took the cap off the tank, pushed in the gas hose, and set it to run automatically. While it was pumping, I leaned on my truck and started going over my conversation with Betty.

There were some things I couldn't remember as I stood there trying to recall it all but at the time I had thought were a bit out of place. Try as I might, I couldn't recall them. Too many other things on my mind, I guess.

I was broken from my thoughts when the chowder head waiting to get gas behind me hit his horn. Being engrossed in thought, I hadn't heard the gas finish pumping. I guess he did and wanted me to know. Mouthing a sorry to him, I pulled the hose, set it back in the pump, and hopped back in the truck.

Pulling a total of probably one hundred feet from the pump, I stopped in front of the pizza place. It was a hole-in-the-wall, but they had great pies. I ordered a large Canadian bacon and pineapple, told them I would be right back, walked back to the mini-mart where I got gas, and picked up a six pack.

I put the beer in the truck, went back into the pizza joint, and picked up my pie. Ready to head home, I set the pizza on the bench seat next to me and started the truck up. Before the engine started, my stomach began to growl. The pizza smelled amazing. Good thing I was only a couple miles from home.

Kate had not arrived yet when I got there, so I set the pizza in the oven just because I didn't want to leave it on the counter, put the beer in the fridge, and I heard the garage door open.

Whew. Close one.

"Hi, darlin'," I called out.

"Hi back."

"How was your day?"

Without a response, Kate walked into the kitchen. "Your got pizza, didn't you? Getting a little lazy, are we?"

"It's not being lazy. It was what sounded good."

"Liar. How did your meeting with Betty go?"

"Great. I want to talk to you about it. I think I am missing something. We talked for quite a while. She filled me in on the backstory. There were even a few surprises."

"Like what?"

"Let's grab a beer and a slice and sit out back."

"Let me clean up a bit, and I will meet you. Don't eat the whole pizza before I get out there," she said with a smile in her voice.

"Better hurry then." I grabbed some plates, the pizza in its entirety and stuck two beers in my pants pockets, the necks protruding like geoduck necks out of the sand. Barely sticking an opener in my back pocket since the pressure of the beers on my front pockets took up all the available stretch my pants had in them, I headed out the back door.

Once Kate came out, sat down, and took a deep breath, almost a sigh, and had a drink of her beer, I started at the beginning. As I told her the story, starting with the tears when Betty realized that the watch was indeed hers but how it couldn't be due to its having been buried with William, the reactions from Kate ranged from "What?" to "Wow" and an occasional "Oh my god."

When I had finally completed the tale, my beer and half the pizza in between sentences, it was Kate's turn to speak.

"And now, Betty wants your help to find who dug up the watch? Why you?"

"I think simply because she doesn't have anyone else to help her."

"What about Sandy? You said that he kept in touch with her."

That was what had been bugging me. Leave it to Kate to pick up on it. Sandy hadn't mentioned that he had been in any contact with Betty. Why would he leave that out when I talked with him? Could it have just been an honest mistake? In fact, he led me to believe that Betty could be dead or alive.

"That is why I want you on my team. You get right to it. That was something that had nibbled at the corners of my brain, but I didn't put two and two together. Probably had just too much information for my pea brain to process. It is curious he made the statement about not knowing if she was alive though."

"Not at all, honey. Betty gave you loads of information. It is natural to have to think your way through it. I just got lucky and hit on the right thing, right off," she replied.

Trying to recall my conversation with Sandy the previous week, I wondered if he tried to tell me or if I just missed it somehow. He talked about all the Bettys he had met over the years, but I couldn't recall him mentioning seeing or talking to Betty of the watch.

"I have to get a pad and pencil. You already hit on one thing I want an answer to. I am sure you will hit on more. You're batting a thousand so far."

Running back into the house for the writing implements, I grabbed two more beers as well and headed back out. The evening was coming on, but being summertime, the light in the sky was still bright enough to sit and write notes. At least for a while yet.

"Okay, first the Sandy issue. Awesome. What else?"

"What do you think, I am some sort of investigator? Let me process the rest of the stuff you told me for a few minutes," she said.

"Let's see. She told you about a bunch of different people. What do we know? William is obviously dead, as is his bucker, Davey."

I wrote on the pad.

"What?"

"I want to figure out how this Davey died. She mentioned it was a freak accident. Just taking notes."

"Do you think there was anything odd in the way William died?" Kate queried.

"Something to think about," I said as I scribbled more notes.

"Besides Sandy, did you ask her if she ever saw anyone else from those days? Do you think there could still be someone else alive who could add insight? Did you ask her if her sister was still alive?"

"She mentioned a couple of other folks. I will jot those names down and ask her, as well as seeing if she knows of anyone else still around. No, I can't believe I didn't, but I never even asked her about her sister."

I wrote down the Bordeaux brothers and Harvey Trumble. Working through the conversation with Betty again in my head, I thought about something else to ask her. She had mentioned that she had moved to Olympia and visited the grave every day for a couple months. Did she notice any sign of the grass being moved? I knew from when I had put in a sprinkler system one time that the grass you cut out, no matter how careful you were with the sod, took time to look "normal" again. If someone had dug up the grave, there would have been sign of it, and it would take some time for the ground to heal back up.

By now it was getting pretty hard to see the paper I was writing notes on. We didn't want to turn on the lights and attract every flying insect in the county, so we headed back into the house.

"Have enough questions but not many answers, huh?" Kate said more as a comment than a question. "Are you going to go back and see Betty on Sunday? I would love to meet her."

"She wants to meet you as well. Said she could always use new friends or something like that."

"Great. Why don't we have her over for lunch? We can eat and then sit and visit a bit."

"Works for me. I want to take her by the cemetery so I can see William's grave."

"Why?" Kate asked.

"Call it morbid curiosity."

CHAPTER FIVE

Sunday could not come quick enough, but it had finally arrived. I had spoken with Betty and was picking her up at around eleven. A quick stop at the cemetery and then home for lunch with Kate.

There were questions that needed answers if we had any hope of finding out who had dug the watch up originally and why. Betty likely had some of them, but not all, so I assumed I would be visiting with Harlan Saunders again as well to get his perspective.

Leaving Kate at home to prepare lunch for the three of us, I headed out to collect Betty. We only lived about four miles apart, and the good news was the cemetery that housed William's remains was between our house and hers. That would make it a quick trip, I hoped. Betty had mentioned spending hours at the grave site. I was praying that wasn't what she wanted to do today.

Rather than park at the capitol this time and hoof it back to Betty's abode, I decided to just double-park in the street. The streets were relatively quiet, and I would not be gone from my truck long enough to create any problems for anyone.

Stopping in the street, and before I could even turn off the engine, I looked over and saw Betty emerge from her house. She waved as she came out, turned to lock the door, and strode up the sidewalk. Trying to imagine what I would walk like when I was seventy-five or so, I could only hope I had the health that this woman had, as well as the sound mind she possessed.

Jumping from the truck, I ran around and barely beat her to the door of the truck.

"Good morning, Jim."

"Hi, Betty. How are you this morning?"

"As well as can be expected, I suppose. I haven't slept much since your last visit," she replied. "Too much on my mind, I guess. Thank you for opening the door for me. What a gentleman!"

She climbed up into my truck, and I shut the door behind her. As I rounded the truck, I thought about how well my parents had taught me manners—respect your elders, open doors for ladies, and so on. With women's liberation in full swing, I had actually been told, in no uncertain terms, one day by a lady that she was "perfectly capable of opening my own door." I didn't let that rock my beliefs, just took it for what it was worth at the time. Little to nothing. Now Betty was a *lady*. She appreciated having her door opened for her, and I would continue to do so for any woman, even those that wanted to prove they were equals by simply opening their own doors.

"Ready to go?"

"Yes. I am excited to meet your wife. Are we stopping at the cemetery on the way to lunch?"

"I thought that would be best." I didn't want her to be thinking about going to William's grave through lunch, and also, I wanted her to have a clearer mind to answer some of the questions Kate and I had.

Turning onto Capitol Way, we headed in the direction of home and, subsequently, the cemetery. The day was going to be another warm one. The nice thing about western Washington is that the temperature is pretty consistent year to year, season to season. Summers are usually warm, maybe in the seventy-five- to eight-five-degree range, and winters can get cold but typically no colder than twenty degrees. There are the odd years where we get superhot summers or super cold winters, but the norm is moderate during all seasons.

Today the sun was out, and the sky was as blue as the Caribbean ocean. A slight breeze moved the trees. It seemed to me that cemeteries usually didn't have a lot of trees out in the open where the graves were, so I thought that it would be best to go early so that we didn't get too hot standing and looking at William's grave.

We made our way up Capitol Way. Betty was sitting with her purse on her lap and her hands gripping the strap. I had heard once before that when women did this, it was a sign of stress or anxiety. I believe it. She naturally was thinking of what lay ahead for us. Another good reason why I thought it best to get the cemetery portion of the day out of the way early, before lunch.

The cemetery was actually a collection of several cemeteries all grouped together. The founding fathers must have decided that this was a good place to bury people a hundred plus years ago. Little did they know that even though this was well out of town at the time, it would be encroached upon by urban sprawl in the years to come. The twelve or so acres were now surrounded by either houses or road. I recalled when they widened the road there was an uproar by some of the people who had loved ones buried near where the road was to be widened, saying that they didn't want their family members remains exhumed and moved just to accommodate progress. Due to these folks' vocal opposition, there were graves within a step of the sidewalk that paralleled the road. That meant that their loved ones, in some cases, were buried under concrete as well as dirt.

Traversing the roads that were now a part of the acreage, I took direction from Betty to get us to William's grave site. "Stop here. We can walk the rest of the way," Betty stated.

I braked and came to a rolling stop. Shutting off the engine, I turned to Betty. She looked stressed, more so than when she was clutching her purse handles.

"Are you okay?"

"Yes. Just lots of things going through my mind just now."

Jumping out of the truck, I did my best to get to the opposite side before this lovely old lady could extricate herself from it without my assistance. I didn't make it. She was standing on the grass next to the road, having left the door to the truck opened. She was staring in the direction that I knew would take us to William's last resting place.

She started walking slowly toward the grave. William was interred near the back of one of the cemeteries, under a large fir tree, one of the few on the cemetery proper.

"I really debated with myself at the time whether or not to bury him under a tree since…" she took a ragged breath. "But William loved the woods so. I felt in the end it was the right thing to do. He would have liked this spot."

We both stood staring at the headstone that was now fifty-five years old. Neither of us spoke. What could I say at this point? Questions would be asked later, but not now.

Betty was the first to break the silence.

"When we buried William, this tree was only about twenty feet tall. Look at it now. It must be at least seventy or eighty feet to the top. Time flies, and life goes on. For some."

Standing in the shade of this tree, which was a godsend since the day was heating up quickly, I took note of some of the headstones around William's. The oldest person whose headstone I could see had died at forty-three. It was a different time back then. People didn't live as long to start with, and then with the other considerations, like available jobs, many of which were dangerous, many folks died before their time. Loggers, mill workers, and sawyers all were in a position to have their lives end too soon. This town, the whole county, was built on the backs or strong young men who put their lives literally on the line every day.

"Can we go now please?" Betty asked.

"Of course."

We turned and walked slowly back to the truck without looking back. Nothing was said by either one of us. I kept my eyes averted so that if Betty wanted to shed a tear, she could do so without having me looking at her or asking if she was going to be okay.

She had left the truck door opened, so she climbed inside and I shut the door with as little noise as possible, trying to be a bit cognizant of what was running through her mind and not wanting to disturb those thoughts.

I jumped in the other side, started the engine, and wove my way around to come back out on the main street once again. Betty was looking straight ahead, and it was as if she were watching a movie unfold in front of her. She was replaying something in her mind, and I wanted to let her have this time alone with her thoughts.

After about a minute, she finally broke free of whatever it was she had been thinking about and spoke.

"So how far do you live from here, Jim?"

"By the time I answer, we will be there," I said, trying to lighten the moment a little. "It is only about a mile or so ahead."

"Good. I am excited to meet your wife."

With that, the day took a turn for the better. It was as if she had shut a book and was going about her day.

Knowing that we had some questions that would perhaps bring her back to the state from which she had just departed, my hope was that Kate and I could keep things as light as possible so that she didn't have to relive too much of the day she had buried her too young husband.

The drive to the house was fairly quiet, and since we only had about a mile and half to go, that was fine with me. Turning into the driveway, Betty let out a gasp.

"Your yard is beautiful!" she exclaimed.

"Thanks, but it is really Kate who does the work. I am more of a hired hand or slave, depending on how you look at it."

"Well, she does a wonderful job of it, that's for sure."

I parked in the driveway to make it easier for Betty to remove herself from the truck. The garage is too small to allow the person on the passenger side to get out real easily due, in large part, to all the junk we have on that side of the garage. Mostly mine.

Not even trying to beat her this time, I let Betty get herself out and I met her, and we sauntered up the walk to the front door. Before we reached the porch, Kate opened the front door and stepped out.

"You must be Betty."

"And you must be Kate."

Both extended their hands in friendship, and they shook with smiles on their faces, as if they were long-lost friends.

"Your yard is gorgeous. Jim tells me it's from your hard work."

"That and the work of my indentured servant," Kate replied. I guessed that would be me.

"Betty's yard is beautiful as well, and she doesn't even have any help."

Knowing I was trying to make a point, Kate gave me a smirk and a look. *Okay*, I thought, *I get it.*

"Come in, come in." Kate ushered us both into the house.

"Oh my, your home is as beautiful as your yard."

"Thanks, Betty. Again, you can thank Kate for that. She is a woman of many talents. One of them is cooking too, and since I'm hungry, I will ask, what's for lunch?"

"I made ceviche. Sound okay?"

Betty said she didn't think she had ever had ceviche, and I told her she was in for a treat.

"What can I get you to drink, Betty?" Kate inquired. "We have lemonade, beer, iced tea, ice water."

"You know what? I think a beer sounds delicious. It is going to be hot today," Betty replied.

I think it may have had as much to do with knowing we were going to start diving into her past again as it did the heat, but I kept that to myself.

"I will join her," I said.

"Okay, we will make it three beers then. Jim, why don't you take Betty out back and have a seat on the patio?"

Betty followed me as I wound our way to the back door. Stepping outside, she took in the backyard, and I could tell by the look on her face was stricken yet again by the beauty Kate had created.

Before she could speak, I said, "She cheats."

"What do you mean?"

"Kate has been a florist for four years, and she is very good at it. Besides doing floral arrangements, she has learned all about the flowers themselves. She knows when to plant, when not to, when to dig up and move plants, and so on. She really is something special when it comes to gardening."

"Indeed, Jim, she truly is."

We strolled over and took our places at the patio table. I had already taken the time to get a pad and pencil and had stashed the notes from the night before in the pages so that they would remain unseen. I didn't want Betty to think we were going to inundate her with questions but wanted to have them close at hand in case we forgot anything Kate and I had spoken about the night before.

Kate came out onto the patio with three bottles of beer on a tray. No carrying in pockets for this girl. Setting them down on the table, she turned to Betty.

"Would you like a glass?"

"No, honey, a bottle is just fine for me. Thanks though."

Joining us at the table, she dispensed the beer. It was a cold and refreshing. After we sat smacking our lips the conversation began.

"As you have probably figured out by now, Betty, I have shared our conversation and the one I had with Sandy with Kate. Unfortunately, that conversation brought about more questions than answers, but that is why we are here, right?"

"Yes, it is. I want to get to the bottom of this so I know who and why someone would dig up my William."

Not knowing exactly where to start, I decided to start with Sandy. "How well did you know Sandy back then?" I inquired.

"Harlan was the bookkeeper for the Bordeaux brothers. He was in charge of payroll, paying the taxes and keeping the expenses in line. He lived in the hotel. As for knowing him, it was just in passing, I guess you would say. Harlan, or Sandy if you prefer, would come into the store to pick up this and that, and he would always be cordial and pleasant. I don't think he was a bad person or anything."

"You mentioned he had stayed in touch," Kate asked in such a way to make it an open-ended question.

"Oh yes. When I moved to Olympia to live with my aunt, he somehow tracked me down and made sure to pay his condolences. I thought that was awfully sweet at the time. Then I sort of lost track of him, and he of me. Then about—oh, shoot—I don't know, maybe in the late '40s or early '50s, I got a wedding invitation from him. He was going to be married to an Olympia woman whom I didn't know.

Sort of thought it odd after all those years that he would send me an invite, but who knows?"

"Did you go to the wedding?" I asked.

"Well, yes, I did. Barbara, his wife, was a lovely woman and a beautiful bride. Once they got married, they moved south to Chehalis. I still saw them once in a while. Them being newlyweds, they had better things to do than hang around with the likes of me."

"Sandy and you both mentioned she passed away. When was that? Do you recall?"

"Certainly. At my age, death of friends becomes almost a daily occurrence, it seems like. She died in 1961. They had only been married around ten years or so. She had cancer. Poor dear."

"You mentioned that Sandy started getting in touch with you more often after Barbara died," I said. So far this was going well, but we had a lot of ground to cover still to get to the bottom of this. At least, that is how it felt.

"Sandy started calling me and then calling on me around 1964 or 1965. I think he, well, I should say I knew he wanted it to be more than a friendship, but I just didn't feel right about it. William was the one love of my life. I kind of felt like I would be tarnishing his memory somehow if I were to get involved with someone else. He persisted, so I finally told him how I felt, and he seemed to understand. We still keep in touch, but he understands now. We are still friends."

"Can you think of any reason why he wouldn't tell me that you were still in touch?"

Betty thought for a moment, then replied, "No, I really can't. Do you think he purposely didn't tell you, or could it have just been something he didn't deem necessary information at the time?"

That was the crux of what I was trying to find out. Why would Sandy not tell me? Did he have something to hide? Was it just an oversight? I couldn't think through this one, so I decided to press on.

"I guess I will have to ask him. You mentioned you had a sister, Clara, I think? How old was she when you got married to William?"

"Clara is two years younger than I am, which would have made her around sixteen or seventeen years old when I was married. Why do you ask?"

"Just trying to gather facts, that's all."

"A minute ago, you said Clara is two years younger than you. So she is still alive? Does she live around the area?" Kate asked.

"Why yes! She is alive and well and lives just over in Lacey."

"Do you think she would talk to Kate and me if we called her and explained the situation?"

"I can't think of any reason why not. Let me call her and let her know what has been going on, and then I will set it up for you to call her."

"Perfect. She might have a perspective on what happened after you left camp. You know, gossip and the like."

"You mentioned a logger named Harvey Trumble. Is he still around too?"

"Honestly, I don't know. I think he was at the funeral, but I don't know if he is still alive or in the area," Betty said in reply.

"How about another beer and some lunch?" Kate inquired.

"Now that sounds good!" I realized I was starved, and I assumed Betty must be as well.

Kate left to get lunch ready to bring out, and I asked Betty about the Bordeaux brothers. She said they were both gone, passed away. So I still had Sandy, Clara, and I would research Harvey Trumble at the courthouse. Things were starting to move, but very slowly.

I did have one last question for Betty, the one about the ground being disturbed after William was buried. She told me that to her knowledge and recollection, the ground was never disturbed.

Kate returned with a large tray I had never even seen. I am not even sure how she got it through the door. She must have picked it up and just failed to tell me about it. Oh well, how she spends her money is her concern. On the tray were the makings for ceviche and three more beers. The conversation turned much lighter with no questions about the watch, people from Bordeaux, or anything else for that matter. We just enjoyed each other's company. Kate got to know Betty a little better, and I ate ceviche like it was going out of style.

There would be more to do on my next day off, but today was a good day. I felt hopeful.

CHAPTER SIX

Work was becoming an annoyance. It was all I could do to keep my head in the game each day until my next day off. Now don't get me wrong. I really love my job, and in this day and age, or any day and age, I would think having someone say they loved their job was not real common. But I did. My customers were more like friends. At Christmastime, I would bring home more gifts from my customers than Kate had under the tree for me. It always kind of amazed me. Here I am, taking their hard-earned money for a piece of jewelry for a significant other, and yet they bought *me* gifts for taking their money. Really, it was more than that. I made sure they were well taken care of and that the person that received the gift was getting exactly what they wanted. I did this by taking copious notes all year long so that when a husband came in and asked what his wife would like, I could tell him in no uncertain terms. This made him happy and her happy, and for doing so, I would get cookies, pies, neckties. Well, you get the picture.

That said, it was difficult to not think ahead to Wednesday and my next day off. I intended to run down to Chehalis and talk to Sandy again. I needed to take his pulse on some issues that we had raised with Betty. In the meantime, I had decided to run to the county courthouse and see what I could find out about Harvey Trumble.

The county courthouse was only a short distance from the mall where I worked, so I took my lunchtime and jetted over to see what

I could ascertain about the aforementioned Mr. Trumble. Having spent some time there in my original search for Betty, I knew that most of the employees in the records department were pretty cool. There was one woman who worked there, however, who was the rudest person I had ever met to date. Who said civil servants had to be civil? I was hoping I didn't get her today. I wasn't in the mood to engage this old battle-ax for information. Luckily, she must have been at lunch as well. I got Sarah to help me. She was awesome, always willing to go the extra mile.

"Hi, Sarah."

"Oh, hi, Jim. How have you been?"

"Just fine, thanks. Say, I am on my lunch hour and wanted to see if you could help me find out if a person was still around. I guess death records would be a good place to start. He would be around seventy-five or so."

"Name?"

"Harvey Trumble."

Sarah started looking through a large file to see what she could find. After a few minutes, she turned and said that he hadn't died in Thurston County. Of course, that meant he could have died in another county.

"How about tax records?"

"You are getting good at this," she replied. "That was my next step."

Opening an even bigger file, she started digging in. After a few minutes, she looked at me and smiled.

"Harvey Trumble is still alive. He paid taxes last year at least. Or I should say they were paid for him out of an account that was set up to deliver them to us right on schedule."

"Any chance there is an address or telephone number of who is making the payments for him?"

"It looks like it may have been set up by Mr. Trumble himself at a bank downtown—First Security on Fourth Avenue."

"Thanks, Sarah. I think I will pay them a visit and see if I can get anything from them. Banks have a tendency to be a bit close-mouthed though."

"I have a friend who happens to work there. She may be able to help, kind of, um, under the table."

"That would be amazing if you could find out where Mr. Trumble is now."

"Let me call her. Give me your work number and I will see what I can do. And try to eat some lunch, Jim. Running all over hells half acre and not eating is not good for a person," she said with a smile.

I removed a business card from my card case and handed it to her.

"Listen. I don't want to get you or your friend in any kind of trouble over this. If she can help, great. But if there is any danger of her or you getting in trouble over this, please just don't worry about it."

"Nothing to worry about. I am not going to lose my job over something like this. But if I can get what you are looking for, I will."

"You are the best, Sarah. Thanks."

Turning and walking out the door of the records department, I had a spring in my step. Maybe I would at least find Harvey and get a chance to talk to him. I wasn't sure what he could add to what I knew already, but at least things seemed to be starting to take shape.

In a not so uncommon turn of events, the weather today was a bit damp. A summer rain had hit town, and as I drove back to work, the streets were slick as glass. I had warned Kate many times that when it rains in the summer after a prolonged dry spell all the road oils, the stuff left behind by cars that leak oil or other fluids, turn the road into a skating rink until enough rain falls hard enough to wash it all off. Today it was slick. Really slick. We hadn't had any rain for about two weeks, and it was perilous driving. As long as I paid attention, I would be fine.

The shower became a downpour in the short time it took me to get back to the mall. I waited in my truck for a couple minutes to see if it would let up, but with no change in sight, I jumped out and made a run for it. As I entered the mall, I shook off like a wet dog might and wiped as much excess moisture off my suit as I could. It would dry. I just didn't want it to shrink.

"Jim." I heard someone calling my name.

I turned and was met with a hand extended out like the person was a knight and was trying to joust with me.

"Oh, hey, Pat. How are you?" I asked.

"Great, great. Hey, it is the wife's anniversary, and I need to get her something."

Pat was an old customer of mine. It always found it funny that a wife could be having an anniversary and not the husband. And needing to get her something rather than wanting to get her something. I let it go.

"Sure, Pat, come on, let's go in and I will see what she has been looking at." We walked into the store, and I headed for my notebooks, my lifeblood for keeping customers happy.

"Ah, she must have known you would come see me. Mary was just in last week and picked out a couple things for you to choose from."

"Oh, man. I don't want to choose. You pick something out and wrap it up. I will be back in ten. I gotta get a card too."

I smiled and assured Pat that I would take care of it. This scenario played itself out tenfold at Christmastime—husbands who want to please their wives but really don't give a damn what they give them as long as she will be happy. Thinking how I would never do that with Kate, I proceeded to pick one of the items Mary had chosen and wrapped it up. Pat returned, thanked me, and headed home to his wife. I wondered how he would react when she opened the gift when he didn't even ask what it was. Go figure.

As I was charging Pat's account for his purchase, the phone rang. I reached for the handset on the wall.

"Good afternoon, Jewelry Design Specialists, may I help you?"

"No, but I can help you." Sarah.

"Hey, Sarah. Wow. Did you find something out already?"

"Yup. Mr. Trumble is in a rest home. Shady Lane out in Lacey."

"Holy cow. That was quick. How did you find out so fast?"

"Remember, you didn't just ask that, and I had nothing to do with it."

"Gotcha. And thanks for nothing."

"No thanks necessary. I didn't do anything."

We both laughed, and I told her thanks again and hung up. I would have to tell her the story sometime about finding the watch, then Betty of the watch, and how Harvey came to be a part of all this.

The rest of the day at work was uneventful. I spent a good deal of time thinking about what Harvey Trumble might have to offer. I decided to talk to Kate about it and see if she wanted to take a spin out to Lacey for a visit with Harvey.

As I left work, the sun was making an appearance again, and the streets were dry. Or at least drying. They had steam rising from them. No more skating rink.

Kate beat me home and had steaks ready to grill. God, I loved this woman. Steak, corn on the cob, and baked beans. Can't get better than that for a summer meal, at least as far as I was concerned.

"Hey, darlin'. Want to take a spin out to Lacey? I found Harvey Trumble."

"You did? Already? How?"

"Okay, you have reached your total allotted questions for the night. And you accomplished it in one sentence." I laughed out load.

"Funny, Mr. Smart Guy."

"Yes, I did find him already, and I can't tell you how. I promised the person who told me where he was at to keep it a secret, and I intend to do so. I may need help in the future, and I don't want to burn any bridges."

Kate pushed out her bottom lip as if to pout. Then she smiled. "I get it, no prob. But where is he?"

"Shady Lane Rest Home. Want to go for a ride after dinner?"

"Sure thing. Let's eat now so we can get a move on."

I concurred and grabbed the steaks and a beer, putting the beer in my pocket—old habits do indeed die hard—and headed out back. Firing up the grill, I could hear Kate through the window as she put the pot on for the corn. We would eat within twenty minutes and be on our way.

CHAPTER SEVEN

L acey is not a big city by any means. Its claim to fame is South Sound Center, a shopping mall that sprung up when developers realized what they perceived to be a need of the people. The city was basically comprised of two main streets, which intersected each other at one end of the mall. The other end of the mall was right up against Interstate 5, making it a popular stop-off point for travelers who thought they needed something that they had forgotten in their trek either toward Seattle to the north or Portland to the south.

Shady Lane Rest Home sat in the woods that were yet to be decimated by progress, just south of the mall. It was a pleasant-enough setting; big Douglas firs and gigantic maple trees enveloped the rest home so that it appeared to be more of a cottage than a semi-sprawling building with two wings. One wing housed the people waiting to die—soon. The other was for the folks who could just no longer take care of themselves for whatever reason. Harvey Trumble was in the second wing.

Kate and I arrived after the inmates' dinner had been served. Obviously, they were not incarcerated, but that is just the way I felt about such places. I guess we could have arrived at four thirty and been after dinner. It seems that the older people get, the earlier they like to eat. Or maybe it is just being regimented. As long as you know when you are going to be fed, walked, perhaps bathed, and put to bed, all was good. To me it seemed like a lonely, horrible existence.

Places like Shady Lane have a smell. I have never been able to put my finger on it, but it is an obnoxious scent that appears to be a mixture of Lysol, alcohol, stale food, and death. It is not, by any sense of the term, pleasant, and I vowed then and there I would never be put in one of these places. In its defense, Shady Lane was clean, sparklingly so, and we would find every employee seemed to smile, which told me they either liked their jobs very much, or were extremely happy to just have any job.

We stopped at the desk and asked where we might find Harvey Trumble. The nurse on duty said that he was likely in his room, but if we didn't find him there, she would be happy to help us locate him. We made our way up a long hallway and found room A27. The door was opened, so we peeked in, saw whom we assumed to be Harvey sitting in a wheelchair, staring out the window at the trees and flowers that surrounded the building. We knocked politely on the door.

The man in the chair put both hands on the wheels of the chair, and moving his left hand forward and his right hand backward, he spun around to the right so quickly it was evident he had been using this chair for a good long time.

Sitting before us was a man who had obviously been a bull of a man in his younger days. His shoulders, although now shrunken with age, still showed a width that bodybuilders would be proud of. Hands the size of my old Vada Pinson baseball glove and fingers the size of Polish sausages told me he had worked his body hard most all his life.

"Are you Harvey Trumble?" I asked.

"Yes. Who are you?"

"Mr. Trumble, my name is Jim Tuttle, and this is my wife, Kate. Could we speak to you for a few minutes?"

"About what?"

He was coming across as adversarial, and I couldn't figure out why that would be. We had just met, had no prior bad history, and were willing to spend time talking to him to help break up what appeared to be yet another monotonous day.

"Mr. Trumble, we would like to speak to you about your time at the Bordeaux Logging Camp. Do you have a few minutes to spare us?" What else was he going to do? Sit alone and look out the window? Then a thought hit me.

"Would you like to go sit outside in the fresh air, Mr. Trumble?"

It was then there was a complete transformation in his attitude. "Why yes, I would like that very much. They won't let us go outside by ourselves. Afraid we are going to hit the road, I guess. Or maybe *get* hit in the road." He chuckled. "Please call me Harvey."

"Deal. If you call us Jim and Kate."

As quickly as that, a new friendship had been made.

"Can you do me a favor, Jim?"

"Sure, Harvey, what is it?"

"Can you grab me a cup of coffee and bring it outside for me? This dang place thinks we shouldn't drink coffee after dinner for some damn reason. Maybe they think we will be up all night, but what is it to them?"

"Where will I find it? The coffee?"

"In a pot." And he laughed out loud at his own joke.

"Sorry, I couldn't resist. It is in the gathering room back toward the main entrance, then take a right at the other wing, and it will be on your left."

"I will be right back."

Collecting his coffee and then Harvey himself, we followed his lead and ended up going out a side door that opened into what was actually a very nice courtyard. It had patio tables and chairs and a collection of flowers in pots that added to the ambiance. I liked it. Harvey pulled up to a table. I set his coffee down, and we started.

Telling the whole story of finding the watch, Sandy, and, subsequently, Betty, he listened without a word.

"Son of a bitch. You mean Sandy is still alive? And Betty is living over in Olympia? I'll be damned."

"Yes on both counts. Now Betty has asked Kate and I to help her try to find out who dug up William's grave to get the watch out of his casket."

"Plus, we want to find out what you can tell us about the loggers and other people who lived up in Bordeaux," Kate chimed in.

"What do you want to know?"

60

"Well, Harvey, it seems that maybe, just maybe, William's death wasn't an accident. Betty said he was a great faller and knew to run when the tree was coming down. But Davey Jones, the only witness said he hadn't run for some reason. Any thoughts on that?"

Harvey set his coffee down, careful to remove his huge finger from the small finger hole in the cup. He looked down at the ground, averting his eyes from us for what seemed like an eternity. Kate and I were both staring at him, waiting for him to come back to us. "Well…"

If it was possible, we stared more intently. Finally, he raised his eyes to meet mine and then Kate's.

"I am getting on in years and will never leave here," he said, gesturing with his hands to show us the courtyard and buildings. "It's not so bad, but what has been inside me too damned long is ready to come out. I was thinking I might take it with me to the grave but now seems like the right time to finally get my suspicions off my chest."

He had us now. We were both leaning forward in our chairs and boring a hole through him with our eyes. Was this it? Were we going to get some answers to some of our questions?

"Davey Jones was a mean son of a bitch. I roomed with him in the hotel, so I had seen and heard firsthand what an asshole he could be. Son of a bitch was in love with Betty, but his way of showing it was being a domineering bastard with her. He would go into the store, and instead of trying to woo her, he would make terrible comments to her about, well, about wanting to have sex with her, among other things. There was one day in particular that I remember he was beside himself with fury. He had gone into the store and, as usual, made a rude comment to Betty. As I understand it, William overheard it and yanked his ass outside and told him if he ever heard him utter words like that to Betty again that he would kill him. Davey came back to the room with his tail between his legs a bit. William was his faller. He worked with him every day. And now here he was, threatening to kill him just for talking to Betty. As that evening wore on, Davey got madder and madder. His eyes were wide, and his whole body shook as he started to think about what had happened.

He asked me who William thought he was, telling him to keep his mouth shut around Betty. He ranted and raved for the rest of the night. Funny thing was, next morning, it was like nothing had ever happened. That scared me, and I don't scare easy."

"What do you think happened overnight?" Kate asked.

"After all these years, I think that that night, Davey plotted to kill William before William could kill him."

There it was. Out in the open. Someone who was there in Bordeaux telling us that he suspected Davey Jones of being a potential killer.

Harvey picked up his coffee and took a sip. He was doing the eye-averting thing again. We waited for him to come around.

"It wasn't long after that night that William and Kate announced they were going to be married. My roommate went even more crazy *that* night than he had before. He said Betty was his girl and so on. Then just like the previous time, he woke up the next morning, got dressed, and went to work as usual. It was damned weird, I tell you."

"Then what happened, Harvey?" I inquired.

"Shortly after that, Davey was sitting in our room, drinking beer and kind of muttering to himself, as I tried to rest. The work was hard, and at the end of the day, I was bushed."

"Drinking beer? In 1924? What about prohibition?" Kate hit on the obvious again while I sat looking at her and wondering how she remembered that prohibition was on. It was thirty-plus years before she was born, but she had that sort of a mind for details.

"The Bordeaux brothers knew how hard their men worked and had a deal with a couple of home brew makers. Old man Willets at the store would sell it out the back door. Cheap. But the rule was, if you got caught drinking by the law, you were on your own. Most everyone just grabbed a couple bottles and went up to their room to make sure they didn't get caught. Not like the sheriff gave a damn, but you know, just to be safe. Anyway, Davey was drinking his beer and looked at me and said something like, 'If a person were to die up here, do you think the cops would get involved?' Now this seemed strange. He knew full well that people had died up here before, and the cops never came up to investigate. That worried me.

If he had something on his mind, something bad like a plot to maybe kill someone, I didn't know if I should tell anyone or not. He was my roommate and kind of a friend. And I had no real proof that was what he was thinking. That night, I made a decision to pay close attention to him for a while. If he said anything else that sounded like he was going to hurt someone, I was damned sure going to turn him in, friend or not."

"What happened next?"

"Nothing. Well, nothing, at least from that angle. Betty and William, of course, got married. Big tadoo. Then seemed like things kind of settled down to normal for a couple months. Then one last night, Davey seemed agitated and nervous. He paced around the room, talking about how unfair it all was. Never said what was unfair, just that it was unfair. Suddenly he got a funny look on his face, said he would be back later, and walked out. He had a smile on his face when he turned around to me as he left and said, 'You ever think of being a bucker?' That smile has haunted me all these years. It was, best an old man can describe it, pure evil. The next day, William was dead."

We all sat and contemplated this development for a few minutes. Harvey had nothing to say. He had gotten it off his chest after all these years. He suspected that William's logging accident was no accident and that his friend Davey had done the unthinkable, killing another human being.

Finally, Kate spoke, "Have you ever given any thought to how he might have done it to make it appear an accident?"

"Ms. Kate, that was all I thought about for a few months. If Davey was smart enough to kill William and not have anyone the wiser, for a long while I couldn't figure out how. He was a ruthless man. If I am right, killing obviously didn't bother him. But it was maybe two months before I finally hit on maybe how he did it."

Kate and I stared at him as if the world would end if he didn't speak in the next ten seconds. He finally went on.

"Now you may have heard William was a good logger. A great faller. No near accidents, no on-the-job injuries to him or any of his buckers over the time he worked at Bordeaux. He did have an interesting thing he did when the tree he was cutting finally came down. You ever watch the Olympics?"

We both nodded simultaneously.

"I like the Winter Olympics best, but I watch them all now that I am here with nothing else to do. How about you? Ever watch the gymnasts do the balance beam?"

"I will never figure out how they get the kind of balance it takes to stay on the darn thing," Kate said.

"Do you remember what is called when they leave beam upon completion of their routine?"

"Are you talking about the dismount?" Kate asked.

"Yup. Well, when William finished a tree and it started to fall, Davey told me how he did this dismount from the springboard. Of course, I didn't know from dismounts back then. Too busy working and all. Anyway, sorry to ramble. William would, as the tree first started to head toward Mother Earth, drop the saw, which was normal, but then you ever see someone go the end of a diving board and spring up and land on their butts and continue on by flying in the water?"

"Done it many times myself," I answered.

"Well, William would kind of jump in the air, and hitting his butt on the springboard, it would sort of propel him up and he would land on his feet and take off. Davey said he did it every time he fell a tree."

"Go on please, Harvey. What did you think caused William's death? Or maybe I should say, how do you think Davey went about murdering him?"

"That night when Davey left with that terrible smile on his face, I think he went and tinkered with William's springboard. If a guy knew how they worked—and trust me, Davey knew since he was a bucker—he could either shave down the end that was stuck into the tree, just a bit, or he could make some cuts in it that would not show up if you filled them with a little mud or something like that. By weakening the springboard tip, when William landed on his butt, it could have busted and he would have fallen straight down. Now a man not expecting that to happen sure wouldn't be prepared for it.

And even someone as well versed in logging as William was might take a second too long to get up and get out before the log kicked back."

"But what if the tree didn't kick back? I know they all don't when they fall. Plus, Davey was taking a huge risk that the tampering wouldn't be discovered. If William had somehow survived the kickback, he would have examined his springboard carefully, wouldn't he? What if the board broke during the falling of the tree?" I asked.

"You're dead-on, Jim. Not all trees kick back. Davey was taking a hell of a risk, but one he was willing to take to accomplish his goals. Once William was dead, no one thought for a second about his springboard, I am fairly certain. I had said Davey might just have been smart enough to pull it off, but it took a great deal of dumb luck for it to work. Now remember, I can't prove any of what I just told you. It is basically the ramblings of an old broken-down man. At least that is what any decent Colombo would tell you."

He was referring to the detective on television portrayed by Peter Falk. A good detective would indeed think nothing of the story without proof.

"Kate and I get that. What I find astonishing is we came here to see if you knew anyone who might have wanted to dig up William's body to steal his watch, someone who was likely a logger since I found the watch at the bottom of an old growth stump. You have given us the perfect candidate. He had a motive, jealousy both professionally and personally. He also didn't like being threatened by William. Like on the cop shows on television, he had means and opportunity. Sad thing is, we can never prove any of that either."

"Speaking of the watch, I will tell you, I never saw it if he had it. He carried an old leather pouch with his cheap old pocket watch in it when we worked together. Now that is not to say he didn't have it. The only time a watch meant anything to me was when it said it was time to be off work."

The mention of the pouch set my mind off. If he really didn't see the watch on a day-to-day basis, how could he know, I mean *really* know, if it was Davey's old watch or the one stolen from William's grave?

"So you never saw his watch? Or you never saw it on a regular basis?" I asked.

"Oh, I saw it once in a while. But no, not on any regular basis as you call it. I guess it is possible he had Betty's watch, but I never saw it personal like"

Wow. We now knew that it was at least possible Davey had killed William and that it was just as possible that he had dug up William's grave to extract the watch from it. The problem was, we could not prove any of this. Kate and I were not getting Betty any closer to knowing for certain who had stolen the watch from the grave. And I sure as hell wasn't going to tell her William might have been murdered by Davey Jones without some sort of evidence that was more concrete than Harvey's recollections of the happenings fifty-plus years ago.

"I understand you and Davey were both promoted the day after William died."

"Yup. Davey walked around with his chest all puffed out like he was some big man. Asked me to be his bucker. By this point, I was more than a little concerned he might really *be* crazy, but money was money, back then as it is now. I made good money from the promotion to bucker. Couldn't turn it down."

Then Harvey said something that gave us another new wrinkle to this already-bizarre story.

"You know, I always thought it was a little ironic, at least I think that is the word, that Davey had asked about the cops coming up to Bordeaux if someone died."

"Why is that?" The inquiry came from my lovely wife.

"Because the only time in sixteen years I worked up at Bordeaux, the one time the cops showed up for a death was when Davey died."

CHAPTER EIGHT

arvey had given us a load of information. How we could come over to see him with one thing on our minds, finding out who dug up the watch and stole it from the grave, and now sitting here with him telling us that it was at least likely that William had been killed by Davey was a lot to process. This latest revelation about the cops may not have seemed like much of a big deal, but men died up in the woods all the time. Why did the police come for Davey's death? I asked Harvey just that.

"Most of the time when men died, like William, it was in the woods. Shit happens. But Davey's accident happened in the hotel. The sheriff and the local undertaker, who was doubling as the coroner at the time, came up to have a look to see if they could figure out how it happened. No one was allowed to move the body, which didn't make much difference. Davey's neck was broken, and it was damn obvious."

Kate shuddered, visualizing the body, I was certain.

"Thing was, back then, it took awhile to get up to Bordeaux. The sheriff covered a large territory. I don't think he rounded up the coroner and got up there for, oh, maybe five or six hours. I know it was pitch-dark when they got there, and in the summer months, it was light until near ten at night."

"What did they discover?" I asked.

"Well, they examined the body, checked out Davey and my room, and came to the conclusion that he had fallen out the window accidently. Done deal."

"What do *you* think, Harvey? Where were you when Davey fell?" Kate said.

"I can't rightly remember exactly where I was, but I do know where I was when I heard all the hollering outside. People yelling 'Get the doctor' and 'Don't touch him' and the like. I was walking up the stairs in the hotel. I double-timed it once the shouting started so I could get to my room and look out the window. Natural enough thing to do, I suppose. As I rounded the corner onto my floor, I caught just the tail end of someone heading down the stairwell at the other end of the hotel. I didn't think about it just then, but as you might be able to tell just from talking to me tonight, things fester in my brain until I can think them out of there. I figured at first that whoever it was had looked out their window and seen Davey, and they were headed out to get a closer look. Now here is the thing. The sheriff came to the conclusion that Davey was sitting, having a beer on the windowsill and smoking a cigarette. Logical enough assumption since there was a bottle next to the body and a cigarette under it that had burned a little hole in his pants. What would the odds be that he fell on a cigarette someone had just tossed onto the dirt outside his window? Not very likely."

"What conclusion did you draw from what the sheriff had to say? You seem to be holding something back on us here, Harvey."

"Not at all. Just trying to give you the big picture as they say. So the sheriff says it was an accident. But here is the deal. I lived with Davey for a couple years. I never saw him ever smoke a cigarette."

"Then how did the cigarette get under his body?" Kate asked.

"That, Ms. Kate, is just what I kept asking myself. After rolling it around for a period of time, I came up with an idea."

Kate and I were both on the edges of our seats. Harvey was going to tell us now that Davey had been killed as well as William. We knew it but had to actually hear the words and reasoning to believe it.

"As I said, I was coming up the stairs to my floor and rounding the corner and saw another person going down the other flight of stairs. It was the full length of the hotel, so I couldn't see much, just a leg and foot going around the corner and down the stairs as I came up. I should tell you that I didn't think much about that person until much later."

"Okay," I prodded with one word.

"I opened the door to my and Davey's room and saw the window open. Now mind you, these were big windows, maybe six by three feet where the lower half slides up when it is open. I went to the window, looked down, and saw what was left of David Jones."

"And your theory is…," Kate said.

"Once I realized Davey was dead, which one look told me, I thought what a dumbass for falling out the window. Then when the sheriff found the cigarette butt under him, that is when I started with my idea. What if the person I had seen leaving the floor as I came onto it had been in the room? What if he and Davey had been arguing and he shoved Davey out the window and, in the process, dropped his cigarette out with Davey?"

"Lot of what-ifs there Harvey," I stated.

"Yes, but it is really the only thing that makes sense. That cigarette butt was *under* his body. The person leaving the floor could have been smoking while talking to Davey, or arguing, and decided it was time for Davey to meet his maker. When he pushed him out the window, his cigarette must have fallen out as well. Still can't figure out after all these years how he got the jump on Davey though. Davey was strong. The person had to be stronger to be able to overpower Davey. There weren't a lot of people up there who could do that. At least since William was dead. William was bigger than Davey, but once he was out of the picture, there wasn't anyone who was as big as him left."

"What you are saying is that Davey's death was no accident."

"Yup. Best I can figure anyway. Now I may be wrong, but I don't think so. Just too many bits of evidence that no one really checked out at the time."

"Harvey, we have to be going. We both have to work tomorrow, and it is getting late. Can we come back another day and visit?"

"Heck yeah. I would love to have someone to talk to who makes sense. Lots of the folks around here carry on conversations with themselves. It is nice to actually have a regular conversation."

"You can count on it, Harvey. We have a lot to think about. Kate and I are still no closer to figuring out who might have dug up the watch, and now we have two potential murders that we would need more evidence to solve. We are going to be busy trying to tie it all together, but we will come back for a visit, I promise."

"Thanks. It was a pleasure to meet you both."

"Harvey, here is my card. If you think of anything else, feel free to give me a call anytime you want."

"Will do, Jim. Thanks again for listening to the ramblings of an old man."

"Goodbye, Harvey. We will see you soon," said Kate.

"Goodbye, Ms. Kate. You take care now."

We left Harvey outside at his request and reentered the building and exited out through the main entrance and back to fresh air. Harvey had filled up our minds to the point there was no room for any more information. We walked to the truck without a word being said. I opened the door, and Kate climbed in. I rounded the truck and got in my side.

We drove all the way home in silence.

CHAPTER NINE

"Boy, did you get more than you bargained for," Kate said as we sat in the backyard, watching the growing darkness. "You tell a lady you will help find out who dug up her husband and stole his watch, and instead you have found out that it is at least possible he was murdered, as was the person who murdered him. *And* you are still no closer to finding out who dug up the watch."

"That pretty well sums it up, all right. Let me ask you, do you think Harvey was convincing about both potential murders? Or either? Could they be the ramblings of an old man as he put it?"

Kate thought for a moment before answering. "Jealousy is a pretty strong motivator. If Davey thought that William was taking everything away from him, his girl and his job, and then you add in the fact he may have built up in his mind that William was going to kill him and he had to beat him to the punch, then yes, it makes a pretty strong case for him to commit murder. Still no proof, of course, but a strong case nonetheless."

"Now as for Dave being murdered," she continued, "that one I am not so sure there is anything to it. Just because there was a cigarette butt under the body doesn't mean anything. Anybody walking by the hotel could have thrown it down just before Davey fell out the window."

Once again, Kate and I were in total agreement on both counts even though I had not said one word yet. There was evidence but no proof of one murder and really nothing to make us think Davey was pushed out his window at the hotel.

"Have you given any thought to the fact Harvey could be lying to cover up the fact he killed William and or Davey?" Kate asked.

"No, I hadn't. But now that you mention it, in my spare time, I will roll that around too," I said with a smile. Of all the things I had, spare time was not one of them.

We were still no closer to figuring out who dug up the watch.

"Let's go back to square one. We told Betty we would do our best to find out who dug up the watch. How do we do that? What is the best plan of action?" I asked.

"Betty told you the ground wasn't dug back up that she could see. What do you think about getting ahold of the cemetery and asking about who dug the original hole that William was placed in? I would think they employed regular gravediggers. Maybe one of them saw someone hanging around before the grass had time to grow back. You know, digging William right back up after just being buried"

Son of a gun. "That is a great idea. I doubt they have records that would tell us that, but it is worth a shot for sure. I will give the cemetery office a call tomorrow and see what they can tell me," I replied. "Digging the casket up immediately would mean that there would be no evidence later. Good call, darlin'."

"I think we need to consider who would really want the watch as well."

"Could be any number of people."

"Start going through them in your mind and see what comes of it. It may be a way to narrow the field at least."

It was again too dark to see out back. The ambient light from the neighborhood gave us just enough to see our way back into the house.

"One person I want to talk to is Clara. Can you check with Betty tomorrow and see if she has alerted her to our calling?" I asked. I was hoping to get Kate and Betty together for purely humanitarian reasons. Betty seemed lonely, and Kate was all about work and the yard. I wanted them both to have someone to share time with other than just me.

THE WATCH IN THE BOX

"Sure. When do you want to talk to Clara?"

"Sooner the better. Besides asking her about the watch, she may add credence to Harvey's story."

"Jim, you are getting off-line again. Let's stay focused on the watch, okay?"

"You're right. But dang, theft, murder, jealousy. There is so much to choose from here," I laughed as I replied.

Of course, Kate was correct. We could start looking into the other facets of this saga once we had found out who had unearthed the watch in the first place. After that, we would have time to research and not feel like we were letting someone down, namely Betty, by not answering the first question on the list.

I wasn't tired even though I usually went to bed around eleven. There were just too many things floating around in my head. I snuck out of bed so I wouldn't disturb Kate and went into the kitchen. Pulling out the phone directory, I looked up the cemetery number and made note of it on a yellow legal pad. If there was a possibility that whomever had dug the grave for William's internment was still alive, perhaps they could tell me if they saw anyone hanging around the cemetery or grave following the service. Seemed like a bit of a long shot, but I recall my dad telling me that when you were a kid back in the 1920s and early 1930s during the Depression, you would do just about anything for work, and once you had a job, you would keep it. Times were hard. Your pittance of a salary could mean the difference to your family of having enough food to eat. Everyone chipped in and worked to make ends meet. Dad even mentioned that kids did a lot of the menial labor. Maybe, just maybe, the person was indeed still on the right side of the grass and could help Kate and me out.

CHAPTER TEN

Waking up the next morning, I had to look at my watch to see what day of the week it was. I knew it was between Wednesday and Saturday, but I couldn't remember exactly what day. Assuming that happens when you brain goes into overload, I was pleased to see it was Friday. Just a couple days until I had another day off to do some more research for Betty.

Showering and eating breakfast in kind of a haze, I finally climbed in the truck and headed to work. The cemetery was on my right as I drove to work. I gazed in the direction of William's grave and thought about calling the cemetery office on a break. Boy, was I shooting in the dark here. What were the odds of ever rounding up the person who dug William's grave? Slim to none came to mind.

Wanting to also catch up with my grandpa was on my mind. He was alone since my grandma had passed away four years earlier but stayed busy working in his yard and garden. I would have to call him around lunchtime and see if I could catch him inside.

With the jewelry taken out of the safe and carefully displayed in the cases, I opened the front gate and started my workday. Summers were never too busy. Nothing like the holidays. During December alone, we did over 26 percent of the entire year's business and most of that in the first twenty-four days leading up to Christmas. The summers accounted for about 10–12 percent of the year's business per month.

When no one came in when I opened the gate, I ran to the phone to call and see if the cemetery office was open. I was a little surprised when someone answered on the first ring.

"Oddfellows Cemetery, Janice speaking, may I help you?"

"Good morning. I am looking for some information that I hope you can help me with, Janice."

"I can sure try," she said with a smile in her voice. I had learned years before, most people liked being called by name. Use their name, you break the ice quicker.

"This may sound a bit strange, but I am trying to locate the man or men that your cemetery might have employed clear back in 1924 as gravediggers."

"Wow. That is, what, fifty-five years ago? I am not sure where to even look for something that old around here."

"It would really be helpful to me if you could come up with a name or two. I promise to tell you the story behind it all if you do. Do you like mysteries?" I said, trying to bait her a bit.

"Oh yes, I sure do. Is it about someone who was buried here?"

"Yes, and then maybe dug up and reburied by someone who didn't work for the cemetery." I didn't want to scare her off looking if she thought she could get a former employee in trouble.

"Yes, sir, I will look for you. Now I want to know all about it." Hooked.

"Okay, my name is Jim Tuttle. I work up at the mall. Take a look around and just give me a call here if you find anything. I sure appreciate it. And thank you."

I gave her my number at the store and at home and told her to call anytime.

One down and one to go. Now I had to wait until lunch time to see if I could catch Grandpa in his house and ask him about the old days.

Time seemed to crawl. Finally, I couldn't wait any longer and called him about eleven thirty.

"Hello."

"Hey, Grandpa!"

"Hi, Jim. Calling me to set up a fishing date, I hope." Grandpa loved to fish, and since I always seemed to have a boat, I was his main man when it came to getting out on the Black River.

"We need to do that. Hey, how about Sunday?" I asked.

"Sounds good to me. I will bring along my bait box." Grandpa had an old friend from his logging days that always would say he wanted to get his bait box out of the back of the truck, meaning his lunch bucket.

"Great. How about I pick you up around six or six thirty?"

"Six would be better. They will bite better in the hot weather in the early morning."

"Done. Great, Grandpa. See you then."

I hung up and realized I would be killing two birds with one stone. Grandpa would be a captive audience for me to tell him my story and get his feedback, and I would get to go fishing with him, which was one of my favorite things to do. He had great stories and was a great storyteller to boot.

The day at work still drug along. Finally, it was time to figuratively punch the clock and I headed for home.

Kate had beaten me home, which was not unusual, and the house smelled of what I assumed was fried chicken. I was correct. *Yes.* I love fried chicken.

"Hello?" I called out. No response.

Stepping into the kitchen, I saw that the chicken was already done and sitting on the counter. I looked out the back window to see Kate resting in a lawn chair and drinking a beer. God, I loved summer. Backtracking and grabbing a beer from the fridge, I popped the top and headed outside in my suit.

"Geez. Aren't you even going to change before you get drunk?" she chided.

"No, I intend to get totally annihilated and then try to take off my tie," I responded.

We both laughed. I gave her a big hug and kiss and plopped down beside her in a chair.

"How was your day?" she inquired.

"Okay. I talked to the cemetery and there is a really nice lady there named Janice who is looking for what we need. Oh, and by the way, I am going fishing with Grandpa Sunday. I figured I could pump him for information while we fished."

"Sounds like you have a plan. I spoke with Betty today, and she has let Clara know we will be calling her in the next few days. Want me to handle that one?"

"Sure, try to set it up for late afternoon Sunday. That way, I can get what, if anything, I can from Grandpa, and then we can meet with her."

"Sounds good."

We sat in silence for a few minutes, enjoying the late afternoon and early evening, and finally I told her I wanted to get changed so we could eat.

"Not going to attempt fried chicken in your suit, huh?"

"No way, Jose."

Kate has an amazing laugh. I love it, and she blessed me with it as I headed in to change.

Dinner was superb. The chicken was fantastic, and we just enjoyed sitting, talking, and laughing our way through the evening. We had enough on our minds that we needed a night to just let it go.

CHAPTER ELEVEN

Saturday at work flew by, thank goodness, and the when my alarm went off at five on Sunday morning, I was ready to simply roll over and go back to sleep. It had been a long last week, and I wanted to sleep in more than just about anything. However, just about was what got me out of bed and plodding into the bathroom to dress. I wanted to see if Grandpa could add anything to the growing list of weird happenings in the Bordeaux Logging Camp fifty-five years ago.

Luckily, I had loaded the boat and motor into the truck the night before, along with all the fishing gear. I grabbed the worms and my own bait box out of the fridge and headed for the door.

"Good luck," Kate said, standing in the bedroom doorway in her Mickey Mouse bed shirt. She looked amazing for five in the morning.

"Thanks. And thanks for scaring the crap out of me. I thought I snuck out pretty quietly and hadn't woken you up." That marvelous laugh again.

"See you this afternoon. Catch me some fish. We'll have them for dinner."

"That's the plan, among other things." With that, I turned and walked out the door.

Grandpa was waiting on his front porch when I drove up at five minutes to six.

"Thought you weren't going to make it," already starting the banter wc would have all day while we fished. I loved the guy. He was something special.

"Yeah, yeah, whatever," was my flashy comeback.

As we made our way out of town toward Black River, I made the decision to get right to the second reason we were together in the truck.

"Hey, Grandpa, do you remember a guy from back in the Bordeaux days named William Walker?"

He turned and looked at me with an unreadable expression on his face. "Yeah, I do. Where did you ever hear that name?"

I decided to give him the whole unabridged story. It took the entire drive to the river to get it all out.

"William was a heck of a nice guy. I met him a few times. Never really got to close or anything. Grandma and I were living in Oakville, so I didn't hang around the camp in those days. It was a long way home in '24 from the camp. Never heard a bad word about him or from him."

"What about the others? Harvey, Davey, Betty?"

"Knew Harvey a little. Never met Davey but word was he was ornery. Betty, why she was as pretty as a picture. She and William made a great pair for as long as it lasted."

"Harlan Saunders lives down in Chehalis. He said to say hi to you and give you his number."

"Barely knew him. Funny he would want my number."

"Maybe he is just looking for someone he can relate to, like Harvey."

"Harlan also told me the story about you saving Henry Decent's life. Said you were a real hero."

"Ah, bullshit. Anyone would have done it. I just happened to be there at the time."

That was all he was going to say on that subject, I could tell. Nothing new in what he had to say about the guys at the camp. We would have to count on Clara to maybe fill in some blanks.

Grandpa and I spent a beautiful summer morning catching fish and jabbing at each other for the fun of it.

In the end, we had both caught our limits, which was not too uncommon. None of the fish were monsters, most around twelve or fourteen inches long. Black River is known to have some mighty big fish in it, and we have caught our share of them over the years. Today, though, we had to be satisfied with pan-sized fish, which was just fine by me.

Dropping Grandpa off a few minutes after eleven, I realized I had forgotten to eat breakfast and was starving. I pulled through the drive-through of the local McDonald's and got a couple cheeseburgers and a shake. A guy has to get his junk food fix sometimes, right?

Kate was working in the garage when I got home, cleaning out some old boxes of junk to see if there was anything we really needed in them. She had that Goodwill look in her eye, so I knew she would be making a trip to drop off some things soon.

"Any luck?"

"Of course, do you really think an accomplished fisherman like me would come home empty-handed?"

"Please."

"I have to clean the darn things now. Did you get a hold of Clara?"

"Yes, sir. Do you really think an organized person like me would shirk that responsibility?" she said as she raised one eyebrow. It was my turn to laugh.

The fish got cleaned. I got showered and decided to rest out back for a little while and think about the watch and all the other aspects of this interesting dilemma. Kate was right. We needed to focus on the watch first and foremost. The rest was all opinion and supposition at this point, so why waste time with it? Thinking about all that we did know about the watch, which was really not that much, my mind began to wander to the potential murders. Lots of moving parts and nothing to show any of it was true.

"Hey, Jacques Cousteau, we have to head over to Clara's place," Kate said as she stuck her head out the back door.

I jumped up and headed into the house.

"Did Clara give you anything over the phone? Is she married? Kids? Anything?"

"She is a widow. Her husband died around the time your grandma did. Lung cancer. Never had any kids."

Laughing, I replied, "I was really only kidding about getting information. How do women do that? A man would call, set up a time to meet, and hang up."

"Thank goodness you didn't call then. We just chatted for a few minutes. I was trying to get to know her a little and to put her at ease for our visit in person."

"Makes sense. Boy, I never would have thought of doing that. Have I told you lately that you are a wonderful wife?"

"Not recently."

"Well, you are a wonderful wife."

She smiled and raised the eyebrow one more time, then whirled around and headed for the garage.

I was not sure what we might get out of Clara since Grandpa had been somewhat of a bust in the Bordeaux gossip department. She was a woman, however, so the perspective would certainly be different than good old Grandpa's.

CHAPTER TWELVE

Lacey, in many people's minds, should have just been incorporated into Olympia. When driving through the tri-cities of Olympia, Lacey, and Tumwater, you could not tell when you left one and entered the other. More like urban sprawl than three separate cities.

Clara lived on Eighteenth Avenue. Another small home but not nearly as old as her sisters. It was probably built in the 1950s. Her yard was the antithesis of her sisters'. The lawn looked like it hadn't been mowed since Hoover was president, the flower beds were more like weed beds, the entire home looking like it was in a state of disrepair. Then I remembered that her husband had passed away just a few years ago, and she was on her own. Not all people deal well with the passing of a loved one. Perhaps she was still in mourning. I would certainly give her the benefit of the doubt.

We turned into the driveway and stepped out. Kate came around to meet me at the front of the truck, and holding hands, we walked to the front door. We hadn't spoken about what sort of tack to use on Clara to get information simply because we knew so little about her. She was Betty's younger sister and had worked in the store at the time Betty and William were married, and then once William had died and Betty had moved away, the story ended from Clara's standpoint. We had no idea whether she had stayed on at the store or moved away; we didn't even know she was married until Kate gleaned that information from her on the phone. So basically we were on a fishing expedition, trying to find out what she knew the goings-on at the logging camp.

Ringing the doorbell, we waited for a response. When the door opened, here stood the polar opposite of Betty. Clara was about the same height as her sister, but there the similarities ended. She was probably tipping the scales at close to two hundred pounds, and on a frame that reached only five feet five at best, she looked like she had never met a doughnut she didn't like. Her skin pallor was almost gray and she reeked of cigarettes. She was wearing what Mom called a muumuu, a billowing dress that covered her from shoulders to mid-calf. Loose fitting in an attempt to cover the fact she was seventy or eighty pounds overweight.

"Good afternoon. You must be Kate and Mr. Kate," she said with a smile.

"Jim. Call me Jim. I don't think I have ever been referred to as Mr. Kate before," I said chuckling.

I held out my hand, and she shook it. Kate followed suit, and we were invited inside.

The house was neat and tidy, but the smell of cigarette smoke was overwhelming. She had ashtrays on just about every flat surface, and they had not been emptied for quite some time.

"Would you like to sit out back? It's such a beautiful afternoon."

I couldn't think of anything I wanted to do more. The fresh air outside beat the smell inside, hands down.

"Sure, sounds great," I said, looking at Kate who was nodding to the affirmative.

We wove our way through the house and exited through a sliding glass door onto a concrete patio. Her backyard matched her front yard perfectly. Clara motioned to some chairs, and we sat down.

"I think Betty told you a bit about why we wanted to talk to you," I said, purposely leaving it an open-ended statement.

"Yes, she did. She said you found William's watch up at the camp. Hard to believe but true, I'm sure."

"I did find it, yes. You were at the funeral. Did you actually see Betty put the watch into the casket?"

"Yes. She had told me that she was going to keep it as a remembrance, then at the last minute, she walked up and put it into William's pocket. She was crying pretty hard. We all were. William was such a wonderful man. It was horrible when he died."

As she was talking, tears welled up in her eyes and flowed down her cheeks. Having seen such a terrible thing at a young age had had an impact on her. Plus, losing her own husband just a few years ago was probably entering into the mix as well.

She reached into the pocket of her dress and removed a pack of Pall Malls. Straights. No filter for this lady. Removing one from the pack, she placed it back into her pocket and, reaching into the other pocket, pulled out a lighter. She lit up and took a long drag, blowing out the smoke sort of over her shoulder so that it wouldn't come toward Kate and me. Wiping the tears away with the back of her hand, she continued.

"Everyone there saw her put that watch into the box. Not a dry eye in the cemetery."

"How long after the service did you hang around?" Kate asked.

"Oh, we all mingled just a bit and then headed back to the camp. William was so special. When we got back to camp, the Bordeaux brothers had set up a huge, well, party I guess you would say. They filled the cafeteria in the hotel with food, and everyone was able to sit and eat and talk about William. It was a fitting tribute to William. Everyone loved him."

"Do you remember if Davey Jones was at the service or the party?" I inquired. With the mention of his name, her face seemed to droop and her shoulders slumped just a little bit. Having been in sales for a while, I was pretty good at picking up body language. It was an advantage when you were selling something to be able to read people. There was no doubt in my mind she had history of some sort with Davey.

"That man was scum. Davey Jones was an awful person. No, I don't recall seeing him at either the cemetery or the party."

"Why do you say he is scum?" Kate asked.

Clara took another long drag on her cigarette and then snuffed it out in an ashtray that was sitting on the little side table next to the chair she was sitting in. She reached in her pocket and pulled the pack out again and went through the ritual again of lighting it and taking a long pull before she spoke.

"He used to come into the store and say horrible things to Betty. And to me. I was only seventeen. He said things to me that would have made a sailor blush. William overheard him one day saying something to Betty and yanked his sorry tail outside and said something to him. From that day on until poor William died, Davey was better. At least in the store. But if he saw Betty or me outside the store with no one else around, he would start up again. Once William died, Davey thought he was the bee's knees and strutted around, bragging about being a faller. No one cared. No one liked him very much, except maybe Harvey, his roommate."

"You said he was better until William passed. What happened afterward?"

"He was back to business as usual. Of course, with Betty gone, I was his only target. He would come into the store and say the rudest things. Even followed me around at times. These days they would call him a stalker."

"How long did you stay working at the store?" Kate said.

"I stayed until I met my Tom. He was a logger. Not as good of one as William but a faller as well. We met when I was eighteen, and we got married before I turned nineteen."

"Did he ever stand up to Davey?"

"They never met. Tom came from a camp down by Aberdeen in the fall. The fall after William died and that idiot Davey fell out his window. He never met William either, of course."

"Did you stay in Bordeaux after you got married?"

"For about a year. Then Tom got injured. Slipped while sawing down a tree and fell off his springboard. Broke his leg so bad he had to stop logging. Limped pretty much the rest of his life."

She spoke in a matter-of-fact, almost monotone when speaking of her Tom. Having a hard time dealing with his passing was what came to my mind.

"I'm sorry. We understand he passed a few years back."

"Yes. Died of lung cancer. Never smoked a day in his life. They say cigarettes will kill you, but he never smoked and still got cancer."

"Were you there the day Davey fell out the window?"

"Yes. I was never happier. He could no longer pick on me."

"We heard the sheriff came up and investigated."

"Not much to investigate. Fool fell out of his window and broke his neck. Good riddance."

"How about Harlan Saunders. Remember him?"

She smiled just a little and then said, "Kind enough man. I think he had a thing for Betty. Never said anything about it, but you could tell. Then William started to come around and Harlan kind of disappeared. Stopped coming in, you know what I mean."

"Sure."

"And Harvey? What did you know of him?"

"Harvey was okay. Kept to himself. Worked hard as far as I know. He got promoted twice in six months. First to bucker when my...when William died. And then to faller when Davey Jones died. Never bragged about it, just did his job."

Kate and I looked at each other. Clara had let slip one word that caught both of our attentions. *My,* Just like she had said "my Tom" she had tried to stop herself, but had said 'my William.' Things were beginning to get interesting.

Clara must have sensed we had picked up on it as well. She looked at us and said, "I do have some errands to run today. Maybe we can talk again one of these days." With that, she stood and made it very evident that the conversation was over.

Kate and I rose as well, thanked her for taking the time to talk to us, and followed her back into the house, reversing the route we had taken earlier and leaving through the front door.

As we buckled up in the truck, Kate uttered a wow. I couldn't have agreed more.

Once again, we drove home in complete silence, both lost in our thoughts. I had a hunch the afternoon, and evening would find us sitting out back, drinking beer and discussing Clara at length.

I was right.

CHAPTER THIRTEEN

"Where do we start?" Kate asked. "There was so much said and unsaid that we might be here all night."

"I think we start at the beginning like we always try to do. First impression?"

"She really didn't want us there or to talk to us."

"Agreed. She didn't offer as much as a glass of water. I know she was raised better than that. Betty is the epitome of manners and always makes sure her guests, well, me, are taken care of properly," I replied. "Why do you think she would agree to talk to us if she didn't really want to?"

"I've been giving that some thought. Best I can come up with is she felt obligated because Betty had asked her to, or maybe there was a sense of guilt for some reason or another that prompted her to say she would."

"One or both of those are good reasons for her to allow us to visit, but why give the impression then that you don't really want to talk to us? I think there is something else going on with our Clara." I had worded it carefully to see if Kate would take the bait. She did.

"Yeah, and what was that whole deal with 'my William'? If I had to guess, I would say she had a thing for William way back when. I wonder if Betty knows anything about that."

"Perhaps way back when she not only had a crush on William but also fancied herself in love with him. Then he marries her sister. That would throw a wrench in the works, don't you think? We need

87

to ask Betty if her and Clara's relationship was ever strained over William."

The late afternoon sun felt good. We sat and pondered a little bit longer, and the conversation took off again. We were missing something. At least that is how I felt. It was right there at the corners of my mind, but I just couldn't get it to become a hard idea or thought.

"Okay, back to the beginning. We jumped from first impressions to leaving without talking about anything in the middle."

Kate laughed.

"You're right, of course, oh, wise one. Besides the impression that she didn't really want us there, I was shocked that she smoked like a chimney. Betty is so prim and proper, and although she drinks beer, I have never seen her smoke, and I doubt she does. Clara, on the other hand, smells so strongly of smoke that you could smell her coming down the block."

"I guess what surprised me was that she smoked at all since her husband died of lung cancer. I have heard that second-hand smoke, the smoke a person blows out of their lungs, if inhaled by another person, is actually more toxic than it is to the person doing the smoking. If that is true, then her smoking killed her husband 'even though he didn't smoke a day in his life.' He did smoke, but it was Clara's smoke he was taking in that was causing the harm."

"Strange how that works isn't it? A person smokes all their life, and it doesn't affect them, yet someone who is living with them and has never smoked dies. Life's mysteries, I guess."

"I wouldn't say it didn't affect her. Did you see the color of her skin? She looked like a December sky. I have never seen anyone as gray as she was. She doesn't get out in the sun much, that's for sure."

"What I find odd is that Betty is in such great shape, and Clara is so, well, fat," Kate said.

"You don't see that too often. Seems to me families tend to kind of follow a certain path. When you see overweight parents, often their children, even the ones only five or six years old, are already overweight. The difference in Betty's and Clara's appearance couldn't be a heck of a lot more opposite."

"What else did you find interesting from our conversation with Clara?" Kate inquired.

"I found it very insightful that Davey picked on her and Betty. Betty never mentioned it nor did Harvey. It seems like Davey wasn't usually too worried about saying what he wanted in front of other people, particularly after William died. So why didn't anyone else notice him being rude with her? Makes you wonder if she was making that up."

"Why? Why would she make up something like that? It doesn't make any sense. In fact, it muddies the water even further in regard to Clara. She came across as not wanting to talk, and then she tells stories about things that perhaps didn't happen? What's up with that?" Kate said.

"Agreed. Clara gave us more questions than answers. Now I am kind of paralyzed as to which direction to go from here. We found out that Betty had indeed put the watch into the casket, but we are no closer to finding out who dug the coffin up and took the watch out. Then she tells us, more or less, what we expected to hear about Davey and all that, adding, of course, the fact he harassed her as well as Betty. Basically it was a wasted trip."

We sat without a word for maybe five minutes. Kate appeared to be deep in thought. Whenever that happened, I let her have at it. She is a pretty smart cookie, and I suspected she just might get to the bottom of this whole mess if she was given time. Without any help from me.

"I don't think so," Kate replied. "I was just thinking through the conversation in my head. How many times did Clara mention William? Four, five times? And each time it was, 'William was such a wonderful man' or 'It was so horrible when William died.' Not to mention, of course, our favorite—my William. In my humble opinion, Clara was in love with William even though he likely didn't know it. That would make her and her sister rivals for one man's affection. Betty won the battle and the war, probably without even knowing that there was a battle with her sister. Jealousy can be a pretty strong emotion."

"So what are you saying?"

"Just that I am not sure yet about Clara."

"Are we still talking about the watch here or are you diving deeper? You don't think she had anything to do with William's death?" I asked.

"As I said, jealousy can be a pretty strong emotion. Could be that Clara felt that if she couldn't have William, then no one could have him?"

"Holy cow, Kate. Do you really think that? How would she have carried it out? She didn't work in the woods. She would have had to enlist someone's help."

"Like maybe from Davey Jones? Who already hated William and would probably kill him on his own if he got the chance. If Clara went to him and offered him something, you can read my mind on that one, maybe she convinced Davey to do the deed."

"Really? Sex for murder, you think?"

"I am just saying that we need to keep an open mind when it comes to Clara. And I think another conversation with Betty is in order to see what she knows, if anything, about Clara's love for William."

"I can keep an open mind, but wow."

"I hear you there."

CHAPTER FOURTEEN

Monday morning had me back at work. As much as I liked my job, and I really do like my job, I couldn't keep my mind from wandering, thinking about the watch and the other strange happenings back in 1924. At lunchtime, I finally called and spoke with Betty. After relaying a good deal of what happened with Clara, leaving out the "my William" piece, I asked her if her and Clara had always gotten along. She said they were close, but not *really* close. In asking her what she meant, she had said that although they spoke often, she didn't go out of her way to go to Lacey to see her, and the same was true with Clara visiting her house in Olympia.

It finally came time to ask the big question: did she ever feel that Clara was after William while he was courting her? She laughed a good solid laugh and replied that no, she didn't ever think that Clara was in any way trying to garner William's attention. She asked me why I had asked such a question. I finally told her about Clara's comment. There was silence at the other end of the line for so long I thought perhaps we had been cut off. When she did finally reply, it was in the form of a question.

"Do you think that maybe Clara was jealous of William and my relationship? Could she have been the one who dug up the watch as a remembrance of a love she would never have?"

The thought of Clara digging up the watch had not really crossed my mind. But it made complete sense put to me the way that Betty had just done. If Clara was indeed in love with William, she might want to have something to remember him by. It seemed so odd since Betty and William's names were on it. Stranger things had happened, I suppose, but it still seemed damn strange. This was something I wanted to think about. Maybe even run by Kate.

Changing the subject, I told her about our visit with Harvey. I tried not to go into too much detail, but trying to keep it cut down in size and content was harder than I thought it would be, so I pretty much opened up the whole book. Everything—Harvey's thoughts that maybe William was murdered and that maybe Davey was murdered as well. I could tell from her reaction that this revelation didn't faze her much. She simply made one comment. "William was a great logger. I have given it a lot of thought over the years. William just wouldn't have made a mistake like the one that took his life. I guess the most important questions are who and why someone would do it."

"Those are the questions of the day for sure, Betty," I replied.

"I know I have asked you to help me find who dug up William's beautiful watch. I can't ask you to do any more than that. You and Kate have been wonderful. If you can just find out who stole the watch, I would be a very happy old lady."

She sounded older. This call had taken a lot out of her. The fact her own sister could have been involved in the theft of the watch and the revelation that she was not the only one who thought that maybe William had died at someone else's hand was just too much for her at once, I felt.

"I can't tell you how sorry I am to have to have asked you all these questions, Betty. Kate and I will find out who took the watch. Then we will see where it goes from there."

After a moment of silence, Betty replied, "If you want to look into a fifty-five-year-old murder, that would be your choice. I am not sure if you will find anything, but it is entirely up to you. And Kate, of course. Again, all I really care about is the watch."

We ended the call saying our goodbyes and with the hope we would find the answer soon. No more than I had hung up than the store phone rang.

"Good afternoon, Jewelry Design Specialists."

"Jim. Is that you?" I recognized the voice immediately.

"Hi, Sandy! Good to hear from you. What's new in Chehalis?"

"Two things. First I wanted to thank you for giving my number to your grandpa. He called and we chatted for, oh, shoot, maybe an hour. Great to talk to him."

"I'm glad." I remembered that Grandpa wondered why Sandy would call him or wanted to talk to him. I really didn't think he would call him. Seems like curiosity got the better of him. I was happy for Sandy to have someone from his generation and the camp call him and visit.

"You said two things. What else is up?"

"Well, I know you said you got Wednesday's off. How about you come on down here and I take you to lunch? A good friend of mine owns a little café that has the world's best burgers."

"Geez, Sandy. That sounds great. I can tell you what we have found out so far on the watch too."

"What say noon at my house?"

"I will be there with a big appetite!" I said.

"Wonderful. See you then." He ended the call.

Remembering that Betty said he called her often, particularly after his wife passed away, I wondered if I was to become his newest pen pal. It would be good to see him again, and I suspected he was lonely. So what if I missed having a whole day off? The thought of the world's best burger kept rolling around in my head.

The rest of the day was pretty uneventful. Making my way home to have dinner with Kate and relax sounded pretty good. The weather was very usual for this time of year, and I knew we would spend time out back, drinking beer and visiting. Kate was a super conversationalist, and I wanted to fill her in on my day.

Arriving home, I found Kate with her feet up out back, sipping on a cool beer. Having made one stop on my way, at the refrigerator, I joined her. Again, still in my suit.

"Hi there, diamond boy. How was your day?"

"Interesting."

"How so?"

"Talked with Betty a bit about the happenings over the weekend with Clara and Harvey."

"You called instead of going over in person? Really?"

"I wanted to see what her thoughts were on Clara. If I waited until Wednesday, her time would have competed with my lunch with Sandy."

"What? Lunch with Sandy? How did that happen?"

"He called and wanted to have me come down to lunch. His treat. Says he knows a place with superb hamburgers. Poor guy is just lonely, I think."

Kate pondered this for a moment and then said, "Or he wants to see how you are coming on the watch investigation." Once again, Kate had cut to the chase. Thinking about it, I just shook my head.

"What?" she inquired.

"When I talked to Sandy today. As soon as I said I would come down, he cut the call off pretty abruptly. I had said just before that I would fill him in on what was going on for the watch. The reason I was shaking my head is that we know he hasn't been in contact with Betty recently, so for all he knew I hadn't made contact with her yet. Why would he be short with me when I mentioned it unless maybe he knows more than he is telling? Just kind of a weird hunch he is holding back on us."

"And because he is or knows maybe even who dug it up, he wants to see where we are in looking for that person. I agree. Something is just not right with Sandy. Want me to take the day off and go with you?"

"No, no need. It's just lunch. It is a little strange though. When I first met him, he was open and, I thought, honest. Now I am getting a different feeling."

"What if he was the one who dug up the watch?"

"Why would he want it? He didn't have any ax to grind with William that we know of. And besides, he was out of town at the time, remember?"

"I hadn't, no."

"So what does he know?" I said as much to myself as to Kate.

We both sat thinking for so long that I realized I was getting hot. I hadn't even loosened my tie yet.

"I gotta change. Need another beer?"

"That is the easiest question to answer of all the ones being asked this afternoon. Of course I want another beer!"

We both laughed and I headed in to change clothes. I noticed the answering machine was blinking, so I changed course and headed in its direction. I pushed the button and was regaled with the automated voice telling me I had one new message. It was from Janice at the cemetery.

"Hi, Jim, this is Janice at Oddfellows Cemetery. I think I have a name and number for you. Unfortunately, I am off tomorrow. If you can you come by or call me on Wednesday, I will give it to you. Okay, uh, bye."

There were beginning to get to be so many pieces to the puzzle that I had forgotten about even calling Janice. Yahoo. Maybe she had the name of one or more of the gravediggers. Perhaps things were looking up after all.

CHAPTER FIFTEEN

As Wednesday arrived, it was evident that summer's grip was taking hold in a big way. The forecast was for nearly ninety degrees, which didn't happen all that often. When it did, people would complain constantly about the heat. Of course, these were the same folks who would complain when it rained. I would suspect the old adage of "Some people are never happy" was never truer.

Personally, I loved it warm. Even hot. We got enough rain and snow in the winter. When it was time for the sun to shine, I wanted it shining like a new penny and hotter than an oven burner on high. That is if I am dressed for it.

Knowing it was going to be a scorcher, I put on a pair of shorts and a loose-fitting short-sleeved shirt. Tennis shoes with no socks was the footwear of the day. Kate had already left for work as I sat eating a small breakfast. I was looking forward to the hamburger Sandy had promised for lunch. Then it would be hop in the truck and head for the cemetery to meet with Janice. If she had found anything, I wanted to thank her in person.

Putting the cassette into the slot on my dashboard, I was ready to go. Steely Dan's *Aja* was one of my favorite tapes. I cranked up the engine and then the tunes and backed out of the driveway.

Chehalis was in sight before I knew it, and I wove through town to get to Sandy's little farm. It had been so dry; the gravel driveway kicked up dust in clouds even though I was only going about ten miles an hour. Once the truck was turned off, I spotted Killer coming around the corner with his head down. As I stepped out, his head raised up, his ears perked up, and he came over to the gate with his tail wagging. He remembered I was a good guy, I guess. I scratched his head and ears and, as I bent over to get closer, was graced by his purple-and-pink tongue on my cheek.

"Hey, Killer. Good to see you too."

The front door opened, and Harlan "Sandy" Saunders walked out.

"Looks like my big tough watchdog likes you now. Just like I told you, once you are invited in, he figures you are okay with me, which means you are okay with him too."

Opening the gate and entering, Killer fell in behind me like he was on heel. I had always loved dogs, and although our first meeting scared me to catatonia, I now liked this big old mutt a lot. He had befriended me simply because I was accepted by his master. No one had to tell him to sit, stay, or any other command. He just did it on his own volition.

"If you want, Jim, head around back and we'll have a quick beer before we go to lunch."

"Sounds perfect. It is a hot one, and the ride didn't cool me down much. I am going to have to spring for a truck with air-conditioning one of these years." With Sandy's dog, Killer, on my heels, I headed around back. As I made the corner, Sandy was already coming out with a couple beers. He must have known I would say yes.

We sat in the same chairs we had during my first and only visit here. It just seemed right. Sandy set my beer down on the table in front of me, and Killer took up his position at my side, within arm's reach so I could pet him, I assumed.

"How big is your property, Sandy?" I asked as I picked up the beer.

"Just over three acres. I go clear back to those fence posts you can barely see there in the back," he said, pointing.

"Really. I would have thought it was more like two. Shows what a city boy I have become."

"No, it's just a little deceiving with all the grass growing up so tall. Pretty close guess, I think."

We both took drinks of our beer and set them down.

"So tell me, Jim, ever get ahold of Betty?"

"Oh, heck yeah. I gave her the watch and you know what she told me?"

Sandy just shook his head. But there was something else there. His face was shadowed, but it appeared as I asked the question, and he responded, he squinted just a bit. Like I said, I can read people pretty good.

"She started crying and told me the watch was buried with William. Can you believe it? I have spent the last ten days or so trying to figure out who and why someone would do such a thing. And how it ended up back up in the Bordeaux woods."

Watching him very closely, I saw no change this time. Who knows? Maybe he had just inadvertently squinted the first time.

"Any luck yet?"

"No. My wife, Kate, and I have talked to Clara, Harvey Trumble, and Betty. I have talked to Grandpa a bit, but that led nowhere."

"You saw old Harvey? Where is he living now?"

"In a rest home in Lacey. All those years of logging, the poor old guy is pretty bunched up with arthritis."

"He was an okay guy. Got promoted when William died and then again when that fool Davey Jones fell out of the window. Never bragged about it though. Just went about his work."

Interesting. Harvey had said that Davey walked around bragging about being a faller when he got promoted after William's death. Very coincidental that Sandy would use that term to say Harvey had not gone around bragging, unlike Davey.

"I will have to look him up next time I am up that way. So few of us old dogs left around here anymore. What did Harvey have to say?"

This time, a distinct interest coming from Sandy that had not been there previous to this moment. He leaned forward in his chair, his eyes widened a bit, and he was staring at me, waiting for me to answer.

"Harvey has some pretty big suspicions about what happened up in Bordeaux but knew nothing about the watch, which, of course, was why we went over to see him." I was staring at Sandy now to see if he was going to take this conversation any further in a different direction. He did.

"What do you mean by 'what happened up in Bordeaux'?" If he could stare any harder, I would have been terribly surprised.

"Seems Harvey thinks that maybe William and Davey met with untimely deaths." A blind man could have seen the reaction from Sandy when he heard that statement. His whole body tensed up considerably.

"What in the heck would make him say something like that?" Sandy asked as he reached into his pocket for his Marlboros. He shook one out of the pack and lite it. Taking a long drag, he blew out the smoke and reached for his beer. He took a drink as he waited for my response.

"Oh, it's mostly his theories. He just has been in that home so long that I think his mind gets to thinking about the old days, and he has become a man who thinks everyone has something to hide, I guess."

I had tried to frame the response so that maybe Sandy would let it go. I wasn't ready to share the entire story since I still had reservations about Sandy's possible involvement in something. Nothing doing.

"So exactly what does he think he knows?"

"As I said, mostly his theory is that William was killed for some reason and that Davey fell victim for another. Nothing solid at all." Again, trying to soften what I really knew from Harvey.

"Oh, for God's sake, William was killed by a tree. How could anyone have killed him? No man I know is strong enough to pick up a Doug fir and swing it at a person."

"Yeah, I tried to tell him that too, but nothing doing. He thinks someone messed around with William's springboard. Maybe sabotaged it. Seemed pretty far-fetched to my wife and me."

"I would think so. William would have noticed it. He was too good of a logger to not."

Sandy seemed to be calming a bit since I used the word *far-fetched*. Now he appeared to be agreeing with me. Only thing that crossed my mind was that he was trying to cover something and thought he had an opening now.

"What does he think happened to Davey?"

"He thinks someone pushed him out the window, that he didn't just fall."

"That's ridiculous. No one could push someone out one of those windows at the hotel. They were too small to start with, and Davey was a pretty big guy," he said.

"Again, I agree with you. I measured out the dimensions that Harvey had told me the windows were on a sheet of plywood. Pretty tough to get a person through anything so small." I had done no such thing but wanted Sandy to think I had. He had, in the course of the conversation, gone from a man whom I liked to one I suspected could have been involved in a murder. Maybe two. But I didn't have any more evidence than I did when I arrived when it came right down to it. Just call it a hunch. I figured I had better play it close to the vest until I could get some answers.

Sandy visibly relaxed. He thought I was on his side again. That was a good thing. If I could find any true evidence, I didn't want him to know about it until I was ready to confront him one last time.

"I would think a person would have to have a pretty strong motive to kill a man. Nothing I can think of off the top of my head to help you find out the answers to your questions."

"Oh, I'll get there. It may take awhile, but I want to help Betty out if I can. She is just such a nice lady."

Mr. Saunders tensed up again. Then he slowly took a long breath and blew it out.

"She is that indeed. Listen, Jim, I didn't realize when I called you that I had a doctor's appointment this afternoon. I apologize, but I am going to have to miss lunch."

"That *is* a shame. I am starved now. Had too small a breakfast."

"Nothing to worry about. I will give you directions to the café, and you can go eat. I'll call my buddy and tell him you are still coming. He will take care of you, and it will still be on me."

"No need for that, Sandy. I can pay my way."

"Absurd. I invited you to lunch. I am just sorry I won't be there to see you eat one of his burgers."

With that, he rose up and started to slowly head for the side of the house. Unlike Killer, I didn't immediately heel. I stood and finished my beer, looked around the back pasture for a minute, and then slowly followed his lead.

Once out front, he told me how to get to the café as promised. Then he shook my hand and turned to walk back inside. I had still not even gotten out of the front yard. Strange behavior indeed. I gave Killer one last good petting and exited the yard, jumped into my truck, and made my way to the café. The food was as advertised. The hamburger was as good as or better than any I had ever experienced. And it was, in fact, an experience. My taste buds thanked me with every bite.

Finishing my delightful lunch, I got back into the truck and opened both windows. It was like an oven inside, and although I liked heat, not the type without benefit. I would lay in the sun at eighty-five degrees, but to get nothing out of the heat except sweaty, which is what was going to happen if I didn't open the windows, was not my idea of a good time.

Twisting and turning my way back to Interstate 5, I was thinking about nothing now but the why. I was pretty sure Sandy had something to do with the death or deaths at Bordeaux, but any good cop worth his salt will tell you that there has to be a motive. Even Sandy had said that.

Just north of Centralia, the sister city to Chehalis, I was listening to Steely Dan and tootling along when, all at once, my arm that was enjoying the sun, sitting on the open window frame stung. Bad. It is amazing how the human mind works. Immediately to my mind came a story from my younger days. I was working on a strawberry and raspberry farm as an irrigation changer. The foreman didn't show up on time for work, and the boss was annoyed. Then we got word the foreman had totaled his car on the way to work. Seems a bee had flown up inside the sleeve of his short-sleeved shirt, the sleeve that was outside on the window frame and gotten inside and onto his chest. He was going a little fast anyway, but trying to drive and kill the bee that was stinging him on the chest and stomach, he has driven off the road and into a tree. He escaped with several stings and a totaled car. Other than that, he walked away.

Thinking those thoughts had taken only an instant. Now many years later I thought something similar had happened to me. I looked down at my arm to see it was bleeding from a pretty good scratch on the top of my forearm. I suspected a passing car had clipped a piece of gravel and thrown it up and it had hit me. It hurt pretty badly, so I decided to stop at the rest area that was conveniently located about half a mile ahead.

I swung into the rest area and headed for the car-only side. Once I got in a parking spot, I opened the glove box and removed the box of Kleenex Kate insisted I carry. Although I probably hadn't used a Kleenex for six months, I was sure happy they were there.

The bleeding had started to slow a bit. I applied a tissue and held it in place as I walked to the restroom. Being summer, the rest area was packed as usual. I waited for an empty sink, then ran some cold water over the injury.

A little boy, maybe four or five years old, made his way to the sink next to mine. His eyes grew to saucer size and he turned around to meet the gaze of an older gentleman standing behind him.

"Look, Grandpa, he has a boo-boo." The man leaned over my shoulder and took a look at my arm.

"I bet you don't see that a lot up here." I had no idea what he was referring to exactly.

"Excuse me?"

"I am a retired emergency room doctor. Wife and I are heading up to our granddaughter's wedding in Seattle and to drop this little fellow off at my other granddaughter's house. He has been spending some time with Grandpa and Grandma. Worked in the LA County hospital for most of my life. Saw lots of gunshot wounds down there."

"Gunshot wounds!" I hollered. "What are you talking about? I just had a rock or something hit me on the freeway."

"No, you didn't. You have been shot, son. If you want to come out to my car, I have a very good first aid kit, and I can take care of that for you. My name is Thomas. You can call me Tom. When I retired, I dropped all pretense of being Dr. Davis."

"Uh, sure. You really think I was shot?"

"Yup. No doubt in my mind."

We went out to his car, and he spoke to his wife through the open driver's side window. She got out of the car and walked toward the restrooms. Opening his trunk, he pulled out a suitcase and set it on the ground. Digging to the back of the trunk, he pulled out a first aid kit that it was obvious he had put together himself. It was large for a first aid kit and had things in it that I am sure you couldn't find in any over the counter kits you could get at Woolworths.

The boy was heeling as well as Killer had earlier. He was so close I was afraid if I started walking and stopped, he would plow into my backside.

"Daniel, please stand away from this young man." He took a small obligatory step back.

"I'm sorry I didn't introduce myself to you. My name is Jim. Jim Tuttle." I held out my right hand, and he shook it with a strong grip.

"Pleased to meet you, Jim. Where did this happen?"

I pointed south and said, "About half a mile or so back."

He continued to rummage around in the first aid kit, setting things aside I figured he would be using on my arm. Finally, he turned to me. "Let's go sit in the shade. Damn hot out here in the sun."

"Grandpa!"

"Sorry, little man. Dang hot out here in the sun," he said with a smile.

He gathered everything he had set aside, and we walked to a nearby picnic table that was under a large maple tree. Lots of nice shade. Mrs. Davis walked back toward us from the restroom, and as she approached, I noticed her eyes meet Tom's and she nodded. He returned the nod.

Tom had me sit so my right arm rested on the table, giving him access to my left arm. He first cleaned it up with some sort of alcohol-based cleaner that stung. Great case of the cure being worse than the injury itself.

"I should let you know so you aren't too surprised. I had Maggie call the local sheriff and report this." He looked at Maggie. "They are on the way." Maggie nodded again.

"You have to report all gunshot wounds to the authorities. Plus, I am sure they will want to figure out what happened. How in the world you were shot on the freeway?"

"Fine with me. And thanks for letting me know they were coming."

Just as I said this, I could hear a siren in the distance. It was coming from the south. The rest area was just over the Thurston County-Lewis County line. It sounded like the Lewis County deputies were responding since they were closer.

The cruiser roared into the parking lot, and Tom waved at them like he was flagging down a passing motorist, which I guess he was. The deputy slammed on his brakes, pulled to the side, turned off the car, killing the sirens, thank goodness. Stepping out, he put on his Smokey the Bear hat and walked purposefully toward us.

He looked to Mrs. Davis and said, "You called in a gunshot wound?"

"Yes, she did," Tom responded.

"How do you know it is a gunshot wound?"

Tom explained his background, and the deputy seemed convinced. He came closer and looked at my arm.

"You are?"

"Jim Tuttle, sir," I said.

"Do you think you were shot at? Did you hear a shot?"

"I thought it must have been a rock flying up from the roadway. I was going, um, maybe sixty, so no, I didn't hear a shot. Had the windows down and the tunes turned up."

"It's a gunshot wound. Guaranteed," said Tom.

"Probably came from Scatter Creek," I said, looking the deputy in the eye. I noticed his name tag said Danforth. "Are you any relation to Jim Danforth down on Garrard Creek?"

"He was my uncle. How do you know him?"

"He was my grandpa's neighbor...until his accident." Ironically, Jim had been killed in a logging accident.

"I'll be danged. My name is Elmer." He held out his right hand to be shaken.

"Please call me Jim," I said as I extended out my hand. After everyone else had introduced themselves, we heard another siren coming from the north. A Thurston County sheriff's car was screaming down I-5 heading southbound.

"He'll be here in a minute," Elmer said. "They called us since we had a deputy closer to the scene. It is there jurisdiction."

Elmer was right. The cruiser had taken the exit just south, the overpass I had just gone under before I was hit by a stray bullet, and came skidding to a stop behind Elmer's cruiser.

As with Elmer, when the deputy turned off the engine, the siren died. He got out and walked over to us all.

"Hey, Elmer. What's going on?"

"Hi, John. This man was shot in the arm," Elmer replied.

After introducing us all to the new deputy on the scene, they had me recount what had happened.

"He thinks it was a stray bullet from Scatter Creek," Elmer said, pointing west.

Scatter Creek was a state-run game range where hunters could sign up and enter to hunt pheasants mostly. No high-powered rifles were allowed. It abutted the freeway, but having hunted there myself on occasion, I knew that the birds were well back on the property, the farthest area from the interstate.

"Was it a stray pellet you think?" John asked.

"This was no pellet," Tom replied. He was still cleaning up my arm, getting ready to bandage it up to help stop what little bleeding was still seeping out of the wound. "Is this game range over there?" Tom said, pointing toward the game range.

"Yes," came the dual reply from both deputies.

"No way it came from there. By examining the wound, the shot came from that direction," he said, pointing east.

"How can you tell?" I asked.

"The way the skin is pushed what would have been, let's see, west, I guess, it is completely evident to me that the shot came from the east."

105

"How could that be?" I asked. "That would mean that it came through my passenger-side window."

"Which tells me that someone may have deliberately shot at you," Elmer said.

"What makes you say that?" Deputy John said.

"Think about it. What are the odds a stray bullet passed through a speeding car window? Not very likely, I would say. Do you have any idea who might want to harm you or worse, Jim?"

My mind was already reeling with the thought of someone trying to shoot me. Now they wanted to know who might want to kill me. There was only one person who came to mind, but I wasn't quite ready yet to say because, once again, I had no proof. Telling them the entire story would take hours with all the questions I knew they would ask. I really wanted to get to the cemetery before Janice went home. If I stopped to tell them everything, I would miss her.

"Boy. No clue, sorry. I am still a bit shocked you think someone would want to shoot me." As we had been talking, Dr. Tom had wrapped up my arm and taped the bandage in place.

"You are going to want to get this looked at in a day or so by your doctor to make sure there isn't an infection starting. I think it will be fine, but just in case. Do you know when your last tetanus shot was?"

"I had one a year or so ago. Stepped on a rusty nail sticking out of a board while I was out using my metal detector."

"You're covered then. Listen, if you all don't need us anymore, we have to get a move on," Tom stated.

The two deputies looked at each other, and Elmer spoke for them. "I think you are good to go. Here is my card," he said, handing him an official Lewis County business card complete with their county seal embossed on it. "If you want to check with us in a week or so, we can tell you what has been found out about all this."

"Thanks," Tom said, taking the card. "Let me give you my contact information as well just in case you need anything else from me."

Tom went to his car and came back with a piece of paper that I was sure contained all the pertinent information the deputies might need. He handed it to Elmer, who, in turn, handed it to Deputy

John. Thurston County would handle any investigation since it occurred there.

After we all said our goodbyes and thanks for the help, Tom, Maggie, and the little man, who had remained on the sidelines throughout the entire conversation with the deputies without saying a word, all jumped into their car to continue their trip to points north.

"Listen, Mr. Tuttle, we will want to follow up with you. I need you to really think about who may want to do you harm. If you think of anyone, here is my card. Give me a call. The case will be handled by the detectives, but I can sure aim you the right direction."

I took the card from John, and Elmer offered one of his own, stating, "Best watch out for yourself. It sure looks like someone is out to get you for some reason."

Thanking them both, I stood up and realized I was a bit shaky on my feet.

"You okay?" Elmer asked.

"Yeah, just need to get my legs under me. Not every day someone shoots at you. I guess I am in a little bit of shock. I will walk around a few minutes to make sure I am okay to drive before I take off."

"Good idea. Pleasure to meet you. Wish it was under different circumstances," Elmer said.

"Thanks again, both of you." I shook their hands and slowly walked away from them in the general direction of my truck. Wanting to get on the road as soon as possible to go and meet with Janice, I was acutely aware I wanted to get there in one piece. I was in shock, at least a little, and I wanted to make sure I wasn't going to pass out or something while I drove the last seventeen or eighteen miles to Olympia.

When I finally felt more like my old self, I climbed up into the truck. Looking at the open window on the opposite side of the truck, a shudder went up my spine. I had been maybe six inches from being shot through my right arm, with the bullet continuing on into my chest. At sixty miles an hour, I would have almost assuredly driven off the road with the results being, well, not good.

I turned over the engine and shut off the cassette player. No noise for me right now. I just wanted to make it to the cemetery before Janice went home. The rest of the ride to town was, thank God, uneventful.

Pulling through the gate at the cemetery, I drove straight to the office. As I entered, I was welcomed by a lady about my age. She had a slight smile on her face.

"May I help you, sir?"

"Are you Janice?"

"Yes. Oh, I'll bet you are Jim." She rose from her chair and came out from behind her desk. She was dressed appropriately for the situation and job she was doing in a conservative black dress.

"I am so glad to meet you. You gave me something really fun to do. Not too much good ever happens here as you might imagine. Mostly folks looking to bury their loved ones and looking for a plot. You took away some of my monotony for a day or so."

"Glad I could help," I said, smiling. "Um, you said you had some information for me?"

"Yes. Oh my gosh, what happened to your arm?"

"Just a bad scratch. Nothing to worry about."

"Looks like more than a scratch to me." By not replying, she took the hint that the conversation regarding my arm was over.

"I had to do a lot of digging, no pun intended, to find out who was doing the grave digging in 1924. It was kind of fun though. I don't get to do many fun things around here as you might suspect. I went through the archives and found an old ledger book from the '20s. It was a little hard to decipher, but once I figured out the way the entries were made, I was able to determine that we had two regular men who did our grave digging. Well, not men really, boys. One was fourteen or so and the other was fifteen or so. I figured that out by the notes the person entering their information, start dates, addresses and so on into the ledger. The person who was keeping records actually did a very good job."

"That is fascinating," I replied.

"Anyway, I started looking through the phone book and found out that one of them appears to still be alive and living in the area. There is no sign of the other one. He must have moved away."

"Why do you say that?"

"Because one of the benefits of working here at that time was you were given a plot. Even if you quit working, which didn't happen much during the '20s and '30s, the Depression, you know, you got to keep the plot. Since the second person is not buried here, at least not yet, I assumed he probably moved away since he is not in the phone book."

"Makes sense." Janice liked to ramble, and since she was doing me a favor, I let her go on.

"The person who is still alive lives in Tumwater. His name is Charles Kirk. I called his phone number and got an answering machine. He left on a trip with his wife to California, *but* he left a number where he can be reached." She looked at a calendar on the wall. "Starting today. Wow, what timing!"

This was great news. Finally, something good happening today beside a great lunch, which seemed like a decade ago.

"That is awesome, and I can't thank you enough for your work on this. If you ever need a piece of jewelry, come up to the store and you will get my discount on whatever you want."

"Why, thank you so much! As I said, I should be thanking you for making my humdrum existence a little fun for a few days." She handed me a page from a notepad with the cemetery name on it, along with the name Charles Kirk and the contact number.

"I really appreciate all your work on this. You have been a huge help. I promise to fill you in once all the details of the story become a little clearer."

"I can't wait. Please do."

"I promise," I said, extending my hand once again for shaking.

She shook it like you used to see on the old comedies from the '40s when people were trying to make you laugh—the overexaggerated up-and-down motion where your arm goes up almost to your shoulder before starting its descent. I smile and said goodbye.

There was still time to get home and call Mr. Kirk before Kate got home from work. I was excited to try to reach him. Speeding home, I jumped out of the truck and banged my arm, the bandaged one, on the door as I got out. The pain was immediate, and I prayed I hadn't hit it hard enough to get it to bleeding again.

Running to the house, I unlocked it, went directly to the phone, and then stopped. The pain was intense in my arm. I decided I needed a little "medicine" first. Opening the pantry door, I pulled out the brown liquor. Dad had gotten me drinking McNaughton whiskey when I started drinking at twenty-one. I never drank it much, actually preferring beer, especially in the summer. Now, however, I felt like the higher-proof liquid could help ease the pain in my arm.

I poured two fingers into a glass and took a sip. It tasted good, so I took about half of it in a gulp. Then I went back and picked up the phone. Dialing the number, I waited for someone to answer at the other end.

"Hello?"

"Hi. I was given this number as a contact number for a Charles Kirk. Is he there by chance?"

"Yup, Charlie is here." He must have held the phone out at arm's length because, although quieter than when he answered, I heard him summon Charlie from somewhere else in his house.

"I'm Charlie's brother, Daniel."

"Thanks, Daniel. I am pleased to make your acquaintance. I'm Jim Tuttle."

There was silence for maybe ten seconds, and then I heard a different voice.

"Hello, this is Charlie."

"Good afternoon, Charlie. My name is Jim Tuttle. I am doing some research for a friend, and it ended up that perhaps you might aid me in getting some answers."

Again, there was silence for a few seconds. "What is this about?"

"I am told you spent some time as a gravedigger back in the '20s. Is that correct?"

"It is. Man, that was a lifetime ago"

"I know that it has been a long time, but I am hoping you might remember a particular grave that you dug."

"Boy, I dug a lot of graves, along with my buddy. I guess the only way to know if I remember it is to have you tell me the details."

"Okay, great. And let me tell you up front how much I appreciate your taking your time to help me. Back in 1924, there was a death at Bordeaux Logging Camp."

"There was more than one. Sorry, go on."

"I'll bet there was," I said, thinking of Davey. Was he buried there too? "This was a young logger named William Walker. From what I understand, they had a big graveside service. Loads of people came down from the camp, even the Bordeaux brothers."

"Oh hell yes, I remember that one. Never saw that big of a crowd."

"You were there?"

"Yup. My buddy and I stayed on the outskirts, so to speak. Once the ceremony was over and everyone was gone, we went over and covered the grave."

"Were you able to watch the service? Did you hear any of it?"

"We could see it, but we were too far away to hear anything."

"Do you recall seeing the widow open the casket and put something inside?"

"Sure do. We couldn't see what it was at the time, but yes, we saw her walk up and open the casket and put something inside." This was going even better than I expected.

"So let me ask you. If there were no graves to be dug, were you still at the cemetery daily?"

"Yes. We used to use an old push mower to keep the grass down if there were no holes to dig. But we were there every day."

"After the grave was filled in, did it ever appear that the grave had been tampered with?" I recounted my story of the grass and my sprinkler system.

"Not that I know of. Why do you ask?"

"Well, the widow had put her husband's pocket watch into the casket. She had originally thought of keeping it as a remembrance but decided that it belonged with him. About two weeks ago, I was using a metal detector up in the old logging works, and believe it or not, I found his watch. I have been trying to figure out who dug up the grave and took the watch out of the casket ever since."

"I can tell you for sure now that the grave was never dug up."

"How can you be so certain? How else would the watch have ever gotten out of the casket and clear back up to Bordeaux?"

"She came and took it out."

"Betty? The widow?" I asked.

"No, the younger girl who had stood with her during the ceremony. Once everyone had gone back to the place where everyone parked the cars and trucks, the younger girl came out and told my buddy and me that the widow had changed her mind and asked if she could open up the casket and get the watch back out. No skin off our noses, and since we hadn't even lowered it into the hole yet, we said sure thing."

I wasn't sure if this information was hitting me or the whiskey. But what Charlie was telling me was that Clara had taken the watch out of the casket. Without Betty's knowledge obviously. It was making my head spin a bit.

"Is there a problem with what we did?"

"No, Charlie, not at all. It's just that the widow never knew that watch had been removed. It appears her sister did it on her own accord."

"Oh boy. Had I known that at the time, even being a kid, I would have walked over and talked to the widow myself. Geez, I'm really sorry about all the trouble."

"You have nothing to apologize for. You were hoodwinked by the widow's sister. Not your fault. I can't tell you how helpful you've been. I had done some research and was able to determine who the watch's original owner was. I found the widow, Betty, and she has asked me to find out who had dug up the grave. Now we know the answer to that, no one. The watch was removed before the burial. The only really bad news here is that it was her own sister."

"I appreciate you telling me the back story. As I said, we never would have let her have it had we known."

"Charlie, thank you so much. I will let Betty know where I got the information and answers to the mystery surrounding the watch. Have a wonderful vacation."

"Thanks. I'm sure we will. I haven't seen my brother for a few years. We intend to catch up and have a good time doing it."

"Goodbye, Charlie."

"Goodbye, Jim"

The conversation that gave me the answer I had been looking for the last two weeks was over. I couldn't wait for Kate to get home to share what I had learned.

CHAPTER SIXTEEN

"You were *shot*? What the hell do you mean you were shot?" Kate was screaming, not so much at me but at the situation. I hadn't had time to give any thought to what her reaction was going to be with the news of my being shot. I was too excited about the news Charlie had given me an hour ago. But she had seen the bandage on my arm, and I still hadn't had the chance to share the news with her.

"It was no big thing, just a little scratch."

"Your *little scratch* is bleeding through that bandage. You didn't do that yourself. It wouldn't have looked so professional. Did you go to the hospital?"

"No. Listen, I'm fine. I understand your concern, but I am fine now. Grab a beer for each of us and come outside. I will tell you the whole story.

"But—"

"No buts. Just come outside and listen. It will answer all your questions."

With that, I turned and walked out the back door. I hoped she would follow. She did, with a couple beers in her hands and tears in her eyes. As she set down the beers on the side table, between our two lawn chairs, the tears flowed freely from her eyes. I had not sat down yet. She turned to me and almost whispered, "Oh, Jim." I took her in my arms and she cried. "I don't know what I would do without you. I promise to listen. Please tell me what happened and ensure me it won't happen again."

"I will tell you everything, and it won't happen again, I promise. Once I do tell you everything, you may understand why getting shot sort of slipped my mind."

She pulled away and sat down. I sat in my chair and picked up my beer with my left arm. "See, it doesn't even hurt enough to keep me from drinking my beer, darlin'." At that, she smiled at me. Time to tell her what happened to me today.

I relayed the story of meeting with Sandy, my suspicions about him perhaps being involved in some way and, of course, the fact we had no more evidence of his involvement than we had previously. I told her about my great lunch that I ate by myself since Sandy had backed out at the last minute. Then I got to the fun part—the "getting shot" part. She remained completely silent throughout the entire shooting episode. I paused for questions the way any great orator or instructor might do. She had plenty of questions.

"Let me start with the meeting with Sandy. Based on body language, you are ready to make Sandy suspect number one. Why? Why would he want to kill William or Davey for that matter? How are we ever going to prove it? It happened fifty-five years ago."

"I'm just saying he acted very strangely. One might even say he acted like he might be guilty of something. Then backing out of lunch was really strange to me. He had invited me down there to go to lunch. People don't usually forget doctor's appointments. As to why he would have murdered someone way back when, that, my dear, we are going to have to figure out. Without evidence, he will die an old man sitting in his backyard."

"Out of curiosity, you mentioned he said he would buy you lunch. Did he?"

"Indeed. I tried to pay, and they said it had been taken care of. Why do you ask that?"

"It is pretty obvious to me that Sandy *is* the number one suspect for shooting at you. If he thinks we are getting too close to an answer, it may have spooked him enough to act irrationally. Having killed before, it would probably be easier the second or third time. I was just thinking the lunch might have been a symbolic way of making sure you had your last meal—on him."

"I agree with your logic on all counts," I said while picking up my beer for another long pull. "Plus, he was smoking. I hadn't really picked up on that the first time even though we talked about it when he lit up. The cigarette that was under Davey's body could have come from the mouth of our own Harlan Saunders."

"Yes, it could have. But again, oh, wise one, no evidence." I was glad she was kidding me a bit. It meant her mind was engaged on something other than the shooting and "trying to kill me" part.

"The deputies, one of which I liked a lot, asked me if I had any idea who might have shot at me and I said no. Main reason, no evidence. Sandy could just say he didn't do it, and there would be no way to prove it. I suppose they could bring him in for questioning and see if he had a doctor's appointment and so on. Somehow, though, I think our Mr. Saunders is smarter than that. He would have some sort of alibi."

"Now to tell you the big news. I know who took the watch."

"What? Why didn't you tell me first?"

"Because there was a lot leading up to that point, and I wanted to tell you in chronological order."

"Who did it? Tell me."

"Nope," I said smiling. "I have to finish the story in the order in which it happened."

"Jerk."

"Thanks. Here goes. I went to see Janice at Oddfellows. She told me that she had found a man who used to dig graves back in 1924 who still lived in Tumwater. He was on vacation, but he had left a forwarding number on his answering machine. He assured me that no one had dug up the grave. Ever."

"Then how in the world did the watch ever get out of the casket? Oh my gosh, are you saying it was never *in* the casket and Betty has been lying all this time?"

"Nope, it was in the casket for sure. After the service, when everyone else had walked away, our favorite sister had gone back and asked Charlie, uh, that's the gravedigger's name, Charlie Kirk, if it was possible to open the casket that the widow had changed her mind and wanted the watch back."

"Wow! Clara? Why would she want the watch?"

"That is something I hope to ask her Sunday. In person."

"Should you tell Betty now, or are you going to invite her to go along with us to visit her sister?"

"No, neither. I think we need to get some answers from Clara before we spill it to Betty. I can't think of any good reason to take her along. I think Clara might keep shut if Betty was there but may open up when we confront her, just you and me."

"Should we call her to set something up?"

"I don't think she would be too receptive to our coming back. No, I think we need to pay an unannounced visit to her house. I am thinking she doesn't get out much. We can probably catch her at home and off guard."

We both stared at each other, then both broke into big grins. Then we started laughing. We had done it.

We had solved the mystery of the watch. All that was left now was to tie up some loose ends and we could be proud of what we had done. Of course, there was still the little matter of getting shot at and trying to find out if someone had killed William and Davey.

CHAPTER SEVENTEEN

I had thought it was hard to work Tuesday knowing I was to meet with Sandy on Wednesday, but working Thursday through Saturday was excruciating knowing that on Sunday we would be meeting with Clara and hopefully solving the mystery of why she had taken the watch from the casket.

As it happens, time passed slowly but had finally arrived. Kate and I were both unusually quiet milling around the house that Sunday morning, waiting for what we considered an apropos time to go over to Clara's house in Lacey. We had settled on high noon. Having breakfast and cleaning up around the house seemed so mundane compared to what we expected might happen when we confronted Clara. We were both lost deep in thought.

It was finally time.

"Ready to go?" I asked.

"I've been ready since I got up," Kate replied.

Without another word, we both walked out into the garage and climbed into my truck, backed out, and started on our way.

"Nervous?"

"Not really," I said. "We don't have anything to worry about or be nervous about unless she won't let us in."

We made the drive in just under fifteen minutes. No sign of Clara outside, but that didn't seem unusual remembering the color of her skin. Pulling into the driveway, I turned to Kate as I shut off the engine.

"You want to do this, or do you want me to?" I asked.

"Maybe both. I might have questions as we go along, but why don't you take the lead?"

We strode up her sidewalk and knocked on the door. It took about thirty seconds for Clara to answer the knock. When she opened the door, she looked much different than during out first visit. Dressed in a very nice dress that fit her figure, she actually had cleaned up pretty nicely.

"Oh, hello. What brings you two back?"

"May we come in, Clara? We just have some information that may interest you in regard to the watch," I replied.

Although I watch people closely to read their body language, once again, there was no need. Kate spotted it as well. Clara's shoulders slumped down maybe half an inch to an inch, and she lowered her gaze to our feet.

"Yes. Please come in."

The house was definitely cleaner than it had been the first time, but the underlying stench of cigarette smoke was still there.

"Would you like something to drink? Water, beer? I think I have some lemonade."

"Some water would be great," Kate said.

"You know what, I think I'll take you up on the beer." My arm had been hurting all morning, and I thought the beer might help dull the pain.

"How about you two go on out back? You remember the way, and I will be out in a minute with the drinks."

"Sure thing. Thanks, Clara."

We walked through the house, happy to exit into the sunshine and fresh air on the other end of our journey. Kate was abnormally quiet. I could sometimes read body language pretty well, but minds were an entirely different thing, especially one that was as cognizant and active as Kate's is.

Clara stepped out, and although she was built completely different than her sister, this time she seemed more in the mood to entertain. I was wondering what was up with that. She set a nice tray with the water and two beers on it onto the table that was surrounded by chairs. We all sat down. This was it.

"You say you have some information about Betty's lost watch?"

"Well, Clara, it's like this. We have irrefutable evidence that you were the one who removed the watch from William's casket before it was lowered into the ground."

She seemed almost stunned for a moment, then took a deep breath and said simply, "Yes, I took the watch." Nothing more, just that.

She took out her ever-present Pall Mall cigarettes, and tapping one out of the package and reaching into the pocket on her dress, she produced a book of matches and lit it up. The gray smoke surrounded us all as she exhaled it out of her lungs. Still, not another word.

Finally, she started talking. We sat quietly and just listened to her story.

"I loved William from the day he walked into the store looking for something to help ease the pain of cracking skin on his hands. Betty had helped him that day, but I was there, and I always thought if I had been the one to assist him, he may have fallen in love with me instead of her. I haven't always looked like I do now. I used to be just as thin and pretty as my sister. As time went along, and I could see quickly that they were going to be an item, I slowly let myself go to seed, so to speak.

"For a big man, for any man, he was the gentlest, kindest, sweetest person I have met in all my years. He treated Betty like a queen, doting over her all the time. All I could do was watch them and, in the end, become even more jealous of their relationship.

"You have to remember, this was a logging camp. Many of the men were respectful by just as many were cut from the same cloth as that despicable Davey Jones. I wanted nothing more than to find a good man like Betty had, but I knew that would never happen. There would never be another William who would walk through the door of Daddy's store and sweep me off my feet. That's really all I wanted—a good man to sweep me off my feet.

"Once Betty announced that she and William were betrothed, I really took a turn for the worse. I knew my chance was gone. Even though I was only seventeen, I started stealing beer when the shipments came in and hiding them in the back of the store. After we closed and went home to eat supper, I would find some reason to have to go outside, take a walk, get some fresh air, you get the picture. Instead, I would sneak back into the store and drown my sorrows with a couple beers. That caught up with me later on that summer, but I am jumping ahead of myself."

I took a quick look at Kate. She was watching Clara closely and nodding as the old woman spoke. My guess was Kate had figured most of this out for herself, at least this far into the story. She likely had been putting the rest of it together in her mind or trying too as we sat down out back, hence her quietness.

"The wedding was a beautiful affair for the times and location. They got married on the porch of Daddy's store, with everyone attended, even the Bordeaux brothers. In fact, Betty had eluded to the fact they had given William a pretty great offer to help pay his way through college and then employ him after. They were going to be set for life. I didn't hear the details of the wedding gift for a few days. It was very generous of the Bordeauxs.

"Betty and William were blissful for the time they had together. Then that horrible day when we heard the news someone had died on the hill and found out it was William. Betty was beside herself, as you might expect. I tried to help ease her pain, but the problem was, I was in just as much pain and couldn't show it. No one knew, or at least I suspected no one knew, that I was in love with William too.

"Betty left the camp the next day when they came to retrieve William's remains to get them ready for the burial in Olympia. She never came back. I was left on my own with the likes of Davey Jones and the rest of his kind. No one to help me fend them off. The funeral was a couple days later. Darn near the whole camp was there. William was very well liked. The Bordeaux brothers brought down a pickup truck loaded with beer so that after the service people could have a beer and reminisce before heading back to the camp and a cafeteria full of food and more beer. I guess they weren't too worried about prohibition. To them it was the least they could do.

"The service went off without a hitch until Betty decided to put the watch in the casket. Everyone watched her walk up and open it and place the watch inside. The Bordeauxs had sprung for a nice box, one that you could open to look at the remains. At that time, many of the dead were simply placed in an old pine box still. They thought Betty might want to say one last goodbye to her husband. Little did they know she would open it and place the watch inside with William. Everyone saw her do it.

"The service ended, and everyone headed for the parking area. The beer was there, so I knew no one would be leaving anytime soon. Just like at night when I snuck out to have a beer or two on my own, I sort of snuck at first back toward the burial site. Then it came to me that no one would think anything of the sister of the widow walking back over and paying her last respects on her own. I strode over and walked right up to the casket. A couple boys, younger than me, I suspected, were getting ready to lower the box down into the earth. I told them that Betty had changed her mind and that she wanted to get back something she had put inside. They didn't question me about it. Who would? I was the widow's sister. They were kind enough to open the coffin and let me reach in and take out the watch. I slipped it into the little black purse I had brought to the funeral and slowly turned and walked away."

After her long story, Clara needed a smoke. She lit up another one and then picked up her beer. She had a hit of each and sat looking old and tired. Kate and I said nothing. The silence lasted quite some time until I finally ended it with a question that would open another can of worms.

"Well, that answers the question of how the watch got out of the ground. It was never *in* the ground. Clara, I can't imagine that you took it just to bury it up under a tree though. How did it end up buried in Bordeaux?"

Clara sat collecting her thoughts before speaking. "No. I never had any intentions to do such a thing. Even though the watch had

Betty's name on it, it also had William's. I wanted a keepsake from the man I loved to carry with me forever."

"How did it end up where Jim found it then?" Kate asked.

"It was that horrible Davey Jones."

Kate and I looked at each other and then back to Clara. This was where the story could lead us to the answers about William's death and maybe even the death of Davey himself.

"That watch was never out of my sight. I usually carried it around in the pocket of my jeans while I worked in the store. Just the feel of it in my pocket, even though it made me sad, gave me a certain amount of respite from my grief. William was always with me."

Here, love was deep even though it was unreturned. It made me feel sad for this woman who sat in front of us.

"One night, as had now become a habit, I went back out after supper, went to the store, and then walked into the woods and leaned against a tree and had a couple beers. I had to be careful that when I went back to the house that no one smelled it on my breath. And of course, I could never let anyone see me drinking it either. I was sipping on a beer and looking at that beautiful watch and thinking of what could have been when a voice whispered in my ear. I was so startled I almost dropped the watch. Davey Jones had evidently seen me leaving the store and followed me. He had snuck up behind the tree, then peered around it to see me looking at the watch."

"What did he whisper in your ear?" Kate inquired.

"He was a horrible man. He said, 'I know whose watch that is, and now you are mine.' Besides being startled, now I was scared. I asked him how he knew whose watch it was, and he said not to forget he worked with 'that asshole William' in the woods. He said he had seen it many times as William pulled it out to check the time."

"What did he mean by 'now you are mine'?" I asked.

Clara visibly shivered even though it was running up to eighty degrees outside pretty quickly. "Davey Jones had always said rude things to me before, but that night, it was the worst. He said if I didn't give myself up to him, not with those nice of words, though, that he would tell my father I had the watch. I was scared and ashamed. Scared he would take me anyway and ashamed now that I had ever taken the watch in the first place. I hadn't given a moment's consideration to what would happen if someone caught me with it. I told him that I would never let him have me in that way and if he touched me I would scream and he would end up in jail."

"Davey didn't rape you, did he?" Kate asked in a quiet voice.

"No. I think when he realized that I meant business, he changed his tack. He said, 'Okay then, give me the watch or I tell your pa that you stole It.' He didn't know how I had gotten it since he wasn't at the funeral. He just knew that it was William's and that he probably thought I had stolen it from Betty."

"What did you do, Clara?"

"What I had to do. I looked down at the last remnants of William that I had, kissed the watch, and handed it over to Davey. I didn't think the fool realized that all I had to do once he had it was turn him in and he would be arrested for grave robbing. But I was wrong. He said, 'Don't get any ideas about telling anyone I have this now, or I guarantee I will come back here and take it out on you in so many ways that you will never forget who Davey Jones is.' I believed him. As I have said he was despicable. That night, I was truly afraid I might still be raped, but instead he just gave me an awful grin and turned around and disappeared into the night."

"Did he continue to harass you after that?"

"You know, he kind of left me alone, which surprised me. I figured he kind of had me over a barrel in a sense. If I told on him, I was sure he would come back and do God only knew to me. But I think what actually happened is he realized if he was ever caught with the watch and tried to say I had given it to him, no one would believe him. It made my life a little better. I was still missing William, but at least I wasn't under Davey's thumb much anymore."

"You didn't know then that he lost the watch?" I asked.

"He certainly didn't tell me that he did. But you have to remember that he was dead just a short time later."

"Did you ever think that maybe someone killed William? Or Davey?" Kate asked.

"Never really gave it much thought. I was so distraught over William that it never occurred to me that someone might have wanted to do him harm. As for that idiot Jones, it figured he was stupid enough to fall out a window. Why? Do you think someone murdered William? And Davey?"

"Well, Harvey said it was a possibility. He has several theories, none of which can be proven."

"But who would want William dead? He was a gentle soul."

"Anyone with something to gain from his death would have a motive. Seems Davey could get promoted if something happened to William, so he would be what the police call a prime suspect. But with him dying shortly after, it makes us wonder if maybe there was more than one person involved if, in fact, William was murdered."

"Well, I don't know anything about that." Clara lit another Pall Mall and blew the smoke out of her old tired lungs.

"Are you going to tell Betty about all this?"

"Clara, we pretty much have to. She wanted to know who would take the watch out of the casket and why. I assumed she thought it was someone who wanted the watch because it was gold and silver. Now that we know the real reason, I think Kate and I can spin it so that she doesn't think you are a terrible person, just someone who had a hidden love and wanted a keepsake. If we stick to what you have told us, I'm sure she will understand the motive behind you taking the watch from the casket was not to ever hurt her but to help you cope with William's death in your own way."

Sitting with a cigarette in one hand and picking up the nearly empty beer with her other, she looked at us and tears began to fall from her eyes.

"I loved him so. Just let her know I never wanted to hurt her."

We all sat there for a couple more minutes and then realized the conversation was over. Kate stood first and I followed, and then very slowly Clara rose.

"Clara, thank you for telling us the truth. I know it hurts to talk about it," Kate said.

"I should actually be thanking you. Finally getting all this off my chest and having Betty know the truth after all these years, I think I will sleep better at night. Maybe, oh god, I really hope that it will bring Betty and me closer together. I miss her, but it is so difficult seeing her and looking into her eyes and knowing that she had no idea of my love for her husband."

We walked back into the house and then straight out the front door. Clara followed us all the way. As we stepped onto the porch, I did something I wasn't really planning on doing. I turned around and reached out to Clara and put my arms around her. She hugged me back, and I could feel her shudder a little as I knew tears were now falling from her eyes.

"Clara, can we keep in touch?"

"Oh, I would like that very much," she said, wiping the tears away. "Please do."

"Will do," I replied.

Kate led the way down the walk and we got into the truck. Once inside with the doors shut and the windows open, Kate turned to me. "Have I told you lately you are very sweet?"

"Not lately, maybe not ever," I chided.

"Ha ha, funny man. Well, you are very sweet. You just made Clara's day with that hug."

"Makes me feel pretty good too," I replied.

"Now then," Kate said, "when do we tell Betty this whole story?"

"I think we go home, grab a bite of lunch, and give her a call and see if she is going to be home this afternoon. The sooner the better."

"Agreed."

CHAPTER EIGHTEEN

We ate lunch, had a beer, and chatted about Clara's story. There was an air of finality as we spoke. We had done it. Solved the mystery of the buried watch. I didn't want to bring up that there was still some unfinished business, and I sure wasn't going to bring it up to Betty unless she did. I still wasn't sure if she really wanted to know or not if William had been murdered. You would think most people would want to know, but Betty wasn't most people. She had lived her whole adult life missing a man that had died way too young and had dealt with it admirably. To open a new chapter to the story might be something that she just didn't want to do. We would find out very soon.

Kate had called and spoken with Betty and found out she would be home, so as soon as we ate our very relaxing lunch, we locked up the house and headed out once again. This time to deliver news that might be rather shocking to a very lovely and sweet old lady.

We decided that we would park on the capital grounds again and take the walk up Capitol Way to her neighborhood. The day was hot but with very little humidity in the air, making it a really pleasant stroll.

Betty was peering out the window as we strolled up the walkway. She opened the door with a pensive smile on her face. She knew we had the information she wanted us to get for her, but it also appeared she wasn't sure she wanted to know the answer to her question of who had dug up the grave of her deceased husband.

"Hello, Kate. Hi, Jim. Oh my, what in the world happened to your arm?" Betty exclaimed.

Rats. I had worn a long-sleeved linen shirt to Clara's so it wouldn't draw attention to my arm. Before eating lunch, I had changed to a T-shirt so I would get food on it. Whether I had forgotten on purpose or subconsciously, it didn't matter. It would open up the subject I had intended for Betty to bring up if she was interested in pursuing an outcome. I looked at Kate, and she was glaring at me. Whoops.

"Good afternoon, Betty. It's nothing. We can talk about it later," I said.

"Hello, Betty," Kate chimed in, still glaring at me. I was assuming by her look that she had wanted me to keep it covered up for sure.

We entered the small immaculately clean house.

"What do you say we sit out back? The rains will be back soon enough, and I just love sitting outside," Betty said.

"Of course. That sounds great," I said.

She already had three cold beers sitting on the counter on her little tray, along with usual barbecued potato chips in a small bowl. She picked up the tray as Kate opened the back door, and we walked back to her little oasis.

We sat at her little lawn table with the nice chairs that had the peekaboo view that I had noticed on my first visit. It really was a lovely setting.

"Am I to assume that you have found out the answer to who dug up William's grave?"

"Well, yes and no. We know how the watch ended up in Bordeaux, more or less, but no one dug it up at the cemetery."

This explanation was the truth, but Betty certainly didn't understand it.

"Betty, the watch was put in the casket by you. Correct?"

"That's correct."

"You asked me a few days ago if I thought Clara could have been the one to dig up the watch. At the time, I hadn't given it much thought. But through some investigative work, we found out that Clara had taken the watch out of the casket before it was buried."

Betty let out a slight gasp. After our talk the other day, I was sure she spent time thinking about Clara, William, and 1924.

"When you called and you asked me about Clara trying to attract William away from me, I got to thinking about it. She was almost always at the store when William came in after work. The more I thought about it, the more I realized she would insinuate herself into our conversations a good deal. Go on please."

Kate started up now, "Betty, it seems Clara was infatuated with William. In love really. When he died, she was heartbroken. When you put the watch into the coffin, she decided that she had to have it as a remembrance of William. She is very remorseful. She knows he was your husband, but she couldn't help herself."

Betty sat quietly and listened to what Kate had to say. I was so glad she had chosen to tell this part. I knew I would have stammered and stumbled my way through it, and she had put it very succinctly.

"I guess I was just so in love with William and he with me that neither of us caught on to the fact Clara was in love with him too. My poor sister."

Here sat a woman whose own sister had stolen something that had meant the world to her, and she was feeling sorry for her. I was taken aback by this. *No way*, I thought, *that under the same sort of circumstances I could have been so forgiving.*

"Betty, you are a saint. To forgive so quickly is just, well, it's just so unusual," I said.

"I am not a saint, not by a long stretch. But Clara was in love and her love, even though he was my love as well, was taken from the earth too soon. I should call her later."

"You have no idea what that would mean to her," Kate replied.

"You didn't tell me how the watch ended up buried back in the camp."

"I wasn't sure you wanted to hear it. You had asked for my help to find out who had dug up the grave. I can tell you if you want to know, however."

"I do please."

"Davey Jones forced Clara to give him the watch. He told her he would tell everyone that she had it if she didn't." I left out the part about him offering an alternative on purpose. "Clara said once she gave him the watch, he left her alone. He probably figured out that she could tell someone he had dug up the grave, and he would be in terrible trouble for it."

"That man was horrible. When I heard he had fallen out the window, I'm sorry to say, I was happy."

"What must have happened is he took the watch and started carrying it in the woods as William had. His bad luck came when the leather pouch fell from his pocket. He probably looked for it but never found it. Now he had nothing. No watch, no Betty or Clara to antagonize, nothing."

"Good riddance."

"That was the same thing Clara said," Kate spoke up.

"Of course then the watch stayed in its resting place until I happened upon it and started this whole affair in motion."

Up until now, the three beers and the potato chips had sat untouched. In an almost robotic fashion, we all reached out and grabbed our beers, and all took long drinks. It was almost comical. We set them down and silence ensued for maybe two minutes.

"Well, I guess that's it then. I have to thank you both for all you did to help me," Betty said.

"It was our pleasure," Kate replied.

"Jim, now you can tell my about your poor arm."

Trying to keep it light and airy, which is difficult to do when it ends with getting shot at, I told her about my meeting with Sandy and then driving home and getting shot. Her eyes grew big, and she sort of hugged herself.

"Do you think Sandy knows something about William's death that he doesn't want to get out? Do you think maybe he had something to do with it?" Betty asked.

"After our conversation with Harvey and then meeting with Sandy, I would say yes, most definitely he either knows or was involved. Problem is, we have zero evidence that he did anything to William or Davey for that matter."

"I told you the other day that I didn't care about that and wasn't sure I would want to know after all these years. I lied. Is it too much to ask to see if you can find out if he did something to my William? If you think it is going to be dangerous, though, I want you to stop right now."

I looked at Kate, and she sensed it and turned to look at me. She nodded slightly. Atta girl.

"Betty, we will see what we can find out. First sign of any danger, though, we will back out and let the police handle it, *if* they are interested in a fifty-five-year-old cold case that was never really a case to start with."

"Thank you, both. Please be careful though. I don't want anything to happen to my two new friends," she said, smiling.

"We will be ultracareful, Betty. I was so upset the other night when Jim told me he had been shot it took me hours to calm down. It still bothers me. But if we hang together, we can watch out for each other."

Sitting staring out at Capital Forest, the conversation turned to the mundane—weather, politics, that sort of thing. We drank our beer and polished off the potato chips and talked and laughed. It was finally time to go home and leave Betty to her thoughts.

"We need to get going, Kate."

"Yes, we do. Betty, thank you for your hospitality. It is always nice to see you."

"You two take care of yourselves," she said, standing. "I want to be talking to you still in ten years. I plan to live to at least eighty-five, you know," she said with a light chuckle.

"The way you take care of yourself, I bet you live to be one hundred," I shot back with a laugh.

Kate and I left Betty to think about whether she would call her sister or not, whether Harlan "Sandy" Saunders had murdered her husband and perhaps another man fifty-plus years ago, and what the rest of her life would look like now that she had part of the picture in clear view.

CHAPTER NINETEEN

Returning to work Monday, my mood was subdued. Although Kate and I had solved the watch mystery, we still now had two murders, or not, to investigate. I had to believe that there was something there for us to find. I mean, I was shot at.

After kicking several things around, I came up with a plan. Hopefully it would not end with me getting shot at again. I needed to make a call. Digging my wallet out of my pocket, I pulled out the business card I needed, grabbed the phone, and dialed the number.

"Lewis County Sheriff dispatch," the voice at the other end of the line stated.

"Good morning. I was wondering if I could speak to Elmer Danforth."

"I'm sorry, he is out on patrol."

"Can I leave him a message?"

"Certainly," the most monotone voice I had ever heard replied.

"My name is Jim Tuttle. Can you have him call me when he comes in? And can you tell me what time that might be so I can give you the correct number to call?"

"Yes, I can give him the information. He comes in at two thirty this afternoon."

"Okay, great. Have him call me at this number." I gave her the number at the store and hung up. Now it was just a matter of getting my ducks in a row for when he called. I wanted and needed his help if I was to get out of this without any more holes being poked in my body. At least that was going to be the case if Sandy was the person who had actually shot at me.

The day dragged on. Finally, about three o'clock, the store phone rang.

"For you, Jim," the office manager stated quietly.

"Jim Tuttle, may I help you?"

"Hello again, Jim, Elmer Danforth."

Geez, I liked this guy. No Deputy Danforth. He was treating me like a friend. Maybe it was due to the fact I had known his uncle.

"Oh, hi, Elmer. Listen, I was wondering if I could ask a favor of you."

"If I can do it, I will," he replied.

Telling Elmer what I had in mind, he listened without interruption. When I was done, he simply said that he could do what I was asking. We agreed to meet at the sheriff's office Wednesday. I would have to get back to him with the time because I had one more call to make first. Now that I knew he was in, it was time to make that call.

Saying goodbye to my new friend, I pushed down the button where the handset goes, released it to get the dial tone, and made my next call.

The phone rang six times, and just when I expected there to be an answering machine at the other end to tell me my party wasn't home, Sandy answered.

"Hello."

"Hi, Sandy. Jim Tuttle."

There was a moment of silence, then, "Hi, Jim, what can I do for you?"

"First I wanted to thank you for lunch last week. It was delicious, just like you said it would be."

"Glad you liked it," he replied but with a note of hesitation in his voice.

"Say, I was wondering if I could stop down Wednesday around noon. Kate and I solved the mystery of the watch, and since you were instrumental in our finding Betty, I thought it only right I tell you the whole story." Again with the dead silence. This time a bit more prolonged.

PAT ELY

"Uh, sure, Jim. See you at noon." He hung up. Unusual but not totally unexpected. He didn't even say as much as goodbye.

I had done it. I had set the wheels in motion. Now I had to call Elmer back and tell him when I would meet him at the office.

After I made the call to Elmer, I could feel a lump growing in my stomach. Was I doing the right thing here? I wasn't a cop. I wasn't trained to do what I was going to do. It still seemed right. Now I just had to explain it to Kate.

Work finally ended, and I headed home. How was I to explain to Kate what I had in mind, especially since it meant I would be putting myself in harm's way? It finally came to me to just be honest with her and include her in the process.

Kate was pulling in just as I did. She must have had some errands to run after work. She normally beat me by half an hour or so.

"Hi, darlin'."

"Hi yourself." We embraced and kissed in the driveway.

"How was your day?" I asked.

"Good, yours?"

"Interesting."

"How so?"

"Let's get our liquid refreshment and sit out back. I'll fill you in."

We went into the house. I headed for the bedroom for a quick change into shorts and a T-shirt, and Kate grabbed the beer and headed out back. I joined her once I was out of my suit and comfortable in my evening attire.

"Okay, diamond boy, what's going on?"

I had been given the "diamond boy" moniker by the staff of the first jewelry store I worked in when I was promoted to manager of a different location. They had given me a pewter mug with the name engraved on the side. Kate had always remembered it and loved to tease me by using it.

"I called Sandy today. Time to ratchet up the pressure on him a bit. I don't think we have any choice if we want to find out if he had anything to do with the murder of either William or maybe Davey.

You have to think there is something there. Why else would he take a shot at me?"

"So what is your plan?" I could sense a nervousness in her voice. Did I have the same in mine?

I laid out my ideas to her. It was going to be a little fluid once it all started in motion. Knowing that, I wanted to try to ease her mind. I threw Kate a bone.

"Can you take Wednesday off? I would really like you in the vicinity, not right on site but close by."

She took a deep breath and blew it out slowly. She wasn't visibly shaking, but I could tell she had the same sort of lump I had growing in her stomach now.

"Of course. Jim, it's not that I think your plan is a bad one, but it is dangerous. Who knows what Sandy may do once you confront him? It scares me to think about it. Do you think Elmer will be able to protect you?"

"He will be there, but I really can't say. It depends a bit on how quickly it all goes down. I hope he can help when the time comes, but our only chance of this working is his staying out of the way until the very end."

"I understand, but it still scares me."

We sat in the solitude of our backyard and sipped on our beer. Wednesday was just two days away. It was time to start thinking about all the details that had to be looked at to ensure my not ending up with additional holes in my body.

CHAPTER TWENTY

Wednesday finally arrived. Right on schedule. I had done something on Tuesday that I had never done before. Arriving at work to make sure the store had enough personnel, I told the office manager that I was not feeling well and needed to go home. She said I looked fine, but if that was what I needed to do, then so be it. She could see my visage, and according to her, I looked fine. But had she had X-ray vision, she would have seen my stomach tied in so many knots it would have taken a Boy Scout hours to untie them all.

Tuesday was spent going over and over all the little details that I knew had to be perfect and, of course, hoping that Sandy didn't throw in any wild cards that would make my task more difficult. Getting him to admit that he had murdered at least one man and shot at me was not going to be easy.

After choking down a couple eggs, knowing we would need the energy a little later on, Kate and I went over it all one more time step-by-step.

She would be dropped off at the sheriff's office when I met with Elmer. Then once everything was over, I would meet her back there. As I said to her, I wanted her close, but certainly not in the line of fire.

We were to meet Elmer at ten thirty to go over our ideas with him and get his input. I was to be at Sandy's house at noon. That should give us plenty of time.

Placing our dishes in the sink, we brushed our teeth and headed out to the garage. It was funny to me that we acted as if we were just heading into town, cleaning up, brushing our teeth, and so on. Instead, we were heading in to a situation where the outcome would dictate whether I ever had to brush my teeth again.

Every nerve ending was starting to synapse. All sounds seemed magnified. Starting up the truck I had driven for three years sounded like I was starting up a Caterpillar D8.

Taking a lesson from Kate the previous evening, I took a deep breath and slowly let it out.

"You okay?" Kate asked.

"Yeah, just a little nervous," I said. The most understated statement I may have uttered in my life to date.

"Jim, you are a smart man. You will know if it is getting out of hand. Just be ready in case it does."

I looked at my lovely wife. Tears were forming in her eyes, and I sure didn't need her to start crying.

"I only wish I was as smart as you. You married me, so you have to be *very* smart."

With that, she laughed a nervous laugh, but a laugh nonetheless.

We backed out and headed toward the unknown.

Driving south, I couldn't help myself when we went by the northbound rest area. I turned my head and looked at it as a well as the grass fields that were just south of it. Where had Sandy been hiding? There were a few stunted firs and even a couple pine trees in the field. Had he hidden near one of those?

Kate caught me looking and said nothing. She really was a smart cookie. It was a time for quiet.

Chehalis loomed ahead. I kind of remembered seeing the sheriff's office once or twice as I had gone through Chehalis on previous trips into the town. I knew what street it was on, so that made it easier to find. Elmer was standing outside, waiting for us.

We parked, locked up the truck, and headed toward Elmer. He hadn't moved, almost looking like the proverbial drugstore Indian.

Finally, he turned his head in our direction.

"Morning, Jim. And this must be Kate."

"Morning, Elmer. Yes, this is my wife, Kate."

"Pleased to meet you, Kate," he said.

"Likewise, Elmer. Is it okay to call you Elmer?"

"Of course. Well, we better get started getting set up. I think I have everything set up so we can get a move on in about half an hour or so. By the way, I called Deputy Trabor, John. Remember him? Kind of surprised he is not here yet."

"Yes, of course. But, Elmer, I don't want to get there too early. We can take our time. Sandy's place is only ten or fifteen minutes away."

"Okay. Makes sense."

We walked into the station. Elmer first, then Kate, and yours truly dragging up the rear. An hour later, we were ready to rock and roll. Turning to Kate and meeting her eyes, I saw she had the "deer in the headlights" look.

"Darlin', I will be fine. Wait here for me. I love you more than you could ever imagine. You have to stay here and stay safe so that I can concentrate on the task at hand."

We put our arms around each other and hugged tightly. Neither one of us wanted to let the other one go. When we finally separated like two boxers coming out of a clinch, Kate had tears streaming down her face.

"Don't worry, Elmer here will take care of me. Right, my friend?"

"I'll do anything and everything I can do. I promise, Kate," he replied, looking at Kate.

I gave Kate one last small hug and a kiss. "I'll see you soon."

Elmer and I headed out the door. I went to my truck, and Elmer climbed in his cruiser. He was going to be behind me about five minutes. That would hopefully allow enough time for me to get ready at Sandy's place.

It was yet another beautiful summer day. Eighty was the projected temp. I had worn my linen shirt to hide my bandage. The old arm was feeling better, but as I pulled into Sandy's place, it suddenly started to give me little jolts of pain. Nerves.

Parking, I was met by Killer. His tail was wagging like we were long-lost friends. I reached over and opened the gate. Stepping inside,

Killer wanted some love. I scratched his head and ears and patted his back before finally starting the walk up to the house.

Sandy stepped out. His demeanor told me he was nervous as well. He looked stiff.

Here we go, I thought.

"Hi, Sandy. How are you?" I tried to sound much more upbeat than I felt.

"Hi, Jim. Oh, my poor old back is bothering me some. Say, why don't you just go around the side of the house and I will meet you in back? Beer?"

"Sure." Killer followed me around the side. Once I got out of Sandy's sight, I hustled to the back. It was imperative that I beat him back there and get things set up the way I wanted them to be.

His table and chairs were still where they had always been. I set one chair facing the house, that was to be mine, and the other dead-on to the chair I was to be using. I had just finished and sat down when Sandy came out carrying a couple beers.

"Another great summer day," I said, again trying to lighten the moment.

Without a word, Sandy handed me a beer and then stepped back and sat in his chair. I noticed he sat somewhat sidesaddle. He had mentioned his back was hurting. Maybe that relieved the pressure.

"You said you had some news on the watch getting dug up."

"Yup." I took a small drink of my beer and continued, "Kate and I found out it was never even buried at all. Seems that Clara was in love with William and just wanted a keepsake."

"Really?" Sandy seemed a bit more relaxed as I told him this news.

"Yes, sir. She just wanted a remembrance."

"Well, I'll be danged." Killer had taken his normal spot, just beside my chair, and with my empty hand, the beer being in the other, I scratched his head.

"Wait. How did it get back up into the woods then?" Sandy asked. Good question. Could I be wrong? He asked it with conviction as if he maybe didn't really know.

"Well, it seems Davey Jones saw her with it one night, and it was either she had sex with him, likely an ongoing event, or she had to give him the watch."

"Davey Jones. Leave it to that son of a bitch."

"Sandy, I also wanted to talk about Davey's death. I honestly think you know more about it than you are telling me." It was out of my mouth only an instant when Sandy made a sort of grunt and reached around as if to rub his back. His hand came out with a pistol. A very large one at that. Now I knew exactly why he had been sitting catawampus. This was happening way faster than I thought it might.

"You just couldn't leave me be, could you? All these years and now you want to bring it all out in the open."

"I suspected you knew something. That is why I took a chance at shooting you last week." It was out in the open. But why tell me at all?

"*You* shot at me?" I said incredulously. "That I didn't suspect," I lied.

"Please, Jim. I may be old, but I am certainly not stupid. You knew or at least suspected it right off the bat. You're not stupid either. And I should tell you, I am a much better shot at close range than I am at a moving target going fifty or sixty miles an hour. Please don't move."

This was almost surreal. Although I had a pretty good idea Sandy was the one who took the potshot at me, I didn't think he would admit it so freely. Why was he telling me this? I took a chance and sipped my beer and then set it down. At least he didn't shoot me for doing that.

"So why tell me now?" I muttered, afraid to hear the answer.

With his free hand, he pointed to the back of his property. "Stand up very slowly and look out back." Doing so slowly, I saw a backhoe with a gigantic mound of dirt piled next to it.

"I have no problem telling you I shot at you. See, you are going to just disappear today, truck and all. No one will ever find you back there once I cover you up. At least not while I am still alive. Once I'm dead, the new homeowners may come across you at sometime, but by then, I won't give a damn."

I turned slowly back around and resumed sitting. Sandy was going to kill me and then drive my truck to the back and bury me in it. My mind was racing. If I was going to die today, I needed some answers first, so I told him so.

"What do you want to know?"

"I want the whole story. Why not? I won't be in any shape to tell anyone, right?"

Sandy smirked. "Sure, why not?"

"How about I start at the beginning. I was in love with Betty. She didn't give me the time of day. Maybe it was because I was just the bookkeeper at the camp. Who knows? Regardless, as hard as I tried to show her my true feelings, she just kind of ignored me. Then that damn William came on the scene. Not only did she fall in love with the guy, the Bordeauxs also thought he was some sort of god-send. I heard all the stories about how they were going to help pay his way through college and that he wanted to be an accountant or lawyer. Guy wanted my job! First he takes the girl I am in love with and then that! It was just too much."

So here was the motive. Not only did he think William had stolen his girl, he was also sure he was going to steal his job as well.

Sandy was getting agitated, and it scared me.

"I'm sorry that happened to you, Sandy. I really am."

"Bullshit. You are just trying to save your own hide, but we are past all that now." He stopped long enough to reach over with his left hand and grab his beer. He took a swallow and continued.

"It started to fester in me, you know? Here was a simple logger going to get paid to take my job. I had to find some way to make sure that didn't happen. Then as luck would have it, I was in the store that day long ago when Davey Jones came in and made a comment to Betty. William took him to task on it and dragged him outside. Never knew what was said. The one good thing about being a book-keeper in the camp was I was almost invisible. No one ever remembered I was there that day. It was all about the logging. The only time that anyone gave a shit about me was on payday." He paused and took another sip of beer.

"Davey Jones was a loose cannon. My thoughts were to get him to take care of William. I did it very carefully. I never came right out and said it at first, just sort of needled him about what William had done to him in the store. I knew the guy was damn near crazy, but if I worked it right, I could use that to my advantage. Finally, once Betty and William got hitched, I could see he was ready to do something, so I made him an offer. If he took William out, I would see to it that he was paid $1,000 for his troubles. I ran the books and figured I could make it happen and no one would ever know. It wasn't anytime at all that he came back to me and said we had a deal. He said if he did it and I double-crossed him that he would kill me too. I had no intention of doing that. I just wanted William dead."

"Can I take a drink of beer? You said not to move."

This made Sandy laugh. "Of course. Just move real slow like."

I picked up my beer and took a long drink. It was hot out, and I determined that I was so juiced up on adrenaline that there was no way it would have any real effect on me. I had a feeling in my stomach like a hundred hummingbirds were mating. My brain was working overtime as well. I did my best to remain calm.

"Go on please, Sandy."

"Old Harvey was right. It took awhile for it to happen, but Davey finally figured out a way to do it. He made some cuts on the bottom of William's springboard. Then it was just a matter of time and some real luck. Had the board broken while in the middle of cutting down a tree or had the tree not kicked back, it would have meant Davey was going to go to jail for attempted murder in all likelihood. But it all came together perfectly."

Now Sandy had admitted to my attempted murder and conspiracy to commit the murder of William Walker. Two down, one to go.

"What about Davey? Did he really fall out the window?" I asked.

Sandy chuckled.

"That fool decided he wanted more money. Told you he was crazy. A thousand dollars back then was a fortune. But he got greedy. I had hidden it pretty well in the books so far, but trying to take any more would have been trouble. He came to me and told me if he didn't get another $1,000 he would go to the Bordeaux brothers and tell them to check their books. Of course, no matter how well I had it hidden, some digging would have found it. I would have lost my job and the woman I loved anyway. He would probably try to pin William's murder on me as well even though he was the murderer."

"So you killed him."

"In his case, I always considered it like a rabid dog. More like putting him out of his misery."

Game, set, match. He had told me that he had killed Davey. But my curiosity got the better of me. I had to know how he did it—if for no other reason than to prolong my life a bit.

"I heard Davey was a big man. How did you ever push him out the window?"

Sandy actually laughed a good hardy laugh. He set his beer back down on the table. The gun remained aimed directly at my chest, however.

"I had told him I would meet him in his room when his day of falling was done. I was watching for him, and I saw him get a couple beers from the back of the store and figured I would wait until he had at least one of them downed. Finally, I went up to his room. He was sitting on the windowsill, trying to keep cool. He asked me if I was going to pay him the additional money, and I told him yes. He smiled at me and said he knew I would come around. Then he handed me the last beer. I lit up a smoke and took a sip on the beer. He was watching me smoke and complaining the room was going to stink. Hell, just about everyone in the hotel smoked, so I wasn't too worried about that. Plus I knew that it wouldn't be in the room, one way or the other, long enough for it to stink it up. Betty had been gone from camp for three months or so. He knew it, I knew it, shoot, everyone knew it. But all it took was for me to say to him, 'Hey, there goes Betty,' and he dipped his head down and peered out in both directions. Easy work for me then. I just gave him a shove. My cigarette went out with him, I figured out later. I got the hell out of there, and as I was making my way down the hall, I could hear someone coming up the other end staircase."

"That would have been Harvey."

"If you say so. I was gone before anyone saw me, and my troubles with Davey Jones were over. Until now."

What a story. Jealousy had been Sandy's downfall. A regular guy falling for a girl and losing her to someone else. Then the possibility of losing his job to the same man who had stolen her away was just too much for him to bear. It was almost enough to make me feel sorry for the guy—almost.

I have hunted all my life. Elmer had warned me that if I saw him setting up in my peripheral vision to do my best to not react in any way. When I saw movement to my left, I knew he was in position.

"Sandy, why don't you turn yourself in? If you kill me, you will hang. Literally."

He laughed again. "Now why would I want to do something stupid like that? I told you once that no one wants to live forever, but I sure as hell don't want to spend my dying days in prison waiting to hang either. Time for you to take one last ride in your truck."

He stood and swung the gun from side to side in an effort to make me move toward the side yard, the very same one I had just entered a few minutes previous to hearing him tell me he was a murderer.

"Have you heard enough, Elmer?"

Sandy looked at me like I was from outer space.

"Who the hell is Elmer?"

"I am."

Sandy turned his head to the right and saw Elmer standing with a high-powered rifle aimed at him.

"Don't move, Mr. Saunders."

I opened up my shirt to reveal the wire that we had installed at the sheriff's office before coming over. It was the size of a pack of cigarettes, and I had been worried Sandy would see it. Now I wanted him to.

"Every word was recorded, Sandy. The authorities know everything now."

"Put the gun down now, Mr. Saunders!" Elmer hollered.

Killer had risen and was growling at the new arrival. Sandy's shoulders slumped. But the gun never wavered.

"Like I said, no one wants to live forever." He slowly started to turn the gun toward his own head when I heard Kate scream out my name to my right. Next to her was Deputy John. What was she doing here?

She was supposed to be back at the sheriff's office, away from the danger that now loomed in front of me.

"Jim!"

Sandy was startled for just a second and turned his head to his left. This was not part of the plan, but it gave me the opportunity I needed. I sprang from my chair, and while hitting Sandy dead-on with my body, almost a dive into him, my left hand grabbed the gun and I tried to aim it away from his head. The discharge was so loud it almost deafened me. My left arm was still sore from the gunshot the week previously. I wasn't so sure I had won the battle.

Looking down, Sandy lay sprawled beneath me. The gun was pointing at the house now. As I raised my head and looked up, I saw that the glass in the back door was shattered. Sandy was alive.

Killer didn't know what to do. There were far too many folks who didn't belong around his property. I wrenched the gun from Sandy's hand and then stood. Sandy lay on his back, slowly shaking his head from side to side. I told him to get up. It was a bit of a struggle; maybe his back was truly sore from digging my grave with the backhoe, but he finally regained his feet.

Walking him around the side of the house at gunpoint, he exited the gate and was handcuffed by Elmer.

Kate ran up and threw her arms around me and sobbed.

"I'm fine. And better yet, you saved Sandy's life. Had you not hollered when you did, I am pretty sure Elmer would have taken him out."

"I don't care about Sandy. All I care about is that you are safe."

We embraced for a good long time, and it felt wonderful. Kate and I had solved all the Bordeaux Logging Camp murders that no one ever even knew were murders—until now.

Epilogue

The trees in the backyard were resplendent with their fall colors. Although it was late September and officially fall, God had blessed us with a wonderful Indian summer. Hunting season was on my mind with it being only a couple weeks away, but today I was spending most of my time thinking about the summer just passed.

Sandy was in jail, awaiting sentencing. He had admitted to everything since it was all on tape anyway; he really had no choice. His attorney was fighting to keep him alive and not to be put to death for the murders of William Walker and David Jones. What was to happen was yet to be seen.

Betty and Clara had reconciled to the point where they were making regular trips to each other's homes to catch up and start the living rest of what time they had left in this world together.

We had kept our promise and visited Clara a couple times during the remainder of summer and intended to keep building on the relationship since she and Betty were now working things out. It might have been a bit harder had they not gotten back together.

Kate and Betty had become great friends. They went to flower shows together, gardened together, and even went to movies occasionally. It was a special relationship. I felt that Kate was almost like the daughter Betty was never able to have due to her losing William at her young age, and I was happy for their relationship.

Harvey Trumble had passed one night in his sleep. A heart attack, they said. He was a nice man. I would miss him. We had kept in touch, visiting him a couple times during the summer. He reminded me of my grandpa in a way. More broken down but he still did nonetheless.

Elmer and I had become friends as well. In fact, we were planning on hunting together. He was a really good guy, and I enjoyed spending time with him.

Me? I was sitting out back with what seemed like my ever-present beer. Well, it was a Sunday. Why not?

Our lives had changed dramatically since Sandy was arrested and charged with murder. Elmer had told anyone who would listen that it was Kate and me who had solved the fifty-five-year-old murders. Because of him, we had made the local news. Then the Seattle stations picked up on it, and before we knew it, the national media was interested. Murder, jealousy, unrequited love. I guess it made for good news copy. Or maybe it was just a quiet summer and then needed to talk about something to fill the airwaves. We even made an appearance on a morning show called *Good Morning America*. They had paid to fly us back to New York and put us up for a couple days. Everyone wanted to hear about the jewelry store manager and florist who solved the old crimes.

Due to all the news coverage, we got some attention that was unexpected. Several people had called wanting us to investigate the disappearance of family members years before. Some wanted us to try to determine if their relatives had been murdered even if there was no real evidence to suggest that was the case. It was fun at first, but I was a jewelry store manager, not a detective. Kate was happy when the calls finally slowed, and we started living our more peaceful existence again.

I reached down and patted Killer on the head. With Sandy going to prison, or worse, I felt it was the least I could do for this beautiful big dog. We were inseparable when I was home, and when I wasn't, Killer had become fast friends with Kate, and I had a growing suspicion that he was going to take to her more than me soon. He also guarded our yard in the same manner he had guarded Sandy's. I liked that a lot. No worries about anyone breaking into our house—at least not from the backyard.

Hearing the phone ring, I suspected that Betty was wanting Kate to come over to do one thing or another.

It was maybe five minutes later when Kate came out onto the patio.

"Hey, diamond boy, we just had an interesting call."

"Oh?"

"Lawyer named Robert Reynolds."

"And?"

"Says he represents a client by the name of Kenneth Frank. Ever heard of him?"

"Hey, yeah, I think so. He is the guy accused of killing his sister for an inheritance. Big news. Really rich family. Something about cattle as I remember. Then Kenneth Frank decides he wants it all and kills his sister. At least that is what the new says"

"Very good! Yeah, his family owns a cattle ranch in the valley west of Adna. Big spread. They run about five thousand heads on it, at least according to Mr. Reynolds."

"What does all this have to do with us?" I asked.

"Well, as you might already know from the news, the parents were killed by a drunk driver awhile back. Kenneth Frank and his unmarried sister, Nancy, got the ranch and everything else to split evenly. As Mr. Reynolds tells me, the estate was valued at the sum of nine million bucks."

"Whew. That is some estate. I never realized cattle ranching was so prosperous."

"Almost the exact same thing I said to Mr. Reynolds. Then he tells me that the parents were a wiz at picking the right investments. Everything they touched turned into money."

"Wow. Again, I ask, how does this affect us?"

"Mr. Reynolds wants to hire us. Kenneth says he didn't kill his sister and wants us to prove it."

"What? We aren't qualified to do that. He would be putting his life in the hands of amateur sleuths!"

"The trial starts in two weeks. He is offering us $250,000 if we can prove that Kenneth didn't kill his sister. Even if we can't, he said he will pay us a $75,000 retainer that even if we couldn't help Mr. Frank would be ours to keep."

"Two hundred fifty grand? That is like…six years' wages!" I said, quickly doing the math.

"I know. What do you think?"

I sat unmoving for a minute or so, with the exception of my hand petting Killer's head.

"What do I think? I think I better put in for two weeks' vacation, starting tomorrow, and that you better start calling me detective boy."

PART TWO

Murder in the Valley

Prologue

The Bunker Creek Valley is a long valley that stretches from the town of Adna at the east end to the Doty Hills on the west. It is a fertile land with many types of farms. Chicken and horse farms are prevalent, but by far, the biggest livestock businesses in the valley are cattle and dairy farms.

The valley is flanked on either side by towering Douglas firs, and where the logging companies have already fallen the majestic old growth trees, reproduction units, or reprod, where new seedlings are planted, cover the landscape. By replanting, besides creating a renewable resource, which keeps the timber companies in business, the new trees also keep the ground from eroding away and slipping off the hillsides.

The Frank Cattle Ranch is, by far, the largest of the cattle companies that graces the valley. It is at the far end of the valley from Adna, where the road left the valley floor, swung around into the forest, and then dropped back down at the very end of the road to the valley floor. The family had purchased property from their neighbors to grow their original tract, and now had over one thousand acres of prime valley land on which to run their herd. The ranch is mostly Herefords, what most folks called white face. They were orange in color, except for their white face and, most of the time, white lower legs. Calling them white legs didn't quite have the same ring as white face.

The ranch had grown twenty times its size since the Franks had purchased it from an old farmer who was tired of fighting the land to eke out an existence. The farmer's problem was he didn't have the money to invest in more livestock, making it nearly impossible to get ahead. Finally, he sold his ranch, at the time only fifty acres, to the Franks.

Will Franks and his wife, Julia, had started with the original tract of land and invested money he had saved from working his job with the Union Pacific Railroad, and they never looked back. Besides being good cattle ranchers, Will and Julia had a knack. They could look at companies and just seem to *know* which ones were going to take off. Starting small and spending some of the money that they really needed to reinvest in the ranch, they bought stock in a few of these companies. Literally every one skyrocketed. They invested more in the market, and the stocks continued to soar. Before long, they were worth a sizable amount of money. Purchasing surrounding properties for cash in most cases, they increased the size of their ranch and continued to invest at the same time. They had the Midas touch, and their wealth grew even further.

They started a family, having first a boy and then, two years later, a girl. Kenneth grew to be a strapping man as his father and mother aged. He helped on the ranch, running the ranch for his father so that he and his mother could travel and do the things they had always dreamed of doing. Nancy, the daughter, had gone in the completely opposite direction. She felt she was entitled and treated people she met with disdain if they weren't cut from the same cloth. In other words, if they didn't have money. Then she became a party girl, always wanting to hit the lounges and taverns, spending money on booze and assorted other stimulants and depressants in the form of drugs. While Kenneth worked seven days a week, Nancy had chosen her life of leisure and partying and planned to live it to the fullest each and every day.

As Kenneth made the final turn onto Ingalls Road and then turned right into the driveway of the ranch, passing under the ornamental brick and rod iron entry with the double Fs at the apex of entry, his thoughts were of his parents. Will and Julia, coming home from the city of Centralia a month and a half ago, had been run off the road by a drunk driver. Will was driving his baby, a 1972 Ford pickup, that he had kept in pristine condition. The truck had careened off the road, rolled several times, and then caught on fire. Will and Julia had both been belted in with no chance of escape and had burned up in the accident.

Kenneth was thinking about them, and the fact he and Nancy were at loggerheads over the division of the assets, which were sizable. The estate was valued at around nine million dollars, and Kenneth's concern was not as much for Nancy's share but how she would spend it. He was sure she would party herself into oblivion if she was to get four and a half million dollars all at once.

Pulling up in front of the beautiful ranch home and parking next to Nancy's Mercedes, he exited his truck, taking care to lock it. Being this far out in the county meant anyone who had bad intentions would have plenty of time to carry them out before the sheriff could arrive. Better safe than sorry.

Kenneth strode up the stairs onto the expansive porch, put his key in the lock, and opened the door. He called his sister's name and got no response. He walked through the house to the back and entered the kitchen. He called Nancy's name again and, once again, was met by silence.

Wandering through the house, checking out each room, he finally ended his search with a terrifying discovery. He opened the door to Nancy's room. Nancy was lying on the bed. A knife protruded out from her chest. It was completely evident with just one look that his sister was not going to be partying ever again.

CHAPTER ONE

Yesterday, my wife, Kate, and I were relaxing, enjoying the fact we had helped a new friend solve a mystery. Today, I was on vacation time from my job as a jewelry store manager, and Kate was taking time off from being a floral designer to start a new saga into what has turned out to be an interesting twist in our lives.

Our new friend, Betty Walker, had placed a watch in her husband's coffin in 1924 that I happened to find while metal detecting. It took us about three weeks to determine how the watch had made its way from the grave to the hills that had once been the Bordeaux logging works. In the process, we had uncovered the fact that Betty's husband, William, along with another man, had been murdered. One thing led to another, and we were able to solve the murders as well as the mystery of the watch.

Now today, due to that discovery, we were semi-famous because of national television coverage. The fact we solved the crimes so quickly had led a suspected murderer to hire us to find out who really killed his sister. Kenneth Frank had been arrested and charged with the murder. The evidence he had done it was either airtight if you believed it or fatally flawed if you didn't. Kate and I had taken the next two weeks off work to see if we could help Kenneth out. It wasn't an act of kindness. Kenneth was loaded and offered us $75,000 even if we didn't get him off and $250,000 if we did. It was certainly worth taking the time off work. It was 1979, and $75,000 was nearly two years of toiling in the jewelry store I managed. The amount of

$250,000 was over six years' pay for doing my regular job. No doubt and no question we were going to try to hit the jackpot on this one. Call us gold diggers if you want to. Would you turn down 75 grand for two weeks' work? I don't think so.

We had been contacted by Robert Reynolds, Kenneth's attorney, to see if we could find reasonable doubt that the crime could have been committed by someone else. He made us the offer, and having heard about it on the news and coupled with the money, it was something we just couldn't turn down. We were to meet with Mr. Reynolds at his office at 10:00 a.m.

Although the alleged crime took place in Lewis County, the law offices of Mr. Reynolds were in our hometown of Olympia. As we drove into the parking lot and viewed the building, it was obvious that Mr. Reynolds had a thriving practice. The landscaping alone likely cost more than Kate and I drew in salary in a year.

The building was red brick. None of the old-brick look that seemed to be popular. Nice brand-new red brick were used to build his two-story office. Upon entering the lobby, we were again floored by its opulence.

"Holy cow," Kate said, surveying the entry, "this guy makes serious bucks."

"Well, when you consider he is representing the richest clients for the most heinous of crimes, I am sure he earns his keep—if he gets them off," I replied.

Rolling that thought around in my own brain for a minute, I realized Kenneth Frank was banking on Reynolds and the family Tuttle to get him exonerated. If he was paying us $75,000 even if we didn't get him off and a $250,000 if we did, I could only imagine what Robert Reynolds was making on this deal. Frank was putting his life, literally, in our hands. I don't think there is a price tag that is too high when it comes to saving your own skin.

Before we could get to the desk, I heard another car pull up in the parking lot. It was a Lewis County Sheriff's car. Elmer had made it on time.

We had met Elmer Danforth while helping Betty Walker with her issues a few months back. In fact, he was the responding officer when I was shot by the person who had committed murder fifty-five years earlier. He had been promoted to sergeant due to his expertise and help in solving a have century-old case, and he and I had become fast friends. October we intended to go deer hunting together.

Elmer walked into the lobby and let out a low whistle as he removed his hat. He must have been as impressed as Kate and I were.

"Morning, Butch. Glad you could make it." Elmer preferred his nickname to his given moniker.

"Hey, Jim, hey, Kate. How are you two this fine morning?"

"Great, thanks for asking," Kate said.

"You guys ready to get this party started?" I asked.

They both responded with a yes, and we headed up to the long granite counter.

"Good morning. May I help you?" the receptionist asked.

"Good morning. We are here to see Mr. Reynolds. I'm Jim Tuttle, this is Kate, my wife, and this is Sergeant Elmer Danforth from Lewis County."

"Mr. Reynolds is expecting you. Please go through the door," she said, pointing to her right, "and go down the hall. The door to the conference room will be open. You will find Mr. Reynolds and Mr. Frank inside."

Whoa. I had no idea Kenneth Frank was going to be there. The bail had been set at $1,000,000, which, in reality, meant a bond of $100,000. It never crossed my mind that Kenneth Frank probably carried that much around in his wallet.

We followed her directions and started down the hall. We could hear voices coming from what we assumed to be the conference room before we actually were to the door. I poked my head around to look in.

"Ah, good morning. You must be Jim Tuttle. Come in, come in." He motioned to us to do just that.

"Yes, I am. This is my wife, Kate, and we invited along Sergeant Elmer Danforth from Lewis County. Since the crime occurred there, I figured we could use the help of the sheriff's department."

"Perfect. Welcome, Sergeant. I am Robert Reynolds. And this is Kenneth Frank."

"We have had the pleasure of meeting already," Elmer said in such a manner that it left no doubt it hadn't really been a pleasure the first time. Still, they shook hands again, and I shook hands with both Frank and Reynolds, as did Kate.

"Please, sit."

"Kate and I have a saying that I'm sure you have all heard before. Start at the beginning. Mr. Frank, would you please tell us what happened the night your sister was killed, and tell us every detail you can remember?"

"Since we will be spending a lot of time together, we might as well get the formality out of the way. Call me Ken," he said. "And I will call you Jim and Kate. Sergeant?"

"You can call me Sergeant Danforth."

Now I was pretty sure without asking Butch that he was the investigating sheriff the night the murder occurred, along with the Lewis County detectives. He was keeping it formal for now. It might seem odd to invite a member of the authorities to sit in since they were the ones charging Ken with murder, but I knew Butch well enough to know he was fair-minded and would add insight to our conversation. If, at any time, it appeared he was hindering our cause, I would simply ask him to leave, and I knew it would not jeopardize our friendship. Since this was our first meeting with Mr. Frank, I suspected we would not be getting into the specifics of how we were going to try to prove reasonable doubt. Again, if we did, Butch would be asked to leave.

"Okay then," Ken replied.

"Before Dad and Mom were killed in the accident, Dad wanted to look into maybe purchasing some farmland in central Washington. To honor his wishes, I had gone over to the Yakima area that day to look at some potential land to expand our operations. I left at around four in the morning since it was roughly a two-and-a-half-hour drive; I figured that would give me the whole day to view properties and then drive back home. I did just that. I left Yakima, well, Naches actually, around eight, which was later than I had hoped since, even though it was spring and the days were getting longer, it meant I would be driving in the dark over much of Highway 12. Dangerous at night to do that, lots of elk and deer running across the road. Do you think I could get some water?"

Reynolds rose and went to what appeared to be a blank wall. He pushed on the wall, and a panel opened up. Swinging it open and then folding the panel in half, a full bar appeared. Wow. This guy had really thought about the layout of this place when he had it built. He went behind the bar and opened a cupboard on the wall. He took out a tray, five glasses, and a pitcher. Filling the pitcher, he loaded the whole shebang onto the tray and carried it over to the table. He poured Ken a glass of water, then held the pitcher up and looked at the rest of us. All of us nodded, and he filled the rest of the glasses and set one in front of each of us.

"Go on please, Ken," Reynolds said once he had taken his seat.

"The good news was the drive was uneventful. I made it home about ten thirty. When I pulled into the driveway, Nancy's Mercedes was there, so I knew she had stayed home. For once. I got out of my truck, unlocked the door—"

"So the door was locked? You're certain?" I asked.

Ken sat and pondered this for a minute. "Well, I put the key in the lock and unlocked it, so yes, it was locked."

"But did you really? Could it be the door was unlocked and you put your key in and just *thought* you unlocked it?" I questioned.

Again, he sat for a moment. I could see uncertainty creeping into his mind. "I guess it could have been. I was dog-tired. Maybe it was unlocked. You know, I can't be certain now that you ask it that way."

Butch let out a sound that was somewhat like a quiet grunt. If I was right and he was one of the those who investigated the murder that night, he was now hearing the possibility that the door was unlocked, which went against what they had been told that fateful night.

"Butch, can you add anything?" I asked.

"He told us the door was locked. We worked from that assumption during our investigation."

That meant that here was a chink in the armor of their case.

"Butch, maybe it would be best if you went ahead and went back to work. I will give you a call a little later." I didn't want him hearing anymore about this due to the nature of the way the conversation was going. Even though he was fair-minded, he still was a cop. He would listen and make mental notes that could harm us if this ever got as far as the trial that was scheduled for a mere two weeks from today.

"No problem, Jim." He had known this might happen. He stood and shook hands again with Reynolds and turned and walked out without another word.

"Probably smart to ask him to leave. We don't want to give anything away just yet."

"My thoughts exactly," I replied. "Please continue, Ken."

He went on, "After I unlocked the door, or at least I think I unlocked the door, I walked in and called Nancy's name. Then when she didn't respond, I started checking out the rooms. Nancy liked to listen to music on her Walkman, and I thought maybe she had her headphones on and couldn't hear me calling. When I finally opened the door to her room, I saw her lying on the bed. Dead. I walked over to her body and looked at it. The blood had not yet started to congeal, so I knew she had not been dead long. That was when I realized the killer could still be in the house. We have always had guns around the house since Dad and I hunted every fall. I went straight into my room and loaded my twelve gauge and started checking out the house again. This time more closely and more cautiously. If someone had killed my sister, I assumed they would have no problem killing me as well. The house was empty, so I called the sheriff's office and told them of my sister's murder."

All this was told to us with a very monotone delivery. I was pretty sure this must have been the hundredth time Ken had told the story, and it would likely not be the last, particularly if this case made it to court.

"What did the sheriff do when he arrived?" Kate asked.

"What you might expect—started dusting for fingerprints on the door handles, doors, windowsills. Just about anywhere someone could have touched. They found nothing. They took my prints as well, of course, to be able to determine if the prints they had lifted were mine or someone else's. The knife went back to Chehalis with them. Sergeant Danforth was the one who questioned me the most that night. I told the same story, and he seemed to believe it. Then two days later, two patrol cars pulled into the driveway. I was out in the first barn doing some work on the tractor when they came down the driveway. Sergeant Danforth strode up, told me I was under arrest for the murder of my sister, and then they handcuffed me and took me to the county jail."

"Did the sergeant tell you what evidence they had to arrest you?" I asked.

"Said my fingerprints were the only ones in the house and the only ones on the knife. Once they started questioning me seriously back at the office, I told them that, of course, my fingerprints were on it. The knife had come from the kitchen. I used all the knives all the time. That alone didn't seem like a very strong case. But couple that with the fact Nancy and I were just about through the probate process and were about to inherit more than nine million dollars, they said I had a motive."

"Whew. So is that all they have on you? Fingerprints and a motive? I realize that could look damaging, but I'm sure Mr. Reynolds—"

"Robert."

"I'm sure Robert can make a case for reasonable doubt if that is all they have. With no witnesses and shaky evidence, I don't see why they are so hot on you for the murder."

"You have to remember, I was driving back from the other side of the state. No witnesses to cover for me either."

"Still seems a bit shaky. What am I missing here?" I said.

Ken looked at Robert. Robert nodded. Ken looked back at Kate and me.

"That first night, when the deputies came to the house, Sergeant Danforth asked me about my relationship with my sister. I was honest. I told him I hated my sister."

CHAPTER TWO

"He's not making it easy for us to earn the big payday, is he?" Kate said.

"Nope. But he never said it was going to be easy," I replied.

We had left the law offices of Robert Reynolds shortly after our client had told us that he hated his sister. Now we were sitting in our pseudo office, our backyard, sipping on a beer and trying to figure out what our next move would be. Our dog, Killer, sat at our feet, snoring.

"He makes their case much stronger. If you think about it, he had motive and opportunity. But why take a chance of ending up in prison for killing your own sister when you were a short time away from divvying up almost ten million dollars? It just doesn't make sense," Kate said.

"Agreed. People kill other people for several reasons—greed, hatred, jealousy just being a few. Then there are the killings that are just plain murder, you know, some perceived injustice, insanity, and so on."

"Okay, detective boy, let's start at the beginning. We have to assume that Kenneth Frank didn't commit the murder of his sister. How do we go about doing that? We need evidence that he couldn't have done it, which will be hard to produce since he doesn't have any witnesses when he got home or anyone that saw him at a specific time while he was on the road. Lacking that, we have to find out why someone else would want her dead."

"I think you have nailed it. We need to concentrate on Nancy and her lifestyle and see if there was anyone she was dating, seeing, or maybe simply, um, you know."

"Having sex with?"

"Yes. You just say it much nicer than the way I was thinking it should be said."

"Ken is out on bail. Let's give him a call and see if we can come down to the farm. Tell him we want to look around, which, I think, we should do, and then chat with him about his sister and see where that takes us," I stated.

"Good idea. You know, I will call him. Maybe I can get a handle on whether or not he didn't just dislike his own sister but maybe all women. Just saying."

"Have at it. His number is on the counter in the kitchen."

Kate rose and headed into the house. Killer raised his gigantic head and looked her way as she walked away. Killer had been owned by a man who tried to kill me just a couple months before. I had taken him in since his owner was never going to see freedom on the outside of prison for the rest of his life. He is part German shepherd and part wolf. Long story, but he is big and proving to be a very faithful companion.

It was late September, and the northwest was being graced with a beautiful Indian summer. It was starting to show signs of heading into fall soon; cooler nights had actually started turning cold and the heat of the day was less than it was just a week ago, but it was still in the seventies and eighties and I enjoyed being outside as much as possible.

Kate reemerged from the house with a smile on her face.

"Well, the good news is he seemed very pleasant and cordial on the phone. Just like he was to me at Reynolds's office, so I don't think he hates women in general, just his sister. He invited us to come down around three. He said he had work to do on the farm, but by then he could stop for a time to talk to us."

"Nice of him to take the time," I said a bit sarcastically. "We are only trying to save his life."

"Yeah, no kidding."

Kate had had the wherewithal to bring out two more beers when she had finished the call, and we sat and talked about anything but the case for half an hour or so, just enjoying each other's company. There would be plenty to talk about once we met with Ken again.

* * *

The drive to the Frank farm, or at least nearly to the Frank farm, was one I had taken many times. I hunted literally just around the corner from the farm. The Bunker Creek Valley was beautiful any time of year, but during the fall it was spectacular. The large firs that dominated the landscape had just enough maple and alder groves interspersed to make the colors of the valley walls very beautiful with reds and orange patches dotting the landscape. The road wound first up one side of the valley, then right down the middle, before turning to the other side of the valley as you got closer to the Frank's place. Some of the farms were much larger than others. The smaller ones were folks who had decided to become more self-sustaining, raising their own vegetables, cattle, and fruit. In a way, I envied them. My grandpa and grandma had owned forty acres about ten miles as the crow flies from the Franks, and I had spent a couple weeks every summer since I was around eight helping them with milking cows, hauling hay, and the like. Grandpa had lost his job at a mill in Olympia when the company that owned it moved the entire operation to Oregon and had purchased the acreage when he was fifty-five years old. It took a lot of grit to take on forty acres and fifty heads of dairy cows and start all over again at that age. Maybe, since I was only twenty-four, I would still have a chance to do some farming of my own one day.

Kate and I pulled in right on time. The double *FF*s, which I assumed stood for Frank Farm, was a bit pretentious, I thought, as we turned into the driveway. I was pretty sure Ken had nothing to do with it. He seemed, for all intents and purposes, a pretty grounded guy. I had not met many multimillionaires in my life, but I assumed not many of them would want to meet you after he got done working on his own tractor, which we found out was the work he was doing just before we pulled in. Most would hire someone to do the manual labor.

Ken must have been watching for us because as we got out of my truck he was coming out to meet us.

"Hello again."

"Hi, Ken," we said in stereo.

"Mind if we sit on the porch? Seems like too nice of a day to let it go to waste."

"Perfect," I replied.

"You two look like you could use a beer."

"That would be great," Kate said.

He had figured we would say yes and had already set out a cooler on the porch filled to the brim with bottles of the golden liquid. I liked him more by the minute.

We sat at a rod iron table with matching chairs, and Ken opened and handed us each a Budweiser before opening one for himself and taking a seat.

"What's up?" he asked.

"I think we just need some more details before we can really begin to dig into your case. For instance, can you elaborate on your relationship with Nancy?"

He took a long drink of his beer before setting it down and asking, "So what do you want to know?"

"For starters, why did you hate her?" Kate asked.

Ken sat quietly for a few moments before answering.

"My sister was not a very nice girl. She was what I always called a party animal. Where I worked my tail off here at the farm, drove an older truck, and did my best to help out Mom and Dad before… they died, Nancy was just the opposite. She would stay out every night and close down the tavern or bar of her choice and then get home around two thirty or three every night and then sleep until noon and get up and laze around the house until time to go out and do it all over again. She coerced Dad and Mom into a new car every year and not just any car. Her last one was the Mercedes out in the driveway. Dad never tried to instill in her the values that he did with me. Shoot, Dad drove a 1972 Ford pickup! Mom and Dad had money, but if you had met them, you would have never known they were rich. Nancy wanted everyone to know she was from *the* Frank family, which meant she had loads of money, or at least the family did. We never saw eye to eye. While she slept in, I was up working by six or six thirty every morning. I started to resent her for being so lazy, and I guess that resentfulness turned into hatred at some point. I will say lately, since Dad and Mom were killed, it seemed like she was cleaning up her act a bit."

Kate and I sat quietly as he told us this. It made the cop's job a lot easier if Ken was the only suspect and he admitted outright that he hated his sister.

"What else can you tell us about your sister? Did she have a boyfriend? Did she date regularly?"

"She had a guy the last six months or so. I overheard her and Mom talking once. She said he was fun, and she was falling for him. Mom was none too happy since the only people she met were either in the taverns or clerks at the stores she went to shopping for the latest and greatest clothes. Mom felt, at least from what I overheard, he was not good enough for her. In Mom's mind, nobody was good enough for Nancy though. She was her little princess, which is why they let her get away with all the partying and not working."

I could hear resentment in his voice. If his case ever made it to trial, he was a dead duck. The jury would pick up on it too, and his days sitting on his porch would be numbered.

Kate decided to try another angle. "What can you tell us about your parents' death? Sorry to ask, but the more information we have the better."

"I understand."

Ken finished his beer by simply tipping up the bottle and draining it. Something told me this was going to be hard to talk about for him.

"Dad and Mom died less than a mile from here. Actually died in the south pasture of this ranch they loved so much. They had been to town, Centralia, to do some shopping and just to look around. They loved spending time with each other and would wander the streets of the town and stop and have coffee or ice cream, then maybe do some shopping at the local merchants. They did this almost every week, kind of like a date. Coming home that night, they went off the road and rolled over and the truck caught fire. The both were burned beyond recognition. See, the 1972 Ford pickup had the gas tank right behind the seat of the truck. The filler cap was just behind the door. The police suspect that the filler neck was knocked off the truck as it rolled down the hill. Any sort of spark at that point would have likely ignited the spilling gas and ultimately set the gas in the tank on fire."

"You said they were killed by a drunk driver before."

"Yes. There were skid marks from the truck as well as another vehicle. It looks like the other vehicle swerved into them and then continued on. The sheriff's department figures someone who had been drinking didn't want to stop since it would mean blood tests, Breathalyzers, and potentially a murder charge for running them off the road. Of course, it could have been someone sober. Folks drive way too fast on the valley road. They could have just lost control of their car. But most sober people would be much more likely to stick around and face the music. Or at least that is what the cops think."

"You mean there was no evidence to show it was a drunk driver?" Kate inquired.

"None. The official report still states 'killed by drunk driver' however."

I would have to talk to Butch about that. Seemed strange that they would classify it that way if there was no actual proof. Maybe they were trying to pad the numbers to show driving and drinking was killing more people this year than last. I wasn't sure the reason, but it was something I was going to look into for sure.

"Where were you when they died, Ken?" Kate asked.

"Right over there," he said, pointing to a barn. "That is the equipment shed. I was working on the tractor, which seems to have become a daily part of my life. Dad always said it was cheaper to repair a tractor than to replace it, but shoot, my time is worth something. Sorry. I was in the shed and between having the radio turned up, so I could hear it, and starting and stopping the tractor to work on it, I never even heard the accident or what must have been a pretty decent-sized explosion when the truck blew up. I didn't even know if happened until your sergeant friend and a state trooper showed up at my door."

"Sargent Danforth was the investigator?"

"I think so. Although the trooper did most of the talking."

Time to get a hold of Butch for sure.

"So now what for you, Ken?"

"Can we take a walk?"

"Sure."

We all stood, and Ken walked off the porch and onto the side-walk, took an immediate right turn, and headed off. Kate and I did our best to keep pace. Rounding the house, Ken headed toward the backyard. He stopped when he reached the fence that ran parallel to the back of the house.

"Careful, this fence has a hot wire on the inside."

I had been around enough electric fences to know some were more powerful than others. On big farms like this, my bet was they had the weed burner variety. Normally, if a weed or enough tall grass comes in contact with a regular electric fence, it can actually short it out, leaving the farm vulnerable to livestock escapes. With the more powerful weed burners, if grass touched it for too long, it would simply burn it off and it would fall to the ground keeping the fence from shorting out. Touch a normal fence, it hurts. Touch a weed burner and it *really* hurt. For like a week.

Ken pointed out to the cattle in the pasture. There were hundreds as far as your eye could see.

"If I go to prison, this all goes away. My only living relatives are my cousins. Nice enough folks, but not one of them has spent even a day on this farm. I would have to either sell or give it to them. Either way, the farm my folks built would be gone."

Kate looked at the cattle and then to me. I could see in her eyes that she wanted to help this man keep his family farm. She had a soft spot in her heart when it came to any sort of animal. Not really liking the fact I hunted was one thing that almost kept us apart. I told her I wouldn't give it up. It had been in my family genes for literally over one hundred years. Her response was that if I went, I had to keep all the tales of the hunt to myself and never share them with her. Over the two years we had been married, she had softened enough to at least eat some of the meat. I just never was to mention it was deer or elk while we were eating it. She knew, but it was to be left unsaid.

"Ken, is there anyone you can think of who might have wanted your sister dead? Oh, and while I'm thinking of other people, do you know her boyfriend's name? I think we should have a little chat with him too. See what perspective he might be able to add."

"I never met him. Nancy wasn't much for bringing a boy home to meet Mom and Dad, if you know what I mean. His name is Brian Eckland. He lives somewhere down by Napavine. That's about all I know. Other than him, and I have given it considerable thought as you might imagine, there is no one I can think of who would want to harm Nancy. Not saying he would, you understand, but his is the only name I can give you."

"We understand. We will still pay him a visit in short order." We only had thirteen days now before the trial was starting, so it would have to be soon.

Ken turned away from the cattle and looked me straight in the eyes.

"Jim, I want you to know something. I may have despised my sister, but she was still family…all I had left. I didn't kill her or have anything to do with it. I just wanted you to hear that from me."

"Ken, we know you are under a great deal of pressure right now, and we want you to know we believe you," I said this while turning to Kate. She was nodding her head in affirmation.

"Thanks. Thanks a lot. I barely know you, but I have a good feeling about your finding out why my sister was killed and by whom. You did get the check from Robert for your retainer?" he said. It must have suddenly hit him that he never saw us get paid for our services, and he wanted to make sure we had. Nice guy. As well as honest, it appeared.

"Yes. He handed it to us as we left his office. Thanks for asking. Ken, just know that we really want to get you out of trouble, but not for the money. We can see what this farm means to you. It would be horrible for you to lose it." This was from Kate.

"Thanks, Kate. I sure don't want to lose it, that's for sure."

As we had talked we had walked back around to the front of the house. Kate asked if Ken had a recent picture of Nancy we could take with us. He went into the house and came back out in short order, handing it to Kate.

"It's not real recent, but it should do for you, I hope."

"This is perfect. Thanks, Ken," Kate said as she took it from him.

Kate and I shook Ken's hand and told him we would be in touch if we needed more information.

I opened Kate's door and shut her into the truck. Walking around, I got in the driver's side and slammed the door.

"I don't know why, but I am pretty sure he is telling the truth," Kate said.

"I couldn't agree more. But we aren't the jury. We have to gather some evidence, and fast."

CHAPTER THREE

Since it was only a few miles out of our way, we decided to stop and see if Butch happened to be in the office. Chehalis is the sister city to Centralia. As you drive from Centralia south into Chehalis, if you missed the sign stating it, you would never know you left one and entered the other. It was just like Olympia, Lacey, and Tumwater, where we lived. All jammed in tight together.

Sergeant Elmer "Butch" Danforth was indeed in the office. I hadn't visited him since he was promoted. We had talked a lot since we had become friends during the Betty Walker search for answers about her watch, but I hadn't made the trip down from Olympia to see him in person. It was, in fact, an office. Now that he was a sergeant, he actually had four walls and a desk to call his own instead of being relegated to the main floor of the station and sharing desk time with other deputies.

"Afternoon, Butch," I said as we walked slowly into his office. "Sorry again about this morning. We knew it might turn that way, but I just didn't expect it to happen so soon."

Butch looked at us with a stern look on his face. Then slowly he smiled and stood.

"No worries, you guys. I know you are just trying to help. It was a bit uncomfortable, but I get it. What brings you down this way? Visiting your client?"

"Yup. Got some information from Frank but wanted to talk to you about a couple things too."

"Have a seat."

Kate and I sat in the chairs that were in front of his desk.

"Shoot."

"I'm sure you can't share the report on the murder, but maybe you can give us a rundown from your perspective on how it all went down."

"You're right, it's an ongoing, open case, at least until the trial is over, so I can't show you the report, but I can tell you my thoughts. No law against friends talking, right?"

"Right," Kate chimed in.

"I guess I'll start at the beginning. We got the call from Frank around 11:00 p.m. or so. Said he had come home to find his sister murdered on her bed. I was working swing shift, so it was me who got the call from dispatch to go to the Frank farm. When I arrived, Mr. Frank was waiting for me on the porch. He related his story to me, and then I went in to take a look at Ms. Frank. There was no doubt she was dead."

"Then what?"

"I called the county coroner and told him what was going on. He didn't like getting out of bed, but he showed up around midnight. Took samples of her blood, and, uh, swabbed her, uh, you know where I am going here."

"Yes," Kate said with a small smile on her lips. "It's okay, Butch. It's strictly a medical report at this point."

"Okay, he swabbed her vagina to look for semen, I suppose. He also did some temperature analysis as well as visually checking the blood for coagulation and so on. He determined that she had been killed somewhere between nine thirty and ten thirty. Since Mr. Frank had gotten home by his own admission at around ten thirty, that made him suspect number one in my book. While I had been waiting for him to get there, I had called FIT."

"FIT. What the heck is that?" I asked.

"Forensics Investigation Team. The sheriff started it a couple years ago. Even a backward county like Lewis County has enough suspicious deaths that he deemed it a necessity. Actually took money from other parts of his budget to create the team. At first I thought it was a waste of resources, but after watching them firsthand on this murder investigation, I totally changed my tune. These guys were good."

"What did they find, anything?" Kate asked Butch.

"They spent until around 3:00 a.m. pulling fingerprints, looking for any fibers on the body that didn't match what she had on, which by the way, was not very much. The deceased was wearing a skimpy little pair of pajamas."

"Would it better be described as lingerie?" I asked.

"Well, yeah, probably. Not much material but lots of lace and frills."

"That is the definition of lingerie, I think," Kate laughed as she replied.

Butch smiled at her and continued, "They took Mr. Frank's fingerprints at the very end and then took off. I sat and interviewed Mr. Frank again to see if he remembered anything else. The lock on the door thing you brought up this morning, well, it never crossed my mind that the door could have been unlocked. He was so certain he had unlocked it."

"An easy thing to miss, Butch."

"I still think he did it. He actually told me he hated his sister. My prime suspect to that point was the only one around, said he didn't like her, and said he found her dead."

"Wait. To that point? Was there someone else you looked at?"

"Seems Ms. Frank had a boyfriend name of Brian Eckland. Lives down south of here. Weird duck. When I went to talk to him, he was okay at first, but when I started pressing just a little, he went off. Started hollering that his girlfriend was dead and I was picking on him, that sort of thing. I finally got out of him that he was in a tavern down in Onalaska. His alibi checked out, so he dropped off the radar."

"What would you say if I said we wanted to talk to him?"

"Your neck. If you want me to go along, I can—"

"If you would, we would appreciate it," Kate spoke up. I think she was recalling I had been shot the last time I got close to a murderer.

"When?" Butch asked.

"How about now?" I replied.

Butch sat back down at his desk, scanned a few documents, shuffled a few papers, then said, "Why not? I am not much for paper-work anyway. I will lead you down there. You can follow in your car so you can head home afterward without having to come into town. My bet is you wouldn't much like riding around in the back of my cruiser anyway."

"Good idea, and no, I don't want to sit in the back of your cruiser, ever," Kate said.

We all rose and headed for the door. Kate was in the lead. I was acting as her wingman, and Butch brought up the rear. As we opened the outside door to the station house, or office if you prefer to be precise, the heat of the day hit us like a furnace.

"Wow, I thought summer was over!' Kate exclaimed.

"Just remember that it will get down to forty tonight and you will probably complain it is too cold," Butch said lightheartedly.

We all hopped in our respective vehicles, and Butch led us out to Jackson Highway where we headed south to Napavine, where one Brian Eckland resided. It was a hot day, and I still had a truck with-out air-conditioning. Kate and I had both windows down to mitigate the heat as much as possible. The drive, we knew, was a short one, so we tried not to let the heat get us in a mood before we arrived. There were some things I wanted to talk to Mr. Eckland about him going off as Butch had put it.

The Eckland place was an old two-story cedar-sided house with what appeared to be a barn out back. It didn't look like they farmed any of the fields that were surrounding the place, and there were no livestock present, so perhaps the barn was used for something else.

Turning off our engines, we got out and met at the side of Butch's cruiser. "Let me go first," Butch said. "Kind of stay back a little if you would until I see if he is in a mood or not."

"Surely," I said.

We hung back as he asked, and Butch went to the front door and knocked. I took the time to peer back toward the barn. There were old car parts strewn all around it. I now assumed the barn was used for auto or tractor repair or maybe both. The doors were shut, so I couldn't see inside to further confirm my suspicions. Sitting in the driveway in front of the barn was a GMC pickup. It had seen better days. It appeared to be around a 1970 vehicle with four-wheel drive. Eckland had tried to deck it out with some better wheels and a chrome push bar. The body, however, was dinged up pretty good. Probably used it like a truck. Good for him. Mine was newer, but the only thing it had ever hauled was my lazy tail back and forth to work and a few deer and elk.

Brian Eckland came to the door after the third knocking by Butch.

"What do you want?"

"Good afternoon, Mr. Eckland. We were hoping that we could speak to you for a moment," Butch said while motioning in our direction.

"What do you want to know?"

"These folks here are trying to dig into the murder of Nancy Frank. They just had a few questions for you."

Kate and I walked toward the house now so that we could be heard if Mr. Eckland agreed to talk to us. He watched us approach and then said, "Well, let's have it."

"Good afternoon. My name is Jim Tuttle, and this is my wife, Kate. We have been hired to look into Ms. Frank's death in an effort to clear her brother."

"So you gonna try to pin it on me? Sergeant…"

"Danforth," Butch filled in the blank.

"Danforth here already knows I was in a tavern half drunk when the murder occurred. Why do you want to talk to me?"

He seemed a bit adversarial. Oh well, I probably would too if someone was asking me about a murder.

"Did you go to the tavern alone?"

"Nope. My buddy Roger picked me up and then ended up leaving me there. Had to hitch a ride with another friend just to get home. Good thing I wasn't in any shape to drive by the time I left there."

"Is getting drunk a normal thing for you, Mr. Eckland, or was there a reason you went there that night?"

"I wouldn't say it's normal. I don't get drunk every night or anything, but it isn't out of the ordinary for me to get drunk a couple times a week maybe. Not much else to do here but work on cars. As much as I like doing that, I still get tired of it sometimes and need to blow off some steam. You know."

Being one to seldom turn down a beer, I couldn't argue with him on that accord.

"And to answer your question, no there was no reason in particular that I was getting drunk that night."

As we had spoken, Eckland had moved out onto the front porch. More of a concrete landing actually. He had shut the door and seemed a bit more relaxed as our conversation progressed.

Suddenly the front door swung open, and a young women stepped out and stood next to Eckland. Her demeanor was like a cobra ready to strike. She had her fists clenched and a scowl on her face. I would put her at maybe twenty-five. With bleached blond hair with jet-black roots that looked as if the last time it saw a brush was months before and eye makeup that had run down onto her face, she looked almost scary.

"What the hell do you people want with Brian? You know he was in Onalaska the night that bitch was killed!" *Killed* came out like *kilt*.

As Eckland grabbed this she-devil, Butch took a small step to his right to keep her separated from us. *Nice move Butch*, I thought.

"Please calm down, Miss," Butch said.

"Don't tell me what to do!"

"My name is Sergeant Danforth, and you are?"

"None of your fucking business!"

"Miss, I asked you to identify yourself. You are agitated and getting on the edge of unruly. I need your name please now."

She glared at Butch with I perceived to be pure hatred.

"Jane Tucker."

"May I ask you a question, Jane?" Kate said to the woman.

Whether it was hearing another female voice, one who used her name, or maybe it was just really looking at us for the first time, the woman calmed down a little. Just a little.

"What?"

"Had you ever met Ms. Frank before she was murdered?"

Simple question, but it seemed to send another jolt of energy into this maniacal woman.

"No! I never met her. Now leave us alone!" With that, she stormed back into the house and slammed the door so hard that the windows shook.

"I am done with all this too. Please leave," Eckland said. He turned, opened the door, and walked into the house.

"Well," Butch said, "looks like we're done here."

"It would appear so," Kate stated.

CHAPTER FOUR

After the drive home from points south, Kate and I were relaxing in our "office." Killer was at my feet, and once again, he was snoring. Boy, it truly is a dog's life.

"What a day," Kate said with a sigh.

"Yes, darlin', it was quite a day. And just think. One whole day is gone from the fourteen we are allotted to get Ken off the hook."

We sat and pondered this for a few minutes, sipping our beer and enjoying the way the evenings cooled down so quickly during an Indian summer. Today had been interesting to say the least. We had learned that the Frank's family parents had died on their own property. That Ken had no alibi and that he didn't much care for his sister. Couple that with him being the only candidate that the authorities had spent any time looking at and had concluded he must be the culprit, and we had our work cut out for us. This, of course, was not to mention the run-in with Brian Eckland and his, what, girlfriend? Didn't take him long to pick up a new one after Nancy's death. Had to give that one some more thought.

I was also concerned with the fact the Frank parents were listed as killed by a drunk driver. There was absolutely no evidence to show that, yet the official report said that was the case. I had to remember to ask Butch about that one too.

"What did you think of the woman?" Kate asked. No need to say "what woman" since we had really only encountered one, and she was a piece of work to say the least.

"You know, I don't know. She came out ready to fight. It seemed like she was almost *looking* for a fight. For what reason, I have no idea."

"Did you notice Eckland's response when she came out?"

"No. Did I miss something?" I asked.

"When she first came out, I noticed a really quick reaction from him that appeared to be fright, like he was afraid of her."

"Or maybe just afraid of what she might do? Or say maybe?"

"I was just thinking about that a minute ago. If you are so in love with someone, it doesn't seem reasonable to find someone so quickly. By the look of her, she lived there. I couldn't imagine any woman, even her, going out in public looking like she did. Do you think maybe he was getting cozy with her while he still was dating Nancy?"

"Interesting thought. I agree that she was staying there. Doesn't mean they are boyfriend and girlfriend. Maybe she is just trying to help him out while he gets over Nancy."

"You know, you're right. Heck, she could be his sister for all we know. We need to find out how she is connected to Eckland."

"Do you think he had something to do with Nancy's murder? Butch said he had an airtight alibi."

"He might, but does she? That is the question."

"Why would she want Nancy gone? Unless she *is* his girlfriend. Then jealousy comes into play."

We sat and pondered this for a few minutes, sipping our beer. There were some moving parts to this story that we needed to get locked down if we were to help keep Ken out of prison—or worse.

"So where does tomorrow take us?" Kate asked.

"Let me think about it for a few minutes. Right now, I just don't know what steps to take next."

Kate got out of her chair and took a couple steps over to me, then knelt down and patted Killer on the head. "What would you do, Kill? We need all the help we can get here."

CHAPTER FIVE

T he next morning, day two of our endeavor, I woke early and grabbed a cup of coffee and headed for the office. By now, you know our backyard is our office. The mornings were quiet except for the occasional neighbor leaving for work, so it was time I could spend in solitude thinking about what lay ahead for Kate and me the next thirteen days.

There were so many pieces to the puzzle, and most didn't seem to fit anywhere just yet. Who is Jane Tucker? Eckland's new girl-friend? Why was she so hostile? Was there more than one tavern in Onalaska? Who is Randy, Eckland's friend, who drove him and left him at the tavern? Who gave Eckland the ride home that night?

My head started to ache with all the questions and no answers. I heard a very soft *woof* and knew that Killer had woken up and wanted out to do his morning business. Letting him out, I marveled at the size and structure of this big dog. He was beautiful and very loyal. Stronger than any dog I had ever had or seen. Killer went through his normal routine, and we both went back inside, me for more coffee, Kill for his bowl of food. Kate came out of the bedroom looking beautiful as ever. How was I so lucky catching this wonderful woman when she could have had just about anyone she set her mind to? The old saying "Don't look a gift horse in the mouth" came to mind, and I let it go at that. I was blessed to have her.

"Morning, darlin'."

"Morning to you. What you been up to, detective boy?"

THE WATCH IN THE BOX

"Just doing some thinking about what we should be doing today and which question to look for an answer for first."

"And?"

"It is my considered opinion that we need to drive to Onalaska and see if we can find the tavern that Brian Eckland says he was getting drunk at the night Nancy Frank was killed."

"Butch will tell us which bar. Save us some looking."

"See, that's why I keep you around. You're so dang smart."

"Wise guy."

"Seriously, I was thinking we were going to have to drink our way through all the bars until we found the right one. Your idea saves us time, money, and a potential hangover."

"Your way sounds like more fun, except the hangover part."

"I'll call Butch and get the name of the tav. Then we can head south and see what we can find out."

"Sounds good, but first I need some coffee. Like a pot's worth."

"No worries. Let's have a couple cups, then make another pot and take some with us. I have a feeling it will be a long day."

Killer and I headed back outside, and Kate went in to shower and change. The day was heating up nicely. It had indeed, as Butch predicted, gotten down to near forty degrees overnight, but with the south facing backyard, it was all the way up to fifty-three by the time I checked the thermometer again. The TV weatherman said it would only get to about the low seventies, which was fine with me.

Kate joined us, looking fresh and clean. She had a cup of coffee in one hand and the local paper in the other. Someone had written a letter to the editor blasting Ken Frank as a "rich man who wanted more than his share of the pie," and "He should be hung when the jury gets done with him." Perfect. Nothing like bad press to taint a jury pool. I have, over the years, heard more people quoting letters to the editor than an actual news story. For some reason, in small towns and cities, people tend to value their neighbors' opinions more than the experts who deal in facts. This sort of a letter to the editor will be talked about all over the county. The only saving grace is that Thurston County is one county north of Lewis County where the trial will be held. Maybe these words won't get down there too much. Hopefully.

We jumped into the truck and headed for Onalaska, Washington. The town of Onalaska is a tiny little town which consists primarily of just one tavern (Butch assured us we couldn't miss it) and a gas station that had the US mail office attached to it. As we entered town, I saw why Butch had told us about not missing it. Although it was before noon, the parking lot was fairly full, and the gas station across the street only had one car parked at the pump. Yes, a single pump. Made me wonder if it was the type they had on the old *Andy Griffith Show* when Goober would turn a crank to clear the numbers so they could properly charge the next customer.

Pulling into the tavern's parking lot, we slipped into a spot between two other trucks. Mine stuck out like a swan among a flock of coots. They were a mixture of Chevys and Fords, and although mine was a Ford, it was the only one that was not four-wheel drive and didn't have a push bar attached to the front. They ranged in age from old to decrepit where mine was only a couple years old. Washing them would have been taking time away from tavern time, and although I bet they all ran well, they all looked like they were on the last rotation of their tires.

The tavern was called the Blacktail Tavern. It had a neon light deer's head on the sign, so one assumption I was probably okay making is that it was so named because of the type of deer that hunters sought after in the northwest woods.

Entering the tavern, with Kate in the lead, we were hit by the smell of cigarettes and stale beer immediately. All heads in the place turned in unison, like synchronized drinkers, then turned back to their original positions. Hmm. Maybe a new Olympic sport.

The bar was made of very dark wood. It was either fir or perhaps pine, stained dark by years of spilled beer and smoke. There were a couple open stools available between a couple of patrons, so we bellied up and acted like we knew what we were doing there.

The bartender walked up from the right and asked if he could help us.

"Two Buds please," I replied.

He turned without another word and grabbed two mugs from the back counter, then held them under the tap at a nice angle to alleviate the head a bit. He set them in front of us.

"Wanna run a tab?"

"Sure. Thanks. My name is Jim, and this is my wife, Kate," I said, holding out my hand to be shaken.

He wiped his hand on a bar towel he had over his shoulder and offered his hand.

"Name's Buck."

Interesting name for a man in the Blacktail Tavern. It was then I noticed all the stuffed animals and antlers there were on the walls.

"You the owner?" I chanced.

"Yup."

"Interesting name. Is it your given name or a nickname? The only reason I asked is because of the tavern's name. They seem to kind of go hand in glove."

"Everyone calls me Buck." As he said this, he pointed with his thumb over his shoulder. Mounted on the wall behind the bar was the biggest set of antlers I had ever seen. It was actually attached to what is called a shoulder mount. This had been one gigantic deer. Below the deer was a picture with Buck holding the head up, showing it off, presumably in the woods where he had harvested it.

"Ah, now I get it. That is a beauty. I have hunted all my life and have never seen anything nearly that size in the woods."

"Likely won't either. I think the day of big boys like him are coming to an end. The hunters have all turned into road hunters and few hunters get way back in the brush where I got him."

Buck was referring to the type of hunters my dad and I didn't much care for. We had always hunted the hard way—hiking in maybe two or three miles straight back into places without roads, hoping to find a big buck that wasn't afraid of, or maybe had never seen, a human being. Road hunters drove the logging roads, hoping that a deer would cross in front of them or, even better yet, stand in the road, where they could get an easy shot and an even easier drag to put it in the truck. It was illegal to hunt from the road or from a truck, but it happened all the time. Problem was, typically, only the smaller bucks would be stupid enough to stand on or near a road when a car was coming, so the young ones were killed before they could become old and big like this one on the wall. With all the growth going on in the areas surrounding the cities of western Washington, the woods were shrinking and a good number of the big old deer were taken and now long gone, leaving the little ones to be taken by unscrupulous hunters.

"Can I ask you a question, Buck?" Kate spoke up.

"Sure."

"You ever see this lady in here before?" She held up the picture Ken had given us of Nancy.

"You guys cops?"

"No. We are just friends of Ken Frank and are trying to do a little digging for him about his sister."

"Yeah. I know who she is. Used to come in here before she was murdered by your friend."

We had to tread carefully now. It was a simple statement with tons of implications.

"How often would she come in?"

"She was a somewhat regular. I think she visited several different taverns. At least that was the impression I got listening to her talk when she was in here."

As he spoke, I noticed Buck was looking at the two guys sitting on either side of Kate and me. One, then the other, then back again. In the old days, a detective would say that Buck had shifty eyes. Noted.

"Did she hang out with anyone in particular?"

"The Eckland kid mostly. Once she had a few beers in her, though, she got loud and talked to anyone who would listen to her."

"Does a bleach blond named Jane Tucker come in here?" I asked.

Buck was quiet for a moment. The shifty eyes again.

"Maybe, I don't know everybody that comes in. Just like I didn't know you ten minutes ago."

"But you knew the Eckland kid and Nancy. Seems like you have a pretty good memory to me."

Buck took a deep breath and then wiped is hands again on the bar towel that he had replaced on his shoulder after shaking my hand. Finally, he spoke again.

"Yeah. She is a regular too."

"Looney if you ask me." This came from the guy sitting next to me, kind of under his breath.

"Shut the hell up, Phil," Buck said to the man.

"Geez, Buck, these folks are just trying to help a friend. I know how bad you feel for the Frank woman being killed and all, so why not help them?" Phil replied.

A Willie Nelson song had started on the jukebox that was sitting in front of the window, presumably so folks could read the little song labels so they got what they paid for. Everyone sat silently for a moment. It was Buck who finally broke the silence.

"Jane is a bit of a live wire. She seems to be all about finding a man who can take care of her, you know, a husband. But the guys who come in here are pretty much all regulars and don't want her. Think she was a pass-around pack for too long, if you get my drift."

"Got it," I said. "Ever recall her and Nancy being in here at the same time?"

"Yeah, I do because it was kind of odd. Probably six months ago. Nancy came in with Brian Eckland and took a seat at one of the tables. Jane had drunk a few beers by then and was being her noisy self. When she saw them come in, she got real quiet. Sat here at the bar for maybe ten minutes without making a sound, then got up and walked over to the table and sat right down like she owned the place. Seemed like they all got along just fine, then Nancy and Jane got up and left Brian sitting at the table by himself and they went outside together. They came back in maybe ten minutes later. Jane came back to the bar, and Nancy went back and sat down with Brian. Brian and her kind of got a little, uh, I think animated is the word everyone likes to use now. But they left shortly together. End of story."

"You ever see Nancy and Jane together again after that?"

"Nope. Just that once. Doesn't mean they didn't meet in another tavern though."

"One last question. You know a young man named Randy? I guess he was the one who was supposed to have come here with Brian the night Nancy was killed and then left him here."

"Yup. Randy works over at the gas station. He came in that night with Brian all right, but then he just up and left him here. Randy, being so close by, is a regular for sure. Not too far of a drive from across the street."

We all remained quiet for a few minutes. Finally, Kate looked at me and said that we should depart this wonderful tavern or something to that effect. We removed our backsides from the barstools, and paying Buck for the beer and thanking him for answering our questions, we bid him adieu.

Driving across the street was indeed not a chore in a town with less than three thousand total inhabitants, which included a large number of farms on the outskirts of town. There was, once again, a single car at the pump, so we pulled to the side of the station and parked next to a truck that truly had been taken care of. It was a Ford F-250 that was jacked up with special springs and shocks, four-wheel drive, and clean from the chrome trailer hitch to the chrome push bar on the front. The truck was parked next to an old tow truck that had seen better days. Vintage 1950s I would think.

Once the pump jockey, whom we assumed to be Randy, finished up with his customer, he turned and looked at us. Pretty sure he had seen us come from the tavern; he wasn't overly concerned with us as strangers. Probably figured we just wanted directions or had some other mundane question for him.

"You Randy?" I asked.

"Yes. And you are?"

"My name is Jim Tuttle, and this is my wife, Kate. Do you have just a minute for a few questions?"

"'Bout what?"

"The night Nancy Frank died."

"What do you want to know?"

"Brian Eckland says you came to the Blacktail with him and then left him there. That true?"

"Yup. Same thing I told Sergeant Danforth. We came together. He wanted to stay longer than I did, so I left him there. Plain and simple."

"You drive him there often?"

"We hang out sometimes, go to different taverns. Not much else to do in this backwater town."

"You ever met Nancy Frank?" Kate chimed in.

"Couple times. She was kinda getting close with Brian, so if he was around, she typically was too. Seemed like a nice enough lady, except she bragged some about having money. No one cares about that except those that have it."

"How about Jane Tucker. Ever met her?"

"Shoot, everyone knows Jane."

"You ever...uh...date her?" Kate asked.

"Nope," he said with a chuckle.

Since we really just needed to establish that he had indeed been with Brian Eckland to rule him out of the mix for who could have murdered Nancy, we were pretty much done with Randy.

"Thanks for your time, Randy. By the way, you own this place?"

"Yes. This wonderful marvel from the '40s is mine," he said sarcastically. "My dad owned it first and then gave it to me. It is not what you would call a moneymaker. No shop, just a tow truck and the gas we sell to keep me going. Good news for me is I don't need much. My parents died and left me some money, at least enough to survive awhile and buy my new rig," he said while pointing to his truck.

"That is quite a truck," I said as I gazed at it again. "You sure keep it in tip-top shape compared to those," I said as I pointed at the trucks parked outside the tavern.

"As you can see, I am not overly busy, so I have lots of time to keep it washed and waxed. I like a clean truck. Yours looks nice, but a little small for me. I like the 250s more than the 150s."

"Thanks. And thanks again for your time. Have a good rest of your day."

"Thanks." With that, he spun on his heels and headed for the tiny office inside the station. Our job was done here.

189

Kate opened her door before I could get too it and climbed aboard the little 150. As I entered the cab, she made just one single statement.

"We have a lot to go over, detective boy."

CHAPTER SIX

When we arrived home, there were two messages on our answering machine—one from Robert Reynolds and one from Ken Frank. Both wanted the same thing: an update on how it was going.

Since Ken had paid us our retainer, which, in point of fact, was the entire $75,000 he had promised even if we couldn't get him off, he would be the first call. Kate had suggested wisely that we stop and put the money in the bank right after we had received it. We weren't sure if Lewis County had the wherewithal to freeze Ken's accounts, and since I was taking time off work to do this, it made sense to get it in the bank and cashed just in case they chose to make that move.

Kate offered to take Killer for a walk if I made the calls. Seemed like a fair trade. Killer needed to get out and stretch his legs, and I never worried about anyone trying anything criminal with Kate as long as Killer was with her. I sure wouldn't try to abduct, or worse, a woman who had a dog the size of a small car that looked just as mean as he did big.

I made the calls, told both of the gentlemen that we had made contact with several interesting people, and had gained some knowledge but had yet had the opportunity to sit down together and decipher what we had learned. They both said they understood, and I promised a call in the morning if we came across anything that seemed like it could truly aid Reynolds in helping keep Ken out of the courtroom.

I had retired to the office, and instead of a beer, tonight I had chosen to go with what Kate loved to call brown liquor. My dad, to this day, drinks inexpensive bourbon, and he had me doing the same thing. Why spend money on expensive booze when they pretty much taste alike? At least that's what Dad always said. So I had a McNaughton and 7 Up and was lounging out back when Kate got home from walking the dog.

She came out with a glass filled with clear liquid and ice.

"What's that you're drinking, darlin'?" I loved dropping that *g*.

"I decided since you were drinking brown liquor, I would have a gin and tonic."

"Ooh, cool and refreshing."

"So where is your head at in regard to today?"

"I honestly haven't given it any thought. I needed the second half of my brain here before I started." Kate was an extremely intelligent woman. She had gone to college in horticulture, graduated with a degree from Washington State University, and then decided she liked arranging flowers more than having to remember their botanical names. She went to a floral design school in Portland, Oregon, and got a job right out of school doing floral design. So smart and talented. *How in the world did she ever hook up with me?* Again, I say I am blessed.

"What say we start at the beginning? Buck," Kate said.

"Why not? He seemed a little different. Did you notice his eyes?"

"How could you miss them? I think he was concerned with what Phil and whoever the guy next to me might say."

"I agree. So first question, what could he have wanted them to keep quiet about?"

"Then there was the whole story about Nancy and Jane. Jane was pretty adamant about not having ever met Nancy before. Second question, why would she lie about it?"

"And what was all that about going outside together? If Jane was trying to pick up on Brian, you would think it would have been a more heated conversation. But Buck said they talked and then the two women went outside. What the heck?"

"Drug deal? Wanted to talk in private to tell Nancy to back off? We are getting way more questions than answers right now."

"Let's move on. Randy. I didn't get a bad impression of the guy, did you?"

"No, not really," Kate replied. "At least he didn't want to sleep with Jane. That was pretty evident."

"Geez, I can't imagine anyone wanting to. She was scary and a little bit, or maybe a lot, loose for most men's liking. I'm sure she got herself plenty of one-night stands but not what she was looking for—a husband type. Some guys, not me, now mind you, but some guys just want a woman for one thing."

Kate smirked at the last line. She knows I love her for more than the physical attraction we have to each other.

"So Randy and Buck's story is the same, and Brian has an alibi. Dang. We haven't learned anything new."

Kate was right. It was the end of day two, twelve days to the trial of Kenneth Frank for murdering his sister, and we were no closer than we had been when we started on day one. When we took this on, we thought it would be sort of like a paid vacation. A very well-paid vacation. Now that we had gotten to know Ken and saw what he stood to lose, not only his freedom but also his farm, we were getting a bit distraught and downhearted about being able to get him off. At least I was for sure.

We had hit a dead end of sorts, and now we needed to get jump-started and decide what to do and where to go tomorrow.

"What about tomorrow?" Kate said, reading my mind.

"I'm not sure. I am kind of at a loss right now for ideas. You?"

Kate sat there with her eyes focused straight ahead. Well, not focused really, she had more of a dreamy look on her face, like she was a million miles away. I had seen this look many times over our short marriage. It meant she was deep in thought, and I knew it was best to just let her think. As I have stated, she is a truly smart woman. If she was trying to piece things together, best to let her do so without any interjection.

I stood up without a word and went inside to make another cocktail. As I entered, I stole a look back out the window at my lovely wife. She had not moved. The wheels were really turning in her head. Good. Mine had ground to a halt, and I was about to have another drink of brown liquor that might not be so good to lubricate my brain. Couldn't hurt at this point since I was already at a dead stop, brain cell-wise.

Exiting our abode, I went back out, scratched Killer behind his ears, and sat back down next to Kate in one of our matching lawn chairs.

"I think I have a starting spot for tomorrow," Kate said.

"Really? Let's have it."

"Remember when we were at the Frank farm talking to Ken?"

"It was only yesterday. I may have had a cocktail, but my mind still remembers yesterday."

Kate laughed. She had a wonderful lilting sort of laugh that I loved. I hadn't heard it in two days, and it made me feel, I don't know, good, I guess.

"Ken said that his parents were killed by drunk drivers, right?"

"Yup. And at the time I thought to myself we needed to ask Butch about it. Then with everything else going on yesterday, it totally slipped my mind."

"I had thought the same thing," Kate said. "And like you, it slipped my mind as well. I think we need to see if Butch is available tomorrow and if he will show us the official report. It is a closed case, so it shouldn't be an issue, right?"

"I wouldn't think it would be an issue, except the state patrol headed up the investigation according to Ken. Butch may not have it. I bet he'd get it for us though. Why do you want to look at the file?"

"Just a hunch. I may be way off base, but what if the two incidents, the Franks being run off the road and the murder of Nancy, were somehow connected?"

Now that thought hadn't crossed my mind at all. We could speculate a lot, but it would indeed be much better if we could get the facts as they were presented in an official report.

"Hmmm. Good thought. Not sure why they would be connected, but it is sure someplace to start. We just don't want to get too wrapped around the axle with the death of the elder Franks that we run out of time to save Ken."

"Agreed. But if we do find a connection, then maybe it would help solve Ken's dilemma faster."

"I think I will run in and call Butch right now and see if he is available in the morning and if he has the files or maybe a copy of them we could look at."

"Have at it, detective boy," Kate said, finishing the statement with another of her laughs.

"Hey, you are the one who has all the ideas. You are a regular Ms. Marple. I am getting the impression you should be the one who gets all the accolades, not me."

"Team effort, detective boy. We work very well together."

CHAPTER SEVEN

Having spoken to Butch the night before and finding out that he had a copy of the state patrol report that was, as of now, a closed case, he would be happy to share, Kate and I had decided we would head to the sheriff's office first thing this morning although our first thing in the morning was not quite everyone else's first thing. I didn't see the light of day until eight, which was much later than my normal time of rising, but we were on vacation officially, right?

Kate was behind me by half an hour. We had sat in the office until it was well past dark the night before, drinking and talking about the case. So this morning, we needed our rest. When she finally rose, I had coffee made, bacon cooked and sitting in the microwave, and was ready to cook eggs for both of us.

"Oh, you finally rose from the dead, I see," I said with a smile on my face.

"This is much harder work than I thought it would be. You did most of the work on Betty's case. I thought this one would be just as easy. But, detective boy, it seems you are counting heavily on me as well on this one, and I guess I just wasn't ready for this entirely."

"You are doing perfect, darling," I said. "I couldn't solve this one without you. It is way more intricate than Betty's case."

"No way. Betty's was amazingly intricate, and yet you solved it almost without any help from me at all."

"Then I am glad I have you on this one because I think it is going to prove to be way more intricate and involved than Betty's for sure."

"I guess that is yet to be seen. Where is my coffee anyway?"

"Right here, darlin'."

I poured Kate a strong cup of coffee, and she sat down at the bar in the kitchen.

"So today we go back down and see Butch?"

"Yup. If what you think is true, we should find some evidence of foul play in the deaths of Ken's parents. After giving it some thought, I think you are dead-on. If Ken didn't kill Nancy, then there has to be another motive other than Ken wanting the money from the estate. It may have begun clear back when Ken's parents were run off the road."

We had a good solid breakfast of bacon, eggs, and toast, and then after promising Killer a walk when we got home, we jumped back into my truck and headed south. We had a meeting with Butch at 10:00 a.m., and we were going to be pushing it to get there on time. Butch and I had become good friends during and after Betty's case and were actually going to be going hunting together in October. I knew he would not be upset if we were a few minutes late, but I also wanted to keep on the good side of Sergeant Danforth. Even though we were friends, I didn't want to abuse the friendship.

As it turned out, we arrived at about five minutes to ten and entered the sheriff's office to find Butch waiting for us in the lobby.

"Hey, Jim, Kate. Listen, I'm really sorry, but there was just a fatal accident out on I-5, and I have to get out there. I wanted to wait for you and give you this," Butch said as he handed us a folder about half an inch thick.

"It is my copy of the Frank parents' death on Bunker Creek Road. It is my only copy, so I know you will take good care of it."

"Of course we will, Butch," I replied. "Do you want us to copy it and get your originals back to you?"

"Of course not. I trust both of you. Just make sure I get it all back in one piece."

"No problem, Butch. We will get it back to you tomorrow."

"Thanks, Jim. Hey, I gotta run. You guys take care, okay?"

"We will. Thanks, bud."

So our drive to visit Butch was going to be a down and backer—drive fast to get there on time and then drive right back home. Killer will be happy.

We made good time going back north since most of the commuters were already at work. Centralia, Chehalis, and Rochester are all smaller towns or cities south of Olympia where people looking for a little less hustle-bustle move to. Then they commute each day the twenty-five or less miles to the state capitol to work. Since most employers, especially the State of Washington, count on their employees being at their desks by 8:00 a.m., traffic was much more moderate at 10:30 a.m.

Killer was indeed glad to see us home so soon. We made another pot of coffee and then, file in hand, headed out to the office. Fall was starting to sink its teeth into the weather patterns, and although the sun was shining, it was not going to be a very warm day. Fine with me. I loved fall because that is when hunting season begins, and therefore, the cooler weather made me think more about getting out in the woods and chasing deer and elk. The only thing between me hunting and where I was now was twelve more days, counting today, trying to find reason for a jury not to convict Ken Frank of murder.

Kate had brought out the coffee in a carafe that was insulated so we wouldn't have to get up and down to go back inside to refill our cups. God bless her.

Opening the file, we started by reading every written page, even notes that were attached presumably by Butch. The man loved his sticky notes. He seemed to have questions too even after the case was closed. However, he was smart enough not to take on the state patrol. It had been their investigation after all.

"They seemed to be pretty through with the investigation, wouldn't you say?" Kate asked.

"Agreed. With the Franks being pretty prominent citizens of the State of Washington, I would think they would certainly give them the investigation everything they had."

"I still can't see how they can come up with it being killed by a drunk driver. There is absolutely nothing to substantiate it. Perhaps it was indeed just a way to pad the numbers, and with it being the Franks, it would get more media attention," Kate said.

"Butch seemed to think perhaps that was the reason. Since the state had total control over the case, he likely couldn't fight it. But his notes, or two or three of them at least, mention the same thing. No evidence."

Kate refilled out cups, and I started with the photographs. The Franks' truck was a 1972 Ford pickup. I remember seeing a documentary or news program, maybe *60 Minutes*, doing an exposé on the exact truck. They drove it down a road and then purposely tipped it on its side by hitting a drop-off. The neck to the fuel tank sheared off, and the truck burst into flames. This came on the heels of the Ford Pinto recall for exploding gas tanks, so everyone was taking their shots at Ford now.

What was left of the truck, when photographed from the road above, was just a darkened mass of metal. The case report said that the Franks had been run off the road. There were no trees to stop their rollovers as they went over the edge and down the hill, completing the last rotation by going through the fence and into the field that the Franks themselves owned.

Upon closer examination, as the pictures got to be more and more close up, you could see that the body had remained in pretty decent shape, except the driver's side was dented in. I thought this was interesting since there had not been any trees to dent it in.

"I wonder if there was a boulder we can't see on the photos," I said under my breath.

"Why? What are you seeing to make you ask that one, detective boy?"

"It's just that the whole truck looks amazingly good for rolling side to side down the hill, except the driver's side door. If there was a rock under the ground or hidden by grass, it would make sense. But when I look at the long-range photos from the road, I don't see one."

Kate took the first stack of pictures from me and went through them very slowly. She is meticulous, and I knew if there was something I missed, she was likely to find it.

"I see what you mean."

As I looked through the next batch of pics, which were of the skid marks, I suddenly had a very bad feeling come over me. I actually got one of those little chills that make you shiver all over.

"What?" Kate must have seen me react.

"We need to call Ken and see if he is going to be home. I want him to show us exactly where this happened. Kate, I think there is a possibility that the Franks were murdered too."

CHAPTER EIGHT

H anding the pictures to Kate, I went in to call Ken. Kate was standing and looking at the pictures of the skid marks with a puzzled look on her face.

"What are you seeing that I am not?"

"Ken said he will be home. Let's go right now."

"What do you see?"

"I want to see the accident scene first before I tell you. If I'm right, Ken could be a possible suspect in the death of his parents as well as his sister. I don't want to tell anyone my thoughts until I have a chance to look at the scene."

"Okay, I guess."

Leaving Killer behind once more, we were back on our way to the Bunker Creek Valley. As we drove, we didn't speak. Kate had the photos still in her hands and the rest of the file on her lap. She was staring intently at them as if they were going to come right out and speak to her and tell her what I think I saw.

Drawing near to where we knew the site had to be, I slowed. Of course, the tracks were gone now, but we did have the pictures to help guide us some. We still missed the site and ended up driving to the farm to meet Ken.

Ken heard us drive in the driveway and came out of the barn, wiping his hands on a greasy rag. Poor guy (figuratively speaking only) was working on his tractor again, it appeared.

"Hi, Jim, Kate," he said as he nodded at both of us. "What brings you down again so soon?"

"Still trying to keep you out of prison would be the answer you want to hear, but there may be more to it today," I said. "I was wondering if it wouldn't be too much trouble for you to show us where it was that your parents were run off the road."

Up until then, Ken had a small smile on his face. It evaporated with the question. I knew he had been close to his parents and probably never drove by the wreck site without staring down there toward where the truck made its last trip.

"I suppose. What's this all about, Jim?"

"Can we go look first please? I want to make sure what I think is correct or hopefully disprove what I think happened, then I will let you know. Okay?"

"Okay."

"We can just take my truck. All of us will fit."

Kate took the lead back toward my trusty Ford truck. She slid in the passenger side, and Ken hopped in beside her.

I knew about where the accident had occurred, so I knew which way to turn to get there. When we got close, Ken said to slow down.

"You can pull off right there. It's an old grade." Meaning, an old road grade from sometime in the past a logging operation had built a road to haul out logs. The feeling in the pit of my stomach grew as I pulled into the grade and parked.

Exiting the truck, we all stood across the road from where the truck tumbled to its final resting place. Finally, slowly, Ken walked across the road and stood on the shoulder, peering down toward his pasture.

"Well, this is it. What's going on, Jim?"

Without a word, I walked over the shoulder of the road and down the embankment where the old truck had traveled. I was looking down and stomping, looking like an angry buck who was trying to scare off a competitor for a doe in heat.

"What is he doing?" Ken asked Kate.

"I have absolutely no idea. He mumbled something earlier about a rock. Maybe he is looking for it."

I continued all the way down the hill to the fence line, then doubled back and went up a slightly different path that was not really where the truck was supposed to have gone, but I wanted to be sure before I spoke to Ken. I was huffing and puffing pretty bad by the time I got to the shoulder again. I would need to stop drinking so much beer. I was getting out of shape. Not working in the store, I was getting very little exercise.

"So did you find what you were looking for?" This came from Kate.

"Yes and no."

"Good, a nice straight answer."

I walked back over to the truck and grabbed the case file that Kate had thrown on the dash when we all piled into the cab earlier. Opening it up, I grabbed the pictures from the scene, the ones with the skid marks.

Approaching Ken slowly, just because I really needed some answers to some tough questions but didn't really want to ask him, I finally halted at his side.

"Ken, take a look at these and tell me what you see."

Taking the photos from my hand, Ken looked at them closely. I know *he* knew I saw something, and he wanted to see it as well. But just like Kate, it was getting by him.

"I see skid marks from the truck that my parents were in before they were burned to death."

"Do you notice anything unusual about the skid marks?"

He looked yet again but came back with a simple no.

"Okay, here is what I see. Your parents were coming back from Centralia, or thereabouts, and were just about home. Suddenly, a driver runs them off the road, right?"

"As I understand it, yes, that's correct."

"Take a close look, I mean a *really* close look at their skid marks."

Once again, Ken took a long look at the pictures. Suddenly, his eyes jumped to mine, then back at the pictures and then back to my eyes again.

"Holy cow. How could that happen?"

"What?" Kate felt like she was left outside the party.

"See? That is what I suddenly realized when I was looking at them earlier. It just couldn't have happened the way the state patrol said."

"What?" Kate was getting perturbed now.

"This is a pretty straight stretch of road. If Ken's parents were coming home from the east and they were run off the road to the north by a drunk driver, then one of two things would have happened. They either would have gone headfirst off the road, more or less, or they would have tried to swing around the drunk, which would have put them with the nose of the truck heading southwest."

"What does all that mean?" Kate asked.

"For them to go *sideways* off the road, they would have had to have been pushed. The skid marks confirm it. Look at them closely."

"I have for over an hour." This was Kate not very happy at this point.

"The skid marks start straight and then take an almost sideways move. That could only happen if they were hit dead-on from the driver's side."

Kate looked again at the skid mark photos. "You're right. They started east-west and suddenly went south-north. Wow. I am impressed."

"That is why I have had a bad feeling in my stomach, especially when there was an old grade exactly opposite where they went over the hill."

"I am still a little vague on what you are getting at, Jim," Ken said.

"The way I have it figured, their truck was heading up the valley, and just as they got to where the mouth of the grade intersects the road, someone hit them with a great deal of force. Your dad must have seen the vehicle coming at the last second and slammed on the breaks. That would leave the east-west skid marks. Then when whatever hit them, hit them. The direction of the skid marks made an almost right angle and started going south-to north. Or over the edge, if you want to look at it that way."

The realization suddenly hit Ken.

"You mean someone murdered my parents too?"

"That's how it looks. The reason I went down the hill was to confirm that there were no large rocks or boulders that could have damaged the driver's side door as the car went over the embankment. There is not one anywhere between the shoulder and the fence. So the dent in the driver's side door was from the vehicle that rammed them and sent them over the side."

"Good God."

"Now I have to ask you a really tough question. The night your parents were, well, murdered, I guess we could say now, you said you were working on the tractor and had the radio turned up so that you never even heard it happen. Ken, please tell me there is someone who can substantiate that, or Butch, uh, Sergeant Danforth is going to think you killed both your parents and Nancy."

Ken looked at me with no expression whatsoever. I took that as an immediate admission that he had no one to corroborate his story. I was wrong.

"The night my parents died, I was working on the tractor, like I said. But the neighbor kid from down the road was helping me. Dad hired him awhile back because he had needed to make some money to help out around the house. His dad had been injured when the tongue of a trailer had fallen on the top of his foot. The dad couldn't work for a time, so we hired him to help out around the farm. His dad ended up being fine, but Dad liked his work ethic so much he kept him on. His name is Nathan Holt. You can get ahold of him. He will tell you or Sergeant Danforth he was with me that night. I never brought it up before because there was no need to bring it up. Looks like now there might be."

I was elated. Kate was smiling. Any logical thinker would put two and two together and figure that both murders were committed for a reason that intersected each other. If Ken was free and clear on the first murder, it gave us a huge reasonable doubt on the second.

"Ken, that is great news. We may be able to have enough for reasonable doubt on the murder of your sister."

"I don't give a damn about reasonable doubt. I want to know who killed her. It sure as heck wasn't me, but I won't rest until whoever did this is brought in front of a judge. I may not have liked my sister much, but she was still my sister."

"We understand, Ken," Kate replied. "Jim and I will do whatever you want once we keep you out of prison."

"You find out who killed my parents and my sister, and I will give you a million dollars. It's that simple."

Nothing was that simple.

"Ken, we need to drop you back off at the house. Kate and I need to go see Butch and let him know what we have found. Now."

CHAPTER NINE

K ate had used Ken's phone while I made small talk with him in the yard. Butch was back from the accident on the free-way and would be happy to meet with us. Since neither Kat nor I had enjoyed any food since the night before, they decided to meet at the Country Corral, a great restaurant that served breakfast twenty-four hours a day.

We talked incessantly on the road back to Adna, and then going down Highway 6, we hit Interstate 5 and headed to Chehalis to the sheriff's office. All the talk was around the skid marks, how I had figured it out, and the fact this really helped Ken's case.

Pulling into the Lewis County Sheriff's office, Butch met us in the parking lot.

"Hop in," I stated.

"Can't. Still on duty. If there is a call, I will have to be able to be mobile immediately. I will take the cruiser and meet you at the Corral. What's up anyway? Kate was pretty vague on the phone."

"We will fill you in while we eat. We're starved."

Butch followed us in his cruiser, and we pulled in one right behind the other. The Corral is a very unique restaurant. There are table up front for families with kids. There are two chairs, and there are four spots that are fitted with miniature saddles for kids to sit on while they eat their fill of amazing home-cooked food. Not wanting to sit on a tiny saddle, we chose a booth that was in a corner where we could talk without too much interruption from the noise that was around us. I thought kids were supposed to be in school, but the place was full of kids. Was it a weekend? I had no clue. Our days had come down to counting how many were left of the fourteen days we had to keep Ken a free man.

We waited until after we had ordered to get down to business. Telling the story of what we had found, or hoped we had found, had to go slow. Butch had become a good friend, but that didn't mean he wasn't a cop first and foremost. If we didn't convince him, we were back to square one. We needed his help if we were to solve both murders.

When we were done telling Butch what we surmised to be the truth, we let it all sink in. All of us, it seemed, were hungry. Kate and I were famished, so we devoured our breakfasts in record time. Butch was more quiet than normal. I could tell he was thinking about what we had told him and was trying to formulate questions in a logical manner.

Once the last bit of hash browns were eaten and the last of the toast had cleaned up the plate, Butch finally spoke, "So if I understand what you are saying, Mr. and Mrs. Frank were killed. Murdered. And you are saying that whoever killed them likely also killed the daughter Nancy."

"Yup, that pretty well sums it up."

"If what Kenneth Frank said is true, that would certainly bring reasonable doubt on his trial for murdering his sister."

"Exactly how we saw it," Kate replied. "Look, Butch, Ken loved his parents. He idolized them and would do anything for them. He has absolutely no reason to kill them. I don't care about the money issue. He would have never hurt his parents. This is a man who had worked side by side with his dad every day. He learned his love for the family farm from his dad. Trust me, he loves the farm. He is more concerned about losing it than about spending his life in prison. A man that feels that way would *never* hurt the people who had raised him into that lifestyle."

God, I loved this woman. I couldn't have said it better in a thousand years. She articulated perfectly what I was thinking. She was right, we were a great team.

Butch sat quietly and stared at his coffee cup. He spun his finger around and around the rim as his mind worked on what he had heard from both of us.

"Jim, how the heck did you figure out the skid marks? I looked at those pictures a hundred times and never drew that conclusion. I left tons of notes in the file because I didn't think it was a drunk driver, but the skid marks never left an impression on me like they did on you. You make me feel like a lousy cop."

"Butch, please. You are the best cop, sheriff, trooper, whatever I have ever met. You have compassion and an open mind. Those are rare qualities in most law enforcement officers. I just saw it sideways, I guess, which, ironically, is the way the truck was moved over the embankment."

"But in the end, you still figured it out and I didn't."

"Help us figure out who killed the Franks, and it's all good. If we figure that out, Ken will likely go free, we can close the book on the case, and you and I can hunt as planned in about three weeks."

Bringing up hunting I knew would relax Butch. I understood he felt a little threatened that a jewelry store manager could figure out something he couldn't, but he was a good cop. Law enforcement officers sometimes get single-minded in purpose when they think they have the right man. In this case, Butch was thinking maybe he was wrong, and I hoped he and I were right.

We talked about hunting for a few minutes. We had actually made it through an entire meal without being interrupted by murder, mayhem, or another wreck on I-5. Saying our goodbyes, we knew that we would be seeing each other in the next couple days. Kate and I were down to eleven days now. We had made good progress today but still had work to do.

I knew Butch would check out Nathan Holt. If that proved to be a true story, for which I had no doubt, Butch would start thinking twice about the murder of Nancy Frank.

We were both happily full from our late breakfast. Driving home, we chatted about normal stuff, like getting back to work at our chosen professions, the weather, and so on. When we arrived at home, Killer was definitely ready for a walk, and we had messages. Before we even listened to them, Kate offered to take Kill if I answered whoever had called. Done deal.

The first message was from Robert Reynolds wanting an update. I called him back immediately. To say he was ecstatic would be an understatement. We were giving him something to work with to get Ken off the hook for Nancy's murder.

The other message we had received was from my store, checking to make sure I would be back in twelve days. I called and assured them that indeed I would be back. We only had ten days left, so that gave me one day of leeway in the event it was necessary. Wishing them happy selling while I was gone, I hung up, grabbed a beer, and headed out to the office. Kate and I had a good deal of thinking to do now that we had found out the Franks were all murdered. We had to try to link the murders all together so that Ken got off the hook.

The two Ks got back from their walk, and Kate got herself a beer and a fresh one for me. She sat in her chair side by side with mine. We set our beers down on the table between the two chairs and just sort of looked at each other as if to determine who would speak first. She broke the ice.

"I am really proud of you for figuring out those skid marks. Obviously I would not have, and Butch and the state patrol investigators missed it as well."

"Beginner's luck."

"Bull. You have a good mind for this stuff, Jim. I mean that. Now you just have to figure out how the two are tied together so we can get back to our real jobs. And of course, keep Ken out of prison or the electric chair."

"I have been thinking about that since you left for your walk. Nowhere would be a good way to describe where I am so far."

"Hmmm. No ideas at all?"

"Not yet. Need to think about it more. I have been trying to run scenarios through my head as to who would want them all dead. I keep coming up with Ken even though I think he is honest as the day is long."

With that, we both shut our traps and started thinking. Once one of us hit on something, we could discuss it. We were quiet for an awfully long time. Neither one of us had a clue where to begin. Well, that's not entirely true. It had to start with the Frank parents. Who would want them dead? Why? Since they were loaded, I assumed if we followed the money it might help. But again, that came back to Ken.

"Wouldn't someone have to know that the Franks were coming back from town at just that time? Who would know that? Or would they sit and just wait and hope that they saw them coming, were able to get the vehicle used to push them over the embankment, and then, from there, time their run at them?" Kate had good questions. Maybe an answer to one would lead to answers for the others.

"Didn't Ken say it was kind of like a date? That they did it just about every week?"

"Yeah, I think that is exactly what he had said," Kate replied.

"So just about anyone who knew that could sit and maybe watch for two or three weeks in a row to see about what time they came back from town. Lie in wait, so to speak."

"So there are two questions that spring to mind—how would they know and why would they want them dead?"

"Good questions, both. Time to think some more."

We sat in silence again, which was so not like us. Both of us were outgoing people who loved to chat with each other or visit with friends. Sitting without talking was not something we did much. I had a feeling that if we could answer both of Kate's well-thought-out questions, we might just be able to figure this whole thing out.

Since it was late afternoon, or early evening, depending on how you looked at it, I suggested we table all thought until morning. We needed a night off.

CHAPTER TEN

I t was countdown day 10. Ten days until Kenneth Frank stood in front of a jury of his peers to begin his trial for murdering his sister.

The night before was spent laughing and drinking beer. *Happy Days* was on, and since we both were fans, we watched the Fonz, along with Ritchie, Potsie, and Ralph, going through their routine. It was relaxing and gave us both time to just veg out. Now it was time to get back to the business at hand.

Sitting once again in our chairs in the office, this time with a carafe of coffee instead of a Budweiser, the two questions Kate had come up with last night were foremost in our minds. Who would know the Franks' routine, and why would they want them dead?

"Before we were married, I spent a little time in local watering holes." To this statement, I got a sideways glance from Kate. "There were always those girls in the taverns who, when they had too much to drink or whatever, would get loud and, shall we say, boisterous. So this brings up a what-if question. What if Nancy, out on one of her regular visits to a tavern or bar, started going on about how her parents were on a date and that they went on these dates regularly? I know it's a stretch, but couldn't someone take that information and use it to determine when they might catch them coming home?"

"Really? That would take a load of supposition. I guess it could happen, sure. But even if it did, that would bring us to the who and why."

"If the who wanted to find out the when, they could have just hung around Nancy and asked her. If she was doing drugs and drinking, her defenses would be down for sure. She could give out the information without ever realizing she could be dooming her parents. You're right though. Even if the who did find out, there is still the why. I think it still has to be tied to their money."

"I totally agree. It was premeditated. Whoever killed them wanted them dead. We just have to figure out the who. I think it is the money too."

Kate sat outside in the office, and I went in and made us bacon, eggs, and toast. Call me a regular Denny's chef. Simple but delicious. When I came back out, I found Kate staring blankly at the yard. Cool. She was thinking about something.

"Maybe to find the who, we need to find out the how."

"We know how they pushed them off an embankment."

"Duh, detective boy. What I was getting at was, let's think about what kind of vehicle could do that."

"Ah. I get where you're coming from now. Okay. Let me think for a few minutes while I eat before this wonderful breakfast gets cold."

"Good. You think, I'll eat." Kate ate like a logger. That is to say, she ate a lot. She somehow kept herself at 130 pounds on her 5-foot-8 frame. I am beginning to think her walks with Killer were doing her some good as I sat drinking beer and getting even further out of shape.

We both ate without a word, me thinking, her just plain eating. When she had finished, she went back in the house and made another pot of coffee. This was after she gave me the dregs of the first carafe. Fine with me. It may have been like battery acid, but it was still warm.

To figure out what kind of vehicle it would take to run a truck off a road and push it hard enough to send it over an embankment didn't take too much thinking. A tractor was too slow. By the time the tractor was fired up and ready to go fast enough to get up the speed to push a truck in the way the Franks' truck was pushed, it would have to have a good run at it. So even though there was the old road grade, there was no way that anyone could see them coming from where a tractor would have to be parked up the grade to give it sufficient speed to hit the truck and push it off the road. It was the law of inertia. An object in motion remains in motion unless acted upon by an outside force. In this case, the object in motion (the Franks' truck) travelling at probably close to thirty-five to forty miles an hour would have to be hit *hard* by an object (the outside force) to push it off the road. A tractor couldn't do that. However, a four-wheel drive truck that was bigger and stouter than the 1972 Ford that the Franks were driving would certainly fit the bill.

Kate was gone to get the coffee for quite a while, and when she returned, she had a stack of mail from the box. We had been so busy with Ken's case we hadn't checked the mail for days.

"Hey, something here you might want to see."

"What's that?"

"You got a letter from the county."

I took the letter from her and opened it. After being shot on our last little investigation, I had bought a gun. It was the same gun Clint Eastwood had used in the *Dirty Harry* movies—a Smith and Wesson model 29 in 44 magnum. I figured it was big and bulky, but it would stop a train. Just about. The letter Kate was carrying was hopefully my concealed carry permit from Thurston County. Opening it, I was found to be correct.

"Great. It is getting down to crunch time now, and I am glad I can legally carry my gun now."

"The whole idea still scares me a little bit. Well, actually a lot," Kate said.

"Listen, I don't want to have us in the same situation we had last time. At least I want to have some protection. You know me. I am really careful with my hunting rifles. I will be equally as careful with my handgun."

Kate remained quiet. Good call. She knew she would not win this battle. If I had no way to protect her and ultimately myself, we could be putting ourselves in harm's way.

"I think I figured out a few things while you were gone."

"Like?"

"Maybe what kind of vehicle it would have taken to push the Franks off the road."

"Tell me."

So I did. She listened intently to my logic, smiling occasionally and nodding. This was good. It meant she was buying into my theory. I only hoped I was right.

"Even though there are a pretty large number of four-wheel drive trucks, we, or I should say you, just lowered the suspect pool."

"How so?" I asked.

"Well, we have seen a pretty large number of trucks that fit that description in the last three days, right? But who stood to capitalize on the death of the Franks?"

Now the ball was in my court again. Think Jim. Who could make money by killing the Franks? It took less than a minute to come up with an answer.

"Oh man. You're right on. Let's call Butch and see if he is available to make a visit with us. I think we have motive, means, and now we just have to see if there was opportunity."

CHAPTER ELEVEN

Butch was busy until noon. He had paperwork to catch up on. I knew why. We had kept him running for the last three or four days. We told him we would buy him lunch, and he seemed amenable to the offer.

Kate and I showered and cleaned up the house. Like the mail, it had gone unattended for the last while, and we knew it needed vacuumed and dusted. Then we jumped into my truck and headed to Chehalis.

Butch was once again waiting for us in the parking lot. Geez. It's great to have friends who knew you would be on time and keep their word. We went back to the Corral and had lunch this time since I had done such a fabulous job of making breakfast.

"So what's up with you two today?" Butch asked.

"We have a theory. We wanted you to hear it and play devil's advocate. Kind of shoot holes in it if we were wrong in our thinking," I replied.

"Okay. Let's hear it."

I spent the whole time our meal was being prepared and delivered telling Butch what we had determined. He listened intently. Truly a good friend. He never interrupted, and I could tell he was making mental notes of what we were saying.

"So what I get from everything you just told me is that Brian Eckland may have killed the Franks."

"He had motive and means. But we need to determine if he had opportunity. If he has an alibi for the night the Franks were killed, we are back at square one."

"Sounds like we need a couple things to happen here. First, of course, is the opportunity. Then we have to see if his truck is capable of running the Franks off the road."

"Yup." A simple answer but one I felt fit into the conversation.

"I am going to contact FIT. I want them to test his truck to see if his push bar has any paint residue from the Franks' truck."

"How long will that take?" Kate asked.

Butch smiled. "There are perks to being a sergeant. They will jump on it if I ask them to."

We finished our meal and walked into the parking lot. Butch got on his radio and talked to someone and then, after finishing up, came over to where Kate and I were standing.

"FIT will meet us back at the office. Then they will follow us to Eckland's place. It may take a little while. I want to do this right, so the lieutenant in charge of FIT is calling a judge friend of his to get us a warrant."

"Wow. You weren't kidding," Kate said. "You talk, they jump."

"The lieutenant is an old friend of mine. We have hunted together for years. What say we go back to my office? You guys sit quietly while I try to catch up on some more paperwork while we wait for FIT and the warrant."

"Works for us," I said, looking at Kate.

"Yes, that is fine. You may have to tell Jim to calm down once we get there, but I will help you keep him quiet."

It turned out to be a couple hours before we had the warrant and were on our way to Eckland's. Butch was in charge, and I wouldn't have it any other way. We turned into the driveway, and I spotted Brian Eckland standing back by his barn. Seeing three cruisers and a van, followed by Ford pickup, pulling in probably gave him a moment of fright.

Good.

We more or less roared into his driveway, and Butch drove right up to the barn and jumped out.

"Brian Eckland, we have a warrant to search your property."

"What the hell! Aren't you ever going to leave me alone? You know I have an alibi for the night Nancy was killed."

Butch never said another word. He just walked up to Eckland to keep him right in front of him as the FIT team began their work. They headed straight for his truck.

"Why are you looking at my truck? Nancy wasn't run over from what I hear."

"Mr. Eckland, I haven't read you your rights yet. But I would still suggest you keep your trap shut and let us do our job."

Eckland got extremely quiet. He watched as the forensics team worked on the front end of his truck. The lieutenant looked at Butch and shook his head. Butch strode over to him.

"Nothing?"

"Nope, no paint that would match the Franks' truck."

Butch looked around at all the car parts strewn about.

"Check in the barn and along the sides and back for another push bar." He said it with such authority that the lieutenant must have thought he worked for him. That said, he ordered his team to check out what Butch had suggested. After a few minutes, one of the techs came out from around the side of the barn.

"We have something."

"Don't move," Butch said to Eckland. He went directly at the tech and followed him around the barn. In just a few moments, he came back and walked up to Brian Eckland.

"Mr. Brian Eckland, you are under arrest for the murder of Will and Julia Frank."

With that, he handcuffed Eckland and led him to his cruiser. Once he had him in the back seat, he came back over to Kate and me.

"The FIT team found a push bar with paint that very well came from the Franks' truck. I don't know how to thank you for handing me this guy."

"Just make sure he stays in jail forever," Kate said.

"Trust me. We will give it our best shot. By the way, you are welcome to come back and watch the interrogation if you like."

"We wouldn't miss it."

CHAPTER TWELVE

D riving back to the sheriff's office, Kate asked, "Do you think he will confess?"

"I don't know if he did it."

"What?"

"I was watching him when Butch told him he was being arrested for the murders of the Frank parents, and he had a totally bewildered look on his face."

"So? You would too if you were arrested. You wouldn't believe it was happening."

"It was more than that. I don't know, but my money is on he didn't do it."

"But that takes us back to the start again, doesn't it?"

"Not necessarily. Let's see how the interview goes."

Arriving back in procession, along with the other vehicles, to the office, we parked and walked in the front. Brian Eckland was taken around back. Probably SOP for someone who was arrested. He had to be booked and printed and so on. We went in and walked into Butch's office like we owned the place.

It took forty-five minutes before Butch finally showed up.

"You can follow me. Eckland will be in the interrogation room, and you can watch through the glass."

"Really? Like on television? You guys actually have one-way glass?" I said.

"We are not as Podunk as you might think around here. And yes, we have one-way glass."

Butch led the way, and we followed behind him, duly chastised. He opened a door and ushered us in as if we were dignitaries entering a gala.

"Please stay put. Watch through the glass, but don't touch it."

"Got it."

He left us, and the next time we saw him he was entering the interrogation room.

"Why am I here?" Brian said first.

"I told you, you are under the arrest for the murders of Will and Julia Frank."

"I didn't kill them. I didn't even know them. Never met 'em."

"Do you have an alibi for the night that they were killed?" Butch asked.

"Yes." Then a terrible look came over Brian Eckland's face. "I was with Nancy."

"So you don't have an alibi since the witness you are telling me can put you somewhere other than Bunker Creek Road is dead."

"I tell you, I was with Nancy. I honestly don't remember where, but I remember that the next day, I saw her parents had died. I felt awful for her. I loved her."

"You loved her or her money? With her parents out of the way, if you married her, you would be a rich man, right, Brian?"

"It wasn't about money with us. I loved her. She loved me. We were both trying to turn our lives around. It wasn't easy. She was a drug addict and an alcoholic, and I was just a plain old drunk. We were trying to start over with our lives."

"What a sweet story, except if her parents died, you would have a lot of money to start over with, right? Why should I believe you?"

"Because I didn't do it."

"You sure you don't want a lawyer, Brian?"

"Why do I need some snot-nosed attorney who hasn't cut his teeth yet to botch this? I didn't do anything."

Butch walked around the room without muttering even the least sound.

"We found a push bar on the side of your barn with paint that matches the Franks' truck on it. If you didn't kill them, how did it get there?"

"You're kidding, right? I work on cars and trucks for a living, even tractors. I am a damn good mechanic when I'm not drinking."

"You didn't answer my question. How did a push bar with the same paint as the decedents' truck end up on your property?"

"I just told you. I work on trucks for a living. Let me ask you something. How many push bars did you see in or around my place?"

That was a really good question. I know that the first time we were there, I think I remembered at least two that were sitting outside of the barn. Suddenly, there was reasonable doubt. I could tell by Butch's reaction he felt the same way.

"I'm asking the questions here," Butch said this with a little less vigor than he had been using on Brian.

"All you have to tell me is what it looked like, and I can tell you who it belonged to. I may look stupid to you, but I have a pretty good memory for the cars I work on and what I did to them."

Butch didn't say anything. I could almost see his mind racing. He looked at Eckland and told him he would be right back.

Butch entered the room Kate and I were in.

"Well, what do you make of what he says so far?"

"Honestly, Butch, I would say he was truly in love with Nancy," Kate said.

"No way. He is a scumbag. He wouldn't know love if it bit him in the—"

"I don't agree. He seems totally sincere. And what he is saying about working on trucks and cars is also true. We saw it firsthand," Kate replied. "I would try to find out whose push bar that was. At least get that much out of him so that you will maybe know who really did murder the Franks."

Butch looked down. He was thinking about his next move. "Dang it. I thought we had him."

"So did we, Butch," I chimed in. "Find out whose push bar that is, and I promise Kate and I will help solve the murders as long as it doesn't get in the way of us trying to solve who killed Nancy."

I knew it was dangerous saying that last statement because Butch felt they had the right person for Nancy's murder. But I had to get it in. Kate and I both felt Ken had not killed his sister.

"All right. I will ask him whose push bar it was. But,] do you have any idea how many push bars there are in trucks in Lewis County alone?'

We had a pretty good idea since at the Blacktail Tavern, every truck had one.

"Thanks, Butch," was all I could come up with.

Butch exited the room we were occupying and reappeared in the room with Brian Eckland. Brian looked scared, and he should be. Being arrested for murder is no small charge.

He restated the interrogation by walking slowly around the room. His brow was furrowed like a field ready to be planted. I knew he was thinking. Kate looked at me expectantly. I held up one finger as if to say, "Wait for it."

Finally, after what seemed to be an eternity but was only probably a minute, Butch said, "The push bar was all chrome. It didn't really look too damaged, but it had the paint on it. What can you tell me about that?"

Brian let out a deep breath. "Now there is a question I can answer. The only push bar like that belonged to Randy. I asked him several times why he wanted to replace it since it only had paint on it, but he insisted that I do it. Who was I to argue? Time I ordered the new one and installed it, I made a hundred profit."

Butch looked at Brian. "We will have to keep you in jail until we substantiate your claim. If it proves to be true, you could be out as soon as tomorrow or the next day."

Butch came back into our room. "Holy cow. I have to figure out what our next move is now. Now we have no motive or opportunity. Just the means."

"Listen, my friend, we got you into this. We all know that now it appears more than ever that the Franks were murdered. Give Kate and me a chance to help you. We really have to get going home. Killer needs fed, and Kate and I have to think. With you and us both thinking, we will figure this out. I promise."

"I trust you guys, you know that. But if we don't have some answers by tomorrow, we will have to take Brian's case to the courts and let them decide if he should be charged officially."

"If we have to stay up all night, we will get some answers by tomorrow," Kate replied. She really did feel that Brian and Nancy were in love.

"I will call you first thing in the morning, Butch."

"Okay. Thanks, guys. Drive safe."

With me leading the way, we walked back out to the truck and got in for the drive home. The fact that Randy had the push bar on that really bright and shiny truck, which obviously had plenty of power to push a *little* F-150 off the road, we just had to find out the motive. I was pretty sure we could find the opportunity when the time came. Motive was the issue.

CHAPTER THIRTEEN

Another day had dawned, and it was the first one in quite some time where we awoke to raindrops hitting the roof. Fall was upon us. The night before was spent playing with Killer, and of course, Kate took him for his nightly walk. We refrained from even mentioning the case, or should I say cases, that we were now running out of time to solve. Although I felt time was no longer a question in actuality, we were getting close—both to the Franks' killers and who may have really killed Nancy. I felt that Kate and I would be done with time to spare. Hopefully.

We rose and showered, made a quick breakfast, and sat indoors until the rain subsided a bit, then went out to the office, carafe of hot coffee with us, of course.

So now Randy, not Brian, was the top suspect in the murder of the Franks. Randy of the gas station, who drove a truck plenty large enough to do the deed of pushing a much smaller truck off the road. That took care of means. Again, opportunity was likely there *if* we could find the motive. Why would Randy want the Franks dead? That was question number one. Really the only question we had to get a definitive answer to to have a case against him.

The rain had started back up. More of a drizzle. We didn't mind. Sitting under our covered patio, we could listen to it beating out its rhythm on the cover, and it was somewhat soothing to hear. The area needed the rain, so we were happy in a way to see it come. Even though it signaled the long rainy periods Washington is so known for.

Kate sat sipping her coffee. Both of us, again, were unusually quiet. She finally spoke first.

"Why? Why would Randy want the Franks dead? The only thing I keep coming up with is money. But there is no connection."

"If it's money, there is a connection. We just have to figure out what it is or was."

"I have been racking my brain to the point of a headache since I woke up. I just can't see one."

"Let's talk about what we do know. Randy drives a truck big enough to do the pushing. He even mentioned he liked the F-250s more than the smaller F-150s, which just so happens to be the truck the Franks were driving. He had Brian Eckland change out his push bar even though it only had a little paint on it. Why? Because he was guilty, that's why. But that brings us back to the motive. How was he connected to the Franks? How could be *possibly* think that by killing them he would stand to inherit the money they had?"

We sat in silence for…well, for too long. We loved to talk to each other, but when both of us were deep in thought, it was impossible to converse. Kate looked as beautiful as ever even though she had the same furrowed brow Butch had the last evening. And the blank stare. Her gears were grinding. I was waiting for a revelation. More like praying for one. Kenneth Frank was due in court in a little over a week, and if we couldn't find out who killed Nancy, he was likely going to spend the rest of his life in prison.

Suddenly, Kate spoke, and she had the glint in her eyes that told me she hit on something. "Go back."

"Like what, go back in the house?"

She smiled instead of giving me one of her patented "really?" looks.

"I guess I should say go forward if what I think may be the tipping point is what I think it is."

"Talk to me, detective girl."

That got more than a smile. Kate laughed her wonderful laugh. It was great to hear it.

"Think about the night Nancy was murdered. Who was Brian Eckland's alibi? Randy. When he murdered the Franks, who did he go to to have the push bar replaced? Brian Eckland. There is a connection there. I am not there yet, but I think I am on the right track. Too many coincident have to mean something. Help me here, detective boy."

Now it was my turn to laugh. Kate had hit on a couple great points. Randy had been all over this from the start, but he was peripheral. Now he was front and center. Why would he alibi Brian if Brian had actually killed Nancy? "The murder of the Frank parents was his doing, but why?" We were indeed getting closer, but it still needed work.

I sat and thought for maybe ten minutes, emptied the carafe into my cup, and then went inside to make another pot of coffee. It felt like we were getting close, but whatever we were missing was just outside our grasp.

As I was filling the pot, it hit me. I can't tell you what caused it, but it was a culmination of what Kate had just said and what I had in my pea brain. I dropped the coffee pot, and it shattered in the sink. Hearing it break, Kate came running in the house.

"What happened?"

"My god, I think I have it."

"What?"

"I said I think, but I believe I have motive now, as well as means and opportunity."

Kate just stared at me. Not a word left her lips.

"I need another cup of coffee, but since that isn't happening here, let's go to the Mickey D's and get another cup." My nephew had always called McDonalds Mickey D's.

"No way. Tell me what you think."

"No. I need more coffee and time to really rethink this to make sure I am right."

I turned and walked to the key holder we had on the wall, grabbed my truck keys, and headed out the door. I knew Kate would be pissed, but I really needed a few minutes to think about what I thought I was pretty sure of, and getting away would be a good thing.

Driving to McDonald's, my mind was in overdrive. I think I had it, but there were still some missing pieces I had to put together. Getting out of the house was just what the doctor ordered. I used the drive-through, bought two more cups of coffee, and headed back home. I knew Kate was not going to be happy with me leaving, but I also knew she would get over it. If I was right.

She was upset, but not overly.

"Okay, what's going on?" she asked.

"You brought up a couple valid points that made me start thinking in the abstract. Randy tried his best to cover for Brian. Why? But more importantly, why did he make sure the night Nancy was killed that Brian was nowhere near Frank farm? Think back. When I asked Randy if he drove Brian around often, he didn't really answer the question. When I asked him if he drove him to the Blacktail often, he said something like 'We go to lots of taverns.' See, he didn't really answer the question. Why would someone who works right across the street from a tavern go twenty miles out of his way to pick up someone else just to leave him there a couple hours later? To establish an alibi, that's why."

"But why would Randy want to establish an alibi for Brian?"

"I have an idea on that too. But I need to call Butch to make sure."

"Well, call him. Holy cow!"

I went inside and grabbed our new cordless phone. Coming back outside before I dialed, I took a sip of coffee and dialed Butch's office number. It seemed to ring off the hook, but I knew it was just my impatience, not Butch ignoring me. He finally answered.

"Sergeant Danforth."

"Hey, Butch, it's Jim. I have a question for you. Do you happen to know Randy's last name? I don't think we have ever heard it."

"Sure, just a second." I could hear Butch rummaging around through the piles of paperwork on his desk. "Okay, here it is. Holy crap. I never caught that. How did you figure it out?" He told me the last name and I hung up, telling him we would likely see him later today.

"What are you getting at? What does Randy's last name have to do with this?" Kate asked.

"It has a lot to do with it. I think we are really close to motive now."

"What is his last name? Tell me, Jim."

"Tucker."

CHAPTER FOURTEEN

We were, indeed, really close. Randy's last name was Tucker. The same as the she-devil, Jane Tucker. Now we had to figure out why Randy Tucker and Jane Tucker felt that they would somehow benefit from the deaths of the parental Franks. That would help us determine why they felt Nancy Frank should be killed as well. How were they related? Or was it just coincidence?

"Whoa. Randy is somehow related to Jane Tucker?"

"It would appear so."

"What made you start thinking along those lines?" Kate asked.

"Again, it was the answer to a question I asked Brian. When I asked if he had ever dated Jane, he chuckled and said no. It would certainly make sense that he wouldn't date her if she was his sister."

Kate's jaw dropped. Just like you always hear about. Her teeth separated, and her lower jaw and her upper jaw parted like the Red Sea.

"I never would have caught that, but it makes sense. I just assumed he knew the kind of girl she was and didn't want anything to do with her."

"And that could still be the case. We need to get down and talk to Butch in person. How long will it take you to get ready?"

Kate thought for just a moment and replied, "Uh, ten minutes. This is amazing."

"Okay, I will get ready in ten as well. Time to once again head to points south."

Fifteen minutes later, we were on our way to meet with Butch. I know what you're thinking. Women always take longer to get ready than they think. Wrong. Kate was pestering me at eight minutes. I was the slow one this morning.

As we drove to Chehalis, Kate just kept staring at me. I could see her out of the corner of my eye, having been blessed with really good peripheral vision.

"What?" I finally said.

"What do you mean what?" she asked.

"Why do you keep staring at me?"

"It's not a bad stare. It is actually one of admiration. I still can't figure out how your mind works the way it does."

"Just like yours."

"No. You have a real knack, an ability, to see things and remember things that I sure don't have."

"Maybe. But I couldn't arrange flowers or remember their botanical names if my life depended on it. We are two different people."

"I am just impressed. Maybe your calling is in investigations and not managing a jewelry store. You are good at this."

"Not so sure I am good enough yet to even pay for this vacation with a check from Ken Frank. That is what I am trying to do, remember."

"Listen, Jim. We will get, or I should say we have already gotten, more money than you would make in the next six years at the jewelry store. He had only promised to pay us a $75,000 retainer, but he paid us the whole thing up front. He has faith in you. In us. So do I. Now maybe he felt that they might freeze his accounts and he couldn't pay us, but regardless, he did pay us. The full amount. So we have long since made enough to pay for this vacation as you call it. You are good at investigating things and figuring things out. With me by your side, we are like Batman and Robin. The dynamic duo."

"Wow, which one am I?" I laughed.

"You are most definitely Batman." Then she laughed that laugh I loved to hear.

"Okay, Robin. And thanks for the compliments. I know I could never do it without you."

From then on, Kate stared ahead, as did I. Both of us had smiles on our faces.

We arrived at Butch's office at about eleven thirty. I hadn't told him when we would be there, but he came out to meet us as we walked in through the front door.

"I knew you couldn't stay away long. Come on in my office."

Butch led the way. It wasn't like we didn't know where it was by now, but he had started down the hall first, so he was the leader.

We all sat in Butch's office, and he brought us up to speed on what he had learned since we had spoken earlier.

"Okay, here is what I have learned since we talked. Randy and Jane are brother and sister."

Kate gasped a little gasp and muttered, "My god."

Butch looked at her without a word and then continued. "They were born to Darrell and Jolene Tucker in Aloha, Oregon. They were two of the three children that the Tuckers gave birth to. The last one, a girl, was named Janene. She is living somewhere in Montana. Last known address was in Billings. When Randy, who, by the way, is the oldest, was twelve, Jolene Tucker died from breast cancer. Darrell decided he wanted to start a new life and moved the kids to Centralia. They later moved to Onalaska and bought the station and a nice little house. When Darrell died, he willed the station to Randy and the house to Jane since Janene decided to get out of Dodge as soon as she turned eighteen. When she left, Randy was, by then, twenty-four and Jane was twenty-two." He paused for a moment to go over his notes.

"Randy is now thirty-one, making Jane roughly twenty-nine. Both Randy and Jane have had unremarkable lives. He runs the station and still lives at home with Jane. That is pretty much it so far."

"How old was Randy when his dad passed away?" I asked.

"Let me do the math. Never one of my strong suits."

Butch did some figuring and said that Randy had been twenty-six. That made Jane twenty-four at the time and Jolene twenty. Just trying to keep things straight in my pea brain.

"So Randy has had the station five years. Long enough to realize it was a losing concern. Big stations were opening out on the interstate, and little fish like Randy were destined to die a slow death."

"What's your point?" Butch asked.

"Just trying to find a motive."

Sitting in silence, we could hear the noise from the front of the office. Voices speaking too softly for us to really hear, just noise to us. Finally, Butch spoke, "What are you thinking?"

Not being sure exactly what to say, at first I said nothing. I needed more data. Finally, I took a shot.

"Here is how I see it. Butch realizes that his station is dying. No mechanics shop. One pump. Too far off the main drag to get much business. He would be broke or forced to sell the land for a pittance in no time at all. But he loved his life. Drinking beer, going to taverns to mingle with the local color, so to speak, was what he liked to do. He has to figure out a way for a big score. Enter Nancy Frank."

Kate and Butch looked at me like I had two heads.

"Where are you going with this, Jim?" Kate asked.

"Agreed. Good question," Butch responded.

"Randy likes his life, except the part about living with his loose sister. I think he wanted to get enough money for both of them to have their own lives. Think about it. If they could make a big score, their lives take a different path."

"But what the hell does all this have to do with the deaths of the Franks?" Butch said.

"I am still trying to piece it all together. But if I'm right, Randy and Nancy decided that Nancy Frank was the target. They just had to figure out how to get to the Frank money through her."

CHAPTER FIFTEEN

"We have more issues than just that although what you are saying makes sense, sort of," Butch replied.

"Like what?" Kate asked.

"Like how do we tie the push bar to Randy's truck? All we have is a mechanic who says it was from his truck. All Randy has to do is deny it and we are back to square one."

"Do you think there is anything the FIT can do?"

"I will call them and talk to them, get some ideas and advice maybe."

"You do that, and I will work on the why. Motive is still the key here, I think. As we have said, he had the means and likely the opportunity. We just have to come up with the why. Let's take a walk, Kate."

As we got out of our chairs, Butch already had the phone in his hand and was dialing, I presumed, the Forensics Investigation Team leader who helped us previously. Kate and I headed for the front door of the office.

"Why do you want to walk?"

"Because we can't sit at home in the office and have a beer."

She smiled at me and gave a little laugh.

"Walking helps me think sometimes. We need to piece this all together and fast. Ken's court day is creeping up on us. I can't help but think that if we figure out how they intended to get the money from Nancy, we could solve the other murders."

We strolled through the streets, not really looking into any of the shops. Avoiding people was the goal. It was easier for me to think without any conversation. Kate had that far-off look, so I knew she was definitely engaged in some heavy thinking.

Kate broke the silence first. "Let's play the what-if game. What if Jane was somehow manipulating Nancy to get money?"

"You mean like blackmail?"

"Yes. What if the one time Buck saw them at the Blacktail and they left for a while to go outside, Jane sold her drugs and then wanted to use that to blackmail her?"

"That might work. But how do we prove it, and why would she then want Nancy dead?"

More walking, no talking.

After several more blocks, it was my turn to take a stab at who killed Nancy, no pun intended.

"What if Randy and Jane thought that with Brian getting chummy with Nancy that they could somehow manipulate him into getting money from Nancy?"

"That really makes no sense."

"Okay, I tried," I said as I chuckled. "But there has to be some connection. We are getting close to having some pieces. In fact, we could already have several and just not know it."

"Agreed. What say we walk back and see how Butch is coming along?"

Without realizing it, we had walked probably three miles from the sheriff's office. In fact, we had walked clear into Centralia. "Let's see if we can find a cab."

"In Centralia?"

"They have to have at least one cab company."

And one they did. Kate made the call from a pay phone. A bright yellow older-model sedan picked us up and took us back to the office.

When we entered, Butch met us. Kind of spooky actually. He seemed to always know when we arrived. As smart as Kate thought I was, I hadn't thought of cameras outside the building. Duh.

THE WATCH IN THE BOX

"Come into my office," Butch said with no hesitation whatsoever. He must have something.

Once we took our appointed chairs, Butch filled us in.

"FIT thinks that in a collision like that, paint from the Franks' truck may, and I repeat, *may*, have left the outside of their truck and deposited itself somewhere in Randy's truck. Lots of variables—how much time has passed, if he used a high pressure water hose to rinse off his truck, and so on. If we go out and try to pull evidence, we better have a damn good idea what we have on him or he will walk. What did you guys come up with?"

I looked at Kate. "You go first." Kate shot me a look that if it was a .30-06, I would be dead.

"Fine," she replied. "I think that maybe Jane was blackmailing Nancy. When we talked to the bartender at the Blacktail, Buck, he told us that they had met once when Nancy and Brian were there. Jane and Nancy left together, went outside, and came in a short time later. We, or I should maybe say I, think that Jane decided to blackmail Nancy on her drug use to get money."

Butch only uttered one word. "Jim?"

I looked at Butch with a forlorn look. I had to tell him what I thought now. Kate had said it made no sense.

"I think Randy and Jane were trying to manipulate Brian somehow since he and Nancy were an item. If they thought they could extract money from Nancy, somehow using Brian, they would be home free."

Butch just stared at me. Great. Two people in the room out of three who thought I was a blithering idiot. Finally, Butch took the pressure off me.

"Here is the problem. If we check for paint residue and find nothing, we are dead in the water. I think both of you might be right somehow, but we have to figure out how that can be."

From the time I was a kid, I loved watching *Columbo*, *Baretta*, and just about any cop show I could find on television. I always fancied myself as a detective. But this was the real deal. If we got this wrong and Kenneth Frank went to prison, I would have a hard time living with that, not nearly as hard a time as Ken would have but still a hard time. My mind was going a mile a minute. We just had to figure this out. Now.

I did have an idea. I hoped it wasn't as half-baked as my theory.

"Butch, what if we did what we did to Brian? Go in with guns blazing with the FIT guys and at the same time arrest Jane. That would give FIT the time to do their thing, and we could have Jane here at the office."

"To what end?" Butch asked.

"Well, we could grill Randy about the truck and bring him in too. We don't have to tell him if we do or don't find anything but put the fear of God into him. While we are doing that, we do the same with Jane, who is maybe a little unstable, and perhaps one of them breaks."

Butch didn't make sergeant by accident. He was a sharp guy even if his real name was Elmer. He sat and pondered the scenario for a good two or three minutes. It was an excruciating amount of time if you were in my shoes, but I got it.

"You know, it just might work. I need to make a couple more calls, but it may be possible. It would mean me deputizing both of you for a limited amount of time, and I have to check on the legalities of that."

Most states allowed citizens to be deputized for a specific amount of time. How in the world I knew this was a different matter. I must have read it somewhere. I am a voracious reader.

"So what are you thinking, Butch?"

"If we do what you said, guns blazing at the station, it might just scare the bejesus out of Randy. Then if another team finds and arrests Jane, we bring them both back here and start hitting them hard on the issues. Maybe one of them will break and roll on the other. Only problem is, if FIT doesn't find anything, we have shown our hands and they will know we are onto them. It is a risk, big-time."

The way Butch said this was like a "low budget made for television" movie. I had seen it done tons of times. You try to turn one against the other. My guess was that Randy and Jane had spent a good deal of time watching the same shows I watched, and we would indeed end up dead in the water.

"Ken Frank didn't kill his sister, of that I am sure," I said. "We will just have to grill them hard and be smarter than they are. If we lose this one, Ken goes to trial, and with the press killing him in Olympia, he will be convicted even if he didn't do it. We have to try it, Butch."

What I didn't say to my friend was that I really didn't care as much about who killed whom as long as Kenneth Frank could show reasonable doubt. He had paid us handsomely to save him from going to prison or perhaps death row. All I cared about right now was his getting off, hoping, of course, it never got as far as the trial.

"Let me make a couple calls. If you guys want a cup of coffee, there is some in the outer office." This was Butch's nice way of saying get lost. Kate and I went out to the main office and indeed did get a cup of coffee from a pot that probably hadn't been washed properly for, well, maybe forever. Amazingly enough, the coffee was actually pretty good. After about ten or fifteen minutes, Butch came out and motioned us toward him.

"Okay. Washington State allows for regular citizens to be deputized for limited amounts of time as long as they meet the criteria. You both do. Neither of you have ever even had a parking ticket, so that takes care of the felony portion. Plus, you are both Washington State citizens. The rest of the criteria is so vague that just about anyone can pass that portion. Come into my office so I can deputize you officially."

Inside Butch's office was another deputy. He had some paperwork, and once Butch had administered what he had to go through, we had to fill out the papers, and voila, we were newly deputized members of the Lewis County Sheriff's department for one week. Renewals were possible, but if all went well, we would be done within a day or so, and there would be no need.

"Deputies Tuttle, welcome to the Lewis County Sheriff's Department," Butch said with a big smile. "Now let's get to work. Keep in mind, you work for me until the end of next week."

"What is the pay anyway?" Kate asked.

At that we all broke out in laughter.

"No pay, just work," Butch replied when the laughter had died down. "Now here is the plan."

CHAPTER SIXTEEN

Butch laid out the plan for us. It was almost what we had talked about. He added one caveat: Brian Eckland. He wanted him brought in too.

I had brought my gun along for the trip to Chehalis, but Kate was unarmed. I wanted her to stay with me, and of course, Butch agreed. He figured that if things got bad fast, I would protect Kate. Smart man. I would not only kill for her, I would die for her if need be.

Butch had rounded up all the deputies and detectives he could, and we had an impromptu meeting in the lunchroom at the sheriff's office. A couple of uniforms would round up Jane, along with one detective to add credence to the arrest, while Butch, Kate, and I, together with the FIT, went for Randy at the station. He sent another cruiser to pick up Brian. This was going to happen fast. Damn. It was happening *really* fast. We were to be in constant radio contact until everyone was rounded up, then complete radio silence. I wasn't sure why Butch required that, but hey, he was the man in charge and, for the next week, my boss.

We all rolled out at the same time from the office, not the office Kate and I preferred but the sheriff's office. No lights until we got close to the station. We wanted to make a splash, but not for fifteen or twenty miles. The different groups headed their respective directions when their turns came up, leaving just Butch, the FIT, Kate, and I heading to the station. When we got about a mile out, Butch, leading the way, flipped on his lights, so did the FIT van behind us. We roared into the station with sirens and lights. Randy was just finishing up with a customer, pumping his gas. I actually thought that it would be great if it was the last person he ever pumped gas for.

Randy's eyes were visible as we pulled in, and they had the classic deer-in-the-headlights look—wide-open and not knowing what the heck was going on. At least that was what they looked like. My guess was that he knew exactly why we were there and was hoping he could talk his way out of the mess he had gotten himself into.

As I have mentioned, Butch was pretty sharp. He had contacted his cousin's wife who just happened to be the daughter of a local judge. We had proper warrants to search the station and Randy's truck. Butch presented these to Randy, and you could almost physically see him shrink in size. Good sign if you were on the right team.

"What are you looking for?"

"None of your business, Mr. Tucker," Butch replied. Nothing more was needed or said.

The FIT went to work as Butch handcuffed Randy and placed him in the back of the cruiser. Now we had some time to kill. It wasn't long before we got word on Butch's handheld radio that Brian was in custody. Soon after, we had all the pieces in place. Jane was also under arrest.

Now we found out the reason for the radio silence. Butch didn't want any of the players knowing that the others had been apprehended. Leave some doubt in their minds. If they didn't know that the others were picked up, they might think they were going to get away with it. Once we had them all back at the office, we would slowly leak that we had others under arrest too. Smart.

Randy kept yammering on about things. "What is all this about? Why am I under arrest? What's going on?" Butch never said a word.

Kate and I and Butch all got back into our respective vehicles and headed back to the office, leaving FIT to do their thing.

"Holy cow," Kate said. "That was amazing. What happens now?"

"That is up to Butch." It was the only thing I could think to say, and it was totally correct.

As we arrived back at the sheriff's office, the timing couldn't have been more perfect as it turned out. We were coming in the back door as the team that had arrested Jane came in the front. Right behind them came Randy Eckland in handcuffs.

Jane looked at Randy and said very eloquently, "What the fuck?"

Randy's response was just as eloquent. "Just don't say anything to them, bitch."

Ah, familial love at its best.

The deputies and Butch took each to a different room, and we watched this happen. It was like a chess match with live pieces. In the end, Kate and I followed Butch.

Sergeant Danforth not very gently pushed Randy Tucker down in a chair.

"You want to tell us about the Franks? We know you killed Mr. and Mrs. Frank. If you tell us the whole story now, we will let the prosecutor know you were cooperative. Might just keep you out from hanging at Walla Walla."

The Washington State Penitentiary in Walla Walla, Washington, was the only state facility that had the ability to put an inmate to death. Washington State voters overwhelmingly approved the death penalty just two years earlier, and death by hanging was still the prescribed method to carry out the deed.

Randy may have looked stupid, but he knew a little about the law. "I am not saying another word without an attorney. I have no idea what you are talking about. You local yokels are trying to pin something on me I had nothing to do with."

"Fine. Just remember I tried to help you, Randy," Butch replied. "Once a lawyer gets here, you are on your own. Either way, we will prove our case. If you cooperate, it may help to persuade the judge to go easy on you. If you don't…" With that Butch held his hand up at shoulder level and then pointed his index finger down and swung it like a clock pendulum. My assumption was he was trying to make Randy think of hanging from a noose. It worked.

"I haven't done anything."

"Are you giving up your right to remain silent?" Butch had read Randy his rights at the station. This was getting downright fun at this point. A real cop drama playing out right before our eyes.

"I don't need a lawyer. I didn't do anything!" So much for his asking for a lawyer.

Butch was trying to buy time. I knew he was praying that the FIT team had found something by now. He strolled around the small interrogation room without a word. There was a knock on the door. Butch answered the knock, opening the door just enough to see who was outside. He whispered with someone, then turned to Randy and smiled.

"Seems our forensics team came up with something on your truck. Time to tell us what happened the night the Franks were killed, Randy."

"I don't know what you are talking about!" Randy screamed at Butch.

"Fine. Jim, Kate, would you join me outside the room please?"

"You are leaving me in here?" Randy said.

"Yup. You are not going anywhere but to Walla Walla, Randy. Better get used to spending long hours alone." With that, Butch turned and walked out, holding the door for Kate and me.

We stood in the hallway for a minute with no conversation. Finally, Butch said, "FIT got nothing. We are out of luck with his truck."

"Nice rhyme, Butch," Kate said, trying to lighten the moment.

Butch was not that amused. "I am unsure which way to go now. If FIT was a slam dunk, then we were good to go. Time for plan B, I guess."

"That being trying to turn one on the other?" Kate asked.

"Yup."

"How can we help?" I asked.

Butch told us how it was to go down. He left us in the hall with instructions to wait ten minutes, then set the whole thing in motion. Kate and I went and grabbed a cup of coffee and waited the allotted time in the entry of the office. When the time was up, we dropped our coffee cups in the receptacle and walked back down the hall. Here we go.

I knocked on the door, waited a second, then opened it up. "Sergeant Danforth, can I speak to you for a moment please?"

"Stay put, Randy. I guess it's not like you're going anywhere what with being handcuffed to the table," Butch said as he walked toward us.

The plan was to have Butch step into the hall, ask what's going on, and before the door shut, I was to say loud enough that if Randy was listening he would hear maybe one or two words. Since I was only supposed to say two words, I had to do my part right.

As the door was closing, I stated, "She broke." When the second word was out of my mouth, Butch shut the door. We all went to get another cup of coffee. The idea was Randy would start to sweat a little by thinking that maybe Jane had spilled the beans. We took our sweet time, and after maybe fifteen minutes, Butch left us to do his part. If Randy didn't bite, then we were back to square one. But we were still waiting on FIT's report as well.

Just as Butch was opening the door to the interrogation room, the lieutenant from the FIT team came barreling through the front door.

"Sergeant Danforth, come here a moment please."

Butch shut the door to the room and turned back around toward us and the lieutenant. If that didn't shake Randy up a bit, I wasn't sure anything would.

"Got some good news, Butch," the lieutenant said. "We found fingerprints on the bolts holding the push bar to the front of the suspect's truck. No paint shavings or residue. We matched the prints up with the ones we took last time out. They are Brian Eckland's. Has Mr. Tucker made any statement about not having anyone touch his truck or do any work on it? 'Cause if he says no one has worked on it, we got him dead to rights. We have the old push bar with the paint on it we got from Mr. Eckland's place, which just so happens to be the exact same as the new one on Mr. Tucker's truck. I get it is still a bit circumstantial, but it puts a couple more pieces in the puzzle."

CHAPTER SEVENTEEN

"She was nothing, just a rich fucking druggie."

Unlike Randy, Jane was indeed about to break. She was a druggie who needed a fix—bad.

"So why did you kill her?" This was asked by one of the detectives who was present at her arrest. There was a prolonged silence, then Jane finally spoke again although, this time, in a much more subdued tone.

"I didn't kill her."

"Tell us about what you and your brother, Randy, were trying to accomplish. It appears he killed the Frank parents, and then you killed the daughter, Nancy."

"I...uh, I don't know what you are talking about. I want to talk to my brother."

"Isn't going to happen. As I understand it, he is in the middle of a story blaming you for everything. Your only way to salvage your life is to tell us what happened so we can sort it out."

"Randy would *never* say it was my doing. It was all his—"

The detective took this as the first real break. She was admitting that they did something but was also saying it was all Randy's idea.

"So why not save yourself? Your brother is putting all the blame on you. Why not tell us the truth and tell us what really happened?"

Jane sat there, shaking and fidgeting. She needed drugs and soon, or she would start going into withdrawal. That would mean if she was as bad a drug user as the detectives thought, she would become incoherent soon.

The last words out of her mouth before she basically passed out were "I want a lawyer."

While Jane was starting to go through the hell of withdrawal, Randy was standing firm. Butch had walked back into the interrogation room with a big grin on his face. Randy reacted.

"What? Why are you smiling at me?"

"Because you are as good as convicted of murder, Randy."

"What the hell are you talking about? I didn't do nothing."

"So you say. But the evidence we have gathered says different. That, coupled with what your sister is telling us, puts you right in the middle of murder."

"Bullshit. I didn't do anything!"

"Not what we are being told. No worries. One murder or three carries that same sentence—hanging."

Randy suddenly sat back and got a really vacant look on his face. It was never a possibility to him to get caught. Now he had a sheriff's department sergeant telling him that he was caught dead to rights.

Just as quickly as he had gone mute, he woke up and said the words that most law enforcement officers hate to hear.

"I want a lawyer."

Butch turned and walked out of the room without another word. He hadn't heard that Jane had also invoked her rights, but his suspect had indeed made it impossible to continue to the interrogation. He met us in the hall.

"So?"

"He wants a lawyer."

"From what we are being told, so does Jane. Where does that leave us, Butch?"

The one person who had been arrested today that no one had talked about was Brian. We really had nothing on him, but he, however, might have information that would aid us in finding out the truth about Randy and Jane.

"I think it's time to talk to Brian."

All three of us walked down to yet another room to talk to Brian Eckland. The poor guy had been basically left alone for the past three hours, sitting in a room by himself. He looked very much the worse for wear.

"What am I doing here? Can I get something to eat? Maybe a glass of water?" He really had been left alone. I actually felt pretty bad for him.

"Hang on a minute," Butch said as he walked back out the door. Within a minute, Brian had a pitcher of water, a sandwich, and a bag of chips from the machine in the break room.

"Thanks. I am starving, man. Why am I here?"

"Brian, we think that someone murdered Mr. and Mrs. Frank as well as Nancy. We have some questions to ask you about that."

"I told you, I loved Nancy. I would never hurt her."

"There was a push bar we found on the side of your barn, or workshop if you prefer, that had the same paint as the Franks' truck. Can you tell us whose trucks you have done work on to replace a push bar?"

"How far back?"

"Say six months."

"I can tell you where to find my records or, if you will let me go get them, I can be back here in less than an hour."

"You keep records?" Butch asked.

"I may be an uneducated country boy, but Nancy told me I should keep records on all the work I do. Keep me from getting sued by someone. Also, we had a plan. We wanted to get married, and I was going to open a real shop. She said if I kept records of all the work I had done, it might help the bank to see that I was a good loan risk for starting my own business. I tell you, she was amazing. She was cleaning herself up, from the drugs and booze I mean, and as she did, it was like she got real smart all at once. God, I loved her. She was really good for me. And I would like to think I was good for her too."

Butch arranged for a deputy to drive Brian back to his house to get his records. His story seemed so…I guess I would say genuine that we all believed him.

Randy had called a local ambulance chaser, and Jane had indeed passed out. She never made the call for an attorney. Butch had ordered one of his detectives to escort her to the hospital and stand guard while she was going through her withdrawals.

It wasn't even forty-five minutes and Brian was back. He had a box that had all his records neatly filed in it. He looked and found the only push bar he had replaced in the last year was for Randy Tucker.

"How do you know that? How do you know the one on the side of the barn was the one you took off Randy's truck?" Butch questioned.

"It's all done by part number. I don't have the parts right there at the house. I have to order everything. I pay in advance, and the customer pays me back. When I place the order, I put the customer's name on it so I can keep it straight, just in case I have to order a different model of the same product for another customer. Here is the copy of the order for Randy," he said, handing the order form to Butch. "Push bars look a lot alike, but each one fits a certain model of vehicle."

Sure enough, right there in legible writing was the name Randy Tucker on the order Brian had placed at the wholesaler. It wasn't ironclad proof, but the circumstantial evidence was mounting up against the family Tucker.

Butch asked if we could step outside the room for a moment with him. Of course, we did. That's what you do for friends.

"I think I made a mistake with Kenneth Frank. I at least think you will have reasonable doubt if it goes to trial. Listen, tell his lawyer that we are working on some different suspects and that we will notify the prosecutor about it what we have found out so far."

"I no longer believe that Ken killed his sister."

CHAPTER EIGHTEEN

It was two days since we left the sheriff's office. We had notified Robert Reynolds, Ken's attorney, about what was happening as soon as we had gotten back into town two days previously. He seemed elated. Sure, when you make the big bucks, it's nice to have a winner without going to trial. Kate and I were enjoying sitting in *our* office. Killer was snoring loudly at my feet, the carafe strategically placed between us, and Kate and I were drinking our second or third cup of coffee when the doorbell rang.

I was designated by Kate as the butler, so I went and answered the door.

"Hey, Butch, what's up?" Sergeant Danforth was standing before me, literally hat in hand.

"May I come in?"

"Hell yes, Butch. That is a stupid question coming from a sergeant on the Lewis County Sheriff's Department."

Butch walked in, and I shut the door behind him.

"I have news. Where is Kate?"

"Out back. Come on, I'll grab a cup and get you some coffee."

As we passed the kitchen, I grabbed a cup, and we went out back. Killer woke up long enough to see who it was. When he saw Butch, he fell back into his perpetual state of slumber.

"Hey, Butch! How are you?" Kate asked.

"Fine. Well, honestly, a little embarrassed."

"About what?"

"The fact of the matter is, I was wrong. Kenneth Frank did not kill his sister. I feel really lousy that I did shoddy investigative work to even put him in the position of being a suspect."

"What are you talking about, Butch?" I asked.

"The night Nancy Frank was killed, the only suspect we had was Ken. The evidence pointed to him, so I guess I tried to put it all together to make him be the guilty party to get the conviction. We know better now."

"What have you found out?"

"Remember, the only fingerprints found were his. There was no sign of forced entry. Everything pointed to him."

"And?"

"And I guess I was a little overzealous. I wanted the conviction so that I might make detective. For that, I will forever be sorry. Now mind you, there was nothing pointing to anyone else until you two got involved. We all were so sure we had the right guy that we just didn't work hard enough to find the true answers to all the questions. We had motive, that would be the money left by the Frank parents upon their death. We had opportunity, no witnesses to say that he was somewhere else at the time, and means, his fingerprints were on the murder weapon. But even though it looked perfect, it wasn't. We...I should have dug further. He didn't seem like the type to kill his own sister. Not for money. He worked hard on the farm, and even though he didn't care for her much, she was still family."

"So what are you getting at, Butch?"

Butch had sort of a sheepish look on his face. He continued with his dissertation.

"Here is what we know now. Once Nancy finished going through withdrawals, she started talking like a parrot on speed. This happened late last night. In fact, I haven't slept since the night before I saw you last."

"Holy crap, Butch. Here," I said as I poured him more coffee.

"I should go all the way back to the beginning, I guess. Nancy Frank was, indeed, a party animal. She hit a different bar every night, kind of on a rotation basis. As her brother Ken said, from what he heard, she was loud and would tell everyone within ear range who she was and what that meant, presumably that she had lots of money. Then when she got drunk or stoned, she would talk about her family. Seems that on one of these nights, she met Jane Tucker. Jane is, or was, a very loose woman looking for a man. She felt like Nancy was cutting in on her action, which was far from the truth. But it was what she said she thought was happening. Jane started making fun of Nancy about how loud she was, how nobody cared about how much money she had, or who her family was. Nancy took offense. One thing led to another, and they ended up going outside. Just like in the movies, except no one cared. Everyone else stayed in the bar. When Jane saw that no one was going to watch her kick Nancy's butt, she kind of lost interest. Instead, they started talking. Come to find out Nancy was looking for some kind of high, and Jane just happened to have what she was looking for. After that night, you could almost say they became friends although it was more likely druggie and dealer."

Butch stopped to sip his coffee, and Kate immediately filled his cup back up from the carafe.

"Thanks, Kate. Then Brian Eckland came on the scene. Jane had tried repeatedly to pick him up over the last year, but he didn't want anything to do with her. When he met Nancy that night, he was telling the truth. It was like love at first sight. They both seemed to like each other's company, and they became friends. It appears when Brian was around Nancy, she calmed down a bit and was easier on the ears of everyone else in the bar. They started meeting a few nights a week, and before you know it, they were in love. Brian was good for Nancy and vice versa. Yeah, I know, he drinks too much and doesn't have a real steady job, and Nancy was a drinker and a druggie, but Nancy got him thinking about starting his own mechanic business, and he was helping to get her off the drugs at the same time. Then one night in the Blacktail, Jane walks over and starts talking to Nancy. They get up and leave, and then when they come back in, Nancy sits back down with Brian and they have a conversation that leads to their getting up and walking out. My guess was that Brian was upset because he felt that Jane was selling Nancy drugs. We don't know for sure on that, but we feel like that might have put a strain on their relationship, which is what Jane wanted at that moment."

"So how does this all lead to her murder?" I asked.

"Just about there. As she was getting better, the only one who didn't want her to was Jane. She was losing a customer and a friend, as well as a potential suitor in Brian. She started formulating a plan, but she needed help. Enter Randy. Jane felt like she could manipulate Nancy. However, they needed to ensure that she would have the money that was currently in the Frank family fortune. To do that, they needed to take out the parents."

"So it was all about money," Kate said.

"Yes, it was." Butch replied. "The Tuckers decided that they would murder the Franks first and then kind of go from there."

"So how did they do it, Butch? What was the plan?" I asked.

"Well, Nancy had gone on and on about how her parents went on a date each week. Jane listened. She and Randy had it all planned out. Jane sat down the road with a walkie-talkie and notified Randy when she saw the Franks on their way home. Randy was sitting on the old grade in his big truck waiting for the call. Once Jane called him and said they were coming, he fired up his truck, timed it, and pushed them off the road."

"Wow."

"You saw it first, Jim. I should have caught the tire tracks going more sideways than angled. If they had been sideswiped, they would have looked entirely different. They took a shot dead-on. A T-bone if you will."

"But what if the Franks' truck hadn't caught on fire?' Kate asked.

"Remember, Randy owns a gas station. I am pretty sure he had gas in the back of his truck to make sure there was little or no evidence left once he drove away."

Again, I said, "Wow."

"So once they are gone, how do Jane and Randy figure they will get the money?" Kate inquired.

"Remember, Brian and Nancy were getting better every day. You told me that even Ken said that lately she had been better. It was because she was drying out, getting off the booze and the drugs. Nancy really wanted Brian to open his own repair shop or a gas station and repair shop."

"You mean?"

"Yup. Jane started to work on Brian, telling him that Randy wanted to sell, which, of course, he didn't. Brian was taking this as a sign. His chance to show Nancy that he could do it with her help and love. Randy had no intention of selling the station. All he wanted was to get his crazy sister out of his life. Of course, he didn't tell Jane that. All he was after was the money."

"And what happens then, Butch?"

"Well, several things actually. Another one of the things that you found out actually was a big clue in who killed Nancy."

"Really? What was that? You have our attention, Butch. Don't stop now!" Kate said.

"Let me get there in a minute. First, Nancy convinced Brian to keep records and take pictures of his work so that if he needed to show he was a competent mechanic, he would have them. One of the things she had him do was to put the customer's name on any order that he placed for parts. That is why he knew he had evidence showing Randy had him order the push bar. But what you found out was much more intriguing to us. Why would a guy who worked right across the street from the bar he was going to drive twenty miles to pick up a buddy just to bring him back and dump him? To create an alibi for him. Why? Why would someone do that? Because they were the murderers, that's why."

"You mean Jane and Randy killed Nancy?"

'Well, one of them did. It was Jane."

"How did she do it? She was so strung out and drunk most of the time." Kate asked.

"Wait," I said. "Butch, you have been talking for the better part of two hours. If you haven't slept, I am betting you haven't eaten right either for a couple days. I, for one, am starved. What say we push shoptalk aside for a little while and get some food?"

"You're talking to a country boy. We *never* turn down food."

We all got up out of our chairs and went inside. In short order, we had enough bacon, eggs, and pancakes to feed a small army. Eating without saying one word about the case was almost refreshing. Butch and I talked about the upcoming hunting season and where we might go opening day. Kate talked about going back to work soon. It was just some friends having a nice breakfast together. Once we had completed filling our stomachs, we got one last cup of coffee from the coffee maker and all headed back outside.

"Okay, Butch, it's all you again. You had said Jane killed Nancy. Why?"

"From what she told us, the first part of the plan worked flawlessly. The Franks were dead, and now they needed to get the money channeled to them. This is where it got a little disjointed if you were the Tuckers. Since they knew that Brian Eckland wanted to open his own shop and he didn't have enough money to do so, they started working on him first. Both Jane and Randy told him how he had a cash cow and once he married Nancy that he could fulfill all his dreams and so on. Brian didn't want to spoil what he had with Nancy, but they kept working on him to no avail. They had to come up with another plan."

"Which was?"

"The night that Jane and Nancy left the Blacktail, Jane was going to sell Nancy some drugs. Nancy was trying hard to kick them, but she still liked the feeling once in a while. Problem was, it was a setup. Randy was outside with a camera. Jane made sure that they were under some enough light to get a good picture, and Randy snapped the drug buy."

"Okay, now I am confused. What did that have to do with anything?" I asked.

"If they couldn't get Brian to marry Nancy, then they would blackmail Nancy to get the money they wanted."

"See! I told you!" Kate interjected.

"Yes, you did," Butch replied. "As it turns out you were both right with your thought patterns. Jane wanted to blackmail Nancy *or* manipulate Brian in such a manner as to get the cash from the Frank fortune."

"So how did it happen? Nancy's murder, I mean," I said.

"As Jane tells it, she went to the farm that night to tell Nancy that she was going to go to her lawyer and show the picture of her buying drugs unless she gave her a million dollars. The front door was unlocked, so she let herself in quietly, and thinking that maybe Nancy might be armed in some way, she might need some sort of protection. She found her way to the kitchen, and she had been smart enough to wear gloves. Jane pulled a knife from the butcher block and held it at her side, hidden from view as long as she didn't raise her hand. Jane found Nancy reading a book in bed. Just so you know, her nightclothes were what they were. The fact that they were skimpy had no bearing on the case whatsoever. It was just what she liked to sleep in. When Jane told Nancy what she wanted, Nancy laughed at her. By this time, Nancy was pretty close to completely drug and alcohol free. She told Jane that her lawyer couldn't care less about the fact she was or wasn't a drug user. All she cared about was getting his share of the estate for handling probate. This enraged Jane. She went to the side of the bed and, with no additional provocation, raised the knife and stabbed Nancy to death."

"Oh my god!" Kate exclaimed. "She killed her in cold blood."

"Wait. Why was Jane at Brian's house the first time we went there?" We all remembered the way she acted and that Brian almost seemed afraid of her.

"In talking to Brian about that, he said that when Nancy was murdered, he was devastated. Jane showed up one day, dressed up kind of nice, and offered her sympathy. Of course, Jane was only doing this since she now felt she could perhaps pick Brian up now that Nancy was out of the picture and he was vulnerable. Brian said she was really nice at first, and then she basically planted herself in his house and showed no intention of leaving. He was indeed a little afraid of her. Big guy like that afraid of a woman," Butch said, shaking his head.

"Jane was trying to stay close to Brian, just in case he had already gotten some money from Nancy. Once she realized that hadn't happened, she dumped him. She waited for several months to be sure, hanging on, trying to be a good friend when, in fact, she was just making sure he was indeed broke. That and she realized he had no intention of ever marrying her."

"Yes, Kate," Butch said. "Jane did kill her in cold blood. So now you know, and so does the Lewis County prosecutor's office. It is my guess that Mr. Reynolds's office has already been notified. By the way, as of now you are no longer deputized. No need."

Kenneth Frank was innocent.

CHAPTER NINETEEN

We received a summons, well, not really a summons but a call to appear at Robert Reynolds's law office that afternoon. Kate told them we would be there the next morning at ten. She was so cool. I loved her to death. Probably bad phrasing, but I mean it.

We arrived at the appointed time the next morning and walked in like we owned the place.

"Mr. and Mrs. Tuttle, Mr. Reynolds is waiting for you down the hall. He is in the same conference room where you met last week."

Last week? My gosh. It was only last week. It seemed like months ago. Kate led the way, and we strolled down the hallway. We knew this was our big payday. The $250,000 was a huge sum of money for us, and even when you subtracted the $75,000 we had already received, it was a tidy sum that would make our lives infinitely easier. Take out taxes and all that and we still had at least four years of salary coming in one lump sum.

As we turned into the office, standing with Robert Reynolds was Kenneth Frank. He looked, I don't know, happy? Relieved? Vindicated? Didn't matter. He smiled at us as we walked in the door.

"Hello, Jim. Hi, Kate."

We walked forward and shook hands with the man whose life we had just saved, with a good deal of help from our friend Butch.

"Hi, Ken. So sorry for your loss but so glad we found out what happened."

"I realize now that Nancy was trying hard to get her life back. I am just sorry that I didn't give her more help."

We all stood staring at each other for a few seconds, and then Ken handed us the check. Holy cow. It was real. We were going to have an additional $175,000 in our bank account in just a little while.

"Thank you for all you did. Without you two, I would be facing a trial in a few days that could have gone either way. I can't tell you how thankful I am that you helped me."

"No problem, Ken. We are both glad it turned out this way."

For whatever reason, when someone hands you a check even though you know it is good and for the right amount, a person always looks at it. When I opened the folded check, I was stunned.

"Ken, what is this? The deal was for $250,000 if we got you off. You already paid us $75,000."

"I told you a few days ago when you were down at the farm, if you got me off I would give you a million dollars. I am a man of my word."

I had never seen so many zeros on a check. He hadn't subtracted the $75,000. He wrote us a check for $1,000,000.

"Ken, it's too much. We had an agreement."

"And I altered the agreement a few days ago. Your services were well worth the money. Thank you for all you did for me. Believing in me."

Neither Kate nor I could think of anything to say but thank you. Even with 30 percent of it lost to taxes, we would have nearly eighteen years of my salary in our bank account in short order.

"Ken, are you sure you want to do this?" Kate asked.

"Without you two, I would be possibly spending the rest of my life in prison. The money means nothing in comparison to my freedom. Thank you."

With that, Kate and I shook hands again with promises to keep in touch and so on. Our next stop was our bank.

Once they had confirmed the check was good, we paid off our house. Then we left and headed straight for the local motor home dealer. One thing Kate had always wanted to do was take a motor home across the country. It seemed we would have some time and money to do that now. We had good jobs, could take time off for vacations, so why not? We bought a top-of-the-line motor home, and while Kate led the way in my truck, I drove home in our newest addition.

I had a feeling Killer would love travelling.

PART THREE

What a Trip

Prologue

L ooking across the lake and seeing our motor home parked there and standing at mile marker one of the trail, I was one happy camper. I knew we still had a mile, but it seemed like five as tired as I was.

"That was the most beautiful hike I have ever been on," exclaimed Kate.

We were just finishing a five-hour, twelve-mile hike up into some of the most beautiful country on the continent. Glacier National Park was living up to the expectation we had set for it in our minds. As we finally walked up to the campsite, I thought my legs were going to disconnect from my body. I was bushed.

"It was really cool. Wish I was," I replied, still out of breath. Kate was in great shape from walking our dog, Killer, every night. I, on the other hand, was fast becoming the Pillsbury doughboy. Too many beers sitting in what we called the office, which was really our backyard.

"I'm getting us a beer."

"Can you bring out some water for Killer too please?"

"Of course, darlin'. Uh, if you throw me the keys out of the backpack."

Kate had said she would carry the food and water knowing I would be more likely to agree to the hike if I had nothing on my back. Man, I loved this woman.

Kate tossed me the keys. A nice toss, shoulder high. Had I had to bend to catch them, I have no doubt I would have toppled like a toddler just learning to walk.

Getting everyone's liquid refreshment and returning, Kate and I, along with our faithful dog, relaxed and looked out at the crystal blue waters of Lake McDonald. We were in our brand-new motor home, enjoying a vacation that was well-earned and deserved.

"I wonder how deep this lake is," asked Kate.

"Boy, I have no idea. I haven't read up on the lake depths lately," I said somewhat sarcastically.

Kate raised one of her eyebrows and had a "ha ha" look on her face. Then she did, in fact, break into laughter. Kate's laugh was as good a laugh as I have heard in my entire life. It was one of the things that made me love her even more.

The sky was what I call Caribbean blue and the water was a deep blue. The contrast was spectacular when you threw in the snow-capped mountains and the lush green meadows surrounding the lake. I could stay here the rest of my life and be happy as long as Kate and Killer were here too.

"How long should we stay here do you think?"

"As long as you promise not to make me take any more hikes, forever is good for me."

This brought another laugh from Kate.

We had already been here for about a week. When the park rangers found out who we were, we had visitors almost every day. Guess that what happens when you are thrust into fame at a young age. The rangers had warned us that there were bears of the grizzly variety in the area, so when Kate, Killer, and I went on a firewood hunt, we kept our eyes up, looking for the beasts as much as we did looking down for firewood.

Killer sat with his paws crossed in front of him and his head resting comfortably on top of them, staring out onto the lake. Kate and I were seated in lawn chairs which we store underneath our home on wheels in what is called the basement storage, the doors you see on the outside of a motor home, below floor level. Our beers rested on the bench portion of what appeared to be a decades-old picnic table. Life was hard up here in the winter, the road closing with the first heavy snows. The picnic table could be only three or four years old, but just well weathered by the climate.

"Ready for another beer, darlin'?"

"Sure, why not?"

"Good. I want to kill two birds with one stone as they say. I have to use the facilities anyway."

I rose slowly, the only way I could at the moment, and tried to not look like I was in pain as I made my way back into the motor home.

As I opened the door to the bathroom, something looked dark in the shower. My initial thought was simply, *What the heck?* I opened the door. Then I screamed for Kate. Twice.

Kate ran in, somehow being able to move much better than me, rushed down the hall, and looked in.

Sitting on the little corner bench in the shower, for those who like to sit when they are taking their daily cleansing, was the body of a girl we had never seen before. She was most definitely dead.

CHAPTER ONE

We had just finished what turned out to be our second case as amateur sleuths. It all started with Betty Walker. She was a wonderful old lady who asked us to find out who had dug up her husband's grave and stolen his pocket watch which she had placed in his casket at the cemetery in 1924. During the process, I was shot, adopted a dog, and solved two half-century-old murders. With the help of my lovely wife, Kate, of course. We became overnight sensations, even going on television, which was a pretty cool thing to do. The show was *Good Morning America*, and it had started a few years earlier in 1975. It was popular and had a good following.

Ken Frank, a rich farmer accused of killing his sister, had seen the broadcast and had his attorney call us to help keep him out of prison, or worse. We believed his story and indeed helped him stay out of prison but found the killers of not only his sister but also the murderers of his parents, who had purportedly died in a car accident as well. For doing this, Mr. Frank paid us the tidy sum of $1,075,000.

So like anyone who was in their twenties, with money to burn, we had gone straight to the bank, paid off our house, then headed to Charlies Trailer Sales and purchased the nicest motor home we could find in our price range. There was a surprising number to choose from, but we kept within our budget and found one we liked.

Kate is a florist, and I am a jewelry store manager. Getting paid a little over a million dollars was like getting paid for eighteen years of my salary as a store manager. We decided to take some time off. Both our bosses agreed that when we got tired of gallivanting around they would take us back. I think because we were both good at our jobs, they decided they could always use us. Whenever that happened to be.

We had waited until now, late spring 1980, to go on our first trip since I was not about to miss my beloved hunting season in the fall. Our friend Elmer "Butch" Danforth, a sergeant in the Lewis County Sheriff's Department, whom we had met and become fast friends with during our investigation for Betty Walker and an avid hunter it turned out, and I had mixed luck in October. Butch had taken a nice buck black-tailed deer, and I had been blessed by getting a young three-by-three bull elk. No deer for me, no elk for Butch. Still, all in all, what would be deemed a successful season overall. We had loads of meat in the freezer.

For the first time in my working life, I was able to have Christmas off, the whole Christmas season, and Kate and I had enjoyed it immensely. But now here we were, finally on the road in our new motor home, dog at our side, figuratively speaking, since Killer was actually sleeping on the bed in the back as we drove the winding roads to a place we had never been—Glacier National Park.

We had purposely waited until we found out the roads were open in the park so we could stay and relax for as long as we wanted, take hikes, and just enjoy each other's company for as long as we wanted. The park roads had gotten a good amount of snow the past winter, so it was late spring before we were able to take off. The good news was it was a warmer-than-usual spring, so not only had the snow melted nicely but the weather also was in the mid-seventies already.

We found a lake—Lake McDonald to be precise—which we were able to drive into a campsite right along the shoreline. It was in a campground, but the spot we chose was the most isolated and remote. The view was spectacular with the snow-covered peaks far above us and the beautiful lake in front of us.

Having barely had time to set up the camp, a park ranger truck pulled in and parked behind the motor home. The door opened and a man the size of a huge boulder exited the vehicle.

"Afternoon, folks," the ranger said. "My name is Michael Justice. I am one of the park rangers here in Glacier."

"Hi there," Kate replied. "I'm Kate, and this is my husband, Jim."

"Oh, I know who you are. I caught you on *Good Morning America*."

"How did you even know we were here?" I inquired.

"Ranger that took your money at the park gate recognized you two. Can't be on television and not expect to be noticed," he said with a smile and chuckle in his voice. I like the guy already.

"Well, it is a pleasure to meet you, Ranger Justice."

"Please call me Mike."

"As long as you agree to call us Kate and Jim."

"Done. How long you figuring on staying?"

"We honestly don't know, Mike. Since we are just setting up, we hadn't thought about that yet."

Kate added, "This place is so beautiful. We may wait until the first snowfall."

"Indeed it is. But be aware. The grizzly bears are just out of hibernation, and they have pretty big appetites this time of year. Be cautious as you hike, if you plan to."

"Whoa, thanks for the heads-up. We do have our dog with us."

Again, the ready chuckle, this time more of an outright laugh. "Dogs don't help much against grizzlies."

I walked over and opened the door to the motor home, and Killer jumped over the steps and hit the ground. Without even thinking, just acting on instinct, Mike put his hand on the butt of his service revolver. Killer was the dog we had adopted from the person guilty of the two fifty-year-old murders. He had actually been found in Montana, along the road, and ended up in Centralia, Washington. He was a monster-sized dog, partly due to the German shepherd in him and partly due to the fact the other half was wolf. He had a purple-spotted tongue, which our veterinarian had said was typical of wolves and, therefore, half-breeds. Plus, he was, as I stated, huge, and that is why when Mike had seen him, he put his hand on his service revolver.

"Killer, this is Mike. Go say hi."

Killer had positioned himself between Kate and me and Mike without our even realizing it. He was extremely loyal and protective. Killer could now sense in my voice that all was good, so his tail started a slow wag, and he crept up to Mike's open palm, which had left his gun, and was now reaching as far as his arm could reach to let Killer smell him.

"Hi, Killer."

At the sound of his name from this new stranger, Killer's tail wagged a bit more. Mike took the chance to reach out and pat his head, and Killer responded by moving closer. They were good now.

"Killer, you are one big doggy."

Kate responded to this, "Yes, he is, but he is a great dog and, as you can see, very protective. If a bear was coming after us, we have no doubt he would put himself between us and the bear even if it cost him a mauling or worse."

Killer was now the recipient of a good petting by Mike, and Mike had relaxed a great deal.

"Seems like he likes me though."

"As long as we are okay with you, he is okay with you."

"Listen, I will leave you folks alone. There are four of us who patrol this area, so don't be surprised if you see a few others coming here to introduce themselves. Isn't every day we get to see and meet celebrities up here in Glacier."

"We look forward to it. It was nice to meet you. And thanks about telling us about the bears."

With that, Mike gave Killer one last pat on the head and went back to his truck, slamming the door loudly, started it up, and drove off the way he had come from.

"Nice guy," Kate said.

"Sure seemed to be." I looked at Kate. "Do you feel like a celebrity?"

"I guess we have to feel that way a little, Jim. People recognize us from television or the newspapers, and that is kind of the definition, isn't it?"

"I suppose, but it still seems weird to me. Hey, let's go gather some firewood so we can build a fire later. It may be warm in the sun now, but my guess is that when that sun goes down, it is going to get cold fast."

"Great idea. Just remember, detective boy"—a nickname Kate had given me last year when all the investigative work had started—"I plan to walk your legs off. I found what appears to be an awesome hike that I want to go on. Looks to be ten or twelve miles."

"Oh, wonderful. Give me a heart attack on our first week of vacation."

CHAPTER TWO

"Oh my god, Jim, who is she?"

"I haven't got a clue."

"How did she get in here?"

Same answer from my mouth.

We stood there staring at a girl we had never seen before but had somehow ended up dead in the shower of our new motor home.

"Looks like she took a shower," Kate said with a shaky voice.

She was damp. Not really wet but definitely damp.

"I don't think so. She is not that wet."

Her hair looked as if she had been caught in a light rain, and her clothes were also damp. Weird. As we stood staring, we were greeted by the sounds of a vehicle pulling up.

"Go outside and secure Killer," was all I could think to say. Kate ran back down the little hallway and out the door, grabbing Kill's leash on the way past the door where we always left it hanging.

I heard her first call him, and then I heard her say, "Hello, can I help you?" like she worked at a drive-in restaurant. I was waiting for "Do you want fries with that?"

In the distance I could hear another voice, male. I heard Kate respond with, "Yes, we are the Tuttles, and you are?"

I had heard enough to deduce that it was likely a friend or colleague of Ranger Justice. I hurried down the hall and out the door.

"Hi there," I called out.

"Hello. Ranger Justice said you two had signed in at the station a few days back, and I wanted to come by and, um, introduce myself. My name is Ranger Rick Morelli. Everyone just calls me Ranger Rick. Or just Rick."

"Well, you know who we are, and being a ranger, I would suspect you can figure out real quick like that I am Jim and she"—pointing at my lovely wife—"is Kate."

"Indeed." He looked at us rather strangely and then said, "In the old movies I watch, at this point someone would say, 'You guys look like you have seen a ghost.' What's up?"

Kate and I looked at each other and, with just that glance, decided that the absolute best way to handle the situation was with complete and utter honesty.

"Rick, we have a problem."

I started from where we met Mike, Ranger Justice, and told him exactly what had transpired since that moment. I did leave out the four days since Mike had stopped by to introduce himself since they had no bearing on the body in the shower. It took a good fifteen minutes to tell the whole story, and Rick proved to be a very good listener. When I finished the story with us running out to meet him, suddenly his eyes grew the size of quarters, and he stated, "You mean the body is still in there? Now?" pointing at the motor home.

"Yes, it is. We just found her as you drove up."

"Holy cow! I have to call this in right now." He ran back to his truck, reaching in and picking up the handheld microphone, and spoke into it rapidly. After making the call, he walked back over to where Kate and I stood.

"My supervisor told me to tell you that you cannot go back inside the trailer until we get the sheriff's office and their forensic folks up here."

Kate and I shared another glance.

"Rick, first off, it's a motor home, second, that may sound good in theory, but we just got back from a twelve-mile hike. We are hungry, thirsty, tired, and have a dog that needs fed as well. What are we supposed to do about that?"

Rick looked at his boots and shuffled his feet like a shy high school boy trying to work up the courage to ask a girl to the prom.

"I don't know what to say. If I call my boss back, he is likely to yell at me. I am sure he is trying to contact the sheriff's office in Flathead County as well as the sheriff in Glacier County since no one knows exactly where the dividing line is. Hard to measure up here."

"That doesn't answer my husband's question. What are we supposed to do for food, drink, and shelter until everyone has a look at the crime scene?"

Again with the shuffling feet. I got the impression Ranger Rick was fairly new to the job and didn't want to rock the boat. We waited for a response, and he finally came back with, "It shouldn't take all that long for my supervisor to get here. A little longer for the sheriffs and forensic teams. Unfortunately, there may be a pissing match, um, sorry, ma'am, between the two sheriff's offices since I am sure they would love to be known for the department who, well, who maybe brought down the two amateur detectives on a murder charge of their own."

This time, Kate and I did more than glance. It was obvious that neither of us had even *considered* that the rangers or the police would think we had anything to do with it. Suddenly, I was no longer hot and sweaty as a cold shiver went up my spine.

"Ranger, we told you exactly what happened. How could they possibly even suspect us of anything with the information we gave you?"

"I'm just saying locked trai—sorry, motor home—dead body. If you had the only key, they are going to make you suspects number one and two."

Of course, he was right. Smart even though he was both a bit young and most likely new at the job since he didn't want to call his boss back. Smart young man. And we were in deep trouble.

CHAPTER THREE

"I'm telling you, the top of that peak, to the top of that peak is the dividing line," the man said, pointing first one direction and then turning 180 degrees and pointing in the other direction.

This came from a sheriff that you would probably expect to see in a movie about the south—big stomach hanging over his belt, buttons on said shirt stretched to the maximum breaking point without breaking. We found out he was the sheriff of Glacier County. He was arguing with another sheriff whom we found out was the sheriff of Flathead County. Just as Rick had suspected, there was a pissing match going on over who was going to handle the case of the dead body in the famous people's motor home.

"I'm telling you that you are wrong, Nate. It is the peak to the left. At least you got one right."

"Bullshit, John. I know these mountains, and I know what I am talking about."

We found out from Rick that John was Sheriff John Haskins, the sheriff of Flathead County. Big belly's name was Sheriff Nathanial Tate, or Nate. They continued to argue and point for another five minutes before I had had enough. We wanted to eat and get some food for Killer, who was sitting quietly at the edge of the scene, taking it all in.

"Sheriffs? Can we figure this out please and get to the point where my wife and I can get some food and water for ourselves and our dog?"

"Ain't gonna happen anytime soon," came the reply from Sheriff Tate. "We gotta figure this out, and then one of the forensic guys has to go in and look over the scene."

"And that will be *my* man," said Sheriff Haskins.

"No way, John."

"Please, gentlemen. We are getting to the point of starvation. I'm sure neither of you wants to be seen as a bad guy in the press," I said this hoping that they would think twice about the fact Kate and I had a lot of friends we had made over the past six months. People on *Good Morning America* being the ones I hoped they remembered first. *GMA* had wanted an interview a week or two before we left as a kind of follow-up to the murder interviews that they had done last fall. Let the morning viewers know what was happening with the two young detectives, I think, is how they put it. Not good to get national attention for starving people who had solved several crimes.

The two sheriffs stared at us and then looked at each other.

"Look, Nate, at this point, why don't we let both our guys in to process the scene more quickly and then get the deceased out of these folks' home so they can get back inside?"

Nate thought about this for a moment. I could see the wheels turning. If he thought we were guilty, he would be thinking, *I might get on GMA* (what most folks called *Good Morning America*) *and I will be the famous one.* If he thought we might be innocent, he would be thinking, *I will look like a fool for suspecting these two.* I knew just from listening to the two talk to each other I would rather have Sheriff Haskins be the investigating officer rather than Sheriff Tate. He not only carried himself in a manner more befitting a sheriff, but he also seemed to know his stuff and I felt he would be more thorough.

"Fine," came from Tate's mouth.

With that, the two forensic guys entered the motor home, both trying to be the first in. Kate looked at me and smiled for the first time since before I had gone in to get us a beer.

"It will be okay. We know we didn't do anything."

"But it doesn't look good. As Rick said, locked motor home, no one else around, and so on. I am really nervous about this, Kate."

It took the forensic teams from both offices about an hour and a half longer to take fingerprints, including ours, and process the scene for any fibers, hair, and the like. They finally came out and said they were done. Besides the two sheriffs, there were two other deputies, the two forensic guys, three rangers (Rick, Mike, and one we had not had the pleasure of getting to know yet), and an ambulance and driver to haul the body away, all standing around.

"All right then," said Haskins. "Tim," he said to one of the deputies, "help get the body in a bag and get it out of the home, will you?" Although it was a question, there was no doubt that he wanted his deputy to get on it immediately.

"Sure thing, Sheriff."

"What killed her?" asked Sheriff Tate to his forensics man. This was not missed by Kate or me, not who killed her. He felt that he already had that information, Kate and me. I really didn't want this guy handling this investigation. He already had us hanging from a noose.

"No idea at this point. No blood, no visible puncture, stab or gunshot wounds. Looks like we will have to wait for the coroner to determine cause of death."

"John, should we arrest them now. What do you think?"

Sheriff Haskins looked to be in thought for a few seconds. If he said no and we were to take off in the motor home, he would look like an incompetent. If he said yes and it ended up our story proved to be true, then he would also look bad in the eyes of the public.

He turned to Kate and me. "How long you planning on being here?"

"We just got here a few days ago. There is no time line really although it is going to be a little weird trying to sleep in a place where a dead body was just removed from," Kate replied.

He pondered for a moment longer and looked at Sheriff Tate. "I say we let them get on with their vacation as long as they don't leave this park or this spot for at least as long as it takes the coroner to determine cause of death, and the forensic teams to look over what they pulled out."

Sheriff Tate was not happy about this; you could see it in his eyes. He was also thinking the same things Sheriff Williams had been thinking just a few moments ago.

Turning to me and ignoring Kate, he said, "You agree to that?"

I was sure they would have a conversation with the rangers. There were only two entrances into the park. They would be told to watch for us leaving. We had no intention at this point of going anywhere.

"Sure. We just got here, and we still want to try to see some more of the park. We will stay put until we hear from one of you," I said, looking first at Nate and then John in the eyes. "But we don't want one of you to say it's okay to leave just to have the other one arrest us for trying. You two need to work that out before we will totally agree."

The two sheriffs looked at each other.

"My office is closer, Nate. What do you say we talk, and then I can let them know when they can leave if it turns out they are cleared?"

Sheriff Tate was not really wanting to give up his authority to another sheriff, but in an effort to look decent, I suppose, he finally relented. By doing so, it meant that if we were, in their opinion, guilty, Sheriff Haskins would be the arresting department, which made me feel a little better. At least he didn't have us hanging from a rope yet.

"Mr. and Mrs. Tuttle, you will remain here until what time either myself or one of my deputies comes and tells you it's okay for you to leave this park. Is that clear?"

"Crystal clear," Kate spoke for the first time during this exchange.

"All right then, men, clear out." Then turning to Kate and me, he said "If you leave this park, I will consider it an admission of guilt. Stay put. It will only be twenty-four to forty-eight hours."

I nodded to him and then to Sheriff Tate. This was going to be the longest two days of our lives I had a feeling.

CHAPTER FOUR

"I, for one, need some food and another beer," Kate stated as she walked toward the motor home.

"Make it two. Not too sure I can eat, but a beer is definitely in order after all that."

"If we weren't so tired from hiking, we could ride our bikes to McDonald Lodge and have dinner there."

What she was really saying was, "If *you* weren't so out of shape, we could have a nice meal in the lodge."

We had bought a couple new bikes for the trip so we could venture farther from our motor home on excursions. Trying to drive a motor home on the highway can be stressing enough for a novice, let alone trying to maneuver through traffic.

Kate returned with beer and some barbecue potato chips, my favorite.

"Oh thanks, darlin', but I don't think I can eat just yet," I said this as my hand dove into the bag, pulling out a handful a grizzly would have been proud of. This made Kate laugh. Oh, how I loved that laugh.

We sat quietly for a few minutes, Kate sipping her beer while I devoured some more chips and guzzled my beer to wash them down. Kate finally broke the silence.

"Well, detective boy, we have solved fifty-year-old murders, what do you think our chances are of keeping our own tails out of jail?"

"I was just thinking along those lines myself. We need to look at this objectively, as if it wasn't our necks but someone else's. Let's start with when we left today and work our way through it."

Kate is brilliant. She would never say so, but she is. With her on my side, or our sides, as it were, I felt pretty confident we could draw some conclusions that might make sense. Kate started with the fact that she knew she had locked the door on the motor home when we left. I concurred since I was the one who unlocked it and heard the unmistakable sound of the lock slipping open.

We had been gone from close to 9:00 a.m. and returned around 3:00. Made sense. Nearly twelve miles, half uphill, meant that we went way slower uphill than we did down, but an average of two miles an hour seemed about right. Had to be, we had done it.

There was nothing out of place in the campsite when we returned that would make us think someone had been here while we were away. The firewood we had gathered the night before looked exactly the same, at least we thought so. Does anyone really pay attention to a pile of old dead branches? This truly was bizarre. No sign of anyone having been at or near our motor home, a locked door, and a dead body in the shower. Okay, maybe we couldn't solve this one. There was *nothing* to go on. For the first time today, I thought to myself, *One or both of us are going to be arrested for the murder of a person we had never met.*

CHAPTER FIVE

They came early the next morning. Kate and I, as you might imagine, had had a tough time falling asleep the night before. So when the doors started slamming outside our motor home at seven thirty, it awoke us from a very few hours of sleep. I looked out the window and saw what appeared to be a parking lot of police cars and trucks.

I threw my pants on, along with a Seattle Seahawks T-shirt, and walked down the hall and out the door to greet our visitors. It was the Flathead Sheriff's Department, what looked like all of them. They were led by Sheriff Haskins.

"Morning, Sheriff."

"Morning. I won't say good morning since I don't think it will be for you. James Tuttle, I am arresting you for the murder of Sally Klein."

Kate had gotten up, gotten dressed, and had just exited the motor home when this proclamation came.

"What? What are you talking about? Jim didn't kill anyone! We were hiking up to Avalanche Lake when it happened!"

The sheriff looked at Kate and me and said, "We have enough evidence to arrest Mr. Tuttle. There was no way we could look the other way and chance you trying to run off and disappear. We know you have the money to do so. It was my call, and that is my decision."

"What evidence?" I said to Haskins.

"We can get into all that down at the office. For now, please place your hands behind your back."

Knowing I had done nothing wrong really meant squat at this point. The sheriff had it in his mind I had killed some girl named Sally Klein, whom I had never laid eyes upon until she was found in the shower the day before. No use in arguing at this point. I still had faith in our justice system even though it appeared that I was going to jail for a crime I didn't commit.

First the sheriff read me my Miranda Rights, and then one of the deputies handcuffed me, an experience I had never had before and certainly never wanted to have again. It was humiliating. I had seen it dozens of times on the cop shows Kate and I liked to watch but had never dreamed one day it would be me getting shackles put on my wrists. Once the task was completed, the deputy took me by the arm and led me to his cruiser. Just like on television, he put his hand on top of my head to make sure I didn't bang it while getting shoved in the back seat. I am sure they didn't want any claims later of police brutality.

"You can ride down with one of my deputies if you would like, Mrs. Tuttle. Someone can run you back up here later if you want us to, or you can get a motel room in Kalispell."

Kate was shaken but responded that yes, she would take the ride to Kalispell and make a decision on where she would stay later.

"I'll take her down," said one of the deputies. The sheriff nodded, and everyone headed for their vehicles.

For once in my life, I was speechless. Running a jewelry store and waiting on customers, you learn to talk to people on a very personal level. Being able to converse and listen made you a better salesperson. Now there was nothing I could say.

The drive to Kalispell to the sheriff's office was only about an hour, but it seemed like an eternity. My mind raced as I tried to figure out what evidence they had against me. There couldn't *be* any. I hadn't done anything wrong!

As we arrived at the office and drove around back, a thought occurred to me. This may be the last time I was ever to see the outside of a jail.

Scary thought.

CHAPTER SIX

Once Jim was put into an interrogation room, I sat and thought about what I should do next. Hire him a lawyer? He hadn't done anything wrong, but having a good lawyer in this instance seemed a logical thing to do. Problem was, this was Kalispell, Montana. A long way from Olympia, Washington, where we lived. I did know a good attorney there and thought he would be a good jumping-off point. I made the call to Robert Reynolds, the lawyer we had worked with and for in saving Kenneth Frank from going to prison for a murder he didn't commit. I made the call.

"Kate! Great to hear from you. Saw you on *GMA* telling about where you were going on your little vacation. Where are you calling from?"

"Robert, Jim has been arrested for the murder of a girl that was found in our motor home in Glacier National Park. He is in jail in Kalispell, and I think we should hire a lawyer. Can you help us?"

"What? Tell me what happened."

I went through the entire story for what seemed like the hundredth time. Robert listened with only a few interruptions for clarification. When I was finished, he spoke, "First off, Kate, I am not licensed in Montana, so there is no way I can represent you and Jim. However, a good friend of mine who went to Montana University on a rodeo scholarship moved back after he graduated from law school. Good man. Right at the top of his class at Yale. His name is Gary Davis. He goes by bear, and you will know why the second you meet him. I will call him now and let him know what is going on, and set everything in motion for him to represent Jim. He lives in Helena, so it will take him some time to get there. He may fly in rather than take the time to drive."

"Thank you so much, Robert. I am worried beyond belief. Jim is innocent, but they say they have evidence he did it."

"Any evidence they collected in the first twenty-four hours is oftentimes meaningless, short of having a smoking gun. If all they have is fingerprints, then especially don't worry about that. It happened after all inside your motor home. The cause of death will be the big one, and my guess is that they haven't gotten that back yet, especially if there was, as you told me, no sign of trauma to the body."

"Are you sure? The sheriff is the one who told me they had the evidence."

"Of course, they may have found something unusual that would not normally come out this early, but honestly, Kate, don't worry about it. Let me call Gary. Where are you staying?"

"I have to go back up to the motor home. We brought Killer with us and he needs food and let outside. It is not easy to find, but I am sure one of the Rangers will give Mr. Davis good instructions. They seem, or at least seemed, really nice. Maybe that has changed since a murder took place in their park."

"I will fill Gary in, and you can expect to see him. Is there anywhere nearby with a phone you can get to?"

"Yes, it is about a five- or six-mile ride to McDonald Lodge."

"Stop on your way back to the motor home, and I will have left a message at the front desk. It will be Gary's contact information and where he is and how he is going to get to you, by car or by plane."

"Thanks so much, Robert. I know Jim would want to thank you too. This is horrible. My husband in jail! For murder! I still can't believe it. I am going to go see him now if they will let me. They may be interrogating him still."

"Kate, stay as calm as you can. Think your way through this just like you did Ken Frank's case. You will solve it."

"But that was a collaborative effort—Jim, me, you, and Butch. I am not sure I have it in me to do this by myself."

"You can do it, Kate. Jim always said you were the beauty *and* the brains of your little team."

This made me actually laugh. It sounded like something Jim would say.

"Thanks, Robert."

I hung up.

Jim was still in the interrogation room. I really wanted to talk to him before I headed back to the motor home. What evidence could they possibly have that would make them go back on their word to leave us up in Glacier until it was all sorted out? Who was Sally Klein? How in the world did she get into a locked motor home? I had way too many questions and not any answers. Then I had a thought.

I walked back to the desk where a deputy sat to monitor who came in and out of the station.

"Do you think it is possible for me to use the phone again?"

"Long distance again? It will have to be collect," he responded.

"No problem."

He ushered me back into the little office I had been in while making the call to Robert. Collect of course. I pulled a little address book from my purse, one that I had brought so we could send post-cards to friends while on the trip. I went straight to the *D*s and found what I was looking for. Picking up the phone and dialing *O* for the "operator," I waited until I heard her say that indeed she was an operator, and I told her I wanted to make a collect call. I was hoping beyond hope that Butch was in the office.

CHAPTER SEVEN

"Hi, Kate! I thought I might get an occasional letter or postcard from you guys. Never expected a call!"

Elmer "Butch" Danforth was a sergeant with the Lewis County Washington Sheriff's Office. We had met him the first time when Jim had been shot during our first investigation, and he and Jim had become fast friends. He was instrumental in helping prove Ken Frank was not guilty of killing his sister as well.

"Oh, Butch, I need your help," I said with a slightly cracking voice.

"My god, Kate, what's up?"

"Jim has been arrested for murder."

"WHAT? That's impossible. Jim wouldn't hurt anyone unless they were going to hurt you, him, or Killer. Tell me what happened."

Here we go again, I thought, but I pressed on and told him the entire story. One hundred and one and counting. When I finished, I waited for Butch to say something. Anything. He was silent for maybe fifteen seconds and then there was just a little whistle from him.

"I have some vacation time. I am hopping on a plane today. Uh, they do have an airport nearby, I hope."

"They must because when I called Robert he said Gary Davis, the Montana lawyer he recommended, would either fly or drive. Butch, we will pay for your ticket and any expenses. I just really am glad to hear you are willing to drop everything and come over here."

"Let's worry about the cost of things later. Where can I leave you a message?"

"At the front desk of the Lake McDonald Lodge. It's inside Glacier National Park. That is where Gary is going to leave his message. Butch, once you get over here, rent a car. The only way I can get to the lodge is by bike. It would be great to have wheels to get into Kalispell too. It is way too far to go by bike."

"Sure thing, Kate. And, Kate, don't worry. I know that sounds easy to say and hard to do, but we will get this sorted out. I promise. I can't lose my new best friend."

"Thanks again, Butch. I am going to stay here until I can see Jim. Then I will have someone run me back up to the park. I will check the front desk on my way back to the motor home. I hope you can get here soon. I am becoming a bit of a basket case."

"Kate, I know you well enough that even under the circumstances you are not a basket case. Although you have probably gone over it a thousand times in your head, go over it again. Did you miss anything? Have you maybe met this Sally and just don't remember it? You know what I mean."

"Jim and I went over it last night. And I have been going over it in my head all day, but I will try again. See you soon, Butch."

"You got it, Kate."

We hung up.

Butch is a great friend. He was Jim's best friend for sure, and he and I were also very close. He was a good cop, and I needed one right about now. One who was on our side and not on the side of the Montana cops.

Walking out of the little office, I spotted Sheriff Haskins. I made a bee line to him.

"Are you going to let Jim out now? Are you satisfied he did nothing to that girl?"

"I'm sorry, Mrs. Tuttle, but he will be staying here until he is arraigned at least. Then if bail is allowed and you can post it, then and only then will he be released," he said this with a very stern look. What could they have on him?

"Can I see him?" I asked.

"Yes." Looking around, he spotted one of his deputies standing nearby. "Johnson, please take Mrs. Tuttle to see her husband. Five minutes only." Then looking at me, he said "If you need a ride back up to the park, Johnson here can take you back up."

"Thanks, yes. I have to get back up for our dog. He has been locked in the motor home since this morning. I appreciate it, Sheriff. Again, thank you."

I figured I had better be on my best behavior rather than the ranting and raving spouse of a murder suspect. It may be that I would be able to garner a little more time with Jim or have them realize we are not bad people, just frustrated and worried about a bogus murder charge. And of course, I needed the ride back up to the park. Walking fifty miles was not in my game plan for the day.

Deputy Johnson led me to a door, unlocked it, and then a second door, unlocking it as well, and ushered me through. It was a long hall with cells on both sides. Jim was about halfway down on the left side. He saw me as I entered.

"Kate."

I walked to the door and waited for the deputy to open it. He didn't.

"Can I go inside please?"

"Sorry, Mrs. Tuttle, you have to stay on the outside, and I will be right over there," he said, pointing just a few feet away. "You are not to give or take anything from Mr. Tuttle."

What could I take from him? They had taken everything out of his pockets I was sure when he was brought in. Oh well, just take it as it comes, I guess.

"Hi, darlin'. Like my new digs?"

"Oh, Jim. This is horrible. What evidence to they have or think they have on you?"

Jim laughed. I couldn't believe it; he actually laughed.

"They say my fingerprints were all over the bathroom. Other than yours, they found no others."

"Then why wasn't I arrested too?"

"They assume that you are not strong enough to put the body in the shower, that I acted alone. Totally trumped up."

"Have they gotten a cause of death yet?"

"If they have, they haven't told me about it. What have you been up to, reading a ladies' magazine in the lobby?"

Jim knew I didn't read ladies' magazines, and I am sure he suspected that I had been busy. I filled him in on talking to Robert and Butch.

"Glad to hear Butch is coming over. Maybe you two can put your heads together and get me out of here."

"Time's up, Mrs. Tuttle."

In a strange, almost surreal moment, I kissed Jim through the bars of his cell.

"We *will* get it figured out, and once you are arraigned, I will post bail and get you out of here."

"Thanks, darlin'."

I turned and walked away, and as I got to the door, I looked back. Jim had already sat back down and had his elbows on his knees and his face buried in both of his hands. Although he had put up a brave front for me, he was worried.

So was I.

CHAPTER EIGHT

The ride back up to the park was uneventful. I wasn't in the mood to talk, and Deputy Johnson seemed lost in his own thoughts. The park is beautiful. Trees that seemed as tall as skyscrapers, deer, elk, and even bears running around made it even more incredible.

"Can you do me a favor and stop by McDonald Lodge? I have to pick something up at the desk." I wasn't going to tell him it was information on a lawyer and perhaps from a deputy from another state.

"Sure thing, ma'am."

McDonald Lodge sits on the shore of Lake McDonald, the largest lake in Glacier, which was named after a trapper by the name of Duncan McDonald, who carved his name on a tree nearby the lake in 1878. The lodge was started in 1913 and completed in 1914. It was made to resemble a Swiss chalet, and it did so admirably.

Deputy Johnson pulled up in front of the rustic lodge.

"I will wait here while you run in."

"Thanks so much, Deputy."

I actually *did* run in. I wanted to see if Gary Davis or Butch had left me a message. I needed some help with all that was going on.

Walking up, not running, to the front desk, I was greeted by a woman of about twenty to twenty-five. I am a terrible judge of age. She was pretty, with brownish blond hair, and deep green eyes. She was only about five feet tall and looked to be in pretty good shape.

"Hi, welcome to McDonald Lodge. How may I help you?"

I noticed her name tag. As is common these days in tourist places, her name tag had her name, Janene, and below that, Montana, typically the name of the state or country that the person comes from to spark conversation, I assume.

"Hi…uh, Janene, my name is Kate Tuttle. I was supposed to have a couple messages left for me here. I am staying up the road in Avalanche Campground, and this was the only place I could think that I might be able to have someone send me messages." I was rambling and knew it, but I wanted to get it all out at once. Nerves do strange things to people's brains.

"Oh, okay, let me check." She walked over to a desk that was placed against the wall behind the main counter. As she was looking, I noticed just how really cool the lodge was. There were moose, deer, caribou, and mountain goats on display in one form or another, either their heads or what is called a full body mount. The stairs going up the rooms were actually trees that had been cut from top to bottom, making each stair about six feet wide and, of course, the original width of the tree. It must have taken a large number of trees just to make the stairs in this place. But trees were something Glacier is not short of.

Janene returned to me at the counter. "Yes, Mrs. Tuttle, there are two notes here for you," she said, handing them to me as she spoke. "Is there anything else I can do for you?"

The notes simply had "Tuttle" printed in neat letters on the front. I opened them with great anticipation.

I was not listening as she said this second part; I was in the process of reading first the note from Butch and then the one from Gary. Butch was flying in first thing in the morning and thought it a good idea if he stayed at the lodge. Gary was going to be in later in the day, and he also wanted to stay at the lodge. Gary wanted to let me know he had already booked a room. Butch had not, so I turned back to the woman at the counter.

"I'm sorry, what did you ask me?"

"If I can be of any other assistance," she said this with much less of a smile on her face. I think she was sort of put out that I didn't carry on the conversation with her before reading my letters. Too bad. My husband was in jail, and I had a lot on my mind.

"I'm sorry, yes. Do you have any rooms available?"

"Actually, yes, we do. It is early in the year, so not everything is booked up like it will be when the kids get out of school. How big of a room do you need?"

"Just one with a double bed or whatever. It is for a friend who will be staying. I will be paying for it however. Can I get it for a week?" Figuring Butch wouldn't have an unlimited amount of time, I thought a week was probably plenty.

"Sure. That would be, let's see, seven nights at $50, that's $350."

"Can I write you a check?"

"Sure thing. Just make it out to Lake McDonald Lodge."

I wrote the check, tore it from my checkbook, and handed it to her, saying, "I am sorry I missed what you said earlier. I have a lot going on right now."

She looked at the check, and her eyes widened. "Oh my gosh, you are the wife of the guy who was arrested." News travels fast.

"Yes, unfortunately I am. Well, not unfortunately I am his wife but that he was arrested."

"Well, good luck with all that. Terrible thing. Hope he gets a good attorney."

"Oh, he will. Trust me. I love my husband, and he didn't do anything wrong. It is a total misunderstanding."

As I turned to walk away, I vaguely heard something, an odd comment, but some people just have to get in the last word. I swore she said something about it not being a misunderstanding to the dead girl.

Climbing back into the cruiser with Deputy Johnson, I thanked him for being so patient. He just smiled and put the car in gear. I didn't remember seeing him at the motor home earlier, but I am sure they had to leave *someone* back at the station when the entourage came to arrest Jim. He must have drawn the short straw.

We pulled into the campground and drove toward the motor home, swerving only once when a mule deer doe jumped out in front of the car. Deputy Johnson was a good driver, and he missed her, and we continued on. Stopping behind the motor home, Deputy Johnson said, "Will you be needing a ride tomorrow?"

"No, I have some friends coming who are renting cars. I think I will be good, but thanks for being so considerate as to ask."

"Just trying to be helpful. You have a good night, ma'am."

"Thanks." And with that, he backed up, did a K-turn, and headed back toward the west entrance to the park.

Suddenly, as I walked toward the motor home, it struck me. I was alone. Well, I had my big dog, but not my husband. When Jim went hunting, he went nearby, up to maybe fifty miles away, so he was always home at night. This was the first time in my marriage that I would be sleeping alone.

CHAPTER NINE

When Butch said "first thing in the morning," I had no idea. I heard a vehicle pull up behind the motor home at seven fifteen. Unbelievably, I had slept. Probably since the night before, I hadn't much. The car door opened and shut quietly. I knew if it were the police again, they would have slammed their doors. I jumped up and threw on some clothes, the same ones I had tossed on Jim's side of the bed last night, and grabbed Killer. He was wagging his tail and emitting a low whine. I knew Butch had arrived. Killer loved Butch.

Opening the door to our home on wheels, Butch Danforth was standing there in a pair of jeans and a flannel shirt. He would fit right in here. Killer and I both jumped from the motor home's main floor, missing the steps entirely, and ran over to him.

Giving him a big hug, I said, "Oh, Butch, I am so glad you could make it over here on such short notice."

"Heck, I've been here half an hour, driving around, looking for your motor home. This is one *huge* campground."

"No matter, you made it, and I am so appreciative. I need help, Butch. Jim is in trouble in a semi-small town with a sheriff who is trying to make fingerprints look like a signed confession."

"I am yours until you no longer need me. I made a deal with the sheriff. Turns out he met, uh, is it Haskins?"

"Yes."

"He met him at a sheriff's convention a few years back. Says he is a good cop. He was going to call and tell him I am here helping you. I don't imagine the sheriff likes a lawman helping a suspect, but hey, we are here for the truth, right?"

"Exactly. I booked a room in your name at the lodge. That way you are close to the campground and don't have to go from one place to another just to pick me up."

"I know. I already checked in."

"What? What time did your flight arrive?"

It wasn't until then that I noticed the vehicle behind the motor home. It was Butch's personal truck.

"I thought you were flying? Why did you drive?"

"The flight didn't get in until around eleven. I knew if I drove all night, I could be here in ten or eleven hours. Left last evening around five thirty. Drove almost straight through. And now I'm here!"

"Butch, you must be exhausted. Want some coffee?"

"I have had my share, thanks. Between stopping to get coffee and stopping to off-load it, shoot, I could have been here an hour ago."

Killer stayed outside with Butch, staring out at the beautiful water on the lake, while I went inside to make a pot of coffee. Butch may have had enough, but I needed my morning jolt or I would be worthless.

I wanted to take a shower, but the thought of knowing the last person inside was found dead gave me pause. As the coffee brewed, I washed up in the sink and then put on some fresh clothes. Grabbing a cup, I went back out to talk with Butch, taking Killer his breakfast in his bowl, which was the size of a large hubcap.

"Come, Kill." I really didn't have to say this because when Killer saw his bowl in the morning, he was like a bear who had just found an overloaded huckleberry bush. If allowed to jump up, he would knock me down with little to no effort.

"Sit." He complied. I set his bowl down, and he wolfed down his food, no pun intended.

"Do you know what the timetable looks like today for, Jim?" Butch asked.

"No, not yet. I was thinking if he is indeed going to be arraigned, we should probably be in town by around nine. Gary Davis will be in later this morning, and I was really hoping that he would be here before that happened."

"Well, let's see if we can make that happen. I am sure the sheriff doesn't want to lose his airtight case on a technicality. Seems to me that a person still has the right to an attorney. If we tell him that Jim's won't be in until late this morning, they would want to postpone any court proceedings until he got here."

"The thought of leaving Jim in that cell one minute longer than necessary makes me shiver. You didn't see him, Butch. He put on a good show for me, but he is scared. I could tell. Comes with the territory, I guess."

"So what do you want to do first?"

"I thought we should stop at the lodge and make sure Gary hasn't left any messages for me and then head into town."

"Think I have time to take a shower and change? I have been wearing the same clothes for over twenty-four hours. I would like to at least be presentable when I meet Sheriff Haskins."

"Of course. Let me have another cup or two of coffee and we can head out. Okay with you?"

"Yup." Butch can sometimes be a man of few words.

After sitting outside looking at the lake for as long as it took me to drink another cup of coffee, I finally put Killer in with a pat on the head and then a hug, saying "I will bring Daddy home." He was like the child we didn't have, and I was praying that Jim got out of jail so that someday we might actually be able to have a real child of our own. Tears welled in my eyes as I said goodbye and locked the motor home.

"We can't stay in town for more than about five hours. Killer will need to be let out. Makes it kind of a pain, but we may have to run back up, let him out, and then go back to town if necessary."

"No problem. We will do what needs to be done. Ready to head out?"

"Yup," I responded, taking a page from Butch's book.

We drove the six miles back to McDonald Lodge and parked in the lot. The day was going to be clear, but not real warm. The sky was perfectly blue. No other way to describe it.

We walked passed a long line of red buses, hard to describe vehicles from the '30s. They looked like a car when viewed from the front and have a limousine-type appearance behind where the driver sits. They also were built with roll-back tops of canvas so that the occupants could have unobstructed views while being driven around the park. The National Park Service had purchased eighteen of the vehicles in the 1930s from the White Motor Company for the whopping amount of $90,000. They were the first authorized motor transportation in any national park. The drivers are called jammers because you can hear them jamming the gears as they climbed the steep roads to Logan Pass, which is the highest point in Glacier at over 6,600 feet.

"Those are pretty dang cool looking," Butch said, breaking the silence.

"And they stay busy too. I have heard that in the summertime, they run nonstop from dawn to dusk."

We entered the lodge, and Butch headed up to his room while I went back to the front desk. A different woman was behind the counter this time. Her name tag said Nancy and below that was New Hampshire. Nancy from New Hampshire greeted me.

"Welcome to the lodge. How can I help you?"

"My name is Tuttle. Has anyone left any messages for me?"

"Let me check." She looked under the counter and came up with what some might describe as an out-box. She rifled through several sheets of paper and then checked the same desk Janene had checked the night before, then said, "No, I'm sorry, there is nothing here for you."

"No problem, just thought I would check. Have a great day."

"Ha ha. I think I am supposed to say that to you," she said with a smile.

I smiled and turned away and headed out the big double doors that went out onto a patio that viewed the lake. There were chairs and benches, and since it was so pretty out, I decided to sit and wait for Butch there.

Waiting about ten minutes, I decided Butch may not know where to look for me. I reentered the lodge and sat by the fireplace. The fire was roaring, and although the day was beautiful, the warmth of the fire felt exceptionally good.

"Going to sit there all day?" Butch said as he walked up behind me.

"Nope. Let's go," I said, rising from the wooden rocking chair that had been made primarily from tree branches. *They certainly used everything they could from the trees to build this place*, I thought.

We walked purposefully back to the truck and headed back to Kalispell. The drive is not really all that long, but a feeling of dread or doom seemed to engulf me as we drove on toward the jail. Would we be able to get Jim out of jail? Would they allow bail? How could we prove his innocence? There were so many things on my mind, I was afraid it would just shut down and cease to function. Butch must have sensed my concern.

"Kate, I am here to help, and help I will. We will get Jim out of this. He is too good of a friend and husband to have me let him rot in jail for something he didn't do. We will figure it out. Main thing now is getting his tail out of jail."

We drove the rest of the way to Kalispell in silence. When we arrived at the courthouse, it was obvious word had gotten to the media. There were vans and news people all around the entrance to the courthouse. Butch drove around to the side, hoping to find another way in. Parking, we walked around back and went in the entrance that they had taken Jim through the day before. Whether we were supposed to go in that way or not, we were going in anyway.

No one bothered us as we came in, and we made our way through the halls to the desk where the deputy who sat at a desk, like a secretary, was sitting.

"Morning." Not good morning, just morning from the deputy.

"Hello. Can I see my husband please?"

"I will have to check with Sheriff Haskins on that. Wait here please."

He stood and walked to an office we could only assume was the sheriff's. Upon his return, the sheriff was right behind him.

"Mrs. Tuttle. And might you be Sergeant Danforth?"

"Yes, sir, I am," said Butch, offering his hand. They shook and then separated like boxers in a ring.

"I will bring you up to speed on what's happening. The arraignment is scheduled for eleven. Have you hired a lawyer yet?" The question was asked in such a manner that you might think, in the sheriff's mind, a lawyer was a vile being no matter who they were.

"Yes, Sheriff. He is scheduled to land about eleven. Anyway, can we move the arraignment out an hour so he has an opportunity to speak with my husband before it happens?"

The sheriff turned his head slightly to the side and elevated his chin slightly as he looked up at the lights. It was apparent he would love to have the arraignment before our lawyer got there, but he thought about it and came to the same assumption we had made earlier. He almost had to wait or risk some legal maneuvering that might cost him his case.

"I will speak to the judge. Under the circumstances, I think he will be okay with that."

He made the right decision.

"May we see him?"

"Deputy," he said while turning toward the deputy seated at the desk, "who's available to take Mrs. Tuttle and Sergeant Danforth back to holding?"

"Um, Randle or Johnson."

"Well, have one of them come up here and escort these folks back."

The deputy got on the phone and called back into the bowels of the building. A deputy I recognized from yesterday when the whole gang had come to arrest Jim walked toward us.

"Follow me please." I wasn't sure people in Montana were very friendly. Or maybe it was just those of the police variety who had no room for small talk.

We followed him in through two doors and back into the holding area. Jim was in the same cell. All the others were empty. He almost jumped when he saw us walk through the door.

"Hey, Butch, so glad to see you could make it over to this beautiful state," Jim said this as he held his hands out at arm's length and swiveled at the waist, as if to say, "Beautiful state, and I am stuck in here."

"Hello, Jim," Butch replied

"Hi, darlin'. Did you get any sleep last night?"

"Hi, honey. A little. How about you?"

"Oh sure. Had a wonderful lobster dinner with red wine, and then a small three-piece band came in to serenade me to sleep." Jim could be pretty sarcastic when he felt the need arose.

The deputy finally walked back through the doors and shut them behind himself.

"No, darlin', I didn't get any sleep. I am pretty worried as you might imagine. The food we give Killer is better than what they offered me. Really nasty stuff. Not sure even what it was, and no one would say. I think they are giving me the rough treatment so I will admit to killing that poor girl and be done with it."

"I'll see that doesn't happen anymore," came a reply from Butch. "My sheriff is kind of friends with this Haskins, so if I have to, I will call him to make sure he realizes that, at one point, you both were actually deputies."

This had happened when Jim and I were solving the Frank murders. It had only been for a few days, but we were indeed deputized.

"Any word from my attorney?"

"He will be here around eleven. The sheriff is going to try to move your arraignment so that Gary has a chance to meet with you first."

As if on cue, the inner door opened and the sheriff walked in.

"I was able to move the arraignment to one. The judge wants to go to lunch at noon, so we pushed it out a little further. Hope that is all right with you all." Wow. For a moment, he almost sounded human.

"Yes, and thank you, Sheriff," I replied.

The sheriff left as abruptly as he had entered.

"Well, that's good news. I hope this guy knows his stuff. I sure don't want to spend the rest of my life in this place, or worse."

"From what Robert Reynolds told me, he is as good as they get. Pretty high praise, I would think."

It was by now nine forty-five. I told Jim we needed to get to the airport to pick up Gary Davis. He understood but was sad to see us go. The only person he had had to carry on a conversation with, who was not asking him why he killed the girl, was himself once we left.

"We will be back by twelve or twelve thirty at the very latest. I will find out where the arraignment will take place, and then we should be good to go."

"Okay. And thanks again, Butch, for coming. Once I get out of here, we can all put our heads together and see who would want to put a dead girl in our shower."

"No problem, Jim. I will be here as long as you need my services."

The ride to the airport was only about ten minutes from the jail. The crowd of news reporters had grown even larger, so I ducked down in the seat when we left. Butch and I waited for Gary in the terminal. The only flight from Helena came in at ten fifty. Butch went and got some more coffee. Poor guy, he was running on fumes but still wanted to make sure he was there for Jim.

At precisely ten fifty, a small plane touched down on the runway and made its way to the gate. There were only three passengers—two men whom one would have to consider cowboys, with hats, boots, and big buckles, and a man in a suit carrying a briefcase. We hoped our lawyer was the one with the briefcase. We were not disappointed.

"Mr. Davis?"

"Yes. You must be Mrs. Tuttle."

"Kate please. And may I introduce a friend of my husband and mine. This is Sergeant Danforth from Washington State."

Everyone shook hands, and Mr. Davis insisted on having us call him Gary. Butch told him to call him by Butch and not sergeant. I could see why Gary answered to bear. The man was at least six feet four and must have weighed in at three hundred pounds.

"Robert has actually told me a good deal about all of you. Pretty good team you three make. Let's hope the run continues."

We chatted as we walked to the truck. When Gary saw it and the fact the footwell was full of old coffee cups and snack bags, leftovers from Butch's trip last night, he insisted on getting a car.

"I was going to get a car so I could move about more freely. You all might need to use the truck when I need to go somewhere else. Really, it's not a problem at all."

We drove him to a car rental agency just outside the airport and waited while he got a sedan. Butch spent the time dunging out his truck to make it more appealing to anyone else who might need to ride with us. Amazingly, I hadn't even noticed. Probably the last thing on my mind at this point was cleanliness. There was one thing that needed attention—Killer.

"Once the arraignment is over, I have to get back up to the park and let Killer out. Maybe even take him for a walk. Hopefully, Jim will be with us. I know even a sloth like he has become lately will want to stretch his legs once he gets out of jail."

Butch chuckled at the sloth comment. He knew Jim to be a tough hunter who hiked for hours on end. Yes, he had put on a little weight over the winter, but his muscle tone was still there, more or less.

Gary emerged from the rental car office and hollered he would follow us. It was already eleven thirty. We needed to get him in front of Jim so we could tell him what had happened, and he would, of course, want a few minutes to review the police report. Neither Butch nor I knew which he would want to do first.

Traveling back and parking on the side again, we made it without incident. No reporters saw us, so we felt good about that at least. We entered through the back, went to the desk, and Gary took over.

"I am here to see my client, Mr. Tuttle."

This time, the sheriff needed no one to come get him. Gary had a booming voice, and Haskins came out of his office at double time.

"Good afternoon sir. I am Sheriff Haskins, and you are?"

"Gary Davis, attorney-at-law."

They shook hands and smiled at each other. Professional courtesy? Who knew.

"I will need to see the arrest report please," Gary said in a no-nonsense voice.

"Of course. While you visit with your client, I will get a copy made for you to take with you."

"I will take them back," the sheriff said as he turned to the deputy secretary, who nodded his head without replying.

One more time—and I hoped for the last time—we headed through the double doors and into the holding area. Jim was still the only prisoner. Slow day in Flathead County?

Jim saw us coming and rose from his bunk. This time, the sheriff opened the cage door, and we were allowed inside.

"I will put a deputy out of earshot. When you are ready to leave or if it comes time to take Mr. Tuttle to the arraignment, we will be ready either way."

Gary said thank you to the sheriff and turned toward Jim.

"Hello, Mr. Tuttle. My name is Gary Davis. I am your attorney. Robert Reynolds said you were in a bit of a pickle here."

"Yes, sir, but please just call me Jim."

"Done, and I am Gary." They shook hands, and Gary sat on the bunk, motioning Jim to do the same. Butch and I were left standing, which was fine by me. Sitting was just too…stagnant. Gary quickly looked at the police report, which surprisingly looked fairly small. Maybe three or four pages long.

"Tell me what has happened since you were brought in here. Robert gave me the short story of how the body was found and so on. What I am looking for is what angle they are taking with you."

"Well, they said that my fingerprints were all over everything and that they didn't see Kate as being involved. That is pretty much the gist of it."

Just as Jim said this, the sheriff walked in through the double doors with a file folder in his hand.

"Here you are, Mr. Davis," he said, handing Gary the case file.

"Thanks, Sheriff."

The sheriff turned and walked back out, locking the doors behind him.

"Give me a minute to read this, will you?" Gary said to Jim.

"Of course, take your time."

Gary flipped through the three- or four-page document.

"How old are you, Jim?"

"I am twenty-four and Kate is twenty-three years old."

"And how old do you think the girl in the motor home was?"

"Oh dang, I couldn't say," Jim replied. "I am a terrible judge of age." Sounded like me. "She looked pretty young, small even."

"Would it surprise you to learn she was actually twenty-four years old?"

"Well, since I said I am a lousy judge of age, I guess I would have to say no. But if you had asked me to *guess* her age, I would have said maybe fifteen or sixteen," Jim said.

"Honestly, I don't think age has a lot to do with it. There is something else there," Gary said as his face took on a serious look, and he opened the police report again and reread its contents quickly.

"I am afraid to say that, since they are not charging your wife and since the only evidence is fingerprints, I think they are biding their time. If they end up not making a case against you, they may come back and try to make one against Kate. Cops don't like dead bodies with no answers. Sometimes they do their best to make someone guilty just so they can close a case. I know it sounds sort of cliché, but it happens. They might try to make a case that Kate murdered her out of jealousy."

What did I just hear? Was the sheriff who said I wasn't involved going to arrest me and let Jim out if he couldn't make the case stick on Jim? I obviously was not the only one who had an immediate reaction. Butch and Jim were both talking at once to Gary—things like "that's nuts" and "no way," along with a few expletives, to color it up a bit. Neither Jim nor Butch were big cursers, but given what they and I had just heard, even I was ready to let fly a few choice words.

Just then, the door opened and the sheriff walked back in.

"Time to take the prisoner to the courthouse." Suddenly now, Jim was the prisoner and no longer Mr. Tuttle. I shivered.

"Do you know where the courthouse is?"

"Uh, right across the street, correct?" I responded. I had asked the deputy who was waiting for us well away and, as the sheriff had said, would be out of earshot while Gary had been reading the file.

"Yes, but the only door in is the front door."

That meant that Jim, Butch, Gary, and I would be exposed to all the newspeople outside. Oh god, I was dreading that.

Jim got up as the sheriff opened the cell door. The sheriff pulled the handcuffs off his gun belt and asked Jim to turn around. He then clasped them onto his wrists and spun him around, and grabbing onto his bicep, he escorted him out of the cell, with all of us following closely.

This was it. We headed out the front door of the sheriff's office and walked down the steps in front of all the newspeople. Cameras clicked away, and video was taken. Gary said in a loud voice, "No comment from any of this group. Just move out of our way."

That didn't stop them from hollering and screaming questions at us like we were, well, criminals. We all kept our composure and made our way across the street to see what fate awaited my husband.

CHAPTER TEN

"It will be okay, Kate." I knew I looked like death warmed over, but Kate even looked more concerned and frankly scared than I think I did.

"Oh, Jim," she said, "what if they decide to not let you out?"

I knew that was a big concern for Kate. But it was an even bigger one to me. I didn't want to spend another night in jail. Being behind bars for one day was enough to last a lifetime. It was a great deterrent for me to never actually commit a crime. You felt like an animal in a shelter, especially since the shelter I was in was not of the no-kill variety.

It was great to be outdoors, if only for a moment. The blue sky, the warm sun, the light breeze—all were fabulous after a day and night of fluorescent tube lighting and no fresh air. Of course, the people yelling at us made it a little less pleasant, but I would take the bad with the good.

The courthouse loomed before us. It was an old brick building of undeterminable age. At least to me. Once inside, we were met with dark wood everywhere. It looked like walnut, but it may have been something else stained to only appear like walnut.

Sheriff Haskins had ahold of my arm and led me to the courtroom where I would have my arraignment and bail hearing. As the doors opened, more dark wood. The judge's bench was raised up at least five feet above the floor level. I couldn't imagine being a short lawyer trying to approach the bench and needing a step stool to actually see the judge. It made me smile at a time I should have been fearful and straight-faced. I sure didn't want to appear like a crazed serial killer when the judge walked in.

Gary and I had no more taken our place inside the little railing that separates the combatants from the crowd of people who were curious to see if I would get out on bail or not when the bailiff who was standing by a door near the bench spoke loudly and clearly for all to rise.

When we were all standing, the judge entered. He was an older man. Again, no idea of age—white-haired, cleanly shaven, and in the customary black rope. As he sat, he picked up his gavel once, hit it on the little round piece of wood as was intended, and said, "You may all be seated."

The bailiff then spoke again, "This is the arraignment for case number FL71713 in the matter of bail and trial determination."

Trial determination? "What does he mean by trial determination?" I asked Gary.

"This is to determine if they have enough evidence to hold you over for trial. If it is so determined, then bail will either be granted or not."

"Who is representing the State of Montana?"

I hadn't even bothered to look at the other table. We had sat down and jumped up so fast it hadn't even crossed my mind. It did now. Looking over, I saw a man stand up who was at least six feet four inches tall. He had on a dark gray wool suit and had dark hair with graying temples. My first thought was he looked just like Atticus Finch, the character Gregory Peck played in *To Kill a Mockingbird*.

"Assistant District Attorney Marcus Garth."

"And who represents the defendant?"

Gary rose and, in a very clear voice, stated his name for the judge.

"We are here today to determine if the evidence gathered in this case is substantial enough to hold Mr.... Tuttle"—he had looked down at a sheet of paper on his bench—"over for trial on the charge of murder. We will start with the prosecution."

Garth stood up and said that he felt that the evidence was strong and that I should be held over. There was a girl's body found in the shower of my locked motor home with no one else's fingerprints on or near the shower. The girl had been reported missing in Billings a week or so ago. He also said that the cause of death would be in later today but that it was irrelevant given the fact I had said the motor home was locked up tight when we left to go on a hike in the park.

"Fingerprints? That is your evidence? It was the man's motor home. Of course his fingerprints were inside."

"Your Honor, the defendant admits freely that he had locked the motor home. No one else could have gotten inside. Why would anyone else break in and murder someone? It only makes sense it was Mr. Tuttle who did it."

"What motive did he have to do so?'

I was liking this judge more by the minute. He was grilling the state and making it look more and more like I might even walk out today.

"Your Honor, we feel that Mr. Tuttle and Mrs. Tuttle might have been having issues and that Mr. Tuttle and the deceased were likely having an illicit affair."

"That is not real sound reasoning, Counselor. If he was having an affair, why not break it off? Why kill the woman and leave the body where it would most certainly look as if he were the prime suspect?"

"We speculate, Your Honor, that Mr. Tuttle thought that if it came to light that he was having an affair after she was dead, that his *wife* would be the prime suspect and not him."

This caused the judge to sit and ponder for a moment.

"Do you have anything further? Like proof of the affair?"

"Not at this time, Your Honor. We have nothing further at this time."

"Mr. Davis, your turn."

"Your Honor, my client and his wife are very close. They have been married just a couple years, and by their own admission, the honeymoon is not over." This was totally off the cuff. We had not said one word about our marriage, how long we had been married, or any such thing. This guy was good. Really good.

He continued, "They were away from the motor home for several hours and together the entire time. How does the state plan to prove he put the body in the motor home when it wasn't there when he and Mrs. Tuttle left that morning but was there when they returned? I find it not only unbelievable but also unimaginable that even if Mr. Tuttle was separated from Mrs. Tuttle while he, pardon the expression, relieved himself in the woods, that he was gone long enough to run to wherever he had the body stashed, put it in the motor home, and reappear in that amount of time. That is, of course, unless Your Honor thinks he is from the Starship Enterprise and he beamed himself back and forth."

Of course he was referring to the television show *Star Trek*, which occurred in the future in a time when the inhabitants of the Starship Enterprise could set the machine to a certain destination and beam themselves to anywhere they wanted to go and then back again. I hope the judge knew what Gary was talking about.

"Nice reference, Mr. Davis. I watch *Star Trek*. And I couldn't agree more. But we do have a dead woman, and since the state thinks they can make a case for a jury, I am going to let the case move forward."

"Your Honor."

To Gary's remark, the judge simply held his hand up, showing us his palm.

"They have to prove the case, Mr. Davis,"—and then looking at Garth—"beyond a reasonable doubt."

"In the matter of bail, what would the state like to do with that one?"

"The state would like the defendant remanded. He is a flight risk with assets he could use to either drive off in the night or sell to purchase plane tickets and just, well, just disappear, Your Honor."

"Mr. Davis?"

"Your Honor, my client is a model citizen, even being deputized at one point." I realized he must have gotten a ton of information from Robert Reynolds. "He wants to stay and exonerate himself. He is not a flight risk. He doesn't much care for jail, but at least if he is released, he will be able to try to figure out what happened to help his own cause. Mr. and Mrs. Tuttle are amateur detectives, Your Honor."

"I know. I saw them on *Good Morning America*. Bail is set at $100,000. Trial will be in two weeks."

"Two weeks, Your Honor?" This came from Garth. "We need more time to prepare!"

"You should have thought of that before you decided to charge Mr. Tuttle here."

With that, the judge rose and walked out the door near the bench.

"Sorry to say, you will have to go back to jail until bail can be arranged," said Gary. "It shouldn't take more than an hour if they have a bail bondsman in Kalispell."

"As much as I hate the thought, knowing I will be getting out soon makes it a little easier to take. Did you get the impression the judge doesn't think much of the case or the prosecutor, or maybe both?"

"They are really grasping at straws. I still think they may come after Kate unless you can figure out who did this heinous crime."

Thank goodness at this point we were still standing at the desk in front of the fence. Kate hadn't heard it, and I wouldn't want her to. The only thing worse than being in jail was trying to imagine what it would be like for Kate.

The sheriff walked up and told me it was time to go back to his side of the street. The same sheriff I thought would give me a fair shake in comparison to Sheriff Nate Tate of Glacier County. I realized now this may have been the wrong county to be in. Haskins must have decided he wanted to glory of catching me and maybe getting his face on television. Butch's boss was wrong. Haskins was not a good cop at all.

The sheriff told Gary where the local bondsman was and then, once again, took me by the arm and led me back toward jail.

CHAPTER ELEVEN

"Wow. Outside with no bracelets on, darlin'! Feels like I'm free."

"Don't get too excited there, detective boy. We have work to do to keep you from going back in and only two weeks to do it."

"Hey, we saved Ken Frank in less time than that. No worries here."

"Gary, do you want to follow us to the park? We will take you to the lodge. Jim hasn't had the chance to see it yet, and it is something to see for sure."

Gary responded affirmatively.

"I'll ride with Gary," I said. "I want to talk a little strategy, if that's all right with you, Kate."

"Oh great, out for five minutes and dumping me already." Then she laughed. I was pretty sure her laugh had been nonexistent for the past day or so.

We all climbed into our respective vehicles. I was surprised to see Kate get into the driver's side of Butch's truck. Then I remembered he had driven all night to get here. Poor guy was probably exhausted. What would a person do without friends?

The drive back was spent just, more or less, getting to know Gary Davis. He seemed to be a super nice guy, not the kind of lawyer people liked to call snakes, jerks, or whatever came to their minds. He seemed like a genuine person. He said that once he checked in, he would call back the sheriff and try to find out what the cause of death was. That might give us a starting point for our investigation.

Kate pulled Butch's truck into the parking lot and shut it down as we pulled in next to them. Kate was right; the lodge was pretty amazing just from the outside. I couldn't wait to see the inside.

Gary led the way, with Kate and I side by side and Butch bringing up the rear.

As we entered, Kate pointed to the desk and told Butch that we would look around while he checked in.

"Janene from Montana," Kate said in my ear.

"What?"

"Oh, the girl behind the counter's name is Janene, and her name tag says she is from Montana. There is also a Nancy from New Hampshire. Butch has a couple ladies to choose from if he wants to have dinner with someone other than us and Killer. Oh my gosh, Killer. We have to get back!"

"He can hold it another five minutes. I want to look around the lodge, at least for a minute."

Gary walked back over and said he was all checked in. He wanted to unpack and call the sheriff and his wife, and then he asked how to get to where we were staying. Kate gave him good instruction, not wanting him doing what Butch had done—drive around the campground searching for us.

The lodge was indeed beautiful inside. There was a roaring fire, a restaurant, and a lounge, and it seemed just about everything was made out of trees—not lumber, mind you, but trees—from the support beams to the steps heading upstairs. Even the step railings were small trees that had been debarked, then sanded, and had been covered in, I was fairly sure, several coats of high-grade Verathane to keep people who used them from getting a palm full of slivers.

"We should go, Jim. I don't want Killer to be in pain from having to go—"

"All right. We are only a few miles away. We can always come back. Let's head out. Butch? You want to stay and rest or come back with us. We can take your truck and then come back and pick you up, or you can come with us and take a nap in the motor home if you want."

"I think I'll go back with you. If I get really tired, I can sleep inside, outside. It really doesn't matter."

So we all headed back to the truck and loaded in. It was a short drive, as I had said to Kate, but it seemed to take forever. I wanted to see my new motor home and my dog, and most of all, have a cold bottle of beer.

Kate wove the campground roads expertly, and we parked behind our home on wheels and exited the truck.

"Butch, beer?"

"What? You trying to knock me out? I'll pass for now. Maybe after I take a nap."

Kate opened the motor home, and Killer jumped out. When he saw me, he ran full speed toward me. For just a second, I thought maybe he knew I said he could wait five more minutes. But in actuality, he was just ecstatic I was back. He just about knocked me over, and then he did something he had never done. He rose up on his hind legs and put his front paws over my shoulders, like a person might do. And then he kissed me—a lot.

"I never get that sort of reaction from him," Kate said. But, of course, she had never been away from him overnight before.

"If you were gone overnight, I think you would get the same treatment. Only you would end up on your backside. This dude is heavy!"

We all laughed, and Kate went inside. She returned moments later with two beers and the partially eaten bag of barbecue potato chips. This woman *knew* me.

"Thanks, darlin'."

"No problem. I figured we needed to make this as close to our backyard office at home. Beer and chips are staples, aren't they? At least to get your brain going on this case, I know they are."

The food truly had been lousy in jail. Not so much bad food per se, but just undercooked, and then served cold. I was famished, and I couldn't think of a better way to fill my ever-growing belly right now than beer and chips.

Kate ran back inside and came out with a pen and a yellow legal pad.

"We need to get started on this right now," she said this with firmness and conviction. She was right on. I sure didn't want to go back to jail, or worse, anytime soon. Not ever, really.

"Let's start with how the motor home could be locked from the inside by a dead person," I said. "And then we need to figure out who Sally Klein was. The sheriff knew her name but didn't tell us anything else about her."

It grew silent as we all thought hard about how the home could have been locked from the inside. One door. All the windows were locked when we left and the same way when we got back. I looked over at Butch. He was fading fast. He was on the grass, leaning against a tree, with Killer lying next to him. They both had their eyes closed.

"Butch, you want to take a nap inside?"

"Nah, I'm good right here. Just let me listen and sleep for now. I am really out of gas."

"You got it, bud. And hey, thanks again for coming over on the spur of the moment."

"You and Kate would have done it for me. That's what friends are for."

Silence ensued again as we racked our brains. I finally got up and went inside the motor home and locked the door. I tried to put myself in the frame of mind that I had to get out but couldn't use the door. I started in the front of the coach and worked my way all the way to the back, checking every window, every seal, everything. No luck.

Walking back out the door, Kate said, "There has to be a way. There just has to be. That girl, or I guess I should say woman, couldn't have locked herself in. And how did she get inside in the first place?"

Just as Kate finished speaking, we heard a car coming. It turned out to be Gary and not another camper or ranger looking to meet us. We were probably not real popular right now with the locals. At least the media hadn't found out where we were—yet.

"Hello, everyone."

"Hey, Gary," I replied.

"Well, I have some interesting news for you all. Let's start with the cause of death of one Sally Klein."

"Before you tell us that, can you tell us anything about her?" Kate asked. "Like who the heck she was and why she would be in our motor home?"

"I can answer the first, but not the second question. Sally Klein went missing about two weeks ago in Billings. She disappeared without a trace. Seems she liked to frequent a couple taverns, not a drunk I am told, but liked to flirt with the gents and play some pool. Sounded like a relatively typical life for the most part. Just a fun-loving girl. When she didn't come home one night, her room-mates assumed she had...uh, gotten lucky. But when she didn't show up the second night, something Ms. Klein had never done, they got a little nervous, so they called her place of employment. She had not shown up for work, but since she was just a motel maid, the manager just had another maid do her rooms up, figuring Sally would show up the next day. The roommates called the cops in Billings and reported her missing."

When he paused, I took the opportunity to offer him a beer. He said he would love a beer, so I got him one, along with another for myself and one for Kate. Butch and Killer were snoring softly, so I didn't bother to wake either of them to inquire as to whether or not they wanted a beer. Butch had to be really out of it to miss Gary's dissertation on one Sally Klein. I let him sleep. He needed it, and we would need him more later on, I assumed.

I handed Gary his beer; he took a long pull and then continued, "The Billings police did the normal things that police do when a person goes missing. Put out an All Points, talked to coworkers, the gents at the tavern, and so on. The came up with no clues as to her disappearance. It is still, or should I say was, and active case until her body was found here."

"We never met her, have never been to Billings. This continues to get stranger and stranger," Kate said, shaking her head.

"It does get even a bit more interesting when we talk about cause of death."

"How so? Go on please."

311

"Sally appears to have been first knocked unconscious by a blow to her left temple. It wasn't enough in and of itself to kill her. But then the killer, and part of this is only speculation, you will understand why, in a minute, he pinched her nose shut and pinched her windpipe and suffocated her. There was no struggle, so the killer didn't have to wrap their hands around her neck like you might imagine in a—how should I put it?—*normal* murder by suffocation. Therefore, there were no bruises on her neck like you might expect. There was a bruise on either side of her windpipe and on both sides of her nose. Best the coroner can figure that is how she died."

"How awful," Kate said with a visible shutter.

"Wait, there's more. It seems that when the coroner was preforming the autopsy, he ran into something he had seen only once before when a man had gotten lost up here in the park and wasn't found for several days. It happened in late October when the temperature up here, as I understand it, never gets above freezing in most places. You see, what I am trying to tell you is, her internal organs were frozen. More or less solid. Sally Klein had been in a deep freeze before she ended up in your motor home."

CHAPTER TWELVE

K ate and I were stunned by this revelation. She had been frozen. That is why it had looked and felt a bit like she had taken a shower. She was thawing out. Yuck.

"The good news for you is, unless you have a freezer that would accommodate a body *and* they can prove you were in Billings two weeks ago, you are home free, Jim."

"What day exactly did she disappear? Do you know for certain?" Kate asked. "We got here, let's see, six days ago. That would have been the…What day is it, Jim?"

I looked at my calendar watch and did the math. "We got here on the fifth of June. That would have been last Tuesday. We planned our trip to beat the kids getting out of school and the campground being packed."

Gary replied, "Sally went missing on the first or second, best they can figure. Do you know where you were on the first and second?"

Kate and I looked at each other and burst out laughing. I was indeed off the hook.

"Yes," Kate said. "We were in New York being viewed by what I am told is the largest morning audience on television. We were on *Good Morning America* on the second. They flew us back the first—nonstop flight from Seattle to New York. We told them we could do it only if we could fly in the day before and leave the same day the show was on because we were leaving on our vacation. That was the reason they had us back. Kind of a 'here is what the young detectives are doing with their lives' type of show."

I took a huge breath and let it out slowly. No way was I going to be convicted of this crime. But I still wanted to know who did it and why.

Gary finished his beer in one long bottle tipping. "I am going to head back into town and see if I can catch the prosecutor before he leaves for the day. Maybe I can make this go away and get home first thing in the morning."

"Gary," I said, standing and holding out my hand, "thank you. I appreciate all you have done and are continuing to do. Really, thank you."

"My pleasure. If I can get the charges dropped tonight, I will stop back. If not, I will go into town again first thing in the morning and then let you know the outcome. Kate, goodbye for now." He looked at Butch and Killer and just smiled, then turned and walked away.

I walked over, bent down, and gave Kate a big kiss. It felt good to know I was not going back to jail.

"Jim, why would someone try to frame us for murder?"

"Jealous people maybe. People who get it into their heads 'why can't that be me on television? Why can't I catch a break and make a million bucks all at once?' Those types of people might go to any length to make my life and your life miserable just so they can look at us and smile and know they ruined our lives. Sick people, Kate, sick people."

I sat back down in the lawn chair, grabbed the chips, and set the bag on my lap so I could get one hand in the bag while my other was busy holding my beer. Kate was exceptionally quiet, all things considered.

"Jim, whoever did this is still out there. They might try something again. We have to figure it out. We do."

I walked Kate to the door, put her inside, woke Butch up, and asked if he wanted to sleep here. He said no, so he climbed into his truck, started it up, backed up, and drove off. Killer was happy to be back inside with the both of us. I locked the door and then double-checked it and turned out the lights. Time for some real sleep.

CHAPTER THIRTEEN

W aking up to the sound of raindrops on the roof, I slowly rolled over to see if Kate was awake yet. She was not. I eased out of bed in an attempt to not wake her, grabbed my clothes, and exited, shutting the bedroom door behind me. Killer stood and wagged his tail. He knew two things were going to happen—he was going to get fed and he was going to get out. He enjoyed both.

I opened the motor home door, and Killer shot past me, taking a jump to the ground without hitting a step. Poor guy was probably thinking he would be stuck inside again today. Although he was right, it would not be for as long as it had been yesterday. Kate and I had talked before nodding off last night about the plans for the day today. We intended to spend most of our time trying to solve this crime and were going to do so just as if we were at home in our backyard office. Our office was two lawn chairs that we sat in every night after work and had become our go-to place while trying to solve the Walker and Frank murders.

Being as quiet as I could, I made a pot of coffee and poured a bowl of food for Killer. A 120-pound dog that was part wolf ate a lot of food. Lucky our motor home had plenty of storage underneath. Once the coffee was done, I poured myself a cup and grabbed Killer's bowl and headed outside. The awning on the motor home kept me dry from the rain although, in actuality, it had turned into nothing more than a light drizzle now, and I could see breaks in the clouds. Maybe it would turn out to be a nice day after all.

When Killer saw his bowl, he came running up from the edge of the lake where he had been exploring and probably leaving his mark on things. He was such a good dog, never venturing away from the motor home too far. Loyal, smart, and protective, he treated Kate and me just as he had the owner before us, who was now in jail for the rest of his life due to our investigation.

Setting the bowl on a flat spot, Killer waited patiently until I told him okay, and then he attacked his food like it was a two-inch-thick steak. Big dog, big appetite.

I sat down in a lawn chair with my coffee, realizing so much had happened in the past few days that I hadn't stopped to realize how lucky I was to have friends like Butch and a wife like Kate, as well as a loyal dog. Freedom, after being in jail, made me take stock of all these things, and I smiled. I was so glad to be out of a cage and sitting here by the lake.

Once Killer had devoured his breakfast, he came over and nudged my arm, spilling my coffee a bit. "What, Killer?"

I knew what. Killer always came and said thank you in his own way, usually nudging an arm or laying his head on our leg. It was his way of acknowledging that he knew we loved him and took care of him, and he wanted to reciprocate showing his affection toward us.

The motor home door opened and my beautiful wife was standing in the doorway with a cup of coffee.

"Need more coffee?"

"Yes please. Killer decided to try to empty my cup with his big nose just a minute ago."

Kate came out with the pot in one hand and her cup in the other. She poured me a cup, set hers down, and took the pot back inside. As she returned, she inquired as to the time.

"It is…8:27 to be precise." We had both slept deep and well. Or maybe just as deep as a well. We had needed it, both of us.

"I wonder what time Butch will be here. He said he would come out and try to help us with the case. He was pretty tired too though. I don't expect him anytime soon."

We sat for a few minutes in silence. The clouds were clearing out, and there was more blue than gray now. The sounds of other campers starting campfires, chatting, and going about their day filled the morning air. What a great place this was. No wonder it is so busy in the summer months. Kids loved it, parents loved it, and even dogs loved it, I thought as I looked at Killer who was lying between Kate and me with his head erect, staring out at the lake.

"Are you going to shower?" Kate asked.

"Well, I hadn't thought about it, but yeah, probably." The image of Sally Klein came into my head. I had to put that behind us or sell the motor home. We had to be able to get by this and shower in our own travelling home.

"Matter of fact, I think I will do that right now." I had to set an example for Kate so that she would know it was okay to try to move on.

Going inside, I picked out a fresh pair of jeans, a clean Seahawks T-shirt, and some socks and underwear. Doing this slowly, as if I was getting ready for a big date or a state dinner, I realized I was doing so to avoid actually getting in the shower. *Come on, dude*, I told myself, *you got this*.

And I did. I took a long hot shower, and once I had started the water, the image of Sally Klein evaporated like mist in the morning. It felt great to wash the stench, real or imagined, of the jail off my body. I got out, dressed, and poured myself another cup of coffee.

"You ready for some more coffee, darlin'?"

"Yes, sir." I poured Kate a cup and took the pot back inside. Kate never asked me about the shower, so I brought it up.

"Man, that felt great. I can't believe they can build so much stuff into these motor homes, including a really great shower."

Kate took the hint. "Okay, okay. I will go shower too."

When Kate got out of the shower and came outside, the temperature had risen to the upper fifties. It was indeed going to be a beautiful day.

"Know what, you're right. That shower felt awesome." Good. The shower stigma was behind us.

We sat and just chatted about this and that until, finally, Kate said we should start thinking about the case again. We had learned so much from Gary last night about Sally that we started there.

"So she was from Billings."

"And had been killed, it appears, while we were in New York."

"And then frozen," I stated. "Then put in our shower somehow."

"There are two big questions," Kate said. "Who and why? What possible motive could there be to put that poor woman in *our* shower?"

Just as the words came out of her mouth, we heard the unmistakable sound of Butch's truck coming through the park. Funny how vehicles have a distinct sound, almost like a person's voice. I looked at my watch; it was ten thirty. Butch had slept in. Good for him.

"Morning, all!" Butch exclaimed as he climbed out of the cab. Killer got up and ran over with his tail wagging to greet his sleeping buddy from the previous evening. Butch gave him a pat on the head, and Killer led him back to us.

"Coffee, Butch?" Kate asked.

"Sure. Then I need you two to take a hike. Literally."

"What's up?"

"No questions. I want you to go on a hike, just like the day the body was deposited in the motor home. Doesn't have to be nearly as long. I know my hunting partner wouldn't like that much," he said with a smile. "But at least be gone, say, an hour."

Without being able to ask any questions about Butch's request, we decided to go immediately. We grabbed Kill's leash and a soda bottle filled with water and headed out, checking and locking the motor home just as we had done that fateful day.

"See you in an hour," Butch said. "No sooner."

As we walked away, Kate looked at me and said, "What is this about do you think?"

"No clue."

We decided to take the Trail of the Cedars. It was about a mile long, and if we strolled to the trailhead and then took our time on the trail itself, we could make it take an hour.

The Trail of the Cedars was just what it sounded like—a trail that wound through some gigantic cedars that were probably here when George Washington was president. It was cooler in the trees, and I wished I had dressed more appropriately. But Butch had wanted us to leave so fast we had taken off without thinking about such things.

"Wonder why Butch seemed almost giddy when he got here this morning. He had more than his normal amount of energy. Did you notice?" Kate inquired of me.

"I did. He was excited about something. It's been forty-five minutes. Let's head back. Time we get there it will have been more than an hour."

We beat our feet back to the campsite. Butch was nowhere to be seen.

"Now where did he go? His truck's still here."

Suddenly the door of the motor home opened up, and Butch was standing, holding a cup of coffee in the doorway.

"Welcome back!"

CHAPTER FOURTEEN

"The last thing I remembered before falling asleep out here last night was you two talking about how someone could get into a locked motor home. I thought about it driving back to the lodge, and so when I got there, I asked the desk clerk if there was an RV sales office in Kalispell. She said she would look in the phone book and meet me after her shift ended at ten. I was tired, but since it was only a half hour, I went into the lounge and had a beer and waited for her."

"Was it Nancy from New Hampshire or Janene from Montana?" Kate asked.

"How did you know her name? It was Janene," Butch responded.

"I notice things like that. She's a cutie."

"Yes, she is. She told me there was an RV place and gave me the address and directions. After that, we had a beer and got to know each other a bit. She wanted to know if I was buying a motor home or trailer, where I was from, why I was here. Really inquisitive. Probably doesn't get to meet a whole lot of people our age. The lounge was full of the Geritol gang. Not one person within likely twenty-plus years of us."

Kate and I both laughed at that one.

"So anyway, I got up early and drove to Kalispell. Looked at some motor homes as similar to yours as I could find. Then I asked the salesman what would happen if you somehow got locked out, like you lost your keys or something. He had said 'no problem' and showed me that if you went into the basement storage, you guys know that is the storage on the outside, right?"

We nodded.

"You need only a screwdriver to get past the locks. They are pretty easy to turn without a key. Then you climb in. You have underbed storage. Once inside the basement storage, you take your screwdriver and loosen about twenty screws that hold the floor of the underbed storage in place, and the whole floor drops down. Thank goodness you guys didn't have much in your underbed storage. It was easy to let the floor down slowly, reach up, and push the bed on its hinges so that I could squeeze through. And it was a squeeze. I am 6-1 and 180 pounds. Anyone any bigger couldn't have done it. Once inside, I went out through the door and climbed back in the basement storage and put the floor back in place and screwed it in tight, climbed out, and shut the lock with the screwdriver. Of course, whoever put the body inside would have had to go back the way they came in, from under the bed, and then climb back out through the basement storage so they could leave the door to the motor home locked after putting the body in the shower, then crawl out and disappear, leaving no trace they had been inside."

We all looked at each other without saying a word. Butch had found the answer to the first question Kate and I had had the night before. Gary had supplied many of the answers, if not all of them, for the second one about who Sally Klein was.

"Okay, so now we are back to the two big questions, who and why?"

"Anyone for a beer?" I asked.

"I think I will take you up on the offer this time," replied Butch.

"Make it three then," Kate added.

I am not sure what it is about sitting sipping a beer. It just helps me think better for some reason. After getting everyone their drinks, we all sat outside, and although our outward appearance to anyone walking by would have been three people relaxing in the sun, we were all keyed up pretty well. Kate had mentioned what if the person who had done this decided to try again. We really had to come up with something.

Another car pulled up. It was Gary.

"Afternoon, folks."

"Hey, Gary, what did you find out in Kalispell?" I inquired.

"Well, it seems the prosecutor hadn't been given all the facts from the sheriff on where Sally Klein had come from, and he knew nothing about her being frozen. Not too happy a camper when I left, but the good news is, they have dropped all charges and wanted me to apologize to you for any inconvenience it may have caused you."

A sort of cheer went up from the three of us. Killer turned his head first one way, then the other as if he were trying to drain water out of his ears. Seeing this, I started laughing and got up and gave him a good petting. He really is a great dog.

"It looks like you have to sit here and drink beer, detective boy. No more jail for you," Kate said, grinning.

"I can handle that, trust me. Much easier than I could have handled going back into that cage."

"Gee, I thought you looked pretty natural sitting in that cage," Butch joked.

"Very funny, Butch."

Kate strolled in and grabbed a beer for Gary while Butch explained what he had found out about being able to get in and out of the motor home while it was locked. Gary had taken a seat at the picnic table and was listening intently.

"That is incredible. Great police work, Butch. If only Sheriff Haskins and his minions had done their job as well, Jim may have never been in jail at all, possibly."

"You really can't blame them," I said. "They had what appeared to be, on the surface at least, a decent case. I absolutely agree they should have dug more, but it is all in the past now."

"Except trying to figure out who would kill that poor woman and why they would put the body in your home," Butch interjected.

"Indeed, Jim. Someone appears to want you in prison. What enemies have you made?"

As funny as it sounds, I hadn't thought about it from the enemy standpoint. One might think that would be the first order of business, but with having been incarcerated, gone to court, gotten out on bail, and then finally gotten home, I had a good deal on my mind. The word *enemy* hadn't crossed my mind.

"Gary, Kate, and I solved a couple murders last year, as you know. But the folks who perpetrated the crimes are all in jail. At least I think they still are. Butch?"

"Oh, they are. They will all be there for a very long time."

"So who else might there be?" Gary asked. "Perhaps from your other profession, anything there?"

"I don't think so. We go out of our way at the jewelry store to take good care of people. Of course, there is always that one customer who thinks they were mistreated, but to kill someone over that? I doubt it."

"I still think it is a crime of jealousy. Someone who is upset they haven't had the charmed life you have—getting paid big bucks for solving one crime, being able to take time off, and travel. That sort of thing," Butch added.

"You could be on to something there, Butch," Gary said. "Perceived injustices is what we call it as lawyers. Someone thinks they should be the blessed one, and it eats at them until they explode."

We all sat around staring at one another for a few minutes. Killer was still between Kate and me on the ground. Boy, talk about a dog's life. Gets fed, gets to sleep all day. Ah, just what Gary had been talking about. Perceived injustice. I had a pretty good life, and I was jealous of the dog.

Gary announced he had gotten a flight home to Helena and had to leave. We got his card and gave him our address so we could send his compensation for duties performed, telling him it might be awhile until he got our check since we had no idea when we would be home to get our mail. He assured us he wouldn't starve waiting for it. We thanked him several times for his work and said our goodbyes, and he drove off.

"Nice man," Butch said.

"Yes, truly. Where do people get off lumping all attorneys, or any group of people for that matter, into categories? Not all attorneys are bad people. I am sure the ones everyone calls ambulance chasers are decent people deep down. At least as much as anyone else is.

There are good people and there are bad people regardless of their professions," Kate said.

"I couldn't agree more, darlin'," I said. "As the Bible says, 'Judge not lest ye be judged.'"

Kate made dinner for us all, and after eating, Butch said he had to get back and really get some sleep tonight.

"Oh, no dates tonight?" Kate chided.

"I have a date with my pillow. That's it for tonight."

Butch got out of his chair and walked over to Kate and me. We thought he was going to say good night to us, but instead, he squatted down and patted Killer on the head.

"Good night, Killer. Take good care of my friends here."

Killer licked his hand and fell back to sleep. It really is a dog's life.

CHAPTER FIFTEEN

L ying in bed the next morning, listening to Kate's slow, rhythmic breathing, I knew she was still sound asleep. I inched my way out of bed and, once again, grabbed my clothes and exited to dress.

Killer greeted me with a wagging tail, knowing it was time to go outside and then to eat. He was exceptionally exuberant. I told him to chill as I finished getting my clothes on. Standing right behind me as I opened the door, readying himself like a race horse in the gate, he whined like maybe he really had to go. As I opened the door, things happened very quickly.

Killer weighs 120 pounds. I weigh, well, let's just say more than that. But he was so revved up that as the door opened and he made his move to get outside, he bumped me hard on one leg. So hard, in fact, I lost my balance and started to fall to the floor. Just as I muttered "Dang it, Killer," two things happened. First I landed hard on my butt. Second, I heard a gunshot and then the sound of glass breaking.

Having been shot at, and hit actually, on a previous case, I knew that someone had taken a shot at me from somewhere outside the motor home. I heard Kate cry out, "What was that?"

"Get on the floor behind the bed. Someone just took a shot at me." Kate reacted quickly as I heard her hit the floor in record time.

That was when I heard a vehicle throwing gravel as it tore out of the campground. We were safe. For now.

"I think they're gone, Kate. Stay put till I check."

I crawled on the floor to the front of the motor home and retrieved the gun that had become a daily part of my life in a previous case. It was a 44 magnum. Although I knew it was loaded, I checked again. I was not about to go outside with an empty gun even though I was fairly certain all was clear.

Crawling to the door, or more slithering like a snake, I peeked out the door. Killer was nowhere to be seen. Inching my way forward, I finally took the chance to expose myself and stood up. No one shot at me, so gun in hand, I exited into the daylight outside.

I spotted Killer down by the lake. He was sniffing the ground like he was hot on the trail. Assuming that was where the shot had come from, I cautiously walked that direction while keeping an eye all around to movement. Being a hunter has its advantages. I knew that movement meant something was there to be seen. There was no sign of anything moving about except Killer.

Killer had stopped moving, and when he saw me, he barked and wagged his tail while remaining in the same spot. Normally he would run up to me. He had something.

As I approached, his tail was going a mile a minute. He was standing over something he wanted me to see. It was a shell casing. Whoever had shot at me was either not smart enough to realize you don't leave brass behind when you try to shoot someone or figured they had better get out of the campground while the getting was good. Either way, we had some real evidence that someone was trying to kill me.

Kate hollered from inside, asking me if it was okay to come out. I responded it was and told her to bring me a small bag. She was at my side in about thirty seconds holding a baggie.

"Will this do?"

"Perfectly." Using a twig, I inserted it into the end of the shell casing, being careful not to touch it with my fingers, and plopped it into the bag. Then I sealed it. Clean, good, hard evidence. The casing was from a .30-30 caliber rifle. Good gun. Lightweight and accurate in the right hands. I am sure that had Killer not knocked me down, I would be dead or dying now.

We went back to the motor home. I recalled that there had been the sound of breaking glass after the shot whizzed over my head. Yup, broken window on the opposite side of the motor home from the doorway.

"Dang it!" Kate said vehemently. "Now we have to get the window replaced. I hope they can do it in town at the place Butch found." Then she realized it could have been much worse. "Oh, Jim, I am so glad you are okay," she said with tears forming in her eyes.

"I'm fine." I took the pistol from the small of my back, inside by belt and pants where I had put it when I was picking up the casing, and stashed it back in its hiding spot in the side pouch of the driver's seat.

"What do we do now?"

"We wait for Butch to get here. It's eight thirty. My guess is he will be here by nine, knowing Butch."

Kate went about making coffee while I found a role of duct tape I had put in the basement storage. I wanted to try to keep the window in place at least until we could get it replaced. When I had finished and the window looked like it might hold, the coffee was done, so Kate and I went outside to drink it and try to regroup a bit.

"Should you take your gun outside?"

"Probably not a good idea since you are not supposed to have guns in the park."

"Well, it sure didn't stop whoever shot at you!"

"Kate, they're gone. I heard a car or truck pull out fast right after the shot. Hey, maybe someone in the campground saw them tearing out of here. We should ask around."

"Good idea. After I quit shaking and have had some more coffee," Kate replied.

Finishing our first cup, we heard Butch's truck making its way toward us. Kate rose and took our cups to refill and, I was pretty sure, to grab one for Butch.

"Morning."

"Morning."

Killer said his hellos to Butch as he walked over to where I was sitting.

"What's new?"

"Oh, not too much. I got shot at about a half hour ago or so. Other than that, it's been a quiet morning."

"Shot at! You have to be kidding me!"

"If only I were, my friend, if only I were."

"What happened? They missed obviously."

Regaling him with the tale of the morning, Butch sat staring into my eyes. I told him about Killer finding the shell casing and how I had handled it.

"Great. Maybe there will be a print or two on it. We need to get it to the sheriff's office."

"Not before I have had a little more coffee." I had already finished the cup Kate had brought back out for me and got up to get the pot to refill everyone again.

"Did you get some sleep last night?" I asked Butch.

"Yes and no. When I got back, Janene saw me and said she would like to get a beer and asked if I would join her. So being a gentleman, I escorted her to the lounge, and we sat and chatted and drank a couple before I hit the sack."

"Ah. Sounds like someone likes you."

"Yeah, I thought so too until I realized she was wearing a ring on her hand. Maybe it is the kind women wear to keep guys from hitting on them. I never asked. I figured I would figure it out on my own soon enough."

"You said yesterday she was inquisitive. Was she still last night?"

"Not as much as the night before, but she did ask about you two. She remembered seeing Kate when she made my reservation."

"What sort of things did she ask about us?" Kate inquired.

"Oh, the usual—where were you from, how did we all meet, that sort of thing. Nothing too deep. More like just chitchat."

"Why does her name sound so familiar? I swear we have heard it before, but I just can't place it," I said.

"I don't ever recall hearing that name, at least not recently. It isn't at all an uncommon name. You could have heard it and just subconsciously remembered it," Kate said.

"No, it's funny Jim said that. I felt like I knew the name too. Maybe when we head to town we stop and have breakfast at the lodge, call the sheriff, and report the shooting and see if he wants you two to stay and have me run the shell casing in, or all of us stay and he send someone to pick it up. At the same time, let's see if Janene is working, and just chat her up a little. Maybe it will jog our memories. I think she said she started at eleven. We can make it easily by ten thirty."

"Sounds like a plan. I'm hungry now. Should we head out?" Kate asked.

As soon as we all finished our coffee and Killer had been locked inside, we got in Butch's truck for the short ride to the lodge. Once we arrived, things got *really* interesting.

CHAPTER SIXTEEN

Parking in the lot was getting more difficult each day. People flock to this park in summer, and it appeared that it was starting to happen. Butch finally found a spot as someone was pulling out and nosed his truck in.

As we walked in the front door, Butch in the lead, with Kate and me side by side behind him, Kate spotted Janene coming from the area of the restaurant heading toward the front desk.

"There she is," she said, perhaps a bit too loud because Janene immediately looked our way and stopped in front of the glass doors that looked down toward the lake.

"Good morning," Butch said to her. "Do you have a minute to talk to us?"

"Uh, sure. Just give me a minute. Why don't you go sit down by the fire and I will be right there?"

When she said this, like lemmings, we all turned toward the fire. As we did, she bolted out the doors to the lake. We all stood like statues as we watched her run down the thirty or more stairs, taking them two at a time. What she did next was even more bizarre. She ran out onto the dock, pushed an elderly fisherman into the water that was just trying to get into a boat, jumped in, and pushed off.

At this point, we all become fluid again, Butch leading the way as we all ran down the steps toward the floundering old man in the water. Janene started the outboard motor on the boat, turned it up full, and by the time we reached the dock, she was disappearing around the point, heading toward Apgar, the hotel at the western-most point on the lake.

Butch jumped into the water without hesitation, told the man to relax, and dragged him to the dock. Kate and I helped him up and inquired as to his health.

"I'm fine, but someone stole my boat and all my tackle!"

"I'm sure you will get it all back. She isn't a thief. A potential murderer, but not a thief," I replied.

"Murderer? What are you talking about," the old man asked.

"Sorry, it will have to wait. Too long of a story for now."

I helped Butch climb onto the dock. He looked like a drowned rat, as the saying goes.

"What just happened?" was all he could say. What else was there to say?

"My guess? We just found out who took a shot at me this morning."

"Why would she take a shot at you though? None of this makes any sense," Kate replied.

"I think I might know," said Butch.

"Spill it, man!" I almost hollered at him. "We need to take off after her."

"That won't do any good, Jim. This is a big park, and although the road seems to parallel the lake, she could cut across, ditch the boat, and disappear anywhere she wants to. But I will enlighten you. I think I remember where I have heard the name before. If I'm right, you two will remember too."

"When we were working the Frank case, we honed in on two people, remember?"

"Sure, Randy and Jane Tucker."

"And do you happen to recall when I was telling you about how Randy came to own the gas station, I mentioned the rest of his family? He had a sister who lived in—"

"Billings, Montana," Kate finished the sentence. "Her name was Janene. Oh my gosh, she was trying to set us up for murder to send us to jail! When that didn't work, she tried to kill you, Jim! She was vengeful, not jealous like we kept thinking the person was who did all this."

"None of us remembered her because she was not a part of the investigation. Just a sidenote," I said.

"Kate, I think you are dead-on," replied Butch. "She wanted to see you suffer for sending her brother and sister to prison for life. When the first plan failed, then she tried plan B."

"Yup, and she was small enough to crawl easily into the basement storage and then gain entry the same way you did. You said it was tight for you. It would have been easy for her," I added.

The old man had heard all this as he stood dripping on the dock. "I guess I am lucky she only stole my boat."

We had all basically forgotten about him. When he spoke, we had all almost jumped out of our skin.

"Sorry, didn't mean to startle you. I think I better head in and change my clothes and call the cops," he said.

"Actually, I should too. Do both of those things," Butch said while he too dripped on the dock.

Reentering the lodge, Kate and I headed for the fire. We had not been in the lake, but in the process of pulling two men out, both of us had gotten our share of wet. We both stood close to the flames to try to dry our clothes while Butch headed up to his room.

Butch came back down in ten minutes or so, and Kate and I were no longer wet. Damp maybe, but not wet.

"I called the sheriff's office from my room. Haskins said to go back to the motor home and he would send someone to pick up the shell casing and get our statements. He is informing the rangers to be on the lookout for Janene Tucker."

"Great. No we head back without even a chance for breakfast," I said in my best whiny voice.

"Really? You can think about food now?" Kate said incredulously.

"Darlin', I can think about food and drink just about any time," I replied.

Butch chuckled, and Kate gave me one of her fantastic laughs. We walked out the door and headed to Butch's truck.

CHAPTER SEVENTEEN

The motor home looked big as we pulled in behind it. How did I even drive this thing? I am not a bad driver, but it is thirty-two feet long and is more bus than car or truck. The front wheels are actually under and slightly behind the driver's seat. I had told Kate I felt like Jackie Gleason's character Ralph Kramden who drove a bus for a living. I was getting about as big as Mr. Gleason too. I had to go on a diet when this was all over. But not right now. I was famished.

I threw Kate the keys, and she opened the house up and let Killer out. He romped around, wagging his tail and saying hello to everyone in his own way. Then he headed off to explore. We knew he wouldn't go far, so we never worried much about him.

"You guys want breakfast or lunch?"

Although I had been craving hash browns and eggs, I knew they would take longer than a sandwich. Did I say I was famished?

"A sandwich and some chips would be just fine with me. If you add a beer too," I said with a smile.

"Works for me," Butch added.

Kate went inside to go to work on the sandwiches, but not before bringing out a couple of colds ones for Butch and me. I loved this woman dearly.

In short order, out she came again with a tray of sandwiches of different types—peanut butter and jelly, lunch meat and cheese with onion and tomato, and tuna fish. The bag of chips hung below the tray being held in place by a couple fingers as it dangled down.

"How in the heck did you do that so fast?"

"Shoot, it was not a big deal. Cut, slice, and mix, then slap it all on bread. Nothing to it."

I took the chips from Kate and opened the bag up and set it gently on the picnic table. No one likes broken-up chips. Kate set the sandwiches down and produced napkins from her pocket.

"Anyone need another beer?"

"My turn, darlin'. You have done plenty," I said, hustling into the house to grab three beers for us to wash down the amazing sandwiches Kate had made.

We all devoured the sandwiches and drank our beer and waited for the sheriff's deputy or whoever he was sending up to show up to pick up the shell casing.

"Quite a morning. Let me recap. I get shot at, find real evidence, well, Killer actually found it, repair a broken window as best I could, drive to the lodge to talk to the person we assume now shot at me, and she runs down and knocks an old guy into the drink and steals his boat. Pretty much it?"

Butch laughed and replied, "Really condensed version, but yes, I think you hit the high points."

Enjoying the day seemed more special now. Maybe it was because I had lived through the morning. It could have been a whole lot worse. As we were discussing what our next move would be after the shell casing was finally picked up, we heard a vehicle approaching.

A cruiser pulled up, and a deputy got out and walked over to us.

"Hello, Deputy Johnson," Kate said. "Good to see you again." Then she turned to Butch and me and explained, "Deputy Johnson ran me back up here the night you were in jail."

"Sounds like you folks have had an interesting morning. Your afternoon is going to be more memorable." As he let those words fly, he pulled out his service revolver and pointed it at us.

"What's going on?" Butch asked.

"Well, see, it's like this. You, Mr. Tuttle, were supposed to be in jail, hopefully for the rest of your life for murdering Sally Klein. When that didn't happen, we had to go to an alternate plan."

"We?"

"Yes, we. You see, this was to be payback for putting my brother and sister-in-law in prison."

It was all starting to make sense. Sort of.

"Are you telling me you are related to Randy and Jane Tucker?"

"They are relatives by marriage."

The final piece went into place. "You are married to Janene Tucker?"

"Janene Johnson is her name now. That is why it took so long for me to get up here. You see, when she stole the boat, she went straight to Apgar Village and used a pay phone to call the office. She told the deputy she had taken ill and asked if I could come pick her up." Then he craned his head to the side without taking his eyes off us. "Honey, come on out."

Lo and behold, Janene sat up from what must have been a lying-down position in the front seat of the cruiser. She exited and walked toward us.

"Hello, Butch. Good to see you again."

If looks could kill, Janene Johnson would be dead. I have never seen Butch so mad. He turned red as a beet. He was holding himself back, showing great restraint since he had a gun pointed at him, but I could see he was tensed and flexed up just looking at him. His eyes bore a hole into Janene Johnson's head.

"Wish I could say the same," he finally said with venom in his voice.

"What now?" I asked.

"We are all going to take a little ride. There is going to be a tragic hiking accident this afternoon up near the pass."

I knew he was talking about Logan Pass, the highest pass in the park at over 6,600 feet. It also marked the Continental Divide. The road we had heard was treacherous, and they didn't allow motor homes over twenty-one feet. We had resigned ourselves to not being able to see it unless we took one of the buses up there.

"So what, you are going to kill us? Why? Randy and Jane got what they deserved. We just helped pull together the evidence."

"My sister and brother would have been fine if you had let Mr. Frank take the heat for the murder of his sister. Instead, you got involved, figured out what they had done, and now they will rot in prison for the rest of their lives. I didn't like that idea much."

"Your plan wasn't really well-thought-out either. You have to know that the authorities would figure it out sooner rather than later," I replied.

"The idea was to make sure you stayed in the area long enough for us to get a shot at you. I missed. Now we move to a plan that will work—for certain."

"What about Sally Klein? Why kill her?"

"She was a means to an end. I was trying to figure out how to get to you when I saw that you were coming to me on *Good Morning America*. I worked the front desk at the hotel Sally was a maid at. She was a loser. No one would miss her if she was gone. So that night, I told her I would give her a ride home."

"Then you hit her in the head and strangled her." This came from Kate.

"Yes, to put it simply. I had already been hired by the lodge. Originally, I figured I would work at Glacier for a year and transfer to Mount Rainier National Park. That would get me right in your backyard."

She was right. We could actually see Mount Rainier as soon as we hit the main road after we left our housing development.

"Then like it was a sign, you decide to take this thing"—pointing at the motor home with a thumb over the shoulder—"and come right to me. I stuck Sally in my freezer, rented a truck for all my stuff, and got some help loading it. Dale," she pointed this time to the deputy, "was already over here. It worked out perfectly."

"Except it didn't work out at all," I replied.

"Once we saw your motor home, Dale went to the dealership in Kalispell, and they told him how he could get inside without a key. He went in uniform and told them he was doing an investigation. They were more than nice enough to show him exactly how to do it."

"Then it was just a matter of time. I was watching the motor home when you all left for your hike that day. I drove down to McDonald Lodge and used the phone to call Dale. He ran home in his cruiser and loaded up Sally and drove to the lodge to pick me up."

"I was so stupid. I should have caught it," Kate stuttered.

"What are you talking about, Kate?" I asked.

"Everyone who comes up here looking for us gets lost. Butch, the sheriff, everyone. When Deputy Johnson brought me back up that night, he drove straight here. No missed turns. I was still in a state of shock, so I guess since he made the turns, I didn't have to tell him. I should have caught it."

"Kate, you were under a lot of stress. Not your fault."

"Story time is over. Since you know it all now, it's time to take one final ride," Deputy Johnson said with a very straight face. "And Mr. Tuttle and Deputy Danforth, I know you would do anything to save Mrs. Tuttle, just like I would do anything for my wife here. But so much as a twitch and I will shoot you all and say you attacked me. I have a witness right here with me," he said, motioning to his wife. "Now stand up. Which of you has the keys to the pickup?"

"I do," Butch spit out.

"Kindly throw them gently to my wife. Honey, you can drive the truck. We will put all three in the cruiser and head toward Logan Pass. I will turn off and you follow me up when I turn off the main road."

"Got it," Janene replied.

"Now very slowly, all of you get out of your chairs. Put your hands on your heads. Again, not a flinch. Then slowly walk toward the cruiser."

We did as we were told. Johnson was no slouch. He kept back about fifteen feet. Butch had told me once that if you have a gun and someone has a knife, if they get within twelve feet, shoot them. It was unofficially called the three-step rule. It meant that if a person with a knife was twelve feet away, they were only three steps from being on you. Evidently, at four steps you would have time to react and fire. At three, it was so close you actually had a better chance of missing. Johnson obviously knew this.

As we passed the back end of the motor home, with both Johnsons behind us, I saw a slight movement to the right in my peripheral vision. Being a hunter, I knew to not turn to look. That would spook the animal many times. In this case, I hoped what I saw was correct, but I didn't want to give the Johnsons any sort of a heads-up. The next thing happened so fast that none of us actually saw it happen, but since I knew it might, I was the first to react.

As Deputy Johnson's arm just got past the end of the motor home, while his body was still behind it, Killer made his move. He evidently jumped from a crouching position and in mid-flight, put his considerable mouth over the gun arm of the deputy, and then bit down. Hard.

When the deputy let out a yell, I turned, ran, and tackled him, with Killer still attached to his arm, and we all hit the ground. Butch was only seconds later, stepping on the wrist that somehow still held the gun and pinning it to the ground. He then relieved Deputy Johnson of his sidearm.

Throughout all this, Killer had kept his mouth clamped on Johnson's arm. He was screaming in pain. I got up and told Killer to release. For the first time since we had had Killer, he didn't respond. I said it again, and he finally let the arm go. It was gushing blood at a pretty good rate.

"Good boy, Kill."

"Okay, get up. Kate, you got any rope in the motor home?"

"Better yet, Kate, get the duct tape I had left over from trying to fix the window this morning. I left it on the shelf up front."

Butch said, "Get the cuffs off his belt. Cuff him, and we will use the duct tape on Mrs. Johnson. Better get your first aid kit out. We need to stop the bleeding so he doesn't die before he gets to go to trial and join the rest of his relatives for a nice, long stay in prison."

Kate brought out both the duct tape and our first aid kit. Butch knew me well enough that I didn't ever go anywhere without a first aid kit. I had cut my fingers badly hunting one time and had to use my T-shirt to staunch the flow of blood until I could get back to my truck. Now I was smart enough to carry a small one in my backpack.

Once we had stopped the flow of blood and tied up Janene with duct tape so she had no way to move her arms or hands, Butch walked over to the cruiser and started talking into the handheld microphone.

When he walked back over to us all, he said he had told the sheriff we had one of his deputies in cuffs and he better get up here. He said by putting it that way, the sheriff would double-time it, thinking maybe we were holding him hostage. We could explain it all, so Butch wasn't worried. Not in the least.

Epilogue

We were back home, sitting in our office—Kate in one lawn chair, yours truly sitting next to her with a small table between us—holding our ever-present beer. Both Johnsons were in jail, and I was actually happy to hear that Deputy Johnson wouldn't have any permanent damage to his arm. Evidently, Killer had bitten clear to the bone, so he had considerable pain and a couple surgeries to go through to repair some things in his arm, but he would be just perfect by the time he entered the State of Montana Penal System.

Butch had taken off a couple days later, but not until we drove up the Logan Pass. It was pretty amazing to be that high up and see the views of waterfalls, mountain goats, and bighorn sheep. We were really appreciative he insisted on taking us up. We had said our farewells, and he had left for home. We stayed in Kalispell long enough to get the window repaired. Then we headed for home. We had had enough of vacation. We had been home for a couple weeks, and things were getting back to normal. Killer lay snoring at our feet, and we just sat enjoying the summer day.

"Do you think we were wrong to sell the motor home?" Kate asked.

"Nope. Even though we kind of took a bath on it, I just think it was the right thing to do."

We had made the decision on the way home to sell the motor home. We liked to travel, but short trips could be just as enjoyable as long ones. Having paid nearly $100,000 of our money from the Frank case on it, it was a little depressing to find out motor homes were like cars. Once you drive them off the lot, they depreciate immediately. We had only gotten $80,000 when we sold it. A $20,000, 1,200-mile trip.

"I'm glad we went, all things considered. Glacier was beautiful."

"Indeed. We need to go back sometime. Take the truck, and Killer can sit between us."

Saying his name brought his head up slightly and opened his eyes.

"It's okay, Killer. You are a good boy." And he was. He had saved my life when Janene Johnson had shot at me and then again when her husband had a gun pointed at us all.

"So what now?" Kate asked. "Do we go back to work at our real jobs?"

"I suppose that is the right thing to do. Although we could take the summer off. We have the money, right?"

"Yes, we do. Maybe we could take a trip somewhere."

We both turned our heads and looked into each other's eyes, then burst out laughing.

Man, I loved her laugh.

PART FOUR

A Week to Forget

CHAPTER ONE

"I need your help."

Funny how you never think you will hear those words from certain people. I certainly never expected to hear them from attorney Robert Reynolds.

Robert didn't say, "I would like to hire you." In fact, those four words were all he said—*I need your help.* He wouldn't elaborate over the phone, and since my lovely wife and I were free this morning, as we have been since we solved the Frank murders, I told him we would be there shortly, knowing Kate would agree to go.

"Who called?" Kate said as she came into the kitchen from the bedroom.

"Robert. He needs our help."

"With what?"

"Wouldn't say. Care to take a drive downtown to see him?"

"Of course. Just let me have some coffee and we can go. Got to have my caffeine, you know."

"Boy, do I."

"Ha ha, detective boy. Very funny," Kate said, calling me by the nickname she had given me while working on the first case we had.

We sat outside in our backyard office and drank a cup of Joe and then hopped in my trusty Ford F-150 and headed to town. Robert's office was located on the waters of Puget Sound. A beautiful brick building that had to have cost a fortune to build. Robert and his staff occupied the entire building. Two stories. Robert was a very successful attorney.

Upon entering, we were not greeted by Robert's receptionist. She must have had to run an errand or something. We stood around for a minute or two, and then Robert himself came out from the hallway that leads to his office and conference rooms.

"Hello, Jim. Hello, Kate."

"Hi, Robert," Kate replied

"What's up? You were exceptionally vague on the phone."

"Come on back to my office," he said and turned his back on us and led the way down the hallway.

Robert's office was understated, with dark wood and law books on one entire wall. It had one wall of windows facing the water, and the one behind his back when he was at his desk housed his law school diploma, along with several pictures of Robert and dignitaries—the governor, state senators, and even a few sports stars—thrown in for good measure. On his desk were pictures of his wife and sons. Very Americana.

"Where's Nancy? She didn't greet us," I inquired.

"That is why you are here. Nancy has been arrested for the murder of her husband."

"I heard on the radio this morning while I was getting ready that a man had been shot. That was Nancy's husband?" Kate asked.

"Yes. And she did not kill him. Problem is, her fingerprints were on the murder weapon. She also stands to inherit her dead husband's estate, which is fairly sizable. He owned a construction company here in town."

"How are you so certain that she didn't kill him?" I asked.

"Witnesses heard a gunshot around seven last night. It is not possible because at seven last night, Nancy and I were at the Tyee Hotel. To make matters worse, Nancy was going to tell her husband she wanted a divorce."

CHAPTER TWO

"I assume you were not there on business." Saying this more as a statement than a question.

"No, we were not there on business," came Robert's reply.

Hearing that a man I had grown to like and admire was having an affair hurt me. What about his wife? His kids? How could he do such a despicable thing to them?

"Before you jump to too many conclusions and pass judgment on me, let me tell you some things that you may not know. It appears you may have already passed judgment."

You don't get to be a powerful attorney without being able to read a person. I had already passed judgment, and I could see by Kate's body language she had as well. She had crossed both her arms and her legs, and her lips were pursed.

"Go on," was all I could think to mutter.

"Without going into great detail, Nancy and I have worked together for three years and started meeting after work about two months ago. There was just a chemistry, if you will, between us." At that, he paused, walked to a table near the window, and poured a glass of water from a pitcher that sat on a wooden tray. "Can I get you a glass of water?"

Both of us shook our heads.

Robert returned to his leather chair behind his desk. "My wife and I have been married twenty-five years. We got married right after

I got my bachelor's degree and before I started law school. To say we were madly in love would be an understatement. Still are."

Kate looked out the corner of her eye at me, shaking her head slightly as if to say, "Yeah, right."

"Mary, that is my wife's name, was diagnosed with Parkinson's disease before I graduated from Yale with my law degree. She was only twenty-four."

I thought to myself that I had just turned twenty-five and Kate was now twenty-four. How would I feel if she suddenly was diagnosed with such a horrific disease? What would I do? I would like to think I wouldn't have an affair.

"Mary turns forty-seven in January, if she makes it. The Parkinson's is in its advance stages now. She was diagnosed with uterine cancer three months ago. Stage four. She refuses to take any sort of treatment. She is a strong-willed woman, always has been. Wants to go out naturally, as she calls it, rather than spend her last days sick from chemotherapy or the like. She will not be on earth much longer, I'm afraid. I have been a faithful, loyal husband for twenty-five years. Never had I even thought about having an affair with anyone over all those years. One evening, as I was leaving the office, Nancy invited me to have a cocktail and just talk. We went to the Tyee Hotel, knowing that the restaurant had a nice lounge. We sat and talked for an hour or so. She told me she was thinking of leaving her husband, that he didn't love her anymore, and the feeling was mutual. However, he never mentioned divorce because that would mean giving her half his company. He loved money more than her."

Robert took the rest of the water in his glass in one long drink, then continued, "I talked about how much I loved my wife and how I had cared for her during her illnesses. Nancy said she only wished her husband would be so kind. As they say, one thing led to another, and we started having a cocktail maybe once a week. Both of us noticed how easy it was to talk to each other and not about business, but about everything that really matters. Soon, the drinks escalated to…" He let out a long sigh.

"We never considered it to be an affair. After the first time, Nancy said she was going to get an attorney and file for divorce. I told her that I would never leave my wife. Now it appears she may leave me soon." Saying this, Robert had tears rolling down his cheeks. "Nancy already knew I wouldn't leave my wife. Divorces usually take around ninety days, and in all likelihood…" More tears.

"Jim, Kate, I have been blessed with a wonderful woman for twenty-five years. It is evident she will not live much longer. Please do three things for me. First, my wife must never know about my time with Nancy. I would never want to hurt her. Second, don't judge me too harshly. I am a lucky man to have had Mary, and I feel the same way about Nancy now. Yes, it was an affair, but it will become much more once… Third, I would like to hire you to help keep Nancy out of prison. You have to find out who killed her husband and why. If I lose Mary and Nancy goes to prison, my life would be over."

CHAPTER THREE

H eading home was a quiet affair. We had decided to go home, have some breakfast, and then try to lay out a plan of action.

Kate made hotcakes and eggs while I made another pot of coffee. We hadn't said anything to each other since getting home. We had agreed to take on Robert's case. What else *could* we do? The man laid open his heart to us and although we had prejudged him, we both realized that sometimes there are extenuating circumstances. Two sides to every coin as they say.

Loading our food onto plates, we grabbed a carafe, filled it, and then took everything out on a tray. I liked making one trip, not two or three, just to eat.

After a few bites, Kate broke the silence.

"I feel so sorry for Robert. His whole world has been turned upside down."

"Indeed. He is a good man. Lots of guys once they realized what they were in for would probably have divorced their wives and left them to their own devices. Robert stuck by Mary all these years as she steadily declined. Then he meets someone who he cares for, and she ends up in jail."

"I couldn't help thinking about Mary's age when she was first diagnosed. She was *my* age. What would you do Jim if that happened to me?"

I smiled at my wife and told her I had signed on for better or for worse, in sickness and in health. She could always count on me. That made her smile.

"Let's start formulating a game plan. I think we need to go talk with Nancy first and see what, if anything, she has told the police."

"I agree. Then we need to dig into her husband's life to see who would want to kill him. Maybe Nancy can give us some idea on that too."

"Okay. I need to brush my teeth and we can go."

"Should we check with Robert to make sure we can get in to see her? I remember when you were arrested in Montana, it took a while for me to get in to see you."

"Yes, I will call him and see if she has an attorney and make sure Robert paves the way with him or her. Don't want to waste a trip."

We both shined the pearly whites. Then I called Robert, and he told us that Nancy was going to be represented by Jake Cummings, the second best defense attorney in town. When pressed about why he wasn't going to do it, Robert just said it might make it hard to keep his story about being with Nancy private. That was going to be hard if they ended up in court regardless since her only defense is that she couldn't have done it because she was sleeping with another man at the time.

We were back in the truck in record time, heading for city hall where the local jail was housed. When we got there, we both realized we didn't even know Nancy's last name. Geez.

The officer at the front desk had a name tag neatly placed above his right shirt pocket. It read "Officer Tomlinson." We inquired about seeing Nancy, and he filled in the last name—Michaels. He said that Mr. Cummings had called and told them that we worked for him as investigators and we should be allowed in to see Nancy when we arrived. Of course, all the cops in the county knew who we were after solving a few murders.

We were escorted to an interview room. Officer Tomlinson told us to wait and someone would bring in Mrs. Michaels. So we sat and waited. About fifteen minutes later, Nancy was brought in by a female officer named Officer Wentz. She told us that she would be outside the door and just to knock when we were done talking to Nancy.

"Hi, Nancy. How you holding up?" Kate asked.

She had the classic deer-in-the-headlights look—eyes big, pupils dilated. "Thanks for coming. I'm okay, I guess. I just can't believe I'm here."

"Can you tell us what happened last night?" I inquired.

She took a deep breath. "I got home around eight fifteen or so. I walked in through the garage like I do every night, and I smelled gunpowder. I knew what it was because I love to go shooting and do it as much as possible. I was afraid of what I might find. My husband, Clifford, was not the type to shoot himself. I suspected foul play as soon as I smelled the powder. Do you think I could get a glass of water?"

I rose and knocked on the door and made the request to Officer Wentz. She said she would see to it. I returned to my chair to listen to what was coming next.

"I looked in the family room first. Nothing there, so I went into the living room. Clifford was lying on the floor dead. He had been shot once in the chest. That is when I noticed *my* pistol lying on the ground next to the body. I love that gun. It is a pearl-handled revolver like a cowboy might have carried back in the day. I keep it in my night table so that if anyone broke in at night, it would be handy. Without thinking, likely from being in shock, I picked it up and placed it on the end table."

"Hence your fingerprints on the murder weapon."

"Yes. I immediately called the police. They said someone had called in a gunshot at around seven, and they had cruised the neighborhood but didn't see anything out of place, like a body in the gutter, I suppose. They arrived in short order. The police took pictures, asked me what happened, where I had been, that sort of thing. They took my fingerprints so they could rule them out when they fingerprinted the gun. I told them I had picked it up and placed it on the table. In the end, I guess it really didn't matter. They had a murder weapon with my prints on it, my husband was dead, and, according to them, the motive was money. I obviously have now been arrested for murdering my husband."

"When they asked you what happened, what did you say?" Kate asked.

"I told them my husband was shot. That was all I knew. I hadn't been home."

Now the big one. "Where did you tell them you were?" I asked, already knowing the answer.

"Well, I, um, told them I was up at the mall shopping. That I didn't find anything so I came home."

"Did they ask if anyone can corroborate your being there?"

"Yes. I told them I just wandered from store to store and never spoke to anyone."

So, we knew she had lied to the police. All the more important that we find the killer fast. If this ended up in court and her involvement with Robert was made public, she would not only look like she had reason to kill her husband, but it would be found that she had lied to the police the night she was arrested.

"Is that really where you were?" asked Kate.

Nancy looked down at the table. She wrung her hands sort of like she was trying to wash them, but without the aid of soap and water. Probably wondering what we did or didn't know and trying to decide if she should tell us the truth or lie to us as well as the police.

"Nancy?"

She finally spoke, "I don't want you to think I am a bad person, not trustworthy. I lied to the police."

"Where were you?" I pressed.

Once again, she wrung her hands. She was nervous about telling us. I decided to let her off the hook. We needed her help.

"Nancy, we spoke to Robert."

"Then you know?"

"Everything."

Letting the air out of her lungs in a rush, Nancy Michaels finally relaxed. "I am so sorry I lied to the police, but I had to protect Robert's and my secret. I promised I would never speak about the fact we were, you know, lovers before Mary died. If all worked out and we were married after a legitimate grieving period, which Robert will most assuredly need, we would take to our graves the fact we had met that way before her death. And no one would ever know. But now you two do."

"We can keep secrets, Nancy." Looking at Kate, I said, "We promised, right, Kate?"

"Absolutely."

"Thank you. Now what can I do to help you find who really killed my husband?"

"Let's start with people you think maybe didn't like Clifford and would have reason do to him harm."

"Well, that may be harder than you think. There is not a person on earth who liked my husband."

CHAPTER FOUR

K ate and I were planted in our backyard office with our dog Killer at our feet. Killer was a tremendous dog who had actually saved my life twice while we were in Montana—once by accident and once very much on purpose. He is half wolf and half German shepherd and tips the scales between 110 and 120 pounds, depending on the season. Wintertime, he put on a little weight, along with growing a beautiful winter coat.

It was cold out, but not freezing. We were dressed for warmth. Sitting out back was our way to connect and think. We had always done it since we got married and bought the house. Kate, being a florist, loved to be outdoors, and I enjoy hunting, fishing, and even an occasional round of golf, so you could call us both outdoor enthusiasts. There is just something about the fresh air that clears your head.

Our conversation with Nancy had gone on for about an hour and a half. She told us how Clifford had owned his own company, a construction company that did everything from build houses to bridges and even large office buildings. Olympia was growing, and the competition for work was fierce with other companies. Clifford had built his from the ground up. He now employed around fifty men and an office staff of five. He had indeed done very well for himself.

However, growing pains were numerous. As his company grew, he irritated most all the other companies by underbidding them for jobs. State work orders for bridges and the like were always given to the low bidder. Clifford was always the low bidder, sometimes by mere dollars. The other companies were sure Clifford was doing something illegal to gain knowledge of what they had bid on these jobs but could never prove it. Consequently, the other companies didn't care much for Clifford. Then the thefts occurred. Clifford's men would lock up their tools in an onsite shed wherever they were working, and someone would break in and take their tools. This happened often enough it was costing Clifford a good deal of money to replace the stolen items. He finally hired a security guard on the big projects for protection of his assets, but again, that cost him as well.

Clifford finally let it be known that he knew who was doing the stealing and named every other construction company in the city. Not a good way to make friends. There was talk of a lawsuit or two for slander, but nothing ever developed. Except hatred toward Clifford and his company.

"It sounds like we have our work cut out for us," Kate said with a hint of a smile on her face. "Just like you like it."

"I would like it a whole lot more if someone would turn themselves in and end this now. With so many potential suspects, we may never get around to the right person by the time the trial begins. The good news is, the prosecutor hasn't officially charged her. She has only been arrested for murder. The arraignment is not set up yet. Looks as if it may be in the next twenty-four hours though. Sounds like the prosecutor wants all the ducks in a row before he makes that announcement. Unlike the one in Montana that took me in to court before he had all the facts of the case."

"Where do you want to start with the possible suspects? Use the phone book and just start calling everyone? Mr. Michaels does not sound like a nice person. Maybe even conniving and underhanded."

After giving it a little thought, I said, "Let's start with the other construction companies. You never know, we might get lucky right out of the gate."

We sat with the phone book and wrote down names and numbers, as well as addresses of the construction companies in Olympia. Nancy had told us the ones who were the most vocal on the allegations of cheating them on the bids. Those would be our first visitations.

"It's kind of late in the day. Think we should wait until tomorrow to start?" Kate asked.

She was correct, as usual. It was already after three. Assuming the owners or bosses would be in the office first thing in the morning, instead of the last part of the day, we decided to wait. I knew a few of the names on the list from working in the jewelry store. Some were good customers. I didn't think any of them would be capable of murder. I could be wrong.

CHAPTER FIVE

"Hey, Jim! What brings you to my office? It's usually the other way around."

"Hello, Pat. Good to see you," I said, shaking hands. His hand was more the size of a honey-glazed ham. Pat is Patrick Godwin. He is the owner of one of the construction companies and one of my very good customers. It would be important to tread a little lightly or lose a customer that spent upward of $10,000 a year buying nice things for his wife and daughters.

"Do you have a minute to talk to Kate and me? Oh, I'm sorry, darlin'. Kate, meet Patrick Godwin, the owner of this fine company."

"Pleased to meet you, Mr. Godwin," Kate said as she too shook his enormous hand.

"Call me Pat, and I will call you Kate. Like to be on a first-name basis."

"Great."

"Now what do you want to talk to me about? Finally going to spend some of that detective money and have me build you a new house?"

"Can we speak in private, Pat?"

"Sure, come on into my office." He kind of tipped his head to one side like he might be wondering or trying to figure out what this was all about. He would know in a minute.

His office was the antithesis of Robert's office. There were blue-prints and invoices on a table that was maybe six feet long and four feet wide and had a set of those fold-up legs keeping it upright. His own desk was stacked high with what appeared to be invoices and the like.

"Pat, we are actually here in a sort of official capacity. Jake Cummings has hired us to look into the death of Clifford Michaels."

What little smile he had left on his face from our coming to his office disappeared.

"Good riddance. Guy was a crook. Plus, I thought it was an open-and-shut case? They arrested his wife, right?"

"They did. But we don't think she did it."

"Why not? She probably hated him as much as the rest of us did."

"We have reason to believe she is telling the truth about not being there when the murder occurred. Um, where were you last night, Pat, if you don't mind my asking?"

"I do mind actually. You know me, Jim. I'm a lover, not a fighter. That guy could bring out the worst in people though."

"How did he do that?"

"Just by being himself. Contractors have meetings all the time to discuss different things going on in the business. New tools, new techniques, ways to save money, that sort of thing. Michaels would listen and take notes and would never share one thing he was doing. He was a jerk. Then have you heard about his bidding practices? He would somehow get the numbers others had put into a sealed bid. A sealed bid is where everyone has to bid by a certain day and time, then whoever is going to be responsible for accepting the bids opens them all one at a time. Typically, whoever has the lowest bid gets the job. That *sob* undercut me by *eleven dollars* on a bid once. There is *no way* he could have won that bid without knowing exactly what my bid was and then bidding just below it. He did it on purpose, making it so slight a difference. He was trying to show me he had the power. Did it to a couple other contractors too. Guy was scum."

Pat was starting to get heated. I was losing a customer if I pushed much more. But I had to. Kate could see I was hesitating, and she took the initiative. Man, I love this woman.

"Pat, you really didn't answer Jim's question. Where were you last night? We want to be able to rule you out as soon as we can. Sounds like we have a number of people to talk to."

Pat took a deep breath and let it out slowly. "Sorry. Talking about that guy gets me riled up. I went out to dinner with a couple other contractors last night. Had a couple projects we are working on together to discuss. Jerry Conigliero and Tommy Stafford. I figured you were going to ask who I was with, so there you go. Right up front. Now listen, as much as it is good to see you, I have to get back to work."

He stood, signaling the end of our conversation, and held his hand with his palm up and pointed us toward the door. We took the hint.

"Thanks for your time, Pat. Always great to see you."

"You too, Jim. Sorry but I really do have to get moving. Time is money. Have to earn more to spend in your dang store!"

I had not lost a customer. That was a good thing. Pat really is a nice guy.

As we walked toward the truck, Kate said, "My gosh, Jim, I couldn't believe the size of his hands! Mine got totally lost in his."

"I know. Lorne tried to measure his ring finger one time, and we didn't even have a size big enough to fit!"

Kate and I got in the truck and perused the list we had written of contractors. Both of the men Pat mentioned were on the list.

"Which one first?"

"Let's do Conigliero first. I know Tommy Stafford. He is an… well, let's just say he is not a nice guy."

"How do you know him, Stafford that is?"

"From the store. Long story. He may not even talk to me, so let's go see Mr. Conigliero."

"Okeydoke."

Conigliero's office address was a house in a, more or less, run-down section of town. Not so much run-down as just old. His house was the jewel of the neighborhood. Pays to know how to build and remodel. We knocked on his door, heard footsteps on what we would soon learn was oak hardwood, and the door opened.

"Hello. You must be Jim Tuttle," the man of around fifty years old stated.

"Yes, and this is Kate. Obviously you had a call from Pat."

"Yes, I did. Told me what you wanted and that you were okay. Come in."

The house was as perfect on the inside as it was on the outside. Mr. Conigliero had done some beautiful wood working inside his home. Large bookcases that had been built floor to ceiling out of what appeared to be walnut. Expensive, but beautiful. They had extensive grooving in them along the top that added to their beauty. His railing going upstairs matched the bookcases and had a high polish on it.

"Your house is wonderful," Kate said, wide-eyed as she looked around. "Did you make all these bookcases?"

"Yes, I did. Thank you. I still love to work with wood even though my company kind of changed directions and we do more now in rebar and concrete."

"Well, it is lovely. This is your office too?"

"Yes, it seemed foolish to rent or buy a building when I can run the company from my house just as easily. Plus, it's paid for."

"Makes sense," Kate said. "And you get to work in such a beautiful atmosphere. Beats a building downtown anytime."

"Thanks again. So you two are trying to pin the murder on someone other than Mrs. Michaels, I hear? To me it is one of those ones they call open-and-shut. Used her own gun and everything."

"Well, as I told Pat, we have reason to believe that she couldn't have killed her husband because she wasn't home at the time."

"Sounds like a likely story to me. Of course she is going to say she was somewhere else. How else could she try to get out of killing him?"

"Pat tells us you went out last night with him and another contractor."

"Yes. Pat, Tommy Stafford, and I all went to Steamboats for a couple beers."

Kate and I loved Steamboats. It was an old paddle wheeler someone had gone to the trouble of getting up into Puget Sound.

From there, they remodeled it and turned it into a really cool bar and restaurant. Actually several bars and a restaurant. Big boat.

"What time did you leave? Do you recall?"

"Said we had a couple beers, not a six-pack. Of course I can recall. Tommy said he had to get home. I happened to look at my watch. It was a little after nine thirty."

"Did Mr. Michaels ever undercut a bid you made for a job?" Kate asked.

Looking at Kate, he squinted his eyes, got a little red in the face, and then replied, "Yes. More than once. It was confounding. He would always bid just below everyone else who put in for the job. Didn't matter if there was out-of-town contractors or just us local companies. He won every dang bid. Just about put me out of business. That is why I quit bidding and started just taking on whatever came my way. Now my contracting company is more of a concrete company. We do driveways, curbs, and the like. Not as much money in it, but no real competition either. Especially that snake Michaels."

"Well, thanks so much for your time, Mr. Conigliero. Is it okay if we come back if we have any additional questions?"

"Sure. Pat was right. You seem like good people. Good luck with finding another killer."

"Thanks." With that, we walked down the aggregate walkway and got back in the truck.

"Seems like an okay guy," Kate said.

"We'll see. There may be something were missing. Should we go see Stafford?"

"It is gaining on lunchtime. What say we go to the Oyster House for lunch?"

"Works for me."

The Oyster House had been in Olympia for sixty years or so. It was right at the lowest tip of Budd Inlet on Puget Sound. Phenomenal food and great views were on the menu, along with a long list of beers. I was getting hungrier just thinking about it.

We parked downtown and made our way to the restaurant. I had heard it had burned down at one time, but in my lifetime, it hadn't changed a bit. Same cool bar, plenty of seating, and fish and chips to die for.

Kate and I both ordered the fish and chips and a couple Olympia Beers. If you stood in front of the Oyster House and peered south, you could see the Olympia Brewing Company. It made a pale ale that was okay. I preferred Rainier Beer from Seattle, but when in Olympia and out in public, one always has to but on a "good local boy" face. The food arrived, and it was just as good as I remembered it being.

"This food is always good. I don't think I have ever had a bad meal here," I said with my mouth still full of cod.

"I agree, and don't talk with your mouth full."

"Yes, Mother," I said with a grin.

Kate does this thing with her eyebrows. One at a time. At my saying this, she raised an eyebrow and put on a good scowl. Then she burst out laughing. Her laugh was like snow on Christmas morning. Always welcome and wanted.

"What did you mean back there about 'we'll see' when I said he seemed like a nice guy?"

"You know how you get those little inklings sometimes? That is all it is. Something just doesn't seem right. As I said, we'll see."

We finished our meal, left a substantial tip, paid our bill, and headed out, likely toward Mr. Tommy Stafford's place of business. He might not be there we realized after chatting about the fact it was afternoon, and most guys were out on the jobsite or sites by then. Kate suggested we get a copy of the police report if possible. We hadn't even thought about it yesterday when had visited Nancy. I wound my way through the streets of Olympia and back to city hall.

I held the glass door open for my lovely wife, and she entered first. Officer Tomlinson, once again, manned the front desk.

"Hello again," I said, trying to see if I could get a smile out of the officer.

"Yes?" No luck. One-word question is as good as it got.

"Can you tell me who the detective or detectives are that are handling Nancy Michaels case?"

"Detective Smith. Through the doors, take a right at the first hall, and he will be on your left." Efficient if not friendly.

"Thank you, Officer Tomlinson," Kate said with a smile on her face.

"Welcome."

Following the officer's directions, we got back to an open door to a room with two desks in it, facing each other. A man in a very sharp-looking suit was sitting at one desk while the other chair across from him remained empty.

"Detective Smith?" I asked.

"Yes. May I help you?" Wow, he actually made a full sentence unlike the robot at the desk.

"My name is—"

"I know who you are. Kate and Jim Tuttle. I hear Cummings has hired you to try to discredit our case."

"On the contrary, we want to help you find the real killer. There is no way Mrs. Michaels killed her husband."

"Why, because you say so? Doesn't work that way. We have evidence, and no one saw anyone else come or go from the house. No forced entry. Need I go on?"

I was not making any points with the detective, so Kate tried her hand.

"Detective, is there any chance we can see the police report or maybe get a copy of it?"

"Not just yet. The press has been told the basics, but not what evidence and so on we have. Can't afford to let it slip out before the prosecutor says it's okay. Maybe tomorrow."

"Is the arraignment tomorrow then?"

He gave Kate a cold, dead-on stare. Then replied, "Yes. But that is also not common knowledge. Please keep it to yourselves." He said this turning his stare to me.

"Of course. Sure," I replied. "Do you think you could give us a call when you can release the report so we can come down and get it?"

"If I have time." I wouldn't count on a call. He really didn't like us nosing around his case.

"Thanks for your time, Detective."

Kate and I made our way back out of the maze that was city hall and exited to my trusty truck. Leaning against it was another man in a sharp suit. He extended his hand.

"Jake Cummings."

"Oh hi! Pleased to meet you. Robert has told us about you." I didn't add Robert said he was the second best defense attorney in town.

"Robert had told me you drove a white F-150, and although there are probably a hundred of them in town, when I saw yours sitting here, I took a chance. Of course I saw you on *Good Morning America* and all over the papers awhile back, so I knew what you looked like. What's new in city hall?"

We relayed the information that Detective Smith had told us.

"Good, saves me a trip inside. That is what I came down for, a copy of the police report. They have to give it to me before the arraignment. Guess it will be tomorrow."

"Looks that way."

"Listen, when you get it, will you give us a call? You can leave a message on our machine at home."

"Of course. Well, duty calls. Gotta run. Nice meeting you two."

"Nice meeting you as well. We will look forward to your call tomorrow."

I started the truck and Kate said, "Oh my gosh."

"What? What is it?"

"We have been gone for six hours. We have to get home and let Killer out."

"Geez. Okay. But can you, next time, just tell me calmly? You scared the heck out of me."

"Sorry. Poor boy is probably in pain from not going."

I drove a little faster than the speed limit to get home as quickly as possible. We pulled into the driveway, and Kate ran in to let Killer out. As I came into the house, I heard her laughing.

"Come, look," she said, bursting out in laughter yet again.

She was calling me from the bedroom. Killer was lying on our bed with his gigantic head resting on my pillow. He raised his head and looked at me with a look of "what?" in his eyes. I joined Kate in laughter.

CHAPTER SIX

The evening was spent in our office going over the case, knowing when the night air got too cold for us we would move inside. We really liked sitting out back and chatting about, well, anything. But when we had a case, it was particularly good for us for some unknown reason.

"So any revelations after today's work, detective boy?" Kate asked.

Nothing I can put my finger on, but I think there is something creeping around the edges of my pea brain, trying to get in."

"Do you think you will lose Pat as a customer?"

"I doubt it. As long as he wasn't involved in the murder of Clifford Michaels, then yup, I will lose him for sure," I said with a grin.

"Do you think he could have been involved, really?"

"At this point, I don't know. He sure hated Clifford. As did Jerry Conigliero. My guess is Tommy Stafford will make it a trifecta of hatred when we talk to him tomorrow."

"Oh yeah, what's the deal with you and this Stafford character anyway?"

I was hesitant to tell Kate the story since she would meet him tomorrow and I needed her to have her wits about her. But in the end, I went ahead and spilled the beans.

"Tommy Stafford was a mediocre customer for the past few years. He has always been the type to want top quality service, even above and beyond service, when he is spending a fraction of what my really good customers, like Pat, spend. In fact, Pat is the exact opposite of Stafford. Pat will spend a good deal of money and then apologize for taking up so much of my time. Stafford wants things delivered to *him* so he can look at them and make a decision. Not even necessarily purchase them but look at them. As I said, polar opposites."

"I already don't like him."

"I need you to keep an open mind. Tomorrow is important, and if all you think about is what I am telling you now, you will be of no use whatsoever."

"Okay, sorry. I will wait to hate him until after tomorrow," she said with a little smile on her face.

I tried to give her a stern look, but it didn't work. Instead, she broke out in laughter.

"Stafford came in on Valentine's Day a year and a half ago, before we took on Betty's case. He had told his wife to give him her rings and other jewelry so he could get it cleaned. Who knows if that was a normal thing for him to do or not, but for sure he had never brought in her jewelry to our store. Mrs. Stafford had always brought in her own things. By the way, she is a sweetheart. Go figure."

"I'm getting a bit chilly, and I need another beer. Do you mind if we move inside?" Kate asked.

"Of course not, darlin'. Anything that gets me closer to another beer is a good thing anyway."

We made the move, our ever-present Killer taking the lead, and we went inside to the family room. It was a comfortable room, which we had decked out in leather chairs and a sofa of the same material. Sad to think several good cows gave their hides so we could be comfortable. But I figure, by the time their hide was gone, that was the least of their worries.

Kate grabbed us a couple more Rainier beers out of the fridge and, then as she opened them, said, "Go on. I can hear you from here."

"All right. So let's see, where was I? Oh yeah, Stafford brought in his wife's jewelry. Looking at it, I realized almost, if not all of it, had come from my store. That was good. Nothing too expensive, but nice pieces regardless. Anyway, he said he had a couple errands to run and he would pick them up later. As is the norm, I filled out a repair envelope and handed it to Lorne to clean and check. As you know, he has been a bench jeweler for, like, fifteen years. Lorne checked the pieces and noticed that one of the diamonds in her five-diamond anniversary band was chipped."

"You have told me before how tough diamonds are. How can they chip?"

"The outside perimeter of the diamond, the thinnest part is called the girdle. A diamond in its natural state is, indeed, extremely hard. But once it's cut, the hardness doesn't really diminish but…It's kind of hard to explain."

"You're doing fine. Keep going."

"The girdle is so thin it is susceptible to a blow, which can cause a chip. For instance, if you were to hit your diamond down on, say, a rock in the yard, you stand a chance of chipping the girdle if it connects with the rock just right or wrong, I guess."

"Really. I will take my ring off from now on when I am working in the yard."

"Anyway, we replace people's diamonds that are chipped for free. It is simply called a diamond guarantee. It gives them piece of mind, and it gives us more satisfied customers in the long run. In Stafford's case, keep in mind this was a relatively small diamond. A fifth of a carat. The total weight of the five diamonds is one carat. It was not like it was one like yours which is a one-carat solitaire. One carat solitaires are pretty expensive. One-fifth carats are not one-fifth of the cost of a one carat."

"Why not?"

"To find a diamond in the rough that will yield a one-carat diamond is much harder than finding one that will yield a fifth carat. It is simply mathematics. If you don't have a lot of big rough, the cost goes up."

"Okay, I get it. Sorry, this is interesting."

It was nice to see Kate so engaged. She was listening to everything I said about diamonds. I had done this with her countless numbers of times as she talked about the flowers she loved so much.

"Lorne set the ring aside, and when Stafford came back in, he showed it to him under magnification. Stafford went off on him like there was no tomorrow. Lorne, who is an ex-marine, stood his ground but was polite as he could be, getting yelled at, and explained that we would replace it at no charge. That still didn't appease Mr. Stafford. He wanted us to replace the whole ring, which, of course, would be, more or less, a total loss for the store. We would have four good diamonds and a little scrap, but we can't just put a diamond in it and resell it as new."

"Geez, what a jerk."

"So I finally got involved and tried to talk some sense into Mr. Stafford. He would have none of it. He threatened a lawsuit, and at that point, I got a little angry and told him to have at it. He grabbed the ring and the rest of his wife's jewelry and took off. Haven't seen him since. And…there has never been a lawsuit."

"Maybe I should go see him by myself tomorrow," came Kate's reply.

"No way. He could fly off the handle at you, and he is the type that would do just that. Hey, how about if I call Butch to go with you? Maybe he can free up and come up and help."

Elmer "Butch" Danforth was a friend of mine whom I met when I had been shot at the first time. The only time I was actually hit by a bullet. He is a sergeant in the Lewis County Sheriff's Office. Lewis County is the next county south of Thurston County, where Olympia is.

"Think I'll call him right now."

Butch was home and said he could swing a couple hours in the morning to go with Kate to see our next interview with a person who might have had a grudge against Clifford Michaels. I filled him in as best I could on what had happened and what we were trying to do, and he was all in.

"Sounds like you guys got another live one," he said.

"Seems like they keep popping up, that is for sure."

"I'll see you first thing in the morning."

We said good night and hung up. Butch is a good cop with great instincts. I was glad he could come up and help us out.

"What are you going to do in the morning when Butch and I interview Mr. Stafford?"

"I might just sleep in or do some Christmas shopping. Who knows? I kind of want to be here if Detective Smith calls to say the police report is ready for our perusal though."

"Be sure you hit your store if you go shopping," Kate said with her patented amazing laugh.

"Oh, I see how it is. You only want me for my jewelry."

"Oh no, I want you because, as a team, we are the best private investigators on the planet."

CHAPTER SEVEN

Butch arrived later than expected, around ten. He had been tied up at his own office for a couple hours. He and Kate, who had been chomping at the bit, took off as soon as he got there. I sat around for an hour or so and decided I was hungry. Steamboats sounded like a good place to go. Gave me a chance to see if I could find anything out there from anyone about the meeting of our first three interviewees.

The restaurant was empty except what appeared to be a retired couple having a Bloody Mary for breakfast or lunch or, perhaps since it was around eleven, brunch. The bartender was a man of about thirty maybe, looking very cliché, polishing glasses with a towel while standing behind the bar.

"Hi there. What can I get for you?"

"I'll take a bottle of Rainier if you've got it." Why not live dangerously and not have an Olympia beer while in Olympia?

"Coming up."

He reached into a large fridge and pulled out a Rainier and popped the top, spun around, and set it on the bar. I had decided he was my only chance for information. The other bars weren't open yet. I plopped down on a bar stool and said a polite thank you.

"You ever work the evening shift?" I asked.

"Yeah, we kind of get scheduled to the shifts, depending on what the boss needs. No set schedule."

"You working night before last?"

He tipped his head back, squinted his eyes just a touch, then replied, "Yes, right here."

"Did you happen to see three men, big guys all, chatting? You might even know them. I know one of them has his picture on the side of his contractor trucks."

"Oh, you mean Stafford? Yeah, he and two other guys were in. Came in around six and stayed, oh heck, I don't know, maybe half an hour."

"You remembered them pretty quickly. Something stand out?"

"You mentioned the truck. I remembered seeing the guy. His trucks are kind of all over the place."

"Ah. Anything else?"

He did the head tipping back, squinty eye thing again. "Well, one thing I did find kind of odd. We weren't very busy, so all but a couple of the window seats were open. Instead of choosing one of them, they sat over there," he said, pointing to a table in the corner. "Most people don't like that table because it is right by the kitchen, and it can be hard to talk and be heard over the noise sometimes."

"Any idea what they were talking about?"

"Not really. They had their heads together real close as they spoke. I figure it was because they couldn't hear each other over the noise."

"And you say they were here for half an hour? Did they have dinner?"

"No. They each had a couple drinks, then just got up and left. Actually, I remember one guy got kind of upset. He got up first, held his hands out like this." He said this with his palms out, about shoulder height. "Then he said something to the other two and walked out. He dropped a fiver on the counter for me as he left. Seemed agitated but was nice enough to give me a nice tip. The others sat for a couple minutes and then got up and walked out. Chintzy on the tip, those two. Go figure. Guys who make the kind of money they must make, and they leave me a dollar as a tip."

"Unreal. Well, listen, thanks for your help." I left, but not before leaving a $2 tip for a $.75 beer. I figure he gave me some good information, and it was well worth the two bucks.

When I got home, there was a message from Detective Smith. The police report, including the autopsy report, were ready for us to take a look at. I would wait for Butch and Kate. I had figured they would beat me home, but I was wrong. They rolled in a couple minutes later.

"Well, that was interesting," Butch said as he entered.

"Yes, yes it was," Kate added.

"Okay, you two, let's have it. What was so interesting?"

"Mr. Tommy Stafford is indeed a jerk," said Butch.

"What happened?"

"Kate and I went to his office. Big place, nicely furnished. Didn't look much like what you might expect a contractor's office to look like."

I thought of Pat's office with blueprints, files, and invoices all over the place.

"Anyway, we introduced ourselves and asked if we could talk to him for a few minutes. Immediately he got all fired up and asked what about, what did we need to talk to him about, and so on. We explained we were looking into the death of Clifford Michaels, and then the fun really began."

"Go on, Butch, please!"

"He says he hated the guy and was glad he was dead. Then he starts pacing around like a caged animal and is muttering under his breath the whole time. I think the guy is unstable. When I asked him where he had been the night Michaels was killed, he said it was none of my business. He wasn't involved, and they already had the bitch who did it. Said he knew she did it because it was her gun and she shot him right in the chest. Then he comes at me like he is going to do me harm. I mean, right up in my face he hollers to get out. Kate asked him again where he had been, and he said he was at dinner with some friends until after nine o'clock, long after the guy had been shot. Then he tells Kate, 'If you want a suspect other than the guy's wife, why not talk to his tramp girlfriend?' That she was wanting more than just being an affair. She wanted the whole enchilada. We asked if he knew what her name was, and he said he didn't, but she worked at Steve and Eydie's Bar and that you couldn't miss her.

She was a bottle blond with a really good body. As far as he knew, she is the only blond working there. Sounds like he frequents the place. After that, he started clenching his fists, got all red in the face, and told us to get out. I informed him I was a police officer, and he had better think twice before he decided to use his fists. If possible, and I would have never believed it would have been, he got even redder and looked me in the eyes and said, 'I'll do what I damn well please, Mr. Police Officer. We left. End of story."

"Wow. I warned Kate the guy was a loose cannon."

"We went to the bar to see if this mysterious blond was working, and the owner said she had taken a couple days off. That she had lost a good friend and needed some time. But we did get her name. It's Heather Norris. Kate wanders off while I am still talking to the owner of the bar and then wanders back and says, 'Let's go.'"

"Seems Kate had wandered to the pay phone and had looked up one Heather Norris in the phone book. That is why we are late. We stopped to talk to her."

"I let Kate talk to her, figured it would be better under the circumstances, and I just sat and listened. Kate, you take it from here. I need another cup of coffee."

"I'll make some right now," I said as Kate started to enlighten me on what happened at the Norris residence.

"Heather Norris looked awful. It was obvious she had been crying and perhaps for a long time. I tried to frame my questions so that I could try to determine if she was crying because Clifford was dead or she was crying because she had killed him. Not an easy thing to do, I might add.

"I started simply with, 'Did you know Clifford Michaels?' which started the waterworks up again. She responded yes, she had known him. Asking her how she knew him was next. She readily admitted she loved him. Seems they met one night at Steve and Eydie's, and for her at least, it was love at first sight. He was strong and handsome, and she found out later he was loaded, but that was after she already knew she loved him, at least according to her. He had been right up front about being married. My assumption was he was trying to have a quick roll in the hay, and he figured he would either turn her off with that fact or she would maybe be the type who just wanted the same thing he did and didn't care.

"Next, I went to where she was the night he was murdered. She seemed a little almost dazed, I guess I would say, at the question. I thought to myself, here we go, she is going to make something up. But instead, she said he had stopped by the bar for a quick beer and left. She was working and didn't get off until eleven."

"We will have to confirm that with the owner of the bar," Butch chimed in.

"I asked her why in the world Clifford's wife would want to murder him. She said because she herself had called and told her about the affair, figuring she might be able to get her so upset at her husband that she would file for divorce. She said she never expected her to kill him. She had called the wife right after Clifford left the bar at around five thirty. It could be the reason she was dazed. She was thinking that if she had never called Nancy that night that Clifford would still be alive. That is a big burden to bear.

"Or she's lying through her teeth because she told Clifford to divorce his wife, and he told her he wouldn't do it. I would bet it would have cost him a pretty large sum to settle up with Nancy had they divorced. Heather could have killed him because he wouldn't leave Nancy. All the more reason to ask her boss about her shift that night," said Kate.

"Oh yeah, one of the top things on the list," I said.

"I have to get back down to the office. Sorry I can't stay and help," Butch said.

"Well, from what Kate and I learned yesterday, which I assume she told you."

Butch nodded.

"And what we all found out today, I can tell you one thing for sure."

"What would that be, detective boy?"

"If this case ever gets near a courtroom, we will be able to give the jury plenty of reasonable doubt."

CHAPTER EIGHT

After a quick lunch of ceviche, Kate and I headed into city hall. We were really hoping that the arrest report and coroner's report would give us even more ammunition to keep Nancy out of jail. This was the first case that we were hired by someone we knew, and although we had no idea what kind of compensation we might get for taking the case, it really didn't matter. We both considered Robert a friend, and therefore, the amount of money really didn't matter.

We parked and started to walk toward the building. The shape of the building was a hexagon. Rather an odd shape for a building, at least for a city hall, I had always thought.

"Do you think you should buy a new truck? You have had this one for quite a while, and it's not like we can't afford it."

"I know, but I really like my truck. Why buy a new one just to have a new one, you know?"

"Whatever you say." I think Kate thought it was unfitting for people who had better than a million dollars in the bank to drive a four-year-old vehicle. My truck was, well, my truck. I loved it. We would have to have this discussion later. We were entering the building.

"Hello," I said to a new officer at the counter. This one's name was Shanks. The irony hit me—a cop named Shanks, working in a jail, since a shank was slang for a homemade knife like instrument used to kill inmates typically. "We are here to see Detective Smith."

"Okay, does he know we're coming, or did you have an appointment?"

"I assume he knew we were coming. He called me a couple hours ago and gave us some information that would lead me to believe he knew we would be down here soon."

"Do you know where his office is?"

"Yes, we do."

"Okay, you can go on back then."

"Thank you, Officer Shanks."

We wound our way back to the detective's office, and he was planted in his chair opposite what I had to guess would be his partner.

"Good afternoon, Detective Smith. Thanks for calling and letting us know the police report was ready to be viewed."

"Not a problem. Do you want me to make you a copy? The newspaper will probably run the whole damn thing this afternoon anyway."

"That would be great. Thank you." Things seemed to be going well. He was almost friendly.

"This is my partner, Detective Jones," he said while gesturing toward the other cop at the adjoining desk. I had a smile start to form on my lips as I tried to say hello to the other detective.

"Nice to meet you," the detective said.

"You as well," I said as I broke out in a big stupid grin.

"It's okay. You are not the first. Let me guess, you like westerns," he said.

There was a show when I was in my mid-teens that I loved called *Alias Smith and Jones*. It just had struck me funny that the two cops handling this case carried the same monikers.

"I'm sorry, yes. I used to watch *Alias Smith and Jones* every week."

He actually laughed. "Usually, no one will admit that. They try to shine us on. Thanks for being honest."

"We always try to be. Honest, that is."

"Any luck with your *case*?" This came from Smith.

"Honestly, yes. We have several people who disliked the deceased. Many had reason to kill him. Listen, we don't in any way want to disparage the work you do. It's just that we are trying to help out a friend whom we felt may have been wrongfully arrested. I know that sounds counterintuitive. Your work is very important, and we feel ours is too."

He took a deep breath and let it out slowly. "I have a funny feeling about this case. Although all roads lead to the arrested individual, I have been doing this a long time, and I have to tell you, I think you may be on to something. Will you do me a favor? Keep me posted on what you find. If we are wrong, I am the kind of person not to admit I made a mistake."

We were treading on some uneven ground here. He was a seasoned police investigator. Was he saying this because he really wanted to get to the correct answer of who killed Clifford Michaels, or was he trying to get us to let our guard down and tell him what we knew so they would have time to find ways to diminish the evidence in court?

"Tell you what, if you keep us up on anything else you find, we will be happy to keep you appraised on what we find. Deal?"

Without hesitation, he responded, "Deal."

"Okay great. Um, when can we get the copy of the report?"

He slid out a desk drawer in his old, gray, worn-out desk and pulled out a file folder. "Right now. I figured you might want a copy, so I had one made for you."

"Thank you very much."

"No problem. Can you fill me in on what you have so far?"

Here we go. I had to tread carefully here. But before I could open my mouth, Kate spoke.

"Everything we have so far is not real evidence. Once we have something solid, we promise to give you a full rundown." Man, I loved this woman.

Although Detectives Smith and Jones were not happy with that, evidenced by the looks on their faces, they both nodded.

"Okay. We appreciate it. Thanks."

"Oh, no problem," Kate said. "You have been very kind to us, and we won't forget it."

How did she do that? Take a potentially explosive moment and turn it around to the point we got a thank-you from the cops. I was in awe of her abilities once again.

We took our file and headed out into the maze that was city hall. I smiled at Officer Shanks as we went by, and he actually gave a little nod. Maybe there were some other really good cops in the world besides our friend Butch.

"Think we'll find anything in this we didn't already know?" Kate asked as we got in the truck.

"I just want to read it. We have had four people tell us where they were the night Clifford was killed, and there is enough contradictory evidence just from those four to fill a file twice this big. We just need to figure out who is telling the truth and who is lying."

CHAPTER NINE

Killer was in heaven. We had gotten home and decided to take him on a walk. Washington State in December can be unpredictable. It can be sunny and really cold, rainy, snowy or just cloud cover and maybe a light mist. Today was one of the first variety. It was a beautiful sunny day, but the high was supposed to only get to about thirty-five degrees. It had been dropping into the teens at night, and some days it never got above the freezing mark on the thermometer. I loved this weather. Rain, I know, is necessary, but it didn't stop me from hating it. When I hunted, I loved the rain. It made the woods quiet and knocked down your scent. But other than that, I hated it. Today was my kind of day. The sun shone as bright as a new dime in the sky. It was not warm, but it was cloudless and, therefore, beautiful. We had come home, and before we opened the file, we decided Killer needed a walk. He is such a good dog. We just couldn't not take him. After an hour in the cold, we headed for the house.

"Hey, I have an idea," Kate said. "How about an Irish coffee?"

"You trying to butter me up for a big Christmas gift? Of course that sounds great!"

Kate got to it and made us a couple of her wonderful Kate's Irish coffee. I am not sure they are much different from anyone else's, but it hit the spot as we sat out back in our office and started to read the police file. I had given the police report to Kate, and I tackled the autopsy report.

We sat in silence for more than a half an hour, reading, thinking, and going over the reports in detail. Kate was the first one to break the silence.

"There is nothing here we haven't already heard. Gunshot about seven o'clock, police called by Nancy after eight, husband shot once in the chest with her gun. I am assuming ballistics proved that in your report."

I nodded.

"So this is really nothing to us. It means we have to find it out for ourselves."

"Maybe not," I said.

"What? What did you find in the autopsy report?"

"I'm not sure, really. But the coroner said this, and I quote, 'There is a stippled pattern approximately one-half-inch wide that was inflicted premortem on the neck of the deceased between the C-4 and C-5 vertebrae. It appears to have been caused by a round object of undetermined length.' And then this, 'It is evident from the blood spatter on the wall and the bullet hole that the decedent was standing approximately four feet from the wall with the blood spatter when he was shot.' There is not any mention of the round object again. No mention of what it could have been, no mention of if it would have incapacitated Clifford, nothing."

"What does that mean?"

I had been asking myself the same question for the last fifteen minutes.

"I don't know for sure. What it tells me is, Clifford could have been hit hard enough with something on his neck to render him either unconscious or incapacitated before he was shot."

"Why would someone knock him out and then wait for him to wake up just to shoot him once he did?"

"Again, I don't know. But what I do know is that if Nancy had killed her husband, I don't believe she would have knocked him out just to wait for him to awaken so she could shoot him. It doesn't make any sense."

CHAPTER TEN

Kate and I had moved inside and pondered all the things we learned from the police and coroner's reports. We were getting tired, so we decided to start fresh in the morning.

I awoke first and exited the bedroom and headed in to make coffee and, of course, let Killer outside. The reports kept rattling around in my head. What was I missing? I got a headache before the coffee was even brewed.

"Morning," said Kate, coming into the kitchen. She pecked me on the cheek, grabbed a cup from the cupboard, and poured herself some coffee. I had grabbed a cup moments before, so we both sat down at the kitchen counter.

"Did you sleep well?"

"I guess so," I replied.

"So what's the game plan for today? I think it is pretty obvious we need to go to that bar, Steve and Eydie's, and find out if Heather Norris was indeed working late the night Clifford was murdered."

"Yup. Tops on my list. I think we need to make another stop too."

"Where would that be?"

I had been thinking about it last night, lying in bed. I hadn't really slept all that well, too many things running through my mind. This one uppermost this morning.

"I think we need to talk to Mary Roberts."

"Robert's wife? Why do we need to talk to her?"

"Kate, we need to cover all the bases. Think about it. If Mary knew that Robert was having an affair, isn't it possible that she would hire someone to take out Clifford, making it easier for Nancy and Robert to hook up once she died?"

"Oh, Jim. I think you are really grasping at straws."

"She might have thought that Clifford would never give Nancy a divorce, and if she truly wanted Robert to be happy and since she is in the last stages of life anyway, why not? It makes a perverse sort of sense."

"If you say so. Shouldn't we contact Robert first?"

"Better not to, I think. Robert told me that Mary has a live-in nurse now that she is fading. We can simply stop over to see her and let the conversation go where it goes."

"Oh, I don't know, Jim. That sounds like a really bad idea. What if we slip and tell her that Robert is with Nancy, you know, in that way?"

"Kate, we won't slip. I feel like we have to do this."

"Okay, if you say so."

We looked up the bar in the yellow pages and saw their advertisement. They opened at 11:00 a.m. Our plan was to be showered, have breakfast, get there when they first opened and hope that the owner was there instead of Heather. That might prove to be uncomfortable all the way around.

Our plan was working out. We got to the bar just as the outside light flickered on to Open. As we entered, Kate whispered to me that the guy behind the counter was the same one she and Butch had encountered yesterday.

"Good morning," he said.

"Hi there. Are you the owner of this fine establishment?" I asked.

"Yes, sir. What can I do for you?"

"Well, I would assume that you are the Steve then and not the Eydie."

He chuckled. "My name is Dan actually. Everyone assumes my wife and I are Steve and Eydie when, in actuality, the bar is named after Steve Lawrence and Eydie Gorme. My wife is a big fan, so I relented and named the place according to her wishes."

"Dan, my name is Jim, and this is my wife, Kate."

He got a puzzled look on his face. Then it dawned on me that he recognized Kate having been in with Butch yesterday.

"Kate and my friend were in yesterday making some inquires." At this, he nodded his head, and I could see he physically relaxed his shoulders. Probably thought he was going to end up in the middle of something he wanted no part of.

"Yes, yes, I remember. Were you able to run down Heather?"

"Yes, we did," Kate replied. "Which actually is why we are here. Can you tell us if Heather worked, let's see, it would have been Monday night?"

"Yea, she worked. I take Sundays and Mondays off."

"How late are you open on Monday nights?" Kate asked.

"Normally until eleven. But now that you mention it, Heather called me and said she wasn't feeling well. She asked if I could cover. She said it was super slow, which is not uncommon on Monday nights. We don't cater to the Monday night football crowd, so they go other places to watch. I told her to shut it down and go home and take care of herself. That was the last time she worked, like I told your buddy yesterday."

"Do you remember what time she called you?" Kate kept on him. I was just standing there like a statue, listening.

"Oh yeah, it was halftime. See, I *do* watch football. It was around six thirty or so. The game had started at five o'clock."

Kate looked at me, and our eyes met. Heather had been off work. She had lied to us.

CHAPTER ELEVEN

W e thanked Dan for the information and left the bar.

"Maybe we should have had a beer," I said. "That information was enough to make me want to calm my nerves down a bit. How could she lie to us and think she could get away with it?"

"Good question. Want to head back over to her place and ask?"

Thinking about it for a few seconds, I replied, "Nope. I still want to talk to Mary Roberts. We can go see Heather afterward maybe."

"Whatever you say."

I didn't much like it when Kate used that statement. It was like she was acquiescing instead of saying what she really felt. 'Whatever you say' is like saying, 'I don't agree but will go along because you want me to.'

Neither Kate nor I had ever been to Robert's house. We did have the thought that if his office was as nice as it was, his home would be better. We were not wrong.

Robert's home sat in the middle of probably a one-acre lot. It too was brick, like the office. Two stories that looked like it could have come out of *Gone with the Wind*. Four big pillars held up a full-length porch cover that actually started top-down from just under the second story windows. That made it roughly twelve feet over our heads. All the trim was bright white. The gardens were meticulous as was the lawn. The house and yard were so perfect it could have been on the cover of *Sunset Magazine* or *House Beautiful*.

The driveway was circular. We came from the right and swung around to the left, which put Kate's door on the front door side of the house. Climbing out, I strolled around the truck and must have looked like a local yokel with my head turning all directions, trying to take it all in.

Kate rang the bell, and after a thirty second or so wait, Mary's nurse answered the door.

"May I help you?" she asked.

"Hello, we are friends of Robert. We are actually working for him at this time as well. We were wondering if Mrs. Roberts could talk with us for a few minutes." Kate smiled as she said this to try to ease any suspicion that the nurse might have.

"She just woke up from a nap. Let me ask her if she wants to see anyone. What are your names?'

"Kate and Jim Tuttle."

She didn't ask us in; instead, she left us standing on the porch. No big deal to me. It was another sunny, cold day, and I always like being outside instead of inside on days like this.

"Ten to one she calls Robert to check us out," Kate said.

"Hadn't crossed my mind, but I bet you are right. We have been out here plenty long for her to ask Mary if it's okay for us to come in."

We waited another five minutes. What Kate had said had to be true. The nurse was calling Robert to check us out. Good idea. Olympia was primarily a safe place, but you never know when someone comes to the door if they could have bad intentions. We did actually, but not of the criminal type. Our type was subtler.

The door reopened, and the nurse invited us in. She introduced herself as Marge. We introduced ourselves officially again, and then she said to follow her.

She led us to Mary's room. It had been converted to what appeared to be part hospital room and, part still, maybe a guest bedroom. Mary was lying in bed with her upper half raised up by the hospital bed she was lying in.

"Hello."

"Hi, Mrs. Roberts. My name is Jim"—and motioning to Kate—"and this is my wife, Kate."

"I have heard nothing but wonderful things about you from Robert. He thinks very highly of you both. Sorry for the delay. Marge wanted to call Robert to make sure it was okay to let you in. Obviously, he said it was."

"We won't stay long. We just wanted to ask you a few questions."

"Fire away."

She looked much better than her prognosis. She had fairly good color and seemed stronger than I would have anticipated knowing her weakened condition. Her fingers were interlaced with her hands resting on her stomach. Likely to diminish the effects of the Parkinson's. Her voice was strong, but she did have a difficult time enunciating. *Fire away* had sounded more like *far way*.

"We are looking into the death of Robert's receptionist, Nancy Michaels."

"Yes, Robert told me he had retained you."

"He doesn't think there is any way she could have killed her husband. We are trying to find out who did in an effort to keep her out of prison."

"Nancy didn't kill anyone. She is a wonderful person. I have known her for almost the whole time she has worked for the firm. We have had her and her husband over for dinner in the past, not recently, mind you."

Now came the tough part—trying to ask if she knew anything about the murder. I wasn't sure how to even start with the questioning. Good news was, Kate picked up on it and decided to take the lead.

"Mrs. Roberts."

"Mary."

"Okay, Mary, do you know the circumstances surrounding the murder of Mr. Michaels?"

What a perfectly framed question. It was not open-ended, meaning it *could* elicit a yes or no answer, but my guess is Robert had filled her in on what he knew, so she would probably answer yes, giving Kate a second whack at another question.

"Do you mean, did Robert tell me about it in detail? Or do you mean the fact that I knew Nancy was not happy with Clifford being her husband anymore?"

Go for it, Kate!

"Both. How did you know Nancy was not happy with Clifford?"

"First, Robert told me what happened. In detail. As for Nancy and Clifford, as I said, we have had them here for dinner. The man was not a nice man. He would belittle his own wife in front of Robert and me. Saying things like, 'All you are good for is buying things for the house with my money' or 'You wouldn't know an arraignment from a jury box.' Things that were demeaning. Nancy took it all in stride at the time, but you could tell it was eating away at her, just like the cancer is eating away at me. Robert and I wished he would treat her better. She is a very valuable employee to Robert. Smart as a whip and does more than just be the receptionist. She and Robert are in love."

She stopped talking. Kate and I were stunned. She had just admitted that she knew that Robert and Nancy were having an affair.

"Excuse me?" I stammered.

"You heard me, and you probably were already aware of that. The reason Robert wanted you to help Nancy is because he loves her. Now don't get me wrong. He still loves me and treats me the same way he has our entire marriage. He doesn't just take care of me and my needs. He has been the love of my life from the day we met and will be until the day I die. I like to think he still feels that way about me too."

"I do." He had tears streaming down his face.

Kate and I whirled around to see Robert standing in the doorway. He must have decided to come home to see what we were up to.

"Robert. Oh, Robert, I didn't mean for you to know that I knew about you and Nancy."

"But how *do* you know?" Robert asked as he walked to her bedside and took one of her hands in his. As soon as she unclasped her hands, she started to move her arms in sort of a wild motion. I knew that was the Parkinson's. Poor lady.

Robert sat on the edge of the bed, and Kate and I backed away just a bit.

"Robert, you have stayed with me through all my maladies. I haven't been able to do my wifely duties for a long time. I couldn't expect that you would remain faithful forever. A man needs what he needs. About a month ago, I had the nurse at the time go to your office and sit outside to watch you when you left work and, if need be, to follow you. She said you left by yourself in your car, but another car with a woman who had walked out with you followed. You know the rest. No need to go there."

"I never wanted to hurt you, Mary. You have to believe me. At first Nancy and I would talk about her wanting a divorce and how bad Clifford treated her. She listened when I spoke of how you were doing and what was in store. It just sort of happened. Honey, I was blessed with you, and I wanted you to live the rest of your days without knowing what a terrible man I am."

"Robert, you are a wonderful man. The best anyone could ask for. Don't be sad I found out. Be happy. I am. Really. Once I knew you were actually meeting someone who makes you happy, I realized I can move on. You deserve someone, Robert. You have been so good to me all these years. You deserve to have someone who can spend the rest of your life with you."

They sat holding hands, and Mary finally looked to Kate and me.

"You see, there is no way I would want to have someone kill Clifford. Yes, I figured it out rather quickly. You were trying to decide if I would send someone to kill Clifford and frame his wife. But it couldn't be further from the truth. I want Robert and Nancy to be together. Why would I set it up? No good reason as you can see now."

Kate and I looked at each other. "Mary, you are right-on, and we are so sorry to have even suspected you could do anything like that."

"Think nothing of it. You are just doing a job for my husband. Under the same circumstances, if they were reversed, I would have done the same thing no matter how hard it must have been to come here."

"You are very understanding, Mary," said Kate.

"Now go out there and find out who killed that awful man so that my Robert can be happy."

That sounded so strange coming from Mary. Mainly because it left off an addendum to the sentence "So that my Robert can be happy...when I pass away and he has a new wife."

CHAPTER TWELVE

Robert had told us that Nancy's arraignment was at three o'clock. It was just afternoon. It seemed like it should have been much later with all that had happened this morning. We decided to go home, let Killer out, have some lunch, and then maybe even take old Killer for a walk before heading down to the arraignment. There was no real reason to go since Nancy was going to be held over for the murder. But in the end, curiosity won out. Heather was going to have to wait as well.

Lunch was a simple sandwich and a bottle of beer. Killer got his walk, and we locked him in the house and headed for the courthouse. I always thought it would be fun to leave the door unlocked, as if to invite trouble. It would be interesting to see exactly what Killer would do if we weren't there for him to protect. Would he protect his den the same way as he protected us? We will never know. Kate always kyboshed the deal.

The parking lot at the courthouse was jam-packed, so we had to park down the street and hoof it back up the hill.

As we entered, we were asked which arraignment we were there for. When we said for Nancy's, the deputy said, "You and everybody else."

He was right. The courtroom was packed. We spied Robert sitting to one side, and it was apparent he was watching for us and motioned us over. He had been kind enough, even after we went behind his back to interview his wife and all that went along with that, to save us seats. We were in the third row back.

"Didn't think you were going to make it," he said as we sat down.

"Parking lot is totally full. We had to park and hike."

"No problem. They are just getting started."

The lawyers were in place. A side door opened, and Nancy stepped out. They had at least given her, what I presumed, were the clothes she had been arrested in instead of making her wear the gray dress she had had on when we visited her. She looked okay physically, but you could see the strain in her eyes and actions. She was visibly shaking. Poor lady.

The bailiff stood and said, "All rise." The judge walked out from a door behind and parallel with the edge of the bench. He walked up a couple steps and picked up his gavel. He banged it once and told everyone to be seated. He was older, which, it seemed, most judges were since to be a judge you usually had to have practiced law for a while and been good at it to get elected. He kind of reminded me of an actor I had seen before, but the name escaped me.

The bailiff told everyone what the case number was, and we got started.

"Who is representing the state?" the judge asked, which I have always found funny. He probably knew every lawyer in town, especially the state ones, since there were a limited number or attorneys representing the state, as well as a limited number of judges hearing the cases. That, coupled with his years of practicing whatever sort of law he had practiced before becoming a judge, made it pretty likely he knew most, if not all, of them. This was done more for the audience than the judge, I had always thought.

"Brian MacAllister for the state, Your Honor."

"And who is representing the defendant?"

"I am, Your Honor, Jake Cummings."

"Are you both ready to proceed?"

They both nodded.

"Bailiff, please read the charges."

The bailiff rose again and told everyone present that Nancy Michaels was being charged with first-degree murder for the death of her husband, Clifford Michaels.

"Mr. MacAllister, does the state feel they have sufficient evidence to take this case to trial?"

"We do, Your Honor. Mr. Michaels was killed in his own home, no sign of forced entry, by a gun that belonged to the defendant, which had her fingerprints and no one else's on it."

"Mr. Cummings, how does your client plead?"

"Not guilty, Your Honor. In fact, my client was not home at the time of the murder and was the one who actually called 911. She had no reason to murder her husband. If there is not motive, there was no murder, at least not by my client."

"Save your opening for the jury, Mr. Cummings."

"Yes, Your Honor."

"The state feels they have a strong enough case to go to trial, and I agree. Now let's talk about bail."

"Your Honor, the state would like the defendant remanded. Mr. Michaels had a very successful contracting business. Who knows how much money she has hidden away to be able to take off and never return. The state considers her a flight risk."

Jake was already on his feet. "Your Honor, that is preposterous. Mrs. Michaels has never even had a traffic ticket. To remand her without bail would be in itself cruel and unusual punishment."

"She is charged with murder Mr. Cummings. Whether she has ever had a moving violation in a car is not the point. However, I agree with you that jail can be hard on someone of Mrs. Michael's background in particular. Bail is set at $750,000."

"Holy cow," I said under my breath. "They might as well have said she couldn't have bail."

I knew bail bondsmen only charged usually 10 percent of the amount of the bail to guarantee that the defendant would show back up in court. If they did, the bail bondsmen kept 10 percent of the 10 percent. So in this case, if Nancy could come up with $75,000 and she showed up in court, it would cost her $7,500 in the end.

"She doesn't want me to help her," Robert said with no emotion whatsoever. "She feels it might shine a light where one shouldn't be shone."

"Are you going to abide by her wishes?" Kate asked.

"Yes. All the more reason you two find out who really did this and the sooner the better."

The judge was talking to the attorneys about a potential trial date. It was settled on that the trial would begin on February 16. That was roughly two months away. Looking at the way Nancy was shaking and the look in her eyes, it came to mind that she might not survive in jail that long. She could have a heart attack.

"We'll hit it hard, Robert, I promise," I said to him while patting his leg. "We'll get this done."

As they took Nancy by the arm and led her back to the doorway she had entered by, we all rose and looked around.

"Holy crap!" I exclaimed.

"What?" said Kate.

"I just saw Tommy Stafford leaving the courtroom. I'm going to run him down."

"Jim, wait!"

But I would have nothing to do with waiting. Why was Stafford here? What did he care other than he was being questioned about the murder of Clifford Michaels?

I pushed and shoved my way to the door. We had been up front. Stafford must have been in the back of the courtroom. He had a sizable head start. Kate was following in my wake with a lot of *sorry* and *excuse us* coming out of her mouth.

We hit the hallway and looked both directions. I am six feet one inch, not tall but certainly not short either. He was nowhere in sight. I took a chance and went right. As I continued to push past and through the crowd, I rounded a corner and ran right into a woman. Heather Norris. She saw who I was and turned away immediately, trying to, more or less, run in a crowded hallway. It wasn't going to work.

"Hello, Heather. What an interesting turn of events. Kate and I were just going to come pay you a visit."

She had the infamous deer-in-the-headlights look. She wanted to run but knew she had nowhere to go.

"Oh really? Why is that?"

"Do you really want to do this here?" I asked.

"I have no idea what you are talking about."

"I think you do. You told us that you closed Steve and Edyie's at eleven, but Dan told us you called him, saying you were sick and he told you to go ahead and close. Plenty of time, I might add, to go to Clifford Michaels's house and kill him."

Her shoulders slumped, and she had a look of total defeat on her face.

"Can we go somewhere to talk?"

"Certainly. Let's all walk over to the Dairy Queen. It's close by, and I don't think you can outrun me in a short distance."

"I am not going to run. I just want to explain."

"Okay, let's go then."

Kate, Heather, and I took our time weaving through the crowd, which now included the media. Even the Seattle stations were outside with cameras. This was going to be on the six o'clock news for sure. It took us twenty minutes to fight our way to the DQ, which was only a block and a half away.

We all sat, and leaving Kate with Heather, I went up and ordered us each a chocolate dip cone. This was going to be entertaining, so why not have some fun at the same time? I love ice cream, especially dip cones from Dairy Queen.

Neither Kate nor Heather had said a word while I was gone, I found out later. But when I returned, the floodgates opened.

"Look, I'm sorry I lied to you. Clifford had stopped by the bar around five and said he wanted to see me that night. He wanted me to come to his house, said his wife was out shopping or something, and he didn't expect her until the mall closed. I told him I wasn't at all comfortable coming to his house, but he said it would be fine. He and his wife were done. Of course I took that to mean he was going to finally divorce her and marry me. By the way, I lied when I said I called Mrs. Michaels. I don't know what I was thinking. Well...I guess I just wasn't thinking."

"So did you go?" Kate asked, ignoring the second lie. At this point, it didn't matter.

"Yes, ultimately, I did. But by the time I got there, there was no answer at the door when I knocked. He had told me if he didn't answer, he might be in the shower or in his office in the back of the house, that there was a key under the rock to the right of the front door in the garden."

"Did you use the key?"

"Yes. But as soon as I entered, I smelled a funny smell. I wasn't sure what it was until I saw Clifford lying on the floor dead. Then I realized I was smelling gunpowder. I didn't know what to do, so I went back out the door, put the key back, got in my car, and drove away."

"Seems pretty incredible that you had the wherewithal to actually remember to put the key back under the rock. Really? I would be trying to get as far away as fast as I could if that happened to me," Kate said.

"What can I say? It was all reflex. I just did it and left. Kind of like getting the milk out of the fridge, pouring it on your cereal, and then putting the milk back. I wasn't thinking. I was reacting."

"For someone who is professing their love to a married man, that seems a bit of a stretch," I replied.

"I really don't care what you think. It is the truth. I didn't find out until the next morning that his wife had been arrested for killing him. When I talked to you last, I was more upset about actually seeing him dead than his being dead. Does that make any sense to you?"

Unfortunately, it did. People react differently under the same circumstances. Having found a dead body in my motor home shower just half a year ago, I know that your mind races. You don't know what to think or do. And it certainly had an impact on me, seeing a dead body at close range. I couldn't imagine what it must be like for someone who actually knew the murdered person.

"Heather, I understand. Listen, if you think of anything else, let us know, will you please? We are trying to save Clifford's wife from going to prison. Now I know you may not like her because she was married to the man you love, but she didn't do this. That is a certainty that will come out if this trial goes to court. Guaranteed. So please help us find out who did kill Clifford."

"I will. If I can think of anything else, I will give you a call. And thanks. No one ever listens to me, probably because I am blond and have a good body. I really appreciate that you two do listen to me. I will keep in touch if you give me your number."

Neither Kate nor I realized she couldn't keep in touch without our contact information. Kate smiled, pulled a pen from her purse, and wrote down our home phone on a napkin.

"Keep this with you. If anything comes up or you remember anything, please call us."

"I promise," Heather said and then rose and walked out. It was the last time we ever saw her. Alive.

CHAPTER THIRTEEN

"Now what?" Kate asked.

"I think we need to have a conversation with Mr. Stafford."

"You want to go talk to him? Really?"

"No, I don't, but I don't see that there are many options. Butch is working, and I want to strike while the iron's hot."

The way I had it figured, Tommy Stafford would go back to his office and pretend he was there all day. He didn't know I had seen him leaving the courtroom. I was pretty sure anyway. We drove to his office and knocked on the door. Tommy opened the door himself.

"What do *you* want?"

"Good afternoon, Tommy. Just a few minutes of your time, that's all."

He didn't invite us in, which was fine by me. It was less likely he would start a ruckus standing on the porch of his office.

"Are you interested in the legal system?"

"What do you mean by that?" he replied.

"You know, you ever go to court to watch proceedings, that sort of thing?"

His eyes closed just a little bit; he was thinking. Does he know? Did he see me?

"Yeah, sometimes I like to follow trials and the like. Makes life more interesting."

So at least he was hedging his bets. He didn't lie, just in case I had seen him in the courtroom.

"What about today? Did you decide to go watch Nancy Michaels's arraignment?"

"What if I did?"

"I guess my question would be why. My wife and friend were here the other day, and according to them, you got pretty agitated just talking about the murder of Clifford Michaels."

"I hated the guy. He was a crook. Everyone knew it, but no one could prove it. Just thinking about him gets me angry."

He was right. His face was starting to get the color of a ripe tomato. His voice rose with each word as he spoke.

"Why did you leave the courtroom in such a hurry today?"

"I had to get back to work, unlike some people." He was making reference that I had left my job at the jewelry store. Jealousy didn't become him.

"Look, Tommy, all we are trying to do is find out who killed Michaels. Any help would be appreciated."

"How the hell can I help? I don't know anything about that." Just as Butch had mentioned, he was getting even redder in the face, ready to explode.

"Okay. I understand. Well, if you think of anything or hear anything, would you let us know?"

This was said only to calm him. I was beginning to believe Mr. Stafford was as guilty as sin, but it was a matter of proving it.

"I don't know how I would hear anything, but yeah, if I do, I will give you a call."

That was a call I was not going to hold my breath waiting for.

"Thanks, Tommy. Good to see you again." It really wasn't. I could have gone the rest of my life without seeing him again, but it seemed like the thing to say at the time.

"Good to see you too."

As we turned to walk away, something very unexpected happened.

"And, Jim," he said, "I want to apologize about that whole thing with my wife's ring. I was under a lot of stress at the time. I'm sorry for being such a jerk."

I turned to face him dead-on, then held out my hand to be shaken. He took it and shook it.

"Apology accepted. Take care, Tommy."

"Didn't see that coming, did you?" Kate asked as she shut the door on the truck.

"Not in this lifetime. Now I wonder if he only apologized as subterfuge. He could be trying to hide something and figured that maybe we would lay off if he seemed more likeable."

"Good call. I still don't like him though."

"Until we know better, I think I will give him the benefit of the doubt. Maybe he was just having a hard time back then and he took it out on Lorne and me. I guess time will tell. Or our investigation will."

"What now, detective boy?"

"I think we should pay Detectives Smith and Jones a visit."

"To what end?"

"We should tell him about Heather. At the very least, it will give him something that will likely lead nowhere, but it will cast some doubt on the arrest of Nancy. Plus, it never hurts to get in their good graces. He might share something with us."

"Worth a shot. Then we have to get home to let Killer out. Maybe we should start bringing him with us."

"What? And keep him away from my pillow? I don't think he would like that very much. A cold truck versus a warm bed? The bed would win every time."

We both had a good laugh. It felt good to laugh. We hadn't had much reason over the past few days. At least the dog could keep a smile on our faces.

The city hall parking lot was nearly empty. We nosed into a spot and walked in. Officer Tomlinson was taking his turn behind the desk again.

"Good afternoon, Officer. Is Detective Smith in?"

"Is he expecting you?"

"I don't think so, but he will want to see us."

He looked at me with an expressionless face. Picking up a phone, he punched in some numbers, presumably for the detective, and asked if it was okay if we came back. It must have been because with his usual friendliness, he said, "Go ahead."

Detective Smith was at his desk. His counterpart was nowhere to be seen.

"Hello, Mr. Tuttle, Mrs. Tuttle."

"Please just call us Kate and Jim," I said in an effort to be friendly.

"Okay. What brings you in today?" he said, sounding more like a salesman than a cop.

"We wanted to share some information with you about the Michaels murder."

He looked at us straight-faced, and then a big grin formed. "I would never have believed you would share anything with the police. You two kind of do things your own way normally, right?"

"Actually, we do have a good friend who works with us from time to time who is a sergeant with Lewis County. So actually, we do share quite often in an effort to help justice for wrongfully accused people."

The smile faded somewhat. Maybe I had overstepped my bounds by putting it that way. He was trying to convict Nancy, and I had just said, in a roundabout way, that she was wrongfully accused.

"Well, fire away."

Kate and I shared the information, filling in where the other either left off or missed telling something. We had started with the first time we met her and ended with the conversation at Dairy Queen, so it took a good deal of time to tell him the story. When we had finished, Detective Smith was not smiling at all.

"Well, thanks for the information. It will give me something to do," he said with a hint of sarcasm in his voice. I was pretty sure he was already busy with other cases, and now he had to backtrack and look into new allegations. Or not. It was in his hands to do with what he chose. Assuming that he wanted to find the real killer, it was a start. But again, at very least, it gave him reasonable doubt in his own mind that he had arrested the right person for the murder.

"I'm sure you are busy with other things, but we had promised we would share if we found anything out," Kate said, a bit irritated at his sarcasm.

"No, you're right. Sorry. Cops, like most people, don't like to be told when they may have made a mistake. I will look into it and let you know if I think this Heather could have committed the murder. Thanks for sharing."

"You have anything new for us?" I asked.

"No, not really. Now that Mrs. Michaels has been officially charged with murder, it is more or less out of my hands, that is until something new comes along." Meaning, the information we had just given him.

"Just let us know if something does please. We still believe that Nancy Michaels is not guilty of anything."

CHAPTER FOURTEEN

We were sitting in our office, drinking a hot buttered rum and talking about what we knew and what we had been told and comparing the two. So far, we had a myriad of suspects who could have had something to do with Michaels murder: the three contractors—Pat Godwin, Jerry Conigliero, and, of course everyone's favorite, Tommy Stafford. Add in Heather Norris and we had an even four. Literally everyone we had spoken to, with the exception of Mary Roberts, whom we now felt was above suspicion, was a potential murderer.

"Let's go back a couple days and think about what each person said to us. Maybe there was something there that we missed, starting with your customer Pat Godwin. He was the first one we interviewed if I remember correctly."

"You do, and he was."

"First impression?"

"He didn't like Michaels. That was evident from the start. He said he had dinner with Conigliero and Stafford."

"Which you found out from the bartender was not true. They only had drinks."

"Right. I don't think he mentioned what time he left the bar."

Kate jotted a note on her ever-present legal pad.

"I wrote it down we can call on him again and ask him."

"Yikes. You really do want me to lose him as a customer, don't you? He was okay about it when we left, but I bet if we went back, that would be the end of our relationship at the store. Let's move on."

"Okay. Second was Conigliero. Now he did say the three of them only had a few beers and that Stafford had left at a little after nine. Again, the bartender said they had come in a little after six and had a couple drinks and then one of them, not Stafford but Conigliero or Godwin, got up and left. Then the other two finished their drinks, and they left as well. Said they were all gone within a half hour or so. Why does Conigliero lie about that? Unless he was trying to hide something." Kate asked.

"Great question. Write it down so we can go visit him again too. He, at least, said we could come back. Speaking of which, the first thing he did admit to was a call from Pat Godwin. Pat had called and told him we were okay. Why would Pat call him? Essentially I think he may have been calling to warn him, but about what? That we were going to be asking him some questions?"

"That does seem odd now that you mention it. Sure they were friends, so maybe you can attribute it to that, but my guess is it was more than to tell him we were okay people."

"Agreed."

"The other thing is, Conigliero never mentioned dinner, and Pat never mentioned drinks. We know it was only drinks, so why would Pat start out with something as simple as that to lie about? And why lie about the time unless there was a good reason?"

We sat in silence for a time, mulling over all the questions we had. It was starting to get cold. They were calling for a little snow perhaps later in the evening. Kate suggested we move inside, and as much as I liked being outside, I had to agree.

Dinnertime was upon us. Kate ordered a pizza to be delivered since we wanted to keep working. It was time to look at what Tommy Stafford had told us.

"You and Butch got very little out of Tommy other than the fact he hated Michaels and was glad he was dead. He never mentioned dinner, drinks, or anything to you two about meeting with Jerry Conigliero or Pat Godwin. Come to think of it, he didn't tell you and me anything about that either. Make a note, secretary, and we will visit Mr. Stafford tomorrow as well."

"Secretary? I may not give you any pizza after that crack," Kate said with a fake scowl on her face. Then she burst out laughing, as did I. She wrote down what we needed from Tommy and set the legal pad aside.

"Enough. Let's take a break from this for the rest of the night. Want a beer or another hot buttered rum?"

"Now that we're inside where it is cozy and warm. I will take a beer. Thanks, darlin'."

"I think I will too. Goes better with pizza."

I had built a fire in the woodstove before we had gone outside, and now the house was very comfortable. We sipped our beer and just talked about whatever came to our minds, except the case. The doorbell rang a short time later, and I got up to pay for the pizza, leaving Kate relaxing on the couch. Only it wasn't the pizza guy. It was Detectives Smith and Jones.

CHAPTER FIFTEEN

"Dead? How?"

"We decided to go have a chat with Ms. Norris after you came in today. When we arrived, the subject didn't answer her door."

"You mean Heather when you say the subject, right?"

"Yes. The lights were on, but no one seemed to be home. Detective Jones decided to go around back to see if maybe she couldn't hear us knocking on the front door. When he looked in the back door to her the subj—to Ms. Norris's kitchen, he saw her lying on the floor. The door was unlocked, so he went in to check her pulse. She was deceased. She looked to have been strangled, but we will know more when the coroner finishes up his piece of the puzzle."

"We called it in. The forensic team is there now. We thought we should at least stop by and tell you what had happened. Adds a little credence to your coming in this afternoon."

That meant that he was now thinking that, somehow, the murders were related.

"Well, thanks for coming by. We really do thank you for that. She wasn't, or at least didn't seem to be, a bad person. Makes you wonder why someone would murder her."

"It sure makes *us* wonder, that is for sure. Since you have had contact with her as recently as today, I hope you don't mind my asking where you have been this afternoon."

"No, I get it. But unless my dog can alibi us, Kate and I have been working on the Michaels situation all afternoon. In fact, we had ordered pizza, and when you rang the doorbell, I thought it was them delivering our dinner."

"Honestly, Jim. We don't think you had anything to do with Ms. Norris's death, but we had to ask."

"We understand. Just so you know, we have more questions than answers with a few other people we have talked to about the Michaels murder. We intend to hit the bricks first thing in the morning and re-interview everyone we have already talked to. If anything should become of that, you will be our first call. Could you let us know when the coroner's report is complete?"

"Yes, I will. Sorry to have spoiled your dinner, but we wanted to let you know what had happened."

"Appreciated. Thanks."

As the two detectives left, our pizza arrived. I paid the delivery boy and brought the box inside.

"Are you hungry?" I asked Kate.

"Would you think less of me if I said yes?"

"Not at all. I am too. It is truly a shame about Heather, but we haven't eaten in too many hours to count, and this pizza smells amazing. I say we eat away."

And we did.

By the time we were done, the whole large pizza was nothing but a memory. We had both been ravenous and ate it all without stopping to breathe.

"Now I'm stuffed," I said, putting a hand on my belly.

"I am too. But it was delicious. Want to work some more? At this point, I'm not sure we have much more to do until we talk to the contractors tomorrow."

"I concur. We wait until tomorrow. There is one thing I want to work on tonight."

"What's that?"

"Another beer."

CHAPTER SIXTEEN

T he next morning, we awoke to a skiff of snow. Not enough to worry about but the roads would be slick for a couple hours until it warmed up enough to either melt it or rain or both. We decided to put our little outing on hold for a few hours and relax.

"What do you want for Christmas, darlin'?" The day was fast approaching, and we had been so busy the last couple days I hadn't given it much thought. It was the nineteenth. I knew from experience the stores would be packed from around ten in the morning on, but if you went in early, like at eight, when the stores first opened, you could find what you wanted and get out before the thundering herds got to the mall.

"Oh, I don't know, use your imagination."

Kate was always an early shopper, so I expect my gifts were already wrapped and ready to go, hidden somewhere in the house.

"We still have to put a tree up. Hey, I have an idea. Once we finish with our talks with the boys of contracting, what say we go get a tree today?"

"Sure, sounds good to me."

I was hoping today might add some clarity to the muddy waters that were the Michaels case. Once we found who really murdered him, things would slow down to a crawl. I was hoping that would be today, but I wasn't totally optimistic it would be. With Christmas so close, I had to have a morning to go shopping.

I started a fire to keep the chill off the house, and Killer planted himself right in front of the woodstove. It truly was a dog's life. Kate was frying up some eggs when the phone rang.

"Hello. Oh, hey, Butch, how goes things in the south? Nope, we haven't even showered yet. Sure, we will wait for you. We could use the help. I will fill you in when you get here. Okay, see you in an hour or so. Bye."

"Butch—"

"Is coming up to go with us on our interviews. He will be here in an hour or so. I wouldn't be a very good detective if I couldn't follow *that* call," Kate said with a laugh.

"I guess you're right. Well, good deal. He is sharp, and we need that right now."

We ate, showered, dressed, and waited for Butch's arrival. He got here, as promised, a little over an hour.

"How are the roads?"

"Fine. The cars are warming up the pavement with their tires. Not even slick at all."

Kate and I filled Butch in on the game plan and the questions we still had for all of the interviews that we hoped would give us a lead to turn over to the detectives. He listened without saying a word.

"So who do you want to interview first?"

Before I could answer, the phone rang again.

"Hello. Great, when can we take a look at it? Okay, we will stop by later. Is he in? Okay, great, just in case we have any questions. See you soon."

"Want to take a stab at that one, Kate?"

She thought for about five seconds and said, "The coroner's report is in. He is in the office, and we will stop by city hall and see it and the detectives at the same time."

"How did you do that? I was actually trying to not give it away, and yet you still hit on every single piece of the call."

"I'm telling you, I'm good at picking up half pieces of conversations and making them whole. I think it is a woman thing. When I go to lunch with my friends, lots of times everyone is talking at once. If you can pick up half a conversation, you can figure out what is being said."

"Well, I sure don't have that ability," Butch chimed in.

"Most men don't," Kate said with an air of superiority. Then she laughed that laugh I love so much.

"Well, shall we?"

"By all means."

Kate went over and told Killer to guard the house, gave him a pat on the head, and we walked out.

"We can take my truck. I think I'm blocking yours anyway," Butch said.

"Okay with me. I seldom get to be a passenger," I replied.

Butch's truck was the same as mine, a Ford F-150. But he had sprung for the four-wheel drive, and I had not. Because of that, it was a little higher to get into, and I had to give my darlin' wife some help up and in. Butch hadn't sprung for running boards.

"Where to?"

"Kate, why don't we start with Mr. Conigliero?"

"Sounds like a plan. Then Stafford and then Godwin."

"Any reason why that order?" I asked.

"You don't want to lose Pat as a customer. I figure, who knows, maybe we get lucky with one of the others and you don't even have to go back to his office."

"Good thinking. I like it."

"Okay, head into town. I will give you directions on the way."

Butch had been right; the roads were fine. I liked sitting up a little higher. Maybe Kate was right. It was time for a new ride. I had just decided my new one would have four-wheel drive.

Pulling up in front of Jerry Conigliero's house, we saw him sitting on the porch, reading the paper in a big buffalo plaid jacket. He had a coffee cup by his side. We all got out and walked up to him.

"Morning, Mr. Conigliero. How are you today?" I started the conversation.

"I'm fine. Please call me Jerry."

"Okay, and you can call me Jim, and you know Kate. This gentleman is Butch Danforth, a friend of ours."

Butch said hello and shook Jerry's hand.

"What brings you by today, more questions?"

"Well, actually yes."

"Shoot."

"We are still trying to piece everything together, and there have been some…discrepancies in what we have been told. Hoping you can help us out."

"I'll sure try."

"First you mentioned Pat called you before we came over last time to chat. Why?"

"Why did he call? He just wanted to let me know he had spoken with you and let me know he had given you my name too. And Tommy's. Just a friendly call. He said you were okay."

That made sense. No reason to doubt what he was saying.

"You also said it was nine thirty or so when you left after dinner, that Tommy was late getting home."

"Yup."

"Jerry, I talked to the bartender. He said you left before six thirty."

"We left *that* bar at six thirty. Pat had already left, and Tommy and I were hungry. We headed to one of the other bars. The one we were in had a kitchen, but it specialized in Asian food. I am not much for that stuff, so we went to Duke's, one of the other bars on the boat, and had nice thick steaks."

That also made complete sense. The bartender saw them leave, but he didn't see them leave Steamboats per se.

"One last question. Why did you say you had drinks and not dinner? Why not tell us you had dinner too?"

He looked around, both directions, and then said, "If my wife found out I went out and had a steak, she would skin me alive. I am not supposed to eat red meat. It messes me up sometimes, not all the time, but sometimes, inside." He pointed to his stomach. "Binds me up. I end up in the hospital about half the time. Got lucky this time, so I just sort of failed to mention that part to you."

The rest of us looked at one another and smiled. We got it. Jerry seemed honest to a fault this time around.

"Jerry, thank you. You have made our day. Sorry you get sick from red meat. Butch and I hunt. We could keep you supplied with a little venison if you want. Would that be better for your stomach?"

"You know, it might work. Doc says it's the fat in the beef that does it to me. Gee, I would love to try some."

"Consider it done. I will bring some by for you. Thanks again."

"You bet, and thank you."

We turned and left, leaving Jerry to think about a thick juicy elk steak, maybe even with some mushrooms. He had told us what we considered the truth. Now it was time for Tommy.

CHAPTER SEVENTEEN

The visit with Tommy would either substantiate what we thought we now knew about what happened that night with the three contractors or tear it apart. Mr. Stafford had given little in the way of details to either Butch and Kate or Kate and me the last time we spoke. A few simple questions might be able to clear up everything, we hoped. As bad as I wanted to get Nancy off the hook, I felt like if these guys were telling us the whole story, and it made sense; we were back to square one. And that would not be good. On the other hand, Tommy's apology kept ringing in my ears. Pat was a loyal customer. Could they be totally innocent in all this? Of course they could. We had laid all our eggs in one basket, well, five baskets if you figured in Mary Roberts and the now-deceased Heather Norris. The one thing I was pretty sure of now is that Heather didn't kill Clifford Michaels.

Tommy was at the office, and I can't say he was real happy we were there, but at least he seemed civil.

"What can I do for you, Jim?"

"Tommy, we are still trying to clear a couple things up. Do you have just a minute to answer some questions? I promise it won't take long."

He shrugged and said, "Go ahead."

"The night you and Jerry and Pat all went to Steamboats, the night Clifford Michaels was killed, what time did you arrive at the boat? Do you remember?"

"Not exactly, no. It had to have been around six." One down.

"Did you guys have dinner or just drinks?"

"We all had drinks. Pat had to leave, so Jerry and I went to Duke's and had steak. All he kept talking about was how pissed his wife would be if he got sick."

"Do you recall what time you guys left?"

"That I do remember. My wife wanted me home by nine thirty, like some little kid with a curfew. Turns out she had gone out with her friends to a meeting of some sort, and the babysitter watching our granddaughter—we have her until Christmas—had to be home by ten. I felt like kind of a heel getting mad at my wife at the time, but I understood once I got home. I was a little late. We didn't leave Steamboats until right at nine thirty."

"Tommy, that's all we had to ask you. Thanks for your time."

"Sorry, Tommy, one last thing. You haven't spoken to Pat or Jerry today, have you?"

"No, I haven't. I spoke with Pat yesterday, but I haven't talked to Jerry for at least a couple days."

"Thanks again."

"No problem, Jim. You going to be at the store soon? I still need to pick something up."

"Tell you what, Tommy, I know you like to shop on Christmas Eve. I will meet you there at eight o'clock when we open. Deal?"

"Deal," he said while reaching out to shake hands.

We walked away from the second interview knowing that these two were telling the truth. Made me wonder if Pat had told us the truth or had omitted some things. We had thought ill of Jerry and Tommy and had been proven wrong. Would we go three for three and be back at the starting gate in the case?

Time would tell.

"Hey, Jim. Pat's office is on the opposite side of town. Think it would be worth our time to stop by city hall and see if the coroner's report is done yet? It's kind of between here and there."

"Good call. Butch, you know how to get to city hall, right?"

"Yes, sir, I sure do."

The parking lot at city hall was, more or less, empty. Was it Saturday? I didn't think so, but we had been working so hard on the case I had lost track of the days. I thought it was Thursday or, at worse, Friday.

"What day is it?"

"Huh, you don't even know what day it is? Guess that happens when you don't work for a living," Butch said. "It's Friday."

"I have lost track of the days. The parking lot is so empty I thought it was Saturday."

"My thought is that since Christmas is just four days away, some people probably decided to start their shopping and took the day off," Kate replied.

Christmas. Dang. I still hadn't gotten anything for Kate, and now it was upon us.

There was a new cop at the front desk—Officer Miller. We inquired on the whereabouts of our detective friends, and he said they were in the back. He didn't even bother to call them, just motioning for us to go ahead.

Detectives Smith and Jones were both in their respective chairs, toiling away on case files.

"Morning, gentlemen."

They both turned and looked at us.

Smith spoke first, "Good morning. Just got the coroner's report. Heather Norris was strangled."

"So your original assessment was correct. Can we take a look at it?"

He sorted through a couple of file folders on his desk and handed me one.

I flipped it open, and Kate and Butch were peering over my shoulders.

"Whoa," said Jones. "You two can look at it, but not him." He pointed to Butch.

"I'm sorry. Remember when I told you I had a friend in the Lewis County Sheriff's Office? Detectives, meet Sergeant Elmer Danforth of Lewis County. He is a good friend and a heck of a cop."

Both of them rose and shook hands with Butch.

"I go by Butch," he said as he shook hands with them.

"Dave," said Smith.

"Roger," said Jones.

Must be a brotherhood of the law thing. Neither of them had given Kate or me their first names, and we had known them all week.

We all went back to looking at the report now that the introductions were out of the way. It was pretty straightforward. Heather had been strangled, of that there was no doubt. The report went on to say she had a series of bruises on her back that had occurred premortem and a bump on the back of her head. The strangulation had been done in the typical way as described by the coroner as asphyxiation.

"I don't see anything that does us any good here. Is the coroner working still? Or did he take the rest of the day off? I only ask because the parking lot is so empty."

"Coroner is county, not city. Let me call. Did you want to talk to him?" Smith asked.

"Yeah, I want to see if he left anything off the report that might be of help. I doubt it, but I have to ask."

Smith looked in his rolodex and punched the number into the phone.

"Hi, Gene. It's Dave. Hey, I have a person who would like to ask you a couple questions about the Norris autopsy. Do you mind?"

Evidently he didn't, and Dave handed me the phone.

"Good morning. My name is Jim Tuttle. Yes, that Jim Tuttle. Yeah, it seems a lot of people saw us on television. Kate and I are investigating another murder, and we are trying to see if this one might somehow be connected to it. The Michaels murder. Well, that is what we are trying to find out."

I heard Kate telling Butch what the coroner was asking or saying on the other end of the line. She was spot-on. Her ability to do so was uncanny.

"You mention that Heather died from asphyxia. Anything strange in the manner? Was she strangled with a rope or…"

I listened intently as the coroner went over his findings. Suddenly I got a chill and literally shook.

I was pretty sure knew who killed Heather Norris. And maybe Clifford Michaels.

CHAPTER EIGHTEEN

"We have to go."

"Hang on, Jim," said Smith. "What did the coroner tell you? I saw your reaction."

I thought quickly. "I was just reacting to his description of what happened to Heather. We had kind of become friends with her."

That seemed to appease him a bit, but I could tell he wasn't convinced. I didn't care.

"Thanks for letting us see the report."

He was looking through me, boring a hole into me with his eyes. I wasn't going to talk, and I think he knew it.

"Whatever," he said with the coldest voice I had ever heard. Maybe I was wrong, but I was going to stick to my guns.

We all said goodbye and headed for Butch's truck.

"What was that all about?" Kate whispered to me as we were crossing the small lobby.

"Wait. I need to make a call."

I went to the pay phone in the lobby and looked up the number. Putting in my dime, I figured this was it. If I got the response I expected, I would be able to close the loop completely.

We got outside, and I asked Butch if he had his gun with him.

"Always. Required to carry it at all times. You know that."

"Just making sure."

We climbed into Butch's truck literally. I filled them in on what the coroner had told me. That, coupled with what we had read, painted a pretty clear picture for me. For all of us now.

"So are we heading to his place now?" Kate asked.

"Yes, right now."

Butch drove across town, and we pulled up in front of Pat Godwin's office. I was sure he killed Heather and, if I was right, Clifford Michaels as well. Now we just had to have him tell us why. Talking to the cops, he would have invoked his right to an attorney. I was hoping he would talk to us.

We walked into Pat's office, and he was nowhere to be seen. He was actually in *his* office in the back, I was hoping.

I called out, and sure enough, he came out from the back.

"Oh, hi, Jim, Kate." He looked at Butch and then went on, "What brings you guys back?"

I decided to take the direct approach.

"We are here because we know you killed Heather Norris."

"What? What are you talking about? I don't even know any Heather Norris."

"My guess is, you killed Clifford Michaels too. I think I can piece most of it together. You will have to fill in the blank spots."

"Listen, Jim, we have been friends for quite a while, but you have just ended the friendship. How dare you come in here, my own office, and accuse me of killing someone. Or two someones." The last sentence he practically yelled at us.

"Let's start with Clifford. You told us the first time we came here a couple days ago that you had been at dinner with Jerry Conigliero and Tommy Stafford. That wasn't true. I went to Steamboats and found the bartender who had served you that night. He said that you left before six thirty."

"I—"

"Please don't lie anymore. Let me continue. He also told me that you guys picked a table that was the least desirable in the place due to its proximity to the kitchen and the noise that arose from it. He said you guys had your heads in real close together and that you did most of the talking."

"I told you, we had things to discuss. Business."

"Yes, but your business was killing Clifford Michaels. You were trying to convince them to join in and kill Clifford. Why? Was it because he stole all your bids somehow? Anyway, you finally rose and told them, 'Fine, you two stay here and drink' or something to that effect, but you probably added something about how you would implicate them if they said anything to anyone."

"You're talking crazy, Jim. Why would I kill Clifford?"

"I think it was a number of things. The underbidding you, the fact he was a jerk to everyone he met, but most of all, I think it had to do with all the invoices I saw stacked up when I was here last time. I think you are in financial trouble, and you figured the only way out of it was to off one of your competitors and get some of the jobs he had underbid you on.

"I think you staged the whole thing. There was no forced entry at the Michaels house, which made it look even more like it could be Nancy who did it. It took me until today to figure out how you did that. When I realized how, I realized you had killed Heather. I'm still not sure why, but I do know how. See, the coroner told me that whoever strangled Heather had done it with one hand on her neck and one covering her mouth. He said the odd thing was that the killer's hand was so large it covered her entire neck. I have always thought your hands were as big as a baseball glove. It was when I was talking to him, I realized why you had killed her. The key."

"What key? I don't know what you're talking about, Jim." But I could see he did know.

"My biggest question was how did you know *she* knew where the key was? Then I got the whole picture. You were still there when Heather came to the Michaels home. My assumption is you were afraid she may have seen you too."

"That's ridiculous. I was nowhere near her house. My assumption is that Jerry or Tommy decided to do this and pin it on me."

"Their story checks out. See, after you left, they *did* go have dinner. They were there until nine thirty, so they couldn't have killed Michaels."

"Still doesn't mean I did."

"We interviewed both of them again yesterday. I asked Tommy if he had spoken to you or Jerry that day. I figured maybe Jerry had called to warn you like you had done for him a couple days ago. Tommy said no but that he had spoken to you the day before. I called him a few minutes ago and asked him what you guys talked about. He said you chatted about several things, but the most important one in this case was, you wanted to know the name of Clifford Michaels's girlfriend. He said he told you where she worked but didn't know her name."

Pat Godwin suddenly shrunk. He was a big man, but it looked as if someone had let the air out of him.

"That stupid key." Then he continued, "That bastard Michaels. I'm broke. I going to have to declare bankruptcy. The son of a bitch stole so many of my contracts I can't pay my bills."

"Tell us what happened, Pat," said Kate.

"The three of us met—me, Jerry, and Tommy. I told them I had a proposition for them. What I really wanted to do was have them go with me to Michaels's house and scare him. Figured if we all went together maybe we could put the fear of God into him. But they said no. See, their business is fine. It was mine that was the most impacted by Michaels."

"So you went by yourself," I said.

"Yes."

This was it. If he told us what happened, we would go to jail for murder.

"I went to his house and rang the bell. He answered the door with a big smile on his face. It faded when he saw it was me. He asked me what I wanted, and I asked if I could come in. He said I could for a minute, that he was expecting someone. I had a length of rebar in my hand, hiding it right behind my leg. It was dark out, so he didn't see it. As he turned to lead me into his house, I hit him on the back of the head. I wanted to scare him, not kill him, but this guy had stolen my life's work from me. I dragged him over in front of the couch, locked the door, and started to look around for something to tie him up with. The first thing that came to mind was a bathrobe belt or a regular belt, anything really. I wasn't thinking too clearly, obviously.

I just happened to open one of the nightstand drawers, and lo and behold, here sat a gun. My mind was racing. I grabbed the gun, went into the kitchen, got a little water in my hand, and walked out and sort of sprinkled it on Michaels's face. I knew I hadn't hit him real hard, and sure enough, he woke up. He saw the gun in my hand. 'My wife's gun,' he had said and started trying to talk to me about working out a deal or going into business with him. I knew he was full of bullshit, so I told him to stand up. He no more than did—"

"And you shot him," Butch said this.

Pat looked at him for the first time. "Who are you?"

"A friend of Jim and Kate." He left of the part about being a cop. Good idea. Pat hadn't admitted to shooting him yet.

Pat stared at him and replied. "Yes, I shot him."

We all exchanged glances as he continued with the story.

"I remembered he said he had company coming, so I grabbed a towel out of the kitchen and wiped anywhere I had touched. I was in the middle of that when the doorbell rang. I stepped back into the kitchen and hid so that if they person looked in, they wouldn't see me. Then I heard the damn door open. Figuring whoever it was would now be looking at Clifford's body, I dared to take a peek. It was a blond-haired woman. She had on a big coat and gloves. She was holding a single key in her hand. She stood openmouthed, looking at the body, then turned and went out. I heard her lock the door. I quickly ran to the window and saw her placing a rock in the garden. I finished wiping anything I thought I touched, left by the front door, and took the towel with me, wiping off the door handle. I picked up the rock that the blond had just set down, and here was the key. People do that all the time, hide a key outside in case they lose theirs or whatever. I took the key and locked the door."

"Which is why there was no forced entry. Clifford had let you in, and you had locked up on your way out," Kate said.

"Yes. Except for two things. I forgot to wipe off the key, and I started thinking about what if she saw me."

"You mean Heather?" I asked.

"Yes. The next morning, I called Jerry and Tommy and told them what happened. I also told them both that if they said anything to anybody, I would implicate them. Now they were accessories after the fact, I believe it's called."

"And they must have believed you. All they had to do was go to the cops and tell the truth, but neither did so. The fact that you told them the details is why they knew how Clifford had been killed."

All of us had missed it. Jerry and Tommy had mentioned that Michaels had been shot in the chest. That detail didn't come out until two days after the shooting in the coroner's report. He had told us the day before the report came out. Dang. Pretty lousy detective work.

"The key had me worried. I was afraid to go back and wipe it off, that someone might see me. In the end, I decided no one knew it was there but this Heather, so I decided to have a talk with her. I needed to know if she had seen me."

"But instead of just talking, you killed her," Butch said.

"I went to talk to her. Her boss at the bar told me her name, and I looked up her address in the phone book and drove over and rang the bell. She wasn't home or not answering the bell, so I sat in my car and waited. She drove up a little while later. I got out and walked over to her and introduced myself and asked if she had a moment to talk. Of course she asked, 'What about?' I told her it was about Clifford Michaels, specifically about *her* and Clifford Michaels. She immediately got agitated and said to leave her alone. Now mind you, I didn't represent myself as a cop or anything like that, but she really didn't want to talk about Michaels. I figured at that point she had never seen me at Michaels's place that night. But then, she starts saying she is going to holler rape if I didn't leave her alone. As I watched her take in a deep breath to holler, I knew she wasn't kidding. I grabbed her by the throat with one hand and covered her mouth with the other."

What Pat had just said jived with what the coroner had told me. The murderer of Heather Norris had huge hands. Kate had mentioned it the first time she met Pat. The coroner said whoever strangled her used just one hand to do so.

"I didn't want to hurt her, but I couldn't have her screaming in her neighborhood that she was being raped. I pushed her to the ground, kinda behind in front of her car where no one could see me, and I held on to her throat until she stopped moving. I guess it was too long. I had given her my real name, so once I realized she was dead, I knew I had to get the heck out of there. I picked her up and went around back. She had a number of keys on her chain, but I found the right one and opened the door at the back of the house. I carried her in and tried to make it look like she was killed there. Then I wiped off her keys and replaced them in her pocket. I walked to my truck and got in and drove off."

When he said this, tears started streaming down his cheeks.

"You have to understand…this was my *life*. That bastard Michaels had ruined what I had built up over the past thirty years. Now he was dead, she was dead, and I had killed them both."

Pat Godwin now had tears streaming out of his eyes. He was, or had been, a good man. That had all changed in the last few days.

"You realize that you just told us you killed two people, right, Pat?"

"Yes. It doesn't matter anymore. I'm ruined."

"That's all we needed to hear," said a new voice from the outer office. Detectives Smith and Jones entered.

"We followed you," Jones said to me. "We figured you would try to go do it alone."

"Patrick Godwin, you are under arrest for the murders of Clifford Michaels and Heather Norris," stated Smith. He started on with reading him his rights. Pat looked dejected and just plain worn-out.

Jones pulled some cuffs out from behind his back and started toward Pat.

"Can I get my keys so someone can lock up?" he said, pointing to his desk.

"Sure," Jones replied.

That is when Patrick Godwin—husband, father, contractor, and friend—opened the drawer of his desk, removed a gun, and, putting it to his head, ended his own life.

Epilogue

Christmas morning. When I was a kid, like most any kid, I couldn't wait for that magical day to arrive. Today I was much more subdued. I had lost what I had considered a good friend. His admission of guilt before he committed suicide, however, had gotten Nancy Michaels out of jail.

I was sitting drinking coffee, waiting for my lovely wife to awaken, thinking about the past couple weeks. Robert had paid us handsomely, $500,000, for getting Nancy out of trouble. It seemed excessive, and both Kate and I told him so. He said that it was not all his money. Nancy now owned the business Clifford had built up, and she had insisted on the amount. Kate and I now had over a million dollars in the bank once again. One million, three hundred thousand, and change to be more precise. We had a good deal of money left over from a previous case, so we were sitting pretty well.

Yesterday I had gone to the store and met Tommy Stafford. He had purchased a very nice, high-quality ring for his wife for Christmas. As he was leaving, we shook hands, and he had said he would see me at Valentine's Day.

I spoke with the owner of the store and told him I wasn't coming back. Kate didn't know this yet, but it seemed we were making a pretty decent living as detectives, and maybe it was time we did it full-time. The jewelry business was something I loved and could always go back to if need be. The owner understood although he was disappointed. He asked if I would come in if special customers, like

Tommy, wanted to buy from me, and I told him of course. Then I picked out a new piece of jewelry for Kate for Christmas—a very nice two-carat anniversary band. I was excited to see her expression when she opened the box. I had gone to other stores for some simpler items, like special lotions Kate liked and so on. She couldn't have just one present under the tree.

Kate had gone out early on Christmas Eve as well. I knew she liked to save one gift for the last minute so she could get into the hustle-bustle of Christmas shopping on the last day. She enjoyed it, so when she left, I knew she was in search of that one last gift.

Hearing her in the other room, getting out of bed, I knew I wouldn't have to wait long. Killer sat by my side snoring. I had gotten him a few new toys at the mall as well. For a big dog, he was playful and loved to run around the yard carrying a stuffed toy, throwing it in the air and then trying to catch it. Kind of like playing catch by yourself.

"Merry Christmas, detective boy," Kate said as she emerged from the bedroom.

"Merry Christmas to you, darlin'. Want an Irish coffee?"

"Want me to pass out before we open presents? I need just caffeine first please," she said with a laugh. That wonderful laugh.

I poured her a cup, refilled mine, walked over, and gave her a kiss. Then we both headed for the living room, where we had put a tree up just the night before. It smelled great, like being outdoors. We had vacillated on whether to bother with a tree or not, but in the end, we had gone to a place that sold live trees in five gallon containers so that after you used them for Christmas, you could plant them in the spring.

"Ready to open some gifts?" she asked.

"Ready as I'll ever be."

We each picked out a present from under the tree. "Here, open this one first," I said. It was customary to us to pick out the gift you wanted the other person to open. That way, you controlled the gifts from small to large, ending with the best gift you were giving till the very end.

Opening some new hunting gear and a new fishing pole, we were dwindling down to the end of the gifts. I was happy with what Kate had picked out, but I knew she had to have an ace up her sleeve. There were no gifts left now, except her new ring.

I handed her the package, which I had disguised in a bigger box in the hopes she wouldn't figure it out before she got it opened. She tore the wrapping off, and her eyes lit up when she opened the small inner box.

"Oh, Jim, it's beautiful."

"So are you, darlin'. Merry Christmas."

She slipped it on, admiring the sparkle of the tree lights in the diamonds. Then she looked at her watch and sort of frowned.

"What, darling?"

"Oh, nothing. Can you get me another cup of coffee? Actually, make it of the Irish variety this time."

I jumped up and headed for the kitchen. I had to make a new pot of coffee and get out the other ingredients, mainly good Irish whiskey, and set to work. While I was in the process, the doorbell rang.

"Who the heck could that be?" I hollered into Kate.

"I'll get it."

I heard her open the door and say, "Well, hello. Cutting it a little close, weren't you?"

Now I had to see who was there. Rounding the corner, here stood our friend Butch.

"Hey, Butch! Merry Christmas."

"Back at you, Jim."

"What did you mean Kate when you said he was cutting it close?"

"Butch was to be here at eight thirty. It is eight thirty-five, and I had one last gift that he was bringing."

"Okay, but he didn't bring anything."

"Oh yes, he did. Follow me, detective boy."

We walked back out the front door Butch had just entered from. Down the sidewalk like a conga line, with Kate in the lead, Butch behind her, and yours truly in the back, we rounded the corner of the house. Sitting in the driveway was a brand new 1981 Ford F-150 four-wheel-drive pickup complete with running boards.

"Merry Christmas, Jim."

About the Author

Washington has always been home to Pat Ely. He was born in Olympia and has lived there most of his life. Most of his stories take place in and around Olympia.

An avid hunter, fisherman, and outdoor person in general, Ely spends as much time as possible traveling in his motor home with Katherine, his wife of over forty years, and their three dogs.

Writing started late in life for Ely, not writing his first story until he was in his late fifties. He worked in retail jewelry for nearly thirty years before becoming a program manager for a telecommunications company. Now that he has more spare time, his writing has become something he does to relax and something he loves to do.

CPSIA information can be obtained
at www.ICGtesting.com
Printed in the USA
BVHW030741150921
616747BV00001B/40